CW00523612

Copyright © 2021 by Kerry J Donovan
Published by Fuse Books 2021
ISBN: 9798499337813

PERFECT RECORD

A DCI Jones novel

KERRY J DONOVAN

I'd like to send my particular thanks to Nicole O'Brien for her unstinting help throughout this project. Whether editing, proofing, or supporting my mood swings, she is always ready to offer a helping hand—thanks millions, my cariad.

Chapter One

London, England

DIGBY BERTRAND 'DB' Parrish rapped the butt of his Montblanc on the table to silence the jabbering heads in the boardroom and turned to the final page on the agenda: Any Other Business.

"'Arry," Parrish called to the geezer in question. "Ain't you found no one yet?"

Director of Human Resources, Harry Bryce—slim bordering on scrawny, with a huge overbite and Toby jug ears—wilted under the intense scrutiny. He opened his mouth but didn't answer.

"Well?" Parrish kept his voice low. He'd learned a long time ago that a quiet voice in a big room could travel a long way if you carried a big stick. In Hutch, his ever-present pit-bull terrier of a minder, he had a stick big enough to silence the roar of a lion.

Six directors of *Parrish Enterprises Ltd*—all moderately competent, all men—stared at Bryce, their expressions ranging from studious concentration to relief. Each had been on the receiving end of at least one of Parrish's interrogations and were definitely relieved to

1

avoid the brunt of his wrath. Parrish liked to keep the buggers on their toes. Keep them sharp. Scalpel sharp.

Parrish turned to face the mountain of a man who guarded his back day and night.

"Hutch. Am I speaking Russian?"

The blue-eyed giant with the muddy-blond hair rose from his seat in the corner of the soundproofed, electronically secure room, and positioned himself behind Parrish's right shoulder. He loomed over the hushed table.

"No, Mr Parrish, you spoke English," Hutch said, matching Parrish's low volume. "I could understand you perfectly well."

"So why ain't he answering my questions, d'you think?"

"No idea, sir. Perhaps he's hard of hearing." Hutch curled his fingers into fists, cracking his knuckles.

The hairs on the back of Parrish's neck tingled at the narrow-eyed dread the noise produced in Bryce and the others. "Yeah, maybe that's it. He's gone fucking deaf." Parrish jabbed the Montblanc towards the HR Director. "'Arry?"

"Y-Yes, Mr Parrish?" Bryce's voice cracked, and he kept his eyes fixed on the pen.

"You deaf?"

"N-No, sir."

Parrish looked up at Hutch, the only person he'd allow to stand so close to him outside of a bedroom or a barber's shop. "See, Hutch. He ain't mutton."

Hutch nodded slowly. "I have to agree with you, Mr Parrish. There doesn't appear to be much wrong with Mr Bryce's ability to hear."

"Yeah, right, but if that's the case, why ain't he answering?"

Hutch shrugged his huge shoulders.

"No idea, sir."

"S-Sorry, Mr Parrish," Bryce mumbled. "I was trying to put my thoughts in order."

"You ought to come to the boardroom prepared, 'Arry."

"Yes, sir. Sorry."

"Get on with it, then."

Bryce stiffened his backbone, and not before time.

"We've tried hiring from within the organisation, Mr Parrish, but there's no one as fits the bill, see. They're either useless, past their sell-by date, or banged up inside. I trawled some of the other firms, but none of the applicants was good enough. Their best men didn't even come close."

"Fuck," Parrish said. "Vacancy's been open nearly three months. I need someone in place before I have to pass on yet another job. If I'd known it would take this long I might've given that piece of shit a reprieve." Parrish nodded towards the only empty chair in the room, the back of which rested against the table's edge.

The directors looked anywhere but at the vacant space.

Bryce found his voice again. "I-It's not easy finding an applicant with that particular skill set, Mr Parrish. Cracksmen are a dying breed." He shot a quick sideways glance at the empty chair, blanched, and soldiered on. "These days it's all hacking computers, breaking electronic locks, and money transfers—"

Parrish threw the Montblanc. Bryce ducked too late and squeaked as the fountain pen hit him below his left eye and bounced onto the tabletop.

"Don't fucking tell me what ain't easy, shit-for-brains!" Parrish yelled. "Human Resources is your responsibility. Or are you tellin' me you ain't up to it no more?"

Parrish's gaze returned to the empty chair and wondered whether Bryce had pissed himself yet. Nothing would have surprised him with the little Welsh git.

"N-No, Mr Parrish. It's not that, see. I contacted the Locksmiths Guild last week but they didn't get back to me for ages."

"Why?"

"I-I don't know, Mr Parrish. It took them a while to find the information."

"Give Hutch the name of the tosser what dragged his heels. Hutch has ways of teaching people not to keep me waiting. Don't you, Hutch."

The blond giant grinned and dipped his chin in agreement.

"Yes, Mr Parrish," Bryce said. "All the relevant names will be included in the personnel report."

"So, what they say?" Parrish asked.

"Turns out they *do* have a guy on their books who meets all the criteria." Bryce picked up the Montblanc and stretched to place it on the table in front of Parrish. His mouth turned up at the edges in a weak, chinless smile. "It's just that I didn't want to say nothing until we'd found him."

"What you mean, 'found him'? Where is he? Gone on his 'olidays?"

Bryce shook his head. His shoulders twitched into a minimal shrug. "That's just it, Mr Parrish. Nobody knows. The Guild lost track of him a year or so back. He got into financial bother and they dumped him from their system."

"Financial bother?" Parrish frowned. "Is he inside, too?"

"No, sir. Nothing criminal. Bankruptcy. Turns out his family business failed. He closed up shop and moved away."

"Where from?"

"Redditch, Mr Parrish."

"Where?"

Hutch leaned close and spoke. "It's a toilet to the south of Birmingham, just off the M42."

"How comes I'm only learning this now?" Parrish picked up the Montblanc and twiddled it between thumb and forefinger. He loved its chunky balance. Didn't use it much for writing, though—a ballpoint wrote better.

"My contact at the Guild only called late last night, Mr Parrish. One of my girls is working up a file on the bloke right now. I told her to call me the moment she prints it off."

Parrish dropped the pen. "Give the bitch a bell. Tell her to pull her finger out her fanny and get me that file."

"Y-Yes, sir, Mr Parrish." Bryce pulled out his mobile.

"What's this geezer's name?" Parrish asked.

"Freeman, sir. Sean Freeman." Bryce bowed his head and dialled.

"Right," said Parrish. "I want him found—yesterday. Call in

some favours from our favourite plods. This Freeman sort's gotta be somewhere. Am I right?"

Seven directors nodded. Seven voices chimed out in unison, "Yes, Mr Parrish."

Parrish waited a second before exploding. "Well? Why you all still sitting on your thumbs up your fat arses? Go find me Sean Freeman!"

Chapter Two

THURSDAY 5TH MARCH – *Sean Freeman*
London, England

SEAN FREEMAN DIDN'T SMILE, sing, or whistle—it wouldn't have been professional—but he felt good. Things were panning out exactly as he'd hoped. Were he anywhere but at work he might have launched into a street dance, if he could street dance.

He removed the brass key-blank he'd spent the past two hours roughing out from the rubber-jawed vice, and held it under the doughnut-shaped magnifying lamp. A fine burr still clung to the inner groove of the upper shaft. He worked a piece of emery paper over the edge and blew. Tiny pieces of swarf fell to the velvet cloth lining his workbench.

Freeman compared the blank's double-shafted profile with the insurance photograph from which he worked. They matched perfectly, as he knew they would. The top shaft complete—apart from cutting the notches and ridges—he turned his attention to the lower shaft.

A shadow fell across the bench.

Crap, here we go again.

The ignorant old sod should have known better than to stand over him while he worked. Freeman hated when Archibald did that. He tried to ignore the man's hovering presence and carried on working.

Archibald coughed. "Mr Freeman?"

"Yes, sir?" he answered, without lifting his eyes from the task.

The groove on the lower shaft's outer face was a shade too shallow and needed enlargement. When that was finished he could begin work cutting the twenty-four teeth—six on each edge of both shafts. Satisfied with the basic configuration, Freeman sighed. He returned the key-blank to the vice before pushing away the lamp. He met Archibald's calculating sneer and waited.

The senior locksmith pulled back the sleeve of his Armani suit and pointed at the blue-faced Tag Heuer Monaco adorning the fleshy wrist.

"You've been working on that same key for nearly two hours. How long are you going to be?" He tapped the glass face of the watch. "Time is money, Mr Freeman. Why aren't you using the key-copier?"

Freeman paused and bit back his knee-jerk response. He'd been marking time at *Archibald & Daughter, Locksmiths and Jewellers of Golders Green*, but if things continued working as planned, he wouldn't be there much longer. He'd taken the underpaid job in this specific locksmith's shop for a particular reason, and the key-blank in his vice made all the humiliation worthwhile.

"Mr Archibald," he said, pointing to the insurance photo and then lifting the damaged original key that rested on the bench next to the vice. "The customer had an accident with the original." Freeman pushed the damaged key under Archibald's bulbous nose. "Some moron tried to straighten it with a pair of pliers and sheared off the lower shaft. It's absolutely criminal treating something as beautiful as this as though it opened a flipping padlock."

Archibald reached into his waistcoat pocket for his reading glasses. "Why make all that fuss over a single key?"

"Take a closer look, sir."

Freeman pointed at the lamp, leaned away from his workspace, and waited for the light of knowledge to blind the ignorant old clown.

Archibald polished the lenses of his half-moon specs and perched them on his shiny nose. He took the damaged key and squinted to read the letters and numbers etched into an extra-large head in the shape of the Ace of Spades. Piggy eyes opened wide.

"No. Surely not," he said, grabbing Freeman's work lamp and angling the light to bring the engraving into clearer focus. "My God. A Monarch 1908!"

"Yes, Mr Archibald. It's the real thing," Freeman said, failing to keep the excitement from his voice.

Archibald's expression hardened and his jaw muscles worked as though chewing on a piece of gristle. He shoved the magnifying light away and fixed Freeman with a cold glare.

"My God, man! We have the original key to a Miles & Archer, Monarch 1908 safe on the premises and you don't see fit to tell me? As far as anyone knows, the only Monarch 1908 in the UK is in the vault at Buckingham Palace!" He paused and covered his mouth with a trembling hand. "My word … do you think?"

Archibald's eyes glazed over. Freeman guessed he was wondering what would happen to the profile of his little shop if he had a *Royal Warrant of Approval* displayed above the front door. Freeman could almost hear the words *By Appointment to Her Majesty* rattling around inside Archibald's head.

Freeman understood the man's shocked reaction—it mirrored his own when he first saw the key that opened something the locksmith industry considered the pinnacle of pre-World War One security engineering.

"Sorry, Mr Archibald, but you were at the bank when the customer arrived. He said the job was urgent and he needed it completed by closing time. You know what I'm like when working. I get lost inside the job."

Freeman tried a disarming grin. It wouldn't work, but he didn't mind wasting this one. Today, he had smiles to spare. He decided to twist the knife a little more.

"If you're worried about the bill, Mr Parrish didn't look like he was short of a few quid. Pulled up outside in a Bentley Flying Spur. Chauffeur-driven, it was."

As expected, colour drained from Archibald's face and his skin turned the colour and texture of old putty. He placed a steadying hand on Freeman's bench. Freeman hoped the man didn't keel over. The last thing wanted was to give the wet-lipped old arsehole mouth-to-mouth.

"Are you okay, Mr Archibald?" he asked, feigning ignorance.

"Mr Parrish was here? Digby Parrish?"

Freeman shrugged. "Didn't give me his first name, but the key's letter of provenance had him as one, DB Parrish. Why? Do you know him?"

Duh, look at him squirm, Sean. Course he knows DB Parrish.

The shop's proximity to Parrish's base of operations was the main reason Freeman applied to work for Archibald in the first place. Freeman's day couldn't get much better than this.

"Fuck's sake, man," Archibald shouted, swearing for the first time since Freeman met him. "The whole of North London knows Digby Parrish."

"I'm from Redditch, Mr Archibald," Freeman said, eyes wide and innocent. "It's nowhere near London."

The middle-aged jeweller's lower lip trembled. "Did he ask for me?"

"Who? Mr Parrish?"

Winding up the old man could be such a hoot. Freeman couldn't remember the last time he'd enjoyed himself so much.

Slowly, the colour returned to Archibald's face, a puce stain spread up from loose neck flaps and rushed all the way to the top of his shiny pate.

"Yes. Who else are we talking about, man?"

"Sorry, sir, but no he didn't ask for you. In fact, he turned up a couple of minutes after you left and handed over the damaged key. Didn't say much, apart from that he'd be back at closing time. Seemed to know what time we closed. Of course, I had to start from scratch as we don't have a blank Monarch key lying around the place."

Archibald tried to snap his fingers, but they sweated so much they only managed a damp slap. He waved them at Freeman's bench.

"The photo!" he demanded.

"It's the insurer's scaled image of the original key. The bittings code is on the back as required. That and the damaged original are all I need to make the replacement."

"Mr Parrish was happy to leave *you* with the insurance blue-print?" The arrogant prick stared down his nose at his employee.

Freeman ignored the slight; his good mood trumped Archibald's snide bitching.

"Yes, sir. In fact, I had the impression he wanted *me* to make it rather than you. Any idea why?"

"None," Archibald answered, but his hushed tone smacked of immense relief, and his shifting eyes gave lie to the answer.

"Mr Parrish knew about the shop's Locksmiths Guild certification and I insisted he show me his insurance company's seal of ownership for the key. I asked for Mr Parrish's credentials too. Needed to make sure everything's kosher, sir. Which is why I checked."

Archibald shuddered.

"Oh, God," he sighed, and leaned even more heavily against the bench; it creaked but stood up rather well under the strain. "You questioned Digby Parrish?"

"'Course I did. You wouldn't expect me to take a commission for a Monarch key without checking the client's credentials, would you? That would be breaking the law." Freeman nearly laughed out loud. He hadn't had so much fun in the six weeks he'd been working for Archibald. After all the embarrassment he'd suffered, he needed to take full advantage of any little pleasure he could find, whether it made him feel guilty later or not.

"You don't need to tell me the rules of our industry, Freeman," Archibald snapped. "But to question DB Parrish. Oh, God!"

"Who is this Parrish fellow?" Freeman asked, loving the effect the man's name was having on his arrogant and now sweat-stained boss. "I mean, he appeared legit. He even had the original receipt for the safe. Fantastic piece of calligraphy, by the way. A real work of art. I'd love to have taken a copy, but well, you know. Didn't seem proper to ask."

Archibald tried to push himself away from the bench, but his arms shook so much he couldn't manage the task.

"You okay, Mr Archibald? You don't look well. Want some water?"

"Yes, please."

Freeman strolled to the office at the back of the shop and grabbed a bottle of Buxton from the fridge. By the time he returned, Archibald had taken his seat behind the till and sat round-shouldered, elbows resting on the counter, head in hands. He took the water, cracked open the top with trembling fingers, and took a deep swallow. Water dribbled down all three chins. He pulled a starched white handkerchief from his waistcoat and dabbed them dry.

"So, who is this Parrish bloke?" Freeman repeated.

"A very bad man, Freeman." Archibald kept his voice low, eyes staring through the window as though terrified the man would arrive early to collect his property. "You're doing a good job? Please say you're doing a good job." His eyes pleaded and he used the damp handkerchief to wipe sweat from his brow.

Freeman stood up straight. "Mr Archibald, I'm more than capable of fabricating a key when I have maker's blueprints, the bittings code, *and* the original to work from, even though it's in that state." He hitched a thumb towards his vice. "Care to take a look at my work?"

Archibald shook his fat head. "Absolutely not. Don't even want to touch the bloody thing, but … I have to, I suppose."

Using his hands to brace himself against the straining bench, he worked his way back to Freeman's work area and examined his efforts.

"Before you say it, I know the inner groove on the lower shaft needs work. I was just about to do that when you interrupted me."

"Don't be so damned impertinent, boy."

"Yes, sir," Freeman said, almost managing to sound contrite. "Sorry."

Freeman smiled inwardly. The man's outward show of arrogance was just that—a show.

While Archibald examined the key, Freeman turned his back and studied the people filing past the shop front. *Archibald & Daughter* didn't attract the mass-market punter. This emporium had pretensions. It was less *H. Samuel* and more *Harrods Wannabe*. Still, Freeman hadn't applied for the job here for its up-market appeal. Oh no. He'd chosen it with expectations of this very day.

"Hmmm." Archibald waggled his head. His pate glistened under the shop's subdued lighting. "Good. In fact, excellent. So far. Make sure the finished article's perfect."

Freeman's jaw slackened. To date, Archibald had never passed any of his work as acceptable without pointing out some imagined flaw.

"Thank you, Mr Archibald," he said, trying to hide the sarcasm.

"Now, finish up before Mr Parrish returns. Closing time you say?"

"That's right. Should be plenty of time to make it perfect."

"Which it must be."

Parrish's arrival that morning was exactly what Freeman had been hoping for since starting at *Archibald & Daughter*. Working on something so damned intricate was wonderful, too. And the fact that DB Parrish had actually made the approach in person, gave the treat immense importance. Freeman bent to the task and tried to block out the image of Archibald slumped in the corner behind the till, staring at the door through dread-filled eyes.

There had only been the one customer all day.

———

THE RUMBLE of early evening traffic drowned out the ticking of the display clocks. Freeman finished the key to his satisfaction by four-thirty and spent the subsequent minutes watching the clocks, the passers-by, and the flickering sun poking intermittently through the scudding blanket of cloud.

Archibald shot Freeman another pleading look. "Are you sure it's up to snuff?" he asked for the fifth time.

"Yes, Mr Archibald," he answered, trying not to add a patient sigh. "I stand by my work."

"You'd better. DB Parrish doesn't accept failure."

Freeman wanted to say, 'Neither do I', but decided against it. Arrogance wasn't flattering in Archibald, and he didn't fancy being accused of the same character flaw.

As Archibald checked his Tag Heuer once again, the shop bell tinkled its merry, hopeful warning.

Digby Parrish breezed in, ignored Archibald, and strode straight to Freeman's bench. An expectant glint shone in blue-grey eyes half-hidden behind designer glasses. As before, the shadow cast by a big blond man darkened the doorway, but its owner stayed on guard outside.

Archibald's "very bad man" wore a dark blue pinstripe suit, cut well, and clearly made-to-measure. Middle-aged, lightweight, greying hair cut tight but not severe, Parrish was short, very short. With back straight and neck stretched high, he might have tipped a measuring stick at five foot seven—providing he didn't remove the handmade shoes with the ten-centimetre heels.

Freeman half-rose in greeting, but Parrish waved him back into his seat. "Sit down, son. I ain't royalty. You done here?" His tone was brusque, and the harsh north London twang stood out in sharp contrast to the nicely-tailored suit.

"Yes, sir." Freeman passed Parrish the key together with a key box containing the damaged original. He threw the switch on his magnifying lamp. It flickered twice before shining a halo onto the bench surface.

Parrish held the key under the light, flipped it over, rubbed the working edges between finger and thumb, and compared it with the original. He asked for the insurance photo—scaled to life size —and laid the new key on top, checking both faces carefully. He sniffed, nodded, dropped the new key into the box with the old one, and snapped the lid closed. "Not too shabby, son. That'll do."

Parrish slipped the box into his breast pocket and gave Freeman a one-sided, cool-eyed smile.

"How much for the work?"

"That's not up to me, sir."

He pointed Parrish toward Archibald. The jeweller cowered behind the till, using it as a barricade.

Parrish nodded a curt 'thank you' and turned to Archibald. He crossed the shop but made sure to keep Freeman in his sightline. Archibald seemed to shrink into himself as Parrish approached.

"What's the damage, Archie?"

The shopkeeper raised his hands, palms out. "Nothing, Mr Parrish."

"What's the problem, *Mr* Archibald?" Parrish spoke with a voice so low he almost growled. "My money ain't good enough for you. Is that it?"

Archibald's eyes popped. "No, no. Not at all, Mr Parrish. I wondered whether you would like to accept the key with my compliments."

"Don't want your fuckin' compliments. I pay my way. What's the charge?"

Tears of sweat popped on Archibald's brow and upper lip and glistened under the shops array of spotlights. "What would you say is a fair price, Mr Parrish?"

The short man nodded and looked at Freeman, who guessed Parrish wanted to make sure he was paying attention.

"There ain't no need to quibble," Parrish said, all smiles again. "I'm more than 'appy to pay top wedge for quality work. Five-hundred quid cover it?"

Archibald's jowls wobbled as he nodded with enough enthu-siasm to risk a cricked neck. Parrish peeled ten fifty-pound notes from a roll thick enough to choke a carthorse. "Here you go. And don't you never say DB Parrish don't pay his way."

"Oh no, Mr Parrish," Archibald said, the words tumbling out. "I'd never say…"

Archibald let the sentence trail off as Parrish turned to face Freeman full on. He didn't seem to mind turning his back on the terrified jeweller. Besides, the giant owner of the shadow in the doorway had a perfect view inside the shop.

Freeman stood and walked around to the front of his bench. He towered over Parrish, but made sure to keep a deferential distance. "Are you happy to pay without testing the key, Mr Parrish?" he asked, knowing Archibald didn't have the stones to make the suggestion.

Parrish paused. A gold molar flashed. "Ain't an issue, son. I can see the quality of your work. Job's a good 'un." He leaned closer to Freeman. Spicy cologne wafted across the narrow space between them. Freeman imagined hot mince pies on a winter's night—sweet and sickly. "I'll be seeing you, son."

With Archibald's attention focused on putting the money in the till, Parrish pressed two fifties and a business card into Freeman's hand.

Freeman slipped the cash and the card into his pocket and watched Parrish leave. His heart raced. At long last things were looking up.

About time.

Chapter Three

MONDAY 27TH JUNE – *Early morning*
Holton, Birmingham

DETECTIVE CHIEF INSPECTOR David Jones climbed out of his elderly Rover 415, scrunched up his shoulders, and worked the stiffness out of his aching neck. He stared up at the new police headquarters and, once again, tried to work out why he disliked the place so much.

Eight storeys tall, faced in blue-tinted glass and finished in faux white marble, the building boasted clean modern lines, bullet-resistant windows, and state-of-the-art electronic security. Although cleaner, "future-proofed" against electronic advances, and more comfortable than its predecessor, it lacked the old building's red brick and slate-tiled charm. On the other hand, it also lacked the shabbiness, the chilly winter drafts, and the black mould growing in every dark and damp corner.

Despite the new building's charmless shortcomings, after a week's enforced annual leave, Jones was actually pleased to be back. He'd missed the place. Well, if not the place then certainly the job.

16

That's it, Jones. Lighten up, old man.

He strode across the car park, skipped up the three steps to the covered entrance, and reached for the intercom button to have the desk sergeant buzz him entry.

"Hold on a minute, David," a female voice called out from the car park.

He turned and waited as the HR Director, Helen Ambridge, manoeuvred her wheelchair up the ramp. Good disabled access was perhaps the new headquarters' greatest single improvement over its predecessor. Watching Helen gain entry through the front, as opposed to the rear service entrance as she had to in the old place, lifted Jones' spirits.

"Morning, Helen," he said. "Lovely day."

"Hi, David," she said, breathing hard as she reached the flat section. "I see the holiday did you good. You bounded up those steps like a spring gazelle." She pushed out a hand enclosed in a fingerless cyclist glove and they shook. She held on and Jones covered her hand with his free one.

Helen, a happy, usually smiling woman in her mid-forties, never complained about a medical condition that he knew caused her great pain, and Jones admired the hell out of her for it.

"Nonsense," he said. "I haven't been a 'spring' anything for decades. And don't try to soft soap me, Ms Ambridge. I still haven't forgiven you for forcing me to take the holiday in the first place. Hardly diplomatic. Let me see now, what was it you said?" He glanced up at the clear blue sky as if searching for the memory. "Can't remember exactly, but the phrases, 'your subordinates need the break from you' and 'use it or lose it', spring into my age-addled mind."

"We all need a holiday, David. Even you. Go anywhere nice?"

"Yep," he said, nodding. "Stayed at home and took things easy. Caught up on a little reading, listened to the test match. I think young Ryan Washington would call it 'chilling'."

Helen, still holding his hand, turned it over and traced her fingers over his palm. Her gentle touch tickled and he jerked the hand away. She tutted and finished it off with a heavy sigh. "Oh dear me. Detective Chief Inspectors shouldn't tell fibs. They really shouldn't. Sets a bad example to the troops. Those calluses are fresh. You've been working on your cottage, haven't you?"

"Okay, I confess," he said, lowering his head and clasping his hands together, playing a schoolboy caught in a lie. "You're wasted in personnel. Should have been a detective. If you must know, I did lay a few courses of stonework and nearly finished the roof on the kitchen extension … while listening to cricket on the radio."

Helen's smile brightened an already cheery morning. Jones tried to recall the last time they'd had a decent conversation.

"January 10th," Helen said.

"Excuse me?"

Helen's blue eyes sparkled. "You were trying to remember the last time we chatted. January 10th. DI McDougall's leaving do."

"Added mind reading to your list of accomplishments, I see."

"You always were an open book to me, David."

Bloody hope not.

Detective Inspector Jock McDougall had been Jones' second-in-command until his wife's illness forced him to relocate to Scotland. Jones and Helen had spent the evening of his farewell party deep in conversation and staying relatively sober while everyone else did the exact opposite.

"He's a fine detective. Pity he had to leave, but I do understand his reasons." Jones lowered his voice, uncomfortable discussing personal matters in the open.

"Heard from him recently? How's Sheilagh?"

"Chemo's taking its toll, but being close to their families helps with the kids. Jock sounded almost optimistic on the phone—or at least he tried to. I'll make time to visit soon. He was part of my team for a long time."

The farewell party had been a boisterous and poignant affair. Nobody wanted Jock to go, least of all Sheilagh, who attended the "do" and was little more than a ghost of the vital woman that Jones had first met nearly a decade earlier. He'd seen their three young children at a number of social functions. Surprisingly, their youngest's runny-nosed, bright-faced presence hadn't completely horrified him.

The party had taken place back in the long dark days of winter. In the months that followed Jock's departure, Jones had managed to keep the DI vacancy open for Phil Cryer, Jones' next "chosen one". Unfortunately, as a Detective Sergeant, Phil didn't immediately qualify for the post.

"So, how are you these days?" he asked.

"As well as can be expected, thanks."

Jones reached for the call button on the door release keypad again.

"2-1-3-5," Helen said.

"Right, thanks."

"They change it every night at midnight."

"I know."

"Control would have sent you a text last night."

"I know that, too." The conversation was getting uncomfortable and the south-facing entrance had become an over-warm suntrap.

"Forgot to charge my mobile last night," he lied.

"Still struggling to work the inbox?" Helen asked, lowering her voice to the same level Jones had done earlier.

He frowned.

"Would you like me to book you on an IT refresher course?" she asked, employing her serious face, and her professional tone. "I can make it one-to-one, to save you the embarrassment if you like."

"Yes, please. That would be wonderful. I'll send you a memo with my availability. I'm bound to have a day or two spare next winter."

Or when hell starts spitting out icebergs.

Jones' most recent attempt to familiarise himself with the various police databases—PNC, HOLMES2, PNDNAD, and a lexicon of other ridiculous acronyms created by people with nothing better to do—had lasted all of three hours. The discovery of a dead body in a wheelie bin behind a row of garages in Sandwell had delivered him a wonderful reprieve. That had been six months earlier. He'd sworn the course leader—a fresh-faced sergeant from IT security—to secrecy, and had yet to rebook another course.

Reading from VDU screens gave him a headache. That was his excuse and he'd stick with it until someone higher up called him on it.

Jones dialled in the numbers and the lock mechanism disengaged with an extended *fizz-click*. He held the door open for Helen and accompanied her through the foyer. The tyres on her wheelchair squeaked on the highly polished floor.

They nodded a greeting to the grey-haired desk sergeant, Barney 'Feathers' Featherstone, who pointed to the telephone handset clamped to his ear and rolled his eyes. A fresh-faced constable sat at his right hand, probably trying to look a little less than terrified.

"I'm sorry, madam," Feathers said into the phone, patience itself, "but I'm afraid your dog doesn't constitute a missing person. I am unable to send a patrol officer …"

Jones and Helen exchanged amused glances and continued until they reached the bank of lifts at the far end of the corridor.

"Changing the subject," Jones said, "when are you going to stop trying to foist a new inspector onto my team?"

"That's nothing to do with me, I'm afraid. Superintendent Peyton wants to restore the head count before the next round of funding cuts. Anyway, what was wrong with the last candidate? Came highly recommended from Thames Valley. He has a superb arrest record."

Jones pressed the lift 'call' button and waited for two constables to pass behind them before answering. "There was nothing at all wrong with Inspector Lewis, but I have someone else in mind for the vacancy."

"DS Cryer?"

She really can read minds.

"If I can convince him to take the Inspector's OSPRE exams."

"What's stopping him?"

"Modesty. Thinks he's too inexperienced, but he's wrong. The man's an excellent detective. Always goes the extra mile, and I doubt he's failed an exam in his life."

Helen craned her neck to stare up at him. "You're talking about his gift?"

"Yep," Jones answered, nodding. "Best memory I've ever come across. It's uncanny."

"So," Helen said, removing her gloves. "If my average memory serves, DS Cryer's been your bag man since he made DS two years ago?"

"Yep, sounds about right."

"And he's had nothing but glowing annual reports since he joined the force's graduate leadership programme?"

"As I said, he's good. In fact, one of the best I've ever worked with."

"In that case, I can't see a reason why he shouldn't apply for promotion. One sec." She dug into the suitcase-sized handbag resting on her lap and retrieved a mobile phone. Her fingers tapped and swiped the screen. She nodded. "Thought so. This year's OSPREs are still open to applications. Want me to give DS Cryer a little nudge? I could send him an application form and put in a word with the Deputy Chief."

"Please, but can you do it on the quiet? I can't be seen to show favouritism, but the Serious Crime Unit is my responsibility and I'll make the hiring decisions this time."

"Okay, David, enough said."

Jones knew Helen understood exactly what he meant. Two years earlier, Jones' immediate superior, Superintendent-bloody-Peyton imposed a new member onto his team in the overblown and highly ineffectual shape of Peyton's drinking buddy, DS Charlie Pelham. Jones vowed never to let that happen again. He'd choose the next applicant, or hang up his spurs in protest.

The red light above the lift doors clicked on and the audible warning pinged. "If you don't mind, here's where I leave you," Jones said, pointing to the stairwell.

"Really? You're on the top floor, aren't you?"

Jones frowned as the lift doors slid open to reveal the shiny metal box—the small and enclosed, shiny metal box.

"I need the exercise," he said.

"No problem, I was only waiting for you. I need to use the facilities." She swivelled her chair and headed towards the disabled toilets at the far end of the hall. "These ones are the most spacious in the building."

"Great chatting with you, Helen. Perhaps we could have lunch sometime. I'll give you a call when I have a spare hour."

"That would be excellent," she called, "but I won't hold my breath."

Jones took the stairs two at a time and reached his floor without breaking into a sweat.

Chapter Four

Holton, Birmingham

AFTER SPENDING an hour reading Phil's excellent handover report, Jones left his office, large mug of tea in hand, and strolled to the end of the corridor. He entered the main SCU office, took one look at the mess, and nearly stormed back out. Crumpled papers, chocolate wrappers, used coffee mugs, and rings of dried liquid covered the surface of the conference table in the centre of the room. Phil Cryer's area was an oasis of cleanliness in the middle of the heaving devastation.

Jones closed his eyes to the mess and crossed to the window at the far side of the room. He studied the car park eight floors below and considered how easy it was for little things to ruin his good mood. He drained his mug and placed it on a conspicuously unused coaster on the windowsill, but before he could reach for the bin liners, the door swished open.

The team filed in led by Phil, looking almost svelte in a new suit. Charcoal and expensive, it was no doubt Manda's idea. Manda,

Phil's wife, heavily pregnant with their second child, understood what a well-tailored suit could achieve in terms of hiding Phil's rapidly developing paunch. Unfortunately, she also happened to be a damned fine cook, and Jones couldn't remember seeing Phil turn down an offer of food of any description.

DS Charlie Pelham followed. Belly flopping over the top of crumpled trousers, tie at quarter-mast, he took his usual position at the far end of the table and sat hunched over a steaming cup of black coffee.

Detective Constables Ryan "Wash" Washington and Alex Olganski completed the team. They stood side by side near the door, looked at the mess, exchanged glances, and stiffened in preparation for the inevitable detonation.

Jones didn't keep them waiting long.

"Pity's sakes. I leave the place for a week and you turn it into a cesspit. What's the matter with you all?"

Alex winced. She dug a roll of black bin liners from a cupboard under the water cooler and, with Wash's help, started clearing the desk. Jones glowered at Pelham, who seemed to find the froth decorating his coffee intensely fascinating.

"Detective Sergeant Pelham."

Pelham looked up, innocent as a kitten. "Yes, boss?"

"Most of that rubbish is yours."

"Nah. Don't think so." When he shook his head, both unshaved chins wobbled.

"You're the only one who eats chocolate bars by the armful and who can't be bothered to throw his litter in the bin." Jones pointed at the offending articles. "Jump to it, Sergeant. Clean your own mess. Alex and Ryan aren't your personal skivvies."

Pelham frowned and paused for a moment before levering himself upright and making a desultory effort to assist the housework.

"Don't know why the cleaners can't do this," he murmured.

"They aren't allowed in here unattended." Jones answered the rhetorical question. "Or do you want to stay late every night to supervise their work?"

Phil leaned against the windowsill beside Jones.

"Sorry, boss. I should have reminded them to tidy the place on Friday before we left. We don't see mess the same way you do."

"How long does it take to bin an empty cup?" Jones asked, but regretted it the moment the surly words left his mouth.

Phil's face creased into an apologetic smile.

Jones relented. "How's Manda?"

"Blooming, but taking everything in her stride, unlike me."

"Not long to go now."

"Five weeks and three days, but who's counting," Phil said, and the goofy grin of an expectant father broke out on his softening face.

"How's Jamie coping?"

"You saw what she was like a couple of weeks ago. Can't wait to meet her little brother or sister. She's almost as impatient as I am."

"She certainly was more, how can I put it … effervescent than usual. Barely finished her pudding. Most unlike a Cryer."

"Ouch," he said, sucking in his gut. "No fair."

Jones pushed away from the window. "Tell Jamie her Uncle David said 'Hi' and don't forget to wish Manda well for me, eh?"

"Will do, Uncle David," Phil said, smiling, but keeping his voice low.

With the desk clear, two litterbins emptied, and one full bin bag standing by the door ready for the basement incinerator, Jones took his seat at the head of the table. The others dropped into their normal positions and awaited his lead.

Alex tucked a lock of hair behind her ear. A small stud earring glinted in the sunlight spilling through the window. Jones hadn't noticed her wearing jewellery before. She tended to wear her wavy blonde hair down and preferred sensible clothing. Curvy and athletic, and an inch taller than Jones' five foot nine, she turned heads wherever she went.

Relatively new to the team, her quick and confident responses to his searching questions during her job interview had impressed the heck out of Jones. The fact that she had a current firearms licence didn't hurt either. None of the others in his team were qualified, although Ryan had volunteered to attend the upcoming training course. Jones had completed the paperwork. The next stage was to convince a reluctant Superintendent Peyton to release the funds. Jones would have to choose his moment carefully.

He rubbed his hands together. "Okay. Let's get started, shall we? I've read the handover notes so all I need now is a case-by-case status report. We'll start with the Post Office robbery. Alex, I understand you've identified a suspect?"

"Yes, boss." She stood and took a position by the whiteboard that covered the entire wall, facing the window. In her precise uppercase script, she'd written the case number, date and timeline, and the name and medical condition of the victim, Arthur Crabtree, who was currently in hospital and unconscious. The notes section included the name and mugshot of the suspect, Kelvin Richardson. Below the mugshot, Alex had also taped a telling still from the Post Office's CCTV footage—a clear image of a wild-eyed Richardson wearing a hooded top and staring full-face into the camera.

Jones encouraged verbal briefings in front of the whole team whenever possible. Reviewing the case was an important part of the investigative process and allowed input from members not directly involved with the case. An outsider's perspective could prove insightful.

Alex and Ryan, both good detectives in the making, needed to cover the salient facts and explain their thinking. One day, he hoped, they'd be briefing their own teams.

Halfway through her review, Alex pointed a remote control at the big-screen TV in the corner and played the CCTV recording.

"As you can see, there is a clear coverage of the attack and the assailant," Alex said toward the end of the footage. "His face is in full view, despite the hooded top."

"Did you identify Richardson from his picture?"

"Not at first," she replied. "He left fingerprints at the scene. His record is on the database."

"Do we have much on him?"

Alex opened her notepad, flipped the pages, and started reading.

"He has twenty-seven years of age, and has convictions for robbery, disorderly conduct, and affray. These go back to juvenile court. His first arrest and caution took place when he was thirteen. Wash and I visited his last known address on Saturday afternoon, but he is, what do you say, gone on a runner?"

Jones smiled. Alex's Swedish accent and misuse of colloquial English—that he'd never correct—made a nice change from the sloppy grammar and cockney slang spouted by others he could mention.

Ah, it's good to be back.

"Don't leave anything out, Alex," said Phil, who rolled his hand forwards as an encouragement for her to expand the story.

"Excuse me?" Alex asked.

"Tell the boss how the SOCOs missed the prints first time around, and you had to point them towards the evidence."

"It's true," Ryan agreed. "Alex spotted it after we'd all seen the film a dozen times. The Post Office took their sweet time to release the film. We didn't receive the tape until Friday evening, more than a day after the assault. We've had uniforms searching for Richardson all weekend, but there's been no sign of the bugger."

"He'll turn up soon enough," Phil said. "He's hardly a criminal mastermind if he's resorting to robbing pensioners."

Jones opened his hands in a "never mind" gesture. "Have you interviewed the victim?"

"Not yet," Alex answered. "The poor man is still unconscious. I plan to visit the hospital this morning."

"Okay, fair enough. Replay the tape from the start please."

They studied the monochrome film again—Jones for the first time.

Kelvin Richardson entered the cramped sub-Post Office and stood at the back of a five-person queue. His shuffling from foot to foot, and his hand waving betrayed a man with little patience for standing in line. The elderly victim, Crabtree, turned away from the serving counter, stuffed banknotes into his wallet, and headed for the exit. Crabtree tried to sidestep past Richardson, but the big man blocked his way. Crabtree opened his mouth to speak. Richardson threw a left jab, which connected with the elderly man's chin. He collapsed against a postcard carousel. As Richardson bent to snatch the wallet with one hand, his other hand brushed the carousel—a fleeting movement easily missed. As he turned to leave the shop, Richardson faced the CCTV camera, leaving the very still that currently adorned the whiteboard.

Alex had done well to notice where Richardson left his dabs.

Jones knew solid evidence when he saw it—video footage was a dream for any prosecutor to place in front of any jury. When they eventually charged Richardson, the CCTV pictures alone would be enough to convict him of criminal assault and robbery with violence. It would be a great collar for Alex's record.

"Well done, Alex," Jones said. "Why didn't the SOCOs dust the area on the day of the robbery? Standard operating procedure, I'd have thought."

Alex hesitated long enough for Pelham to grunt the single word, "Ghastly."

"What?" Jones rounded on Pelham, who'd resumed his habitual loose-limbed slouch.

"Sorry, boss. I meant to say our esteemed Senior Scenes of Crime Officer, Reginald Prendergast, arrived alone and performed his usual bang-up examination of the crime scene. Took him all of twenty bloody minutes."

Pelham's decision to stick the boot in when Reg wasn't around to defend himself was typical of the man.

Jones' mood darkened.

"In defence of Mr Prendergast," Alex piped up, "it was late in the day, and at the time we did not know how serious was the condition of Mr Crabtree."

"That's irrelevant," Pelham said. "Ghastly's fuck-up allowed Richardson all the time he needed to 'do a runner'."

Jones glared at Pelham, but the man simply wasn't bright enough to take the hint.

"Honest, boss," Pelham continued, "the bloke's an accident waiting to happen. Someone needs to sort him out before he screws a case completely."

"Thanks for that, Charlie," Jones said. For once, he couldn't argue with Pelham's logic, if not the tone of its delivery.

"All I'm saying's it ain't good enough. We don't need fuck-ups like Ghastly making our job any harder than it already is. Yeah?"

"We all make mistakes, and you don't need to swear," Jones said, trying to keep calm. "Leave it with me. I'll have a quiet word."

"Right you are, boss."

Jones didn't appreciate Pelham's accompanying sneer, but he let it ride and turned to face Alex once more. "I assume you and Ryan have searched Richardson's known haunts. Put out feelers to the usual contacts?"

Alex nodded. "We circulated his description to the media. They ran a short story on the local TV news last Saturday night, but we've had no sightings."

"What about Richardson's next of kin?" Phil asked.

Ryan fielded the question. "His mother lives in a flat in Smethwick. A God-fearing soul. You know the sort of thing. Statues of saints and crucifixes all over her front room. Claims not to have seen her 'troubled boy' for weeks and doesn't know where he might be."

"Friends and acquaintances?" Jones asked.

"The PNC has him as part of a gang on the Orchards Estate," Ryan answered, his eyes bright, happy being in the spotlight. "But no one's giving him up. There hasn't been a single call to the tip line."

Jones waited for Pelham to chime in following the mention of the Orchards Estate, his pet bailiwick. "Nothing to say, Charlie?"

Pelham jerked as though prodded with a fork. "Sorry, boss?"

"What's happening on the Orchards Estate?"

"Nothing much. It's quieter over there than Wash's sex life," Pelham said, his hand shooting up to forestall the younger man's retort. "Kidding, Wash. Couldn't help it. Too easy a target."

"Behave yourself, Charlie, we're not in kindergarten," Jones snapped. "The Orchards, remember?"

Pelham sniffed. "So, as I were saying. The Orchards is too quiet. Me and Wash's gonna chase up a couple of snouts later. I wanna see what's going on over there."

Jones turned to Alex again. She was much easier on the eye than the fat Londoner. "Thanks for that, Alex. Report to me after you've interviewed Mr Crabtree."

Alex returned to her seat.

"Now what about you, Phil?" Jones asked. "Any movement with the Robby Bridgestone case?"

"Not a lot. We had to release him under investigation," Phil answered. "The Crown Prosecution Service said our case wasn't strong enough to meet the criteria."

"What?" Jones said, shaking his head. "We gave them everything. Physical evidence, witness statements. The works. What more do they want?"

Phil shrugged. "You know lawyers. Desperate to cover their backs and keep their conviction rates up."

"I'll give the CPS a call. See if I can find out what we're missing. The victims deserve better that to have Robby Bridgestone wandering the streets." Jones made another note on his pad before pointing at Pelham. "Charlie, the Broxton Paper Mill fire? Any developments?"

Pelham sent a glance to Ryan before answering.

"Fire Investigation Unit took its sweet time, but confirmed it were arson. The accelerant were a lit candle and paraffin-soaked rags. Low tech and old school. The FIU pointed us to a torch what uses the same MO. I reckon the factory owner's in the frame for hiring him. Insurance fraud. Me an' Wash's next job is to pull the guy in for interview. I'll have the status report on your desk by day's end."

Jones studied Ryan's expression during Pelham's report. He made a reasonable job of giving nothing away, but Jones knew Ryan Washington would be the one to produce the report and have done most of the legwork on the investigation. At some stage in the not too distant future, Charlie Pelham would have to start pulling his weight. Being Superintendent Peyton's favourite drinking mate wouldn't save him for long. The SCU wouldn't carry passengers forever.

An hour later, after covering seven other active cases, Jones stood. "I think that's everything apart from a bit of housekeeping. Let me have your overtime sheets by the close of play today and I'll sort them in time for next month's payroll. Anyone have any questions?"

Ryan raised his hand.

Jones sighed. "Ryan, we're not in school. What's up?"

"Are you going to tell us what you did on your holidays, boss?"

The youngster's impish grin made his hooked nose and pointed chin more prominent. When smiling, he made a passable impression of a garden gnome, and lacked only the fishing rod and the pointed hat.

"No," Jones answered, adding a smile. "Class dismissed."

Chapter Five

MONDAY 27TH JUNE – *Alex Olganski*
Queen Elizabeth's Hospital, Birmingham

ALEX STEPPED BACK from the automated doors to give way to a nurse pushing an elderly woman in a wheelchair. The pained expression on the patient and her yellow skin brought back so many unpleasant memories of her dying father. After spending most of her teens watching him being taken to and from medical centres, she had no desire to enter Queen Elizabeth's Hospital, but her job demanded she overcome her irrational personal phobias.

The doors slid open, nurse and patient pushed through the doorway, and Alex followed them inside. She expected the smell of disinfectant and the taint of death to overpower her, but the overarching fragrance of flowers quietened her immediate fears.

She sidestepped the wheelchair and hurried to the reception desk, brandishing her warrant card to deflect the angry muttering of the patients waiting in the long queue. She held the ID against the glass screen and spoke into the germ-protective grill.

"Detective Constable Olganski. I would like to speak to someone about Mr Crabtree, from the Post Office attack. He was admitted last Thursday."

The attractive receptionist, Carla Gilchrist, according to the nameplate on her desk, studied Alex's ID card, compared her face with that of the photo, typed something into her PC, and then fixed Alex with lively hazel eyes.

"You'll need to talk with Dr Chopra. One moment and I'll call her." She lifted a telephone handset and leaned back as she spoke. Not once did she look away.

Alex found the attention both flattering and intrusive. To some civilians, the idea of a tall, blonde Scandinavian police officer would be an idea worthy of a pornographic movie. Others, mainly male police officers and criminals, would see her as a weak link. She was nothing of the sort, but had a continual fight to prove it. Alex could never tell whether women viewed her as a freak, a joke, or a potential partner. Thank heavens she had Julie, on whom she could rely implicitly.

Alex turned away from the appraising eyes of Carla Gilchrist, and studied the admissions area—a wide-open place teeming with patients, visitors, germs, pain, and the aura of death. She held back a shudder.

"Detective Constable Olgany?" Carla asked, smiling.

"Olganski."

"My mistake," Carla said, staring at Alex's lips. The attention, although not entirely unwelcome, brought warmth to Alex's neck and throat. "Dr Chopra's in the doctors' rest room. Follow that corridor." She pointed a manicured finger behind Alex. "It's the fifth, no, sixth door along on the right."

"Thank you."

"You're welcome. I hope you find the man who attacked Mr Crabtree. Such a shame when an old man can't collect his pension safely. And here we are being told that violent crime is on the decrease."

"It is, Ms Gilchrist. We try our best, but there are always a few bad apples."

"Please call me Carla," she said, parted her lips and smiled.

"Your accent. German, is it?"

"Swedish."

Carla's eyes widened. "Swedish, lovely. Are you in here on a work exchange scheme or something?"

"No. I've lived in England nearly eight years."

The attractive receptionist moved closer to the hygiene filter, making sure Alex caught full sight of her deep and enticing cleavage. "Very nice. I finish work in an hour. Perhaps we could meet and maybe discuss the crime figures. Or you could offer me some tips on self-defence. It's a dangerous world out there for a single woman."

"It is and that would be … wonderful, but I don't think my wife would approve. Thank you for your assistance, Carla. I follow that corridor, *ja*?"

"Shame, but if you ever change your mind, you know where I'll be."

"I do." Alex hid her smile from the over-familiar, but rather appealing woman. "But I won't change my mind."

———

THE DOCTORS' rest room was grubby and poorly lit. Full-length grey metal clothes lockers lined two walls, a table surrounded by dining chairs occupied the central space, and a three-panel screen partially hid a camp bed in the darkest corner.

A woman, Dr Chopra Alex assumed, sat at the foot of the bed. Fine-boned and slim, she owned the sunken eyes and rounded-shoulders of the chronically fatigued and decidedly over-worked. Slim arms, sticking through baggy, short-sleeved scrubs seemed more like those of a child than of a full-grown woman, but the care-worn expression on the drawn face put her age at mid-to-late thirties. Alex had seen the same exhausted expression many times—most often in the mirror after an extended night shift.

Alex flipped open her ID once again.

"Dr Chopra?"

The doctor pulled a pair of reading glasses from a pocket in the scrubs and read the warrant card. The glasses hid her tired eyes and took five years away from her age. "Constable Olganski. Please excuse me for not meeting you at the reception desk. I'm coming to the end of a thirty-hour shift. If I go to the admissions area, the first passing consultant will find something else for me to do. I suspect they think I don't need any sleep at all this week."

Alex took an immediate liking to the doctor, whose intelligent doe eyes shone bright behind the glasses.

"You need a prognosis on Mr Crabtree?" Dr Chopra asked.

Alex nodded and took out her notepad. The boss, a terrible technophobe, preferred his team to use pen and paper, but already some divisional commanders within the West Midlands Police had issued their staff with tablet computers. Before too long, even DCI Jones would have to bow to the advances of the information age, hopefully.

"We are hoping Mr Crabtree will be able to make a statement. May I talk to him?"

Dr Chopra shook her head. "An interview is out of the question, I'm afraid. Mr Crabtree suffered a significant myocardial infarction. I would be surprised if he ever regains consciousness."

"Oh dear. We had no idea his condition was so severe."

The doctor sighed. "Arthur Crabtree is ninety-three and extremely frail. An assault of the kind he suffered is extremely dangerous for a man with an underlying heart condition."

"The fall brought on the heart attack? Are you certain?"

Dr Chopra paused before answering, no doubt considering her words carefully. "In court, I think a pathologist could make a strong causal association. If Mr Crabtree dies—as is likely—you should charge the attacker with murder." She stood and the top of her head barely reached Alex's chin. "Forgive me, it's not for me to tell you your job, but it's a terrible thing. The elderly should be revered, cherished."

Alex gripped her pen tighter—her first murder case.

Should the poor man die, Alex would have to hand the case over to Phil and the boss, but until that time, she would work it to the best of her ability. Her investigative procedures and record keeping must be totally beyond reproach.

"Can I see Mr Crabtree?"

"Yes, but you'll get nothing from him. His daughter and son-in-law are there. They've barely left the hospital since last Thursday. I'm sure your presence will show them you're taking the case seriously."

"Of course we are. My boss would lay kittens if I didn't do my best to find the attacker."

Dr Chopra nodded, said nothing, but her thinned lips and raised eyebrow made it clear what she thought. In the place of the doctor, Alex, would also scoff.

———

MRS BERYL PIERCE blew her nose with a wrinkled tissue and dropped it into the full bin beside her father's bed. "This is terrible," she said, staring up at Alex through glistening eyes. "Dad made it through D-Day but will probably die because he didn't trust online banking. It's so unfair."

She buried her head into her husband's chest and the rest of her words were lost, but Alex understood the message.

Mr Pierce, back straight and tie in position despite what must have been a distressing vigil, rested a hand on his wife's back. Tears filled his eyes too, but he did not let them fall. Alex recognised in him a generation of men, men like her own father, who refused to show their feelings.

"What's happening?" he asked, keeping his voice a little more than a whisper.

Alex had to strain to hear him over the background hum of a busy ward and the electronic buzz of the medical equipment attached to his father-in-law.

"Our investigation is in the early stages, sir."

"But you have video footage of the robber, don't you? I mean, the news report said you did." He looked towards the TV mounted high on the wall opposite.

"We have pictures of the incident, but a statement from Mr Crabtree would be useful, if that were possible. I hoped he would be able to talk to me, but …" Alex let the sentence trail away, it was clear that her words were adding further upset to Mrs Pierce.

One glance at the pallor on the skin of the patient told Alex that Dr Chopra had not exaggerated his condition. She would learn nothing from Mr Crabtree. All she could think to do was offer her commiserations and hand her business card to Mr Pierce. "Please call me when Mr Crabtree awakens and is strong enough to talk."

"We both know that's not going to happen," Mr Pierce said without emotion.

His wife stopped crying and stared with fondness at the frail old man on the bed. With a tube in his nose, electrodes taped to his chest, and his light grey skin, he appeared close to the end. Mr Pierce's comment was not bitter, but factual, if insensitive.

Alex's thoughts turned back ten years to a hospital bed in Sweden, and a similar scene with Alex in the role of grieving daughter and her father in the role of terminal patient. She lowered her eyes and made another note.

"Do you know who did this?" Mrs Pierce asked, dabbing at damp eyes with a crumpled tissue.

Alex wanted to, but could not offer the usual platitudes.

"We have identified a suspect and initiated a search for him. We hope to make an arrest very soon. You understand, I can say no more at this stage, *ja?* I'm sorry."

Alex left Mr and Mrs Pierce with hope, which was more than she should have done. She had lost count of the number of times the boss told her not to predict the outcome of an investigation. They could apprehend a criminal, build what they considered as the perfect case, and yet still fail to gain a conviction in the courts. Such was life in the police service.

Alex bunched her hands into fists. For Mr Crabtree it would be different. They were building a strong case and had good, solid evidence. Kelvin Richardson would pay for his crime, of that Alex was as certain as she could be. Neither she nor the boss would accept any other outcome. She owed that much to Arthur Crabtree.

In a strange way, she owed it to her father, too.

Chapter Six

FRIDAY 6TH MARCH – *Sean Freeman*
London, England

FRESH FROM A SHOWER and pleasantly relaxed after an hour spent pummelling the heavy bag at the gym, Sean Freeman entered the near-deserted pub. He studied the place on his way to the bar—oak beams, corroded horse brasses, built-in leather bench seating, and darkened booths hugging the wall opposite the entrance. The sort of pub his father would have loved, it brought back fond memories of lost times.

A middle-aged man—flat cap, dun-coloured sports jacket, white shirt, dark blue tie, suit trousers, and leather shoes buffed to a high polish—sat at a corner table, alone. Head lowered, he worked a crossword puzzle and nursed half a pint of stout.

The fact that the crossword man didn't look up to investigate his arrival aroused Freeman's interest even more than the shiny shoes and mismatched clothes.

The man was too small and too old to be a minder.

A lookout, maybe.

The other chairs and benches stood empty.

The totty behind the counter grabbed Freeman's attention. She wore an entice-the-punters top emblazoned with the name of the establishment, the *Crown & Cushion*. The letters bulged as her breasts pushed against the thin material. She leaned over the bar making sure he couldn't miss the goods.

"Evening darlin', what can I get you today?" Her voice was low and sultry.

Don't tempt me.

She wore her long dark hair loose. A pair of twinkling brown eyes hinted at humour and availability. On any other night, he'd use his killer smile and ask for her number, but for the moment, he had more important things on his mind. A day spent mooching around the shop working on inconsequential repairs and trying to pump a tight-lipped Archibald for information on Parrish, had stretched his nerves.

Although Archibald told him nothing more than he had done on Thursday, it didn't matter. He'd asked the questions as camouflage in case Archibald's fear of Parrish was an act and Freeman's reaction to the situation found its way back to the "very bad man". Freeman already had everything he needed on Digby Bertrand 'DB' Parrish and his legitimate company, *Parrish Enterprises Ltd*, courtesy of the ninja hacking skills of his childhood friend, Corky.

From the day they met at secondary school, theirs had been something of a symbiotic relationship. Freeman protected Corky—a geek with a fear of confrontation and an unfortunate, almost Tourette's way with words. In return, Corky built electronic equipment to Freeman's specifications and provided Freeman with any information he needed. As they grew older, Freeman literally opened doors for Corky, who could barely go a week without losing his keys.

Under Corky's scrutiny, Parrish's activities hadn't remained a mystery for long.

"Evening," he said, and scanned the array of pump handles sticking up from the faded oak bar. He ignored the unfamiliar and ordered a trusted favourite, Old Speckled Hen.

The girl's arm muscles bunched and her breasts plumped when she pulled on the pump lever. He enjoyed the performance and the sparkle in her eyes told him she knew it. Time would tell, but maybe tonight didn't have to be all about the business.

"Quiet in here," he said, keen to take his mind off other things while he had a couple of minutes to spare.

"It's early, darlin'. Be jumping later on. Quiz night. There's a hundred-and-fifty notes on offer tonight. Rollover from last week. Stick around." She leaned her hands on the counter and gave him a second viewing—his night was looking better by the minute.

"Might do," he said. "Depends on how well my spot of business turns out."

"Business huh? Good luck."

"Cheers."

He handed over a fiver and received shrapnel in change.

The tip Parrish gave him came in handy. Though a hundred quid wouldn't last long at London prices, it felt good to have a bit of spare folding stuff for a change. He took a tentative sip and smiled in relief. Bitter, nutty, and full of body.

"Nice?" she asked.

"Nice," he answered, smiling.

He didn't think it possible, but the barmaid's smile widened even more. A dimple formed on her left cheek, giving her a cute, off-centre grin.

"We know how to keep a decent pint here."

Freeman took another full swallow, revelling in his temporary parole. Three years earlier, before the hard times, nights like this had been commonplace, but those days were long gone, or so it seemed. He raised his glass in salute, and eyed a booth furthest away from the main doors—the one in deep shadow, but offering a great view of both the front and rear entrances.

The old boy in the corner added another answer to his crossword.

Freeman leaned his back against the bar, pulled out Parrish's card and reread the handwritten note scribbled on the reverse.

Perfect Record

Crown & Cushion, Peat Street.
Tonight, 19:30.
I'm buying.

FREEMAN HAD a good idea what Parrish wanted, and hoped he could come up with the correct answers. He drained his glass but before he could order a refill and continue his chat with the well-endowed barmaid, the front doors opened and Parrish entered. Freeman checked the pendulum clock above the bar: 19:30. The underworld kingpin kept excellent time.

Crossword man filled in another clue and took a sip of his stout. Again, he didn't look up or turn around.

Parrish wore a different suit from the day before. This one, charcoal grey and beautifully tailored, screamed Savile Row. Freeman stuck out his hand. Parrish ignored it and left him hanging.

Fair enough.

The barmaid repeated her welcome but without the suggestive dip, and poured Parrish his requested whisky—single malt, no ice. Freeman ordered the same again. Parrish handed over a tenner and waved away the change.

He led the way to the booth Freeman had lined up as the most private and they sat. He sipped his beer and waited. Parrish had called the meeting and Freeman would let the older man take the lead.

Silent seconds extended into minutes.

A young couple, loud and colourful, barged through the rear door and demanded their usual. The barmaid, Karen according to the greeting called out by the boisterous newcomers, greeted them as old friends and had two bottles of a blue liquid—drinking straws included—on the counter before they had finished hanging their jackets on the hooks by the door.

Parrish raised his whisky to his nose and sipped. The liquid barely wet his thin lips. He looked at Freeman for the first time since sitting. "Down to business."

"You're calling the shots, Mr Parrish."

"S'right. Ain't you curious?"

"Yes, sir." Freeman studied the thinning head on his beer, but kept quiet.

"Yet you didn't bombard me with questions the moment we reached this booth." Parrish nodded slowly, as if in thought. "Appreciate that. Shows you got patience. A rare commodity in the very young."

"I'm not that young, Mr Parrish."

Parrish spoke quietly. "Sean Alan Freeman. Born 27th June 1982 at the St John's-in-the-Wood Maternity Clinic. Father's name, John, a locksmith. Mother's name, Natalie, State Registered Nurse. Died when you was a boy."

Freeman leaned away, eyes wide. "You've been checking me out."

"'Course I have."

"Why?"

"Why d'you think?"

Freeman shrugged and shook his head, going full throttle. "No idea, sir."

"Guess."

Freeman grew warm under the heat of Parrish's stare. "Is this a job interview?"

"Yeah."

"Really? What kind of job?"

"I'll get to that in a minute."

Two groups of four people entered and the decibel count increased from 'loud' to 'uncomfortable'. One of them headed straight for the gaming machine and started feeding it money. Rippling electronic notes shattered the calm. One part of Freeman's mind counted the coins the gambler fed into the machine's hungry mouth.

Parrish lowered his drink to the table. He rotated his glass between thumb and index finger. The whisky oscillated and he stared, apparently fascinated by the way it caught the light and threw out shards of gold. He waited a couple of moments for the undulating golden liquid to settle before speaking again.

"Wanna ask some questions?"

Freeman accepted the offer before Parrish took offence. "I'm guessing the Monarch key was a test?"

"Yeah, and one you passed or I wouldn't be 'ere. What I saw today makes you one of the best locksmiths in the country."

"Yeah, right," Freeman scoffed and took another gulp.

Parrish's eyes narrowed and his shoulders tensed.

"I ain't no bullshit merchant, sonny. Don't give me that wide-eyed and innocent bollocks. We both know how good you are."

Freeman dialled down the false modesty. No point continuing with an act that wasn't working.

"In that case, thanks, Mr Parrish."

Parrish relaxed. "Credit where it's due, son. Most locksmiths would have bottled out of the job or ballsed it up completely, but not you. I could see the excitement in your eyes when I handed you the knackered original. You're up for a challenge, ain't ya?"

Freeman didn't need to think about the question, but paused before answering, trying to show caution when he really wanted Parrish to get to the point and make the job offer he was desperate to accept.

"Sometimes, Mr Parrish, but it depends on the challenge."

"Good answer. Let's put it this way, son. As a locksmith you're a natural. At least that's what my research tells me."

"Thanks again, Mr Parrish." Freeman took another pull on his beer. It didn't taste as nice as it had before Parrish arrived. Freeman put it down to the creeping sense of unease he'd felt the moment Parrish fixed him with his pale blue-greys.

Focus on the prize, Sean.

"Don't look so worried, son. I always vet my potential employees. It's what them chinless arseholes in the fancy suits call 'due diligence'."

Parrish raised the glass, took a tiny sip, and returned the tumbler to its coaster. He fell silent. Again, Freeman waited.

The background noise grew with the swelling crowd and as the revellers lubricated their brain cells in preparation for the pub quiz. At least the place didn't have a jukebox, or, worse still, a Karaoke machine.

Despite the occasional pay-out, in ten minutes the gambler had lost forty-three pounds.

Moron might as well toss his money down a drain.

Parrish started speaking, but his words were lost as the machine chose that moment to vomit up a small fraction of the coins it had swallowed. Gambling man whooped and yelled, "Jackpot!" The pay-out didn't cover a third of the losses, it never would, but the machine threw out enough loot to entice the twenty-something gambler into feeding it even more coins.

Parrish resumed. "A recent change in personnel has left me short a man with your specific skills."

Freeman nodded, but said nothing.

"The man whose vacancy I'm looking to fill was my company's Chief Security Officer. He looked after the locks and surveillance equipment in my clubs and offices, among other things. You get what I mean when I say 'other things'?"

"I think so, Mr Parrish."

"Unlike you, he didn't know jack-shit about electronics, but given enough time, could open any mechanical lock ever made. Trouble is him and me had us a little falling out. A difference of opinion that's left me with a vacancy to fill. A very well-paid job. Do you understand what I'm getting at, son?"

Freeman chewed the inside of his cheek and considered his answer. Given the information uncovered by his own "due diligence", the missing employee's body was likely propping up a motorway flyover, or rotting in a landfill somewhere. If Freeman had any sense, he would have made his excuses and run for the door, but the offer of a well-paid job by Parrish was something he'd been working towards for three years. He'd honed his skills and wheedled his way into this position and wouldn't—couldn't—run from the opportunity now.

And no one who knew the real Sean Freeman would ever accuse him of being over-endowed with sense.

"I've been looking for a decent locksmith for a while and I reckon you're my man."

"Do you mind if I ask how you found me?"

"Don't matter. All you need to know is I found you and want you to come work for me. What d'you say?"

Freeman allowed excitement to bleed into his voice. "I don't know what … I mean, I'm speechless."

Parrish scanned the pub and sneered. "While you think about things, get another round."

"You've barely touched yours yet, sir. I can wait until you're ready for a refill."

Parrish picked up the glass, and downed it in one. "Worth waiting for," he said, and his words faded into a sigh. "Answer me one question."

"If I can."

"Why are you working for an uppity gobshite like Archibald?"

How else was I going to attract your attention?

Instead of telling the truth, Freeman lowered his head and spoke to the remnants of his beer. "I'm sorry, sir. Don't like talking about it."

"Ain't no shame in it, son. I'll tell the story. Your dad took ill and you had to stop work to look after him." Parrish placed his left hand flat on the table, tapped the surface with his index finger. "You defaulted on your business loan and your father lost the family home."

"That's about the strength of it," Freeman said, jaws clenched.

"The insurance company screwed your dad over, right?" Parrish said.

Freeman made fists. "Bastards accused him of lying about his health on the loan application forms."

"I know," Parrish continued, "and, as a bankrupt, you lost the shop and your Guild certification. You can't set up as a locksmith using your own name, so you have to work for a spineless shit like Archibald. Can't apply for another business loan neither. It's a fuckin' bitch, innit?"

Freeman stared into his empty beer glass, unwilling to meet

Parrish's eyes. "Too right it is."

He battled anger and frustration every day. Most days he fought to an honourable draw, but never won. But DB Parrish didn't know the half of it. He thought he did, but no way. The full story was buried deep, and would remain that way until Freeman decided otherwise.

"And even when you are discharged as a bankrupt, the Guild ain't gonna reinstate your membership for years. Any way you look at it son, your life's fucked for the next fifteen years."

"Yes, sir." Freeman couldn't add anything else and stood. "I need that drink now. Same again?"

"Yeah, go for it."

Freeman returned with the order and Parrish spoke as he retook his seat. "Is it true there ain't a lock, mechanical or electronic, you can't open?"

"Dunno, sir, but if there is, I haven't found it yet."

"Another good answer. What happens if the right bump key, or pick gun ain't on the market? Make 'em yourself?"

"I do."

"You also know how to build frequency jammers, electronic tumbler sensors, video maskers, and motion sensor inhibitors?"

"Yes, sir."

"Excellent." Parrish smirked. "Tell me what's going through that head of yours right now."

"Honestly?"

"Course."

"Why d'you want a Monarch key?"

Parrish smiled and rubbed his angular jaw. "You reckon I'm gonna break into Buckingham Palace or summat?"

"The thought had crossed my mind. Or maybe you're trying to convince me to do it for you?"

Parrish's barked laugh was neither musical nor infectious.

"Nah. The Queen ain't got nothing as takes my fancy. 'Sides, I'm a royalist. Love Her Majesty and all she stands for. Makes me proud to be British."

Freeman was glad his glass was on the table or he might have spilled beer down his shirt.

Parrish downed his second whisky in one. "Back to business," he said, wiping his mouth with the back of his hand and leaning close. "From time to time I come across nuggets of information. If used properly, this knowledge proves valuable. Do you see where I'm headed with this?"

"Yes, sir. I'm listening."

The edges of Parrish's mouth twisted into a smile. He leaned even closer and lowered his voice to a whisper. "Open certain locks, when and where I tell you, and I'll make you rich. What you got to say 'bout that?"

Freeman gulped half his third beer before responding with, "What doors and how rich?"

"Another good response, son. Think I'm gonna like you. We'll talk details later, in private. Interested?"

"Yes, but … there's a problem."

"What's that?"

"I don't do violence."

Unless I'm backed into a corner.

"Neither do I, son," Parrish said, straight-faced.

No, you get others to do it for you.

"Well? What do you say, Freeman?"

"Do you need an answer now, Mr Parrish?"

Parrish glowered. "Fucking hell, boy, I just offered you the keys to the executive shitter. Why ain't you biting my arm off?"

Don't keep him waiting, Sean, you'll lose him.

Freeman shook his head.

"I'm sorry, sir. It's come as a bit of a shock is all. 'Course I accept. When do I start?"

"Atta boy. I'll be in touch."

"Shall I hand in my notice at Archibald's?"

"Well now, ain't you the keen one all of a sudden."

"Sorry, Mr Parrish, but poverty's overrated. You understand, don't you?"

Another smile flickered briefly, but again failed to warm the man's ice cold eyes.

"Yeah, I do. Don't worry 'bout a notice period. Archibald ain't gonna complain." Parrish stood. "Someone'll email you with details for the next meet."

"You have my email address?"

Parrish snorted. "Don't act stupid, Sean. It don't suit."

Freeman rubbed the back of his neck. "And in the meantime?"

"Carry on as you are for now, but keep the weekend after next free."

Freeman closed his eyes for a moment and took a breath. "Thanks for the opportunity, Mr Parrish. I won't let you down."

At the bar, Karen tapped on a microphone. She called for quiet and for the quiz teams to cough up their entrance fees.

Parrish beckoned Freeman closer and lowered his voice. "In the meantime, find out all you can about the Zinfandel Clasp."

"You've a job lined up already? How'd you know I'd say yes?"

"Educated guess." Parrish scanned the room. "I'll be in touch."

"I'll be ready."

"Better be, son." He dropped five twenties on the table. "That's for the drinks and a taxi home."

Freeman folded the cash and slid it into his pocket. "Thanks, Mr Parrish. I appreciate everything."

Parrish nodded. "So you fucking should."

Freeman and Parrish crabbed their way through the crowd. Seconds after Parrish pushed through the main door, the Bentley whispered to a stop in line with the entrance. The driver double-parked, ignoring the queue of angry drivers piling up behind. A man-mountain—the shadow-maker from the doorway of Archibald's shop—squeezed out from behind the steering wheel. Fair-haired, with scar tissue above and below his left eye, and muscles fighting to break free of his restrictive suit, he hurried around the front of the car and held open the rear door.

"Home, Hutch," Parrish said, sliding into the back.

From the doorway, Freeman watched the car until it turned left towards the city. He pumped his fist.

A delighted Freeman scanned the pub for anyone taking undue interest. As expected, crossword man had left at the same time as Parrish, but by the rear exit.

Freeman fought his way to the bar, and waited to catch Karen's eye. It didn't take as long as he feared. The friendly barmaid incurred the wrath of her regulars by allowing him to jump the queue.

"Hi, handsome," she said. "How'd the business meeting go?"

"Bloody good, thanks."

"Same again?"

"Please."

She pulled the beer and leaned over the bar in the same suggestive way as she'd done earlier. The two young lads closest to him craned their necks so far they risked serious injury.

"Anything else, luv?" Her smile made the offer impossible to refuse.

"Is it too late to enter the quiz? I'm feeling lucky."

She winked. "You might well be."

Chapter Seven

FRIDAY 20TH MARCH – *Sean Freeman*
Near St. Margaret's Hospice, London

AFTER WORK, Sean Freeman had spent the early part of the evening at St Margaret's Hospice holding John Freeman's lifeless hand, talking over his decision and wondering why Parrish's email hadn't arrived yet. As it always did, the rust-pitted bed in John Freeman's drab ward, depressed the fuck out of him during the ninety-minute visit, but God knew what it did to the comatose man lying in the same bed month after month. Locked inside his head and with nothing to stare at but the paint peeling from the ceiling and the television set to daytime chat shows and evening soaps, John Freeman must have suffered the torments of hell—assuming he suffered anything at all.

Back in his soulless bedsit, Sean Freeman dragged his mind from the horrors of the hospice and stared at the view through his darkened window. The railway cuttings didn't improve with familiarity or with the orange platform lighting that wouldn't snap off until half-past midnight.

The bedsit, a twenty-five metre square room with a kitchenette, a small table and one chair, and a sofa bed, wasn't much of an improvement over St Margaret's, but at least he could move around, unlike poor John Freeman.

He lowered his gaze to the laptop screen, set to his Internet browser, and willed it to ping at him. It stared back, a blank white screen with a blue border. For the millionth time, he clicked the "Get Mail" icon:

There are no new messages.

"WATCHED POT, SEAN," he muttered to the unhearing walls.

He tabbed across to his research folders and opened the Zinfandel Clasp file. It ran to thirty-three pages, and Freeman could recall every word and photo. Another scan-read passed an hour, but dried his eyes and spiked his thirst. He closed the file and stared at the bottle of red plonk on the tiny surface in the kitchenette. It had been open a week but would still be drinkable, probably. Freeman doubted he'd be able to tell the difference between a fresh and a stale wine anyway.

"Ah, why not?"

He wasn't in the habit of solitary drinking, but if Parrish didn't make contact soon he might just break his rule and take it up. He stretched out an arm to snag the bottle, half-filled his coffee mug, sniffed, sipped, and spat it back into the mug. Vinegar. Perhaps his sommelier skills weren't as undeveloped as he expected.

The electronic *plink* of incoming mail nearly knocked him from the chair. He emptied the bottle and the mug into the sink before double-clicking the highlighted message bar:

Bandstand. Regent's Park. Midday Sunday.
Bring an overnight bag.

. . .

"YES!" he yelled. "About bloody time."

The 21:33 from Euston thundered past not fifty yards from his window, shaking the laptop screen.

He replied, "Okay", and re-read the message.

Hutch, Parrish's pet gorilla, had turned up at the shop that morning to buy a brass padlock and gave an enigmatic message that Freeman hadn't understood until reading the email.

"Add an hour, and take off a day," Hutch had said while paying for the lock. Freeman asked him to repeat the message, but big bugger sneered, grunted, "You heard," and left.

Plugging the code into the email message gave Freeman the actual meeting time, one o'clock tomorrow, Saturday. He struggled to contain the nervous excitement and barely slept a wink all night.

Chapter Eight

SATURDAY, *21st March – Sean Freeman*
Regent's Park, London

THE MILITARY BAND, stuffed into place beneath the octagonal pagoda roof of the Regent's Park bandstand, strangled the life and soul out of a Beatles medley. Freeman tried to blank out the god-awful din and concentrate on the upcoming meeting. When the band segued into an enthusiastic tribute to the late Freddie Mercury, Freeman didn't know whether to laugh or cry.

With only three weeks until Easter, the sparse crowd occupying the scattered deckchairs had wrapped up well against the cold. Nodding heads and tapping feet suggested that at least the tone-deaf members of the audience appreciated the entertainment, as well they might. Precious little else in London came free.

He completed three circuits of the path surrounding the Victorian relic without spotting anyone he recognised. Watch checked for the hundredth time, he wondered what had gone wrong before catching sight of the blond giant.

Hutch stood next to the diminutive Digby Parrish, which made him appear even larger, an impression that only increased as Freeman hurried towards them. Another man stood ten paces behind Hutch—five foot ten or eleven, black hair cropped close, five o'clock shadow darkening an already swarthy complexion.

"Bang on time, son. Nice one."

"Thanks, Mr Parrish. Thought I'd missed you."

Parrish pointed to a row of benches on a rise overlooking the bandstand. "Let's take a seat, and listen to the music."

Do we have to?

Freeman followed the three men, but kept a discrete distance.

Parrish stopped at a slatted bench occupied by an elderly couple, each of whom held an ice cream cone and tapped their feet in time to Mercury's *Barcelona*. Hutch stood one metre from the old folk, blocking their view of the band, arms folded, glowering. The old man's hands shook so much the ice cream fell from the cone and dropped into his lap. He jumped up and ushered his partner away. She muttered something about the "youth of today", and "British Bobbies" in an American accent, but the man kept dragging her away and rubbing at the white stain with a cotton handkerchief.

"That's better," Parrish said. "This is my favourite spot. Best acoustics in the park." He pointed at the row of oaks behind him— a flush of new leaves, fresh and hopeful—and the ten-foot tall brick wall behind them. "The trees fuck up parabolic microphones."

Paranoid much?

"Adamovic, do the business," Parrish ordered.

The dark man rushed forward and waved a scanner wand over Freeman, head to toe, front and back. It emitted a continuous squeal, but didn't spike.

"He is clean, Mr Parrish. Not even an active mobile phone," he said in a strong East European accent.

Adamovic stepped back and took up a position to the left of the bench to cover a view of the right side of the park, and far enough away to be out of earshot. Hutch stood to the right of Parrish, but kept within arm's length. His view overlapped that of Adamovic. Between the two of them, they covered a two-hundred-and-seventy degree arc without making it too obvious. The oaks and wall protected the remaining ninety degrees.

Freeman was glad he'd powered down his phone. "You think I'm wearing a wire? I wouldn't do—"

"Can't be too careful in this game, son. Never know who wants to muscle in on the business. It ain't only the filth as wants to know what's going on. Hostile takeovers don't only happen in boardrooms and banks."

"Sorry, Mr Parrish. All this is new to me, but I'll learn."

Parrish wiped the seat of the bench with a cotton handkerchief, hitched up his trouser legs to avoid stretching the knees, and sat. He indicated that Freeman should sit next to him, but not too close. Like a good little lapdog, Freeman obeyed.

"What d'you find out about the Zinfandel Clasp?"

Straight down to business, good.

Freeman hesitated, pretending to search for the memory. "A brooch. Flawless blue diamond, pear-shaped, radiant cut, high brilliance, plenty of fire. Fraction under eighty carats. Set in a platinum clasp the shape of a crown. Insurance value puts it between five and eight million pounds, depending on which company issues the cover. Currently owned by the Michelin-starred Italian chef, Luciano Montalbano, and stored in a bank vault in Florence."

"Excellent. You're making my mouth water just by talking about it. The only thing you got wrong is the location."

"Really?"

"Ever been to Winchester?"

For effect only, Freeman paused momentarily. "Don't think so, but why? Hang on … no don't tell me, Aldo Pontini, right?"

Parrish smiled. "Very good. I knew you was the right man for this business."

The band broke into a rousing version of Colonel Bogey. Parrish tapped his hand against his thigh and jutted his chin in time with the beat.

Freeman continued. "Aldo Pontini's just opened up a new workshop on the outskirts of Winchester, near a village called Sparsholt."

"That's right, son. Wanted to move closer to his grandchildren. Soft bugger." Parrish stared expectantly at Freeman.

"And you want me to steal the Clasp for you?"

"Too fucking right. The boy's clever, ain't he, Hutch?"

The left side of the big man's face twitched. Freeman took it as the giant's version of a smile.

Parrish continued talking. "Pontini's first job in his new place is to reset the Zinfandel diamond. Turns out Montalbano's butterfin-gered wife dropped the beauty on the floor. Cracked the setting. Damn near broke the floor tiles too, the rock's that heavy."

Freeman could see an obvious flaw in the plan. "Aldo Pontini's one of the best jewel smiths in the world—"

"So what?" Parrish snapped.

"If he's working on the Zinfandel Clasp, the insurance company and Montalbano will have his place locked up tighter than the Prime Minister's lunchbox. How am I supposed to steal it?"

"Figure it out. You have 'til first thing Monday morning."

"What? That's not enough time."

"It'll have to be."

"Why? Is that when Pontini returns the Clasp?"

"Nah," Parrish said. "That's when his new security system goes live. Before then, his place is an open door to a man with your apparent talents."

"Bloody hell. A day and a half? I don't have a hope. There's no time to research or scout the place. I'll be going in blind."

Parrish grinned, but again without warmth. "Would the archi-tect's floor plan and the blueprints to the new security system be of any use?" He patted a bulge in his camelhair coat.

"How in the hell did you get those?"

"None of your fucking business. Well, you up for the job?"

Freeman hesitated, again for show only. He'd passed the point of no return by turning up to the meeting, but if he didn't talk money, Parrish would wonder why.

"If I do, what's my cut?"

"Nothing. Nada. Zilch," Parrish said adding another chilling smile.

"What?"

Freeman leaned forward, preparing to leave, but Parrish grabbed his arm. Hutch half-turned and wagged an index finger.

"You haven't been dismissed yet, Freeman. Sit the fuck down," Hutch growled.

Freeman stared at the monster for a nanosecond before obeying. No way could he tackle the big bugger on equal terms. Besides, he was there for the job and had no real intention of leaving at this stage anyway.

"Oh no, son," Parrish said, releasing his grip. "Think of this as your second and final practical exam. A field-test if you like. You passed the first one, but that were a piece of piss compared to the Clasp. You had the original key and the bittings code, and weren't under no pressure. I wanna check your bottle before putting you on the payroll."

"Payroll?"

"Oh yeah, didn't I say? Fetch me the Zinfandel Clasp and you'll earn a position in the company."

"Officially?"

"Yeah, it's all gonna be totally legit. You'll have a contract and pay your taxes and National Insurance contributions, the lot. As I already told you, there's a vacancy on the Board of *Parrish Enterprises Ltd*. How does SVP of Corporate Security sound?"

"Rewarding?" Freeman's heart raced.

He'd finally made it, providing he could do the deed.

"Yeah, that's right. The post pays two-hundred-and-ten grand a year plus fringe benefits. For a start, you get private health insurance that'll include your old man. You'll be able to move him from that shithole, St Margaret's."

"Bloody hell! You know where John Freeman is?"

Parrish frowned. "You call your father John Freeman, not Dad?"

Freeman nodded and then lowered his head.

"Why?"

"It's hard to explain. You might not understand."

"Try me."

"I ... I ..." Freeman wrung his hands and stared at the crack in the paving slab between his feet. What would a thug like Parrish make of his explanation?

"Out with is, son. I don't got all bleedin' day," Parrish said, the abrupt words softened by a lowered voice.

Here we go.

Freeman took a breath.

"The empty shell lying in that grubby hospice bed isn't my father. I can't think of him as anything other than a patient needing care. Calling him John Freeman gives me … distance. I know it makes me sound like a lunatic. I … can't expect you to understand."

He looked up expecting to see a sneer, but Parrish stared back with an expression close to sympathy.

Bloody hell! A heart inside that narrow chest?

"Don't underestimate me, boy. Me mum died of the stomach cancer thirty-five years back. Me dad buggered off years before and left me to take care of her on me tod. I know what it's like watchin' someone you love rot slowly from the inside out."

"I'm sorry to hear that, sir, but you have no idea how bad it is inside St Margaret's."

"'Course I do. I need to know I can trust my employees. Had a team watching you since the *Crown & Cushion*. They've been sending me reports and pictures. Those wankers in St Margaret's are running a fucking crap-hole. I wondered how you could stand to see your old man in a place like that."

Freeman chose his next words carefully. "Tears my heart out every time I visit him, Mr Parrish. That's why I'm accepting your job offer. I'm no thief, but the bastard insurance company robbed us blind. I need the money and I need it yesterday."

Parrish shot a sideways look at his minder. "Hear that, Hutch? He's upset at an insurance company. You reckon we can help young Sean get some payback?"

Hutch snorted. "If you say so, Mr Parrish."

"The health insurance, Mr Parrish, are you serious about that?" Freeman asked.

"Deathly. Think about it, son. You can get your father out of that cesspit and put him in a private hospital. He'll get the best medical care possible. I'll pull strings and make sure he's part of any new drug trials that might help his condition."

"You can do that?"

"'Course I can. You calling me a liar?"

"Sorry." Freeman jerked up an apologetic hand. "It's just that I've been struggling so long to find him decent care … I can't …"

"Don't blubber, son. It ain't becoming of a grown man. First thing you can do is move out of that crapper you call home. No executive of *Parrish Enterprises Ltd* lives in a chuffin' bedsit. Wouldn't give off the proper vibe, now would it? The company owns a block of apartments in Docklands. You can move into one this afternoon so I can keep me eye on ya, but don't fuck up the job tomorrow night or you'll be homeless. That's why I told you to bring an overnight bag. Adamovic is gonna sort you out a set of keys. What's more, I own a removals company. They'll pack up your personal stuff and have it delivered by Monday night, always assuming you 'liberate' the Clasp without no problems. I'll throw in a car too. Piece of crap Ford, but it'll do until you choose one you like."

Freeman rubbed some feeling back into his face, which had grown numb from the cold and the blood pooling to his stomach.

"I don't know what to say."

"And don't forget the bonus scheme."

"There's more?"

Things were moving quickly, but Freeman took in all the information. He knew what Parrish was trying to do. He was trying to buy his soul with promises of gold and trinkets, but he didn't need to try quite so hard. Freeman had already bought all the goods and didn't need the sales pitch.

"How does five percent of the insurance valuation of any 'off book' job grab you?"

Freeman puffed out his cheeks. "Grabs me by my wallet and won't let go. I do have one question, if you don't mind."

"Fire away."

"Don't get me wrong, I'm not questioning your logic, but who's going to buy the Zinfandel Clasp? I mean, it's one of the most recognisable diamonds on the planet. No fence would touch it. So where's the profit in stealing the bloody thing in the first place? Do you plan to cut it up?"

"Don't be a plonker, son. I'd never butcher something as stunning as a seventy-nine-point-three carat diamond. It'd be like cutting up my own child."

"You've got kids?"

"Nah, figure of speech," Parrish answered. "Diamonds are beautiful. Ever seen one up close? Ever held a big rock in your hand?"

Freeman shrugged. "Far as I'm concerned, diamonds are nothing but shards of carbon. Useful if you need a decent cutting tool, but as jewels they're a waste of space."

"That's blasphemy in my house." Parrish's whispered words leaked menace. The old, hard-nut villain was back, which was good. Freeman wasn't at all comfortable with the empathetic Parrish he'd just met. That version of the man made his skin crawl even more.

Freeman studied the gangland boss. A light sparkled behind his normally dead eyes. In that moment, Freeman saw it. Parrish loved diamonds. He craved them. It was as simple as that.

"I got enough readies, boy," Parrish continued, his voice hushed. "More money than I could spend in two lifetimes: casinos, hotels, bookies, restaurants, boozers. They all earn legit money, and that's just the stuff as passes through the books." Parrish stared in the direction of the bandstand, but his eyes focused on something only he could see. "Between you, me, and Hutch, I got millions salted away from other areas of, what shall we say … 'commerce', but what I don't got, is what people tell me I can't have."

Hutch, who had been standing beside Parrish, hands clasped behind his back scanning the area with a motorised CCTV camera for a head, did his almost-smile thing again. He'd obviously heard the speech before, but to Freeman the insight into what drove Parrish was both enlightening and chilling. He tucked the information away in case he needed it later.

Parrish continued, half to himself. "When I think of that fat Italian cook owning the Clasp just 'cause he can boil an egg or open a tin of sun dried tomatoes, makes me wanna rip his ears off and feed them to him with his zucchini."

The band moved on to *Amazing Grace* and Parrish sighed. "Love this tune. Real moving." He clasped his hands together and turned to face Freeman for the first time since they'd taken their seats. He sneered at Freeman's creased jeans and mock leather bomber jacket. "Once we're back from Winchester, I'll organise a buying trip for you with one of my shopping girls. You can go get yourself some decent threads. Can't turn up to the boardroom looking like you've been dossing in a shop doorway."

"I have a suit, but only wear it for weddings and funerals."

Parrish curled his lip again.

"Can't promise you many weddings, but get yourself half a dozen tailored whistles and you'll be sorted. Now fuck off." He dismissed Freeman with a snapped wave of the hand, interview over. "Adamovic is gonna drive you to your new gaff. Hutch and me will stay here and watch the band play."

Freeman stood and stared at the bandstand, trying unsuccessfully to block out the dreadful cacophony.

"Let me know who wins."

"Huh?"

"Nothing, an old joke courtesy of Len Deighton."

"Comedian was he?"

"No, he wrote the Harry Palmer spy books." Parrish's frown returned and Freeman gave up the explanation as a lost cause. "Thanks for the opportunity, Mr Parrish. I won't let you down."

"I know you won't, son."

Freeman offered his hand, but Parrish turned away, leaving him hanging for a second time.

Chapter Nine

London, England

THREE MILES FROM WINCHESTER, Freeman felt ready to throw up his late supper. It took all his self-control not to lean out the car window and hurl, but that wouldn't have done much for his "cool cracksman" image. It might even have lost him a job he didn't yet have. Adamovic drove while Freeman concentrated on steady breathing and dropping his mind into the zone.

Parrish and Hutch were following in the car behind.

As promised, Parrish had provided detailed plans of Aldo Pontini's new workshop. The paperwork included architect's blueprints, wiring diagrams for the old and the new security systems, and the details of Pontini's safe—a 1975 Chubb Imperial. How on earth Parrish acquired the information, Freeman had no idea and didn't ask again, but the short man had to have some serious juice to obtain it.

When he'd asked about security guards, Parrish told him there weren't any, and said, "Pontini don't want a bunch of goons around the place scaring his grandkids. Told you he was a soppy old bugger."

"What?" Freeman blurted out. "A multi-million pound diamond in his possession and a disconnected alarm system, and he doesn't have guards? Doesn't seem likely to me."

"You ain't doubting me again, are you, son?" Parrish had said in a manner that ended the discussion.

Freeman had spent the previous day and a half in his new home studying the papers. The place Parrish had called his "new gaff" turned out to be a stunning penthouse apartment overlooking the Thames. It had to be worth a couple of million pounds of anybody's money. Furnished in smoked glass, chrome, and marble, it was both elegant and comfortable, and clinical and soulless in the same breath. It was so far removed from the crappy bedsit, Freeman would take a while to get used to the acreage alone, but he'd manage somehow. Every aspect of his life had picked up. All he had to do now was steal the Clasp and he'd be set. The thought turned the contents of his stomach into broken lumps of concrete.

Cool it, Sean. It's a piece of cake. You can do this, easy.

He hadn't taken long to identify the temporary hole in Pontini's security, which would close the moment the system was connected to the security company's control centre. Parrish was dead right when he said the job had to take place this weekend. By Monday afternoon, *Aldo Pontini Studios* would be as secure as any bank in England.

During the weekend, Adamovic—under instructions from Parrish—had only allowed Freeman to leave the apartment twice, once to visit St Margaret's, and once to collect specialist tools from his old rented lockup. Adamovic, who barely spoke, hadn't left his side since Regent's Park. He'd even slept in one of Freeman's two spare bedrooms. Clearly, Parrish didn't trust him enough to leave him unwatched.

———

DESPITE HIS BEST EFFORTS, the ninety-minute drive from London allowed the questions to form. Had he thought of everything? Could he open the safe? What would happen if he failed? Would Parrish let him disappear, or was he staring at a swift end and an unmarked grave in another landfill? What about the cops?

Shut it, Sean. You'll be fine.

On paper, and in the sunlit comfort of his new home, the job appeared simple enough. Snip a couple of wires, open two padlocks, two mortise locks, a couple of internal lever locks, and he'd be in. The Chubb safe itself presented no challenge, not with his special can-opener.

He had no doubt the technical stuff was doable, no bother, but did he have the stones to commit a real-life, in-your-face crime?

Until this point, he'd only broken into the homes of people who'd locked themselves out through negligence or mechanical breakdown. On those occasions, Freeman had the homeowner's permission. He'd even earned their gratitude, but this was a different matter entirely. He tried to relax and think of something pleasant, but nothing came to mind.

As they left the M3 and skirted the ancient town of Winchester, the nerves struck hard. Freeman's stomach cramped and he found the simple act of breathing a chore. No matter how many times he wiped his sweaty palms on his trouser legs, they wouldn't stay dry. He must have looked terrified, because when forced to stop at a red light, the normally reserved driver smirked.

"Suck it up, kid. You are playing in the big leagues now."

Freeman nodded but didn't trust himself to speak.

Eyes on the prize, Sean. Eyes on the prize.

He drummed his fingers on his thighs as their two-vehicle convoy passed through Winchester keeping nicely below the speed limit. Once out on the quiet and dark B3049 heading towards Stockbridge, the earpiece Parrish had given him burst into life for the first time since they left London.

"You there, boy?"

He thumbed the press-to-talk button Velcroed to his index finger and spoke into the microphone clipped to his lapel. "Yes. Go ahead."

"*Be there in five minutes. You okay?*"

"Never better," he lied.

Adamovic, who had his own earpiece, snorted. He dropped the car into third and made a sharp right.

"*Remember, I want a blow-by-blow. Talk me through everything you do. Right?*"

"Yes, sir. No problem," he lied again.

As though he didn't have enough to worry about, Parrish wanted him to run a bloody football commentary.

Fuck's sake, isn't the job difficult enough?

Adamovic pulled the car to a stop two-hundred metres from their target house. Parrish's big Nissan, stolen Freeman assumed, pulled in behind them.

"*Okay son, go get my fucking rock.*"

Chapter Ten

SHORT OF A MAJOR power cut covering southeast England, Penny Pit Lane, Sparsholt, was as dark as it would ever be. The light pollution from Winchester, seven miles east, would never allow many stars to shine or darkness to descend completely. Not quite pitch black, but close enough for Freeman's needs.

Adamovic couldn't have found a better parking spot—a lane bordered on either side by trees and tall hedges. No one could see their cars unless they drove right up alongside.

Freeman retrieved his heavy backpack and the night-vision goggles from the rear seat, switched off the courtesy light, and pushed the passenger door. It opened with a rubber-suction *pop*. A shock of chill night air bathed his face, drying the thin film of sweat. The temperature change from the warmth of the car would have shocked him awake if his overwrought nerves hadn't done so already.

After pulling on the backpack and tightening the straps, he

checked his hands. They were rock steady when he expected to see them tremble. The lack of a tremor surprised him. Even though his brain was mush, his body had switched into work mode. It made no sense, but he wasn't going to risk losing the status by asking any more questions.

He leaned against the car and adjusted the skullcap harness of his wide-field view NV goggles to lessen their front-heavy weight on the bridge of his nose. Waiting beside the car until he grew accustomed to the pale green light didn't do much for his nerves, but he'd developed a plan for the night and would stick with it. The goggles screwed with his depth perception, but he wasn't wearing them for night-time battle, which was their original design purpose.

A cat mewled high-pitched and mournful over to his left, a haunting sound that did nothing to calm his nerves. Further away, a second cat returned the call. Although a hideous noise, it served to mask the sound of his movements. The undulating hum of distant traffic, driven by the wind and filtered through the trees, drowned out whatever noise the cats' wailing didn't. The nearby A34 never emptied. Freeman breathed deep and prepared to start his new career.

Parrish's voice crackled through the speaker in Freeman's ear. *"What the fuck you waiting for? Get on with it."*

"Night vision acclimation," he answered, wondering whether a thug like Parrish would understand the terminology.

"Fuck that, son. It'll be daylight in a couple hours. Get a move on."

Freeman headed down the lane, keeping to the grass verge to stop his footfalls crunching on any gravel. As he padded forwards, he couldn't shift the niggling sensation that the crosshairs of a sniper's scope were etching lines into the back of his neck.

At the first break in the hedgerow, blocked by a three-bar gate, he stopped and took his first live sight of the target property. He'd seen plenty of photos and architect's drawings, but it looked different in reality, at night and through the NV optics. In the daylight it would look postcard beautiful but, dark and hushed, the place was as welcoming as an insane asylum. He took a one-kneed stance and kept it for two more minutes, wondering whether he should forget the whole damned adventure and bolt. Trouble was, he'd have to keep on running and never stop. If he did clear off, where would it leave John Freeman? Rotting in that desperate place until he died, alone and unloved, that's where. Despite everything, despite the harsh reality, he could never allow that to happen.

Freeman waited, vision-enhanced eyes wide, and ears open for the slightest unexpected sound. After the cats' second chorus, the night fell to a windy hush.

"What the fuck's happening?"

"At the gate now," Freeman whispered. He clicked the press-to-talk button a couple of times while he spoke.

"What d'you say? You're breaking up."

Freeman repeated the performance.

"All right, Freeman. Piss, or get off the pot."

He vaulted the gate, unwilling to risk antagonising rusty hinges, and moved with caution down a concrete driveway, on either side of which were large, well-maintained lawns. The sweet, damp smell of early dew reached his nostrils as adrenaline surged through his blood, heightening his senses, making him more alert than ever. The goggles illuminated his way.

Half of him anticipated success. The other half expected a meeting with armed guards and a pack of rabid dogs.

"Reached the end of the path. Here's the security shutters, as your plans showed."

"You doubted me, boy?" Although the electronics filtered out some of the emotion, Parrish's voice spat poison.

After first cutting the alarm cable, it took mere seconds to open the twin Yale padlocks and slide back the bolts that locked the single-width steel security shutters. His bump key made short work of the five-lever mortise lock securing the wooden rear door.

A quick turn of the handle and he was inside.

With the eerie green light throwing flat surfaces back at him, it wouldn't have taken much to bump and shuffle his way into the nearest jail cell. He took his time. Floorboards creaked underfoot and the old building breathed as he moved within its walls. He stopped, listened, stared, and moved on.

Inside, the eight metres by ten work-cum-storage room contained little of interest. The mechanism of a pendulum clock ticked noisily in the background—the only sound, apart from Freeman's hammering heart and stifled breathing.

"*Where are you now?*"

"Outer workroom. Moving towards the studio. Going quiet for a bit while I work the first internal door." Again, he tapped the PTT button on and off while speaking.

"*What the fuck's the matter with this thing? Repeat that.*"

"I don't…" Freeman turned off the radio unit and took a deep, calming breath.

Shut the fuck up and leave me in peace.

He covered the ten-metre distance to the door slowly, sidestepping past a gauntlet of cabinets, workbenches, and a battery of lamp stands.

At the first inner door—wood reinforced with flat metal bolts—Freeman slipped off the backpack and removed his pick gun. He fed the needle into the lock, pressed a button to release the filaments, and pumped the trigger twice to engage the lugs.

He paused again to listen. The oppressive silence deafened.

Only the pendulum clock spoke.

Tick-tock, tick-tock.

Freeman squeezed his eyes shut, grimaced, and slowly twisted the pick gun anticlockwise. The lock turned smoothly, making a well-oiled click.

Silence.

He opened his eyes, breathed again, and wiped sweat from his upper lip with the back of his free hand. He licked his lips and grimaced—the taint left from the latex gloves tasted horrible.

Tick-tock, tick-tock.

"Having fun yet, Sean?" he whispered, needing to hear something other than his heart and the damned clock.

The door's lever handle turned quietly and the internal bolts slid back. The door opened into a small hallway leading to his target. From the plans, Freeman knew that two of the three doors along the left hand wall guarded storage rooms. The third gave access to the studio's toilet. The right hand wall consisted of floor-to-ceiling glass panels that, in daylight, would allow a panoramic view of the extensive gardens.

He paused again to listen.

Tick-tock, tick-bloody-tock.

At the far end of the hallway, another security door barred his progress. He hurried along the corridor, repeated the procedure with the pick gun, and entered Aldo Pontini's private workshop.

Yes! Made it!

A workbench with a velvet-covered surface clear of all but a jeweller's clamp, a ubiquitous doughnut-shaped magnifying lamp, and a desk phone, dominated the room. Here, Aldo Pontini worked his magic. Here, the wizard made beautiful, unique pieces for others' pleasure. Here, Pontini would restore damaged masterpieces. Here, in the safe behind the bench sat the Zinfandel Clasp.

Supposedly.

Built into the wall behind the workbench, the 1975 Chubb Imperial safe, one metre tall and half a metre wide, stared back at him with dull grey indifference.

He checked his watch. Ninety minutes before the dawn would drive away the protective darkness. He studied the safe's door. The only blemishes to its smooth surface were the gleaming steel numbered dial and the chrome three-spoke handle below it. The safe seemed to be laughing out a challenge.

"Think you can break me?" it jeered.

"We'll see," Freeman answered in a hushed whisper and flexed his hot fingers. The latex gloves were uncomfortable and sweaty, but an essential component of his prospective new career.

From the pack at his feet, he removed the "can-opener", a machine he'd taken six months to perfect. The shiny device—made mainly from titanium and tool steel—consisted of a round frame with three legs, each ten centimetres long. The foot of each leg incorporated a powerful rare earth magnet covered by a thin rubber shim. Attached to the centre of the frame was the magic—a vibration-sensitive, screw–threaded, rotating actuator with a digital LCD display. The whole thing was powered by two 1.5-volt lithium-ion batteries.

Freeman rotated the safe's combination dial until the indicator notch aligned with zero. He centred the mechanism of the can-opener over the dial, and offered it up to the door. The magnets clunked against the metal and held the machine firm. He rotated the thread of the motorised housing, working the actuator arm until it contacted the dial.

Then he hit the power switch and set the timer on his watch.

The powerful little motor hummed, ceramic gears spun, and the dial turned slowly. It barely made a sound. The vibration-sensitive mechanics would search out the lock's internal wheel-notches and throw out the combination.

Hopefully, all it needed was time.

How much time depended upon the bucket load of variables he'd plugged into the search algorithm and the individual variance between one hand-built safe and another.

Freeman squatted with his back against the safe and waited, listening to the gentle whir of the can-opener as it rotated the dial clockwise, anticlockwise, and back again in the pattern Freeman had programmed into it.

Aldo Pontini's studio was warm and well insulated both against thermal variations and noise. Nothing moved nor made a sound except the bloody pendulum clock in the outer workshop and the can-opener's electric motor.

His legs started to cramp and his knees ached, but he refused to move until the machine completed its work—a matter of pride.

Eventually, the can-opener bleeped and its motor stopped. Freeman checked his watch—seven-minutes, thirteen seconds. Not bad. Under test conditions, the can-opener's best performance had been a little under six. He read the numbers from the LED display —49-8-23-17-23-38—removed the can-opener, and stuffed it back into the pack.

Freeman's heart punched against his ribcage. If human bones weren't so tough, the muscular pump would have exploded from his chest cavity, beaten a path through to the back door, and hurtled across the garden to the getaway car.

He dialled in the combination, starting with 49-clockwise and ending with 38-anticlockwise.

Sweat pooled inside the gloves, making his hands cool and slippery. He grasped one shiny arm of the safe's handle. If things were going to go horribly wrong it would happen right about now.

He pressed down on one arm. The wheel turned. The safe's internal bolts slid back, making a heavy metallic double-clang.

Freeman held his breath.

No claxons, no flashing lights, no charging security guards with attack dogs or stun guns—only the pendulum's *tick-bloody-tock* and the rush of blood through his ears.

Freeman pulled, the door swung open on silent hinges, and …

…stared into black depths of an empty safe.

Chapter Eleven

SUNDAY 22ND MARCH — *Sean Freeman*
Near Winchester, Hampshire

NO!

Blind, screaming panic brought acid to Freeman's throat as he stared into the open safe—two shelves, three compartments, each one empty.

A trap?

He spun around. Nothing moved apart from the rippled delay caused by the optical parallax of the NV goggles, which increased his sense of nausea. He breathed fast through his mouth and the feeling subsided.

His first instinct was to run, but he rammed the coward's trick down into the pit of his seething gut. The hollow tick of the pendulum clock in the first room grew louder.

Tick-tock, tick-tock.

Had someone opened a door?

No.

Heightened senses played tricks with his hearing. What the hell was he missing?

Freeman stood, took a pace back, and stared down at the empty metal box. Thick walls painted blackboard matt.

Tick-tock, tick-tock.

What did he know about the 1975 Chubb Imperial?

Think, Sean. Think!

Based on the patented 1968 version, but larger and lined with added ceramic tiles for improved protection against fire. Were there any other modifications to the original? What was special about the 1975 Mark II?

The pendulum clock ticked louder. It stopped him thinking.

He wanted to run again, but outside three men waited. None would believe he'd opened an empty safe. He couldn't stay, couldn't go. At any moment someone would burst through the door and he'd be trapped. The room only had one way in and one way out, and he stood on a wooden floor with no trapdoor.

Trapdoor!

The information struck him with the gentle subtlety of a brick to the back of the head.

A false bottom.

How could he have forgotten something so bloody obvious?

He dived forward and tugged at the heavy metal flap. It hinged open to reveal a felt-lined drawer divided into three segments. The middle segment contained the jewellery box he expected, his Holy Grail.

A cube ten centimetres square, the box was finished in red leather and had intricate gold tooling along each seam. Gold lettering on the top face read, *Zinfandel Clasp – Fabergé*. He couldn't make out the colours through the NV goggles, but Parrish's briefing pack included detailed photos in colour.

He grabbed the box and snapped it open, fingers trembling.

Now they shake!

The box contained a velvet sack held together with a tasselled silk string. He tugged one of the tassels and the bag unfurled like the petals of a flower. The Zinfandel Clasp sparkled in the pale green light. It was so damned beautiful. He kissed it, bit off a whoop of glee, and stuffed the box into his pocket.

A fevered mooch through the drawer's other segments showed a number of interesting and expensive pieces: diamond, ruby, and sapphire rings, necklaces in various states of disrepair or creation, and a large, solid-gold fob watch. They were tempting, but he left them where they lay. Parrish had only ordered the Clasp, and that's what he'd receive.

The safe door closed with a satisfactory heavy metal crump. Freeman locked it and spun the dial. He wiped the front with an anti-static cloth to remove any marks made by the can-opener and picked up his backpack. Finally, he checked the room for anything he might have disturbed, found nothing, and locked the door behind him.

Breathing more normally, he retraced his steps to the back door, raised and lowered the shutter, slid the bolts, and clipped the padlocks back into place. For good measure, he reconnected the alarm. Aldo Pontini wouldn't know the Clasp was missing until he opened the safe, and by then, Freeman would be ninety-odd miles away, lost in the vast anonymity of England's capital city.

He sprinted along the path, revelling in the cool morning air and desperate to howl at the cloud-masked moon. He couldn't remember the last time he felt so damned good. Exhilarated.

The three bar gate was no barrier. He vaulted it again and … ran straight into Hutch's piledriver fist.

It hit him in the chest and knocked him flat on his arse. It would have done a lot more damage had Freeman not turned his shoulders at the precise moment of impact and deflected most of the power.

Freeman overruled the reactions of years of fight training. Rather than roll and spring to his feet, he let himself land in a crumpled heap against the bottom rung of the gate. The NV goggles fell from his head and crunched to the gravel, leaving him night blind for a moment. Mouth open wide, he clutched at his chest, feigning an inability to catch his breath.

Above him in the dark, a monster hovered. It grew larger as it stooped, grabbed him by his jacket front, and pulled him to his feet as easily as if picking up a rag doll.

"Hutch. What … the hell … was that for?" said Freeman, gasping and struggling against the big man's grip.

"You went off air," Hutch whispered. Peppermint breath wafted into Freeman's nose. "Mr Parrish doesn't appreciate disobedience."

"The unit packed in the moment I entered the workshop. Put me down."

Hutch let go of the jacket. Freeman staggered. The eastern sky had brightened enough to show Hutch's gleaming teeth. Freeman had never seen a real smile on Hutch and hadn't believed it possible. Before that precise moment, the man had displayed all the emotional flexibility of a paving slab.

Freeman rubbed his throbbing sternum. "What d'you hit me with?"

"It was nothing, a love tap. Stop moaning. You have the Clasp?"

"Yeah."

Hutch grabbed his upper arm and tugged.

"Hang on," Freeman said, jerking free of the grip and taking a pace back. "Give me a minute."

"Mr Parrish wants to see you now."

Freeman smoothed down his jacket front and brushed the dirt from the seat of his trousers. His tailbone hurt from hitting the deck hard. He picked up the goggles. They rattled in a way that suggested the damage was terminal.

Not my goggles, who cares?

Hutch held out his shovel-like hand. "Pass it over then," he growled.

"What? The Clasp? Piss off," Freeman said, taking a second pace back, bracing to avoid another blow. "Nobody gets that but Mr Parrish."

Hutch lowered his arm and nodded. "Fair enough. With me, *please.*"

Freeman breathed deep, and followed the giant along the lane. They passed Adamovic, who sat with the window down, drawing on one of his interminable black cigarettes and flicking ash to the ground.

Freeman paused and pointed at the six butts littering the gravel lane. "Haven't you ever watched CSI? Never heard of DNA evidence? You're going to get us all caught."

Adamovic snorted and hurled up a loogie that landed a centimetre from Freeman's left trainer. Hutch pulled Freeman by the arm and frogmarched him to Parrish in the waiting Nissan.

The Nissan's rear passenger door opened, and Hutch stepped back to allow Freeman entry.

Parrish sat in his favourite camelhair coat, a scowl of thunder on his drawn face. "Where is it?" He pushed out his hand and beckoned with his fingers.

Freeman slid inside. The car smelled of leather and cigars. He shuffled his backside into a more comfortable position and shrugged the backpack from his shoulders. Hutch slid into the driver's seat and Freeman noticed the third man for the first time. Small, narrow-shouldered, hunched, he sat in the front passenger's seat and faced forward, head down, his face illuminated by the white glow of an e-reader. Something familiar about the stranger sparked Freeman's interest, but he couldn't put a name to the profile. The excitement and tension that had built over the past day and a half had screwed with his head. His memory no longer worked properly.

"Come on. What you waiting for?" Parrish said, flicking his fingers again.

Freeman took the jewellery box from his pocket and placed it in the eager hand. Parrish held it up to the Nissan's passenger light and almost dribbled.

"What did you do with the other stuff in the safe?"

"Left it. You didn't ask for anything else."

Parrish sniffed.

"Good. I like an honest man," he said, with no hint of irony.

With trembling fingers and eyes sparkling, anger apparently forgotten, Parrish pressed the catch-release button and the top of the box sprang open. He left the purple velvet bag in its silk bed and pulled on the drawstring, his actions delicate, as though trying to avoid breaking a cracked egg. The bag opened.

Parrish sighed.

The Zinfandel diamond fizzed in the dim light, casting prismatic starbursts of colour over the car's interior. It seemed to glow with an internal power source.

Despite its broken mounting, the Zinfandel Clasp was quite the most stunning, dazzling thing Sean Freeman had seen since, well, ever. Mentally, he took back his "compressed carbon" jibe.

Parrish lowered his head to the box and kissed the rock. Freeman smiled, his kiss had been first and meant so much more.

Parrish turned feverish eyes on Freeman. "Don't know why people call 'em 'ice'. Diamonds ain't made from water. Ain't cold neither. They might look like ice to the morons who've never seen one up close, but not to those in the know. Not to people like me who can appreciate their beauty. Look at her, son."

He held the box up to greet the new sun.

"Stunning ain't she? She's what I call perfection. Look at all them colours? Light diffraction that is. All the colours of the rainbow. Gorgeous. You can take your gold and your precious metals. Nothing's ever gonna beat a perfectly cut diamond. An' that's what I got here."

Freeman knew when to keep quiet. Parrish was confusing the different properties of light—diffraction, refraction, and dispersion—but Freeman wasn't about to correct the man's inadequate grasp of science. He had a pretty good idea what the reaction might be.

Parrish fell quiet. He rotated the diamond up to the light for a few moments more. After giving up another sigh, he tugged on the drawstrings, closed the box, and put it in his breast pocket next to his heart. He patted the outside of his coat and smiled.

"Nice work, son. You passed your exam. Top of the class. Welcome to the firm. What do you reckon, Aldo?"

The senior citizen in the front passenger seat lowered his e-book and struggled around to face them.

"*Eccellente, il signor Freeman*," he said. "Well done indeed. And much faster than we expected."

Aldo Pontini!

Freeman finally recognised the wizened seventy-two-year-old jewelsmith from his Internet profile and from Parrish's dossier.

"Another test? How many do I have to pass, Mr Parrish?" He didn't know how to react so changed the subject. "Is that why Adamovic doesn't mind leaving all that forensic evidence?"

"Fuck's sake, boy. You thought I'd test you on a real job? Aldo and me has this little arrangement. Don't we, Aldo?"

"Yes, Mr Parrish. Can I go now? At my age, these late nights do not sit so well with my bladder."

"Course you can, mate. There'll be a little something extra in the bank at the end of the month for your trouble. Hutch, escort Aldo back home. I need a quiet word with our new SVP of Corporate Security."

Parrish waited until the men were out of earshot.

"Very impressive, son," he started, "but what was that bollocks with the radio breaking down? I saw you turn off the unit." He pointed at the screen embedded in the back of the passenger's head restraint. "Aldo's place has a CCTV loop I kept off the blueprints. I've been watching your every fucking move."

Freeman didn't answer for a while. With all this information overloading his system, he needed time to think, time to assimilate.

"No excuse, Mr Parrish," he said at length. "I need silence when I work. That's it. Can't concentrate otherwise … sorry."

Parrish stared at him, appraising.

"Okay, we'll let it pass for now. I'll be joining you on most of your specialist jobs anyway. Can't let you have all the fun, now can I?"

Freeman pointed at Parrish's chest. "You're keeping the Clasp?"

"'Course. Why wouldn't I?" he answered, showing his brightened teeth. "Aldo's going to report it as missing in transit from his London workshops. Let the security firm shoulder the blame. Remember this, boy. I don't need to nick everything I want. Not when I have friends like Aldo on the payroll."

"And the Montalbanos? Mr & Mrs Butterfingers?"

"Fuck 'em. They'll claim it on the insurance. Anyone treats a diamond like what they did don't deserve to own one. Am I right?"

"If you say so, Mr Parrish."

"I do, son. I do."

Freeman made a point to rub his chest.

"That hurt?" Parrish asked, as though he really cared.

"Yes, sir. Hutch packs a hell of a punch."

Parrish sniffed and squinted into the rising sun. "Just you remember that next time you think about ignoring my orders. Next time he won't be so gentle."

Next time, I might not let him get away with it.

"I'll remember, Mr Parrish," he replied, truthfully. "What are we going to do next?"

"Next, son, we leave this country shithole. So fucking quiet here, I can't hear mesself think. We're booked in for a spanking brekkie at the Dorchester. I'm starving, and you're going to join me. You need to meet the rest of the executive management team."

Chapter Twelve

Various Locations, England

IN THE WEEKS following the Winchester trip, life moved up through the gears.

True to his word, Parrish enrolled Freeman into the legitimate arm of *Parrish Enterprises Ltd*. He signed a contract of employment and sat through an induction course hosted by a stunning redhead from the HR department.

Parrish also arranged for John Freeman to move from St Margaret's into a private sanatorium in the heart of rural Buckinghamshire, where he received close to individual care. Freeman saw an immediate improvement in the patient's condition. He stopped having seizures, gained weight, and even seemed to recognise Freeman during his regular visits. For that delight alone, Freeman might have considered working for minimum wage, but Parrish didn't let him down on the salary front either. The six-figure income pushed him into the high-tax bracket, but left more than enough to indulge in a lifestyle that Freeman, as a mere locksmith, never expected to enjoy.

He decided to keep what Parrish disparagingly called the "piece of crap" Ford—a low-mileage Mondeo Zetec—but only used it to visit John Freeman in the country. The rest of the time, it remained in the secure underground parking beneath his building. In London, he used black cabs, his one voluntary concession to the life of luxury. It was a complete delight to sit in a cab without having to stare at the meter and pray it didn't tick over to the next digit.

With the help of the firm's personal shoppers, he'd filled his wardrobe with bespoke suits, designer clothes and accessories, but he only bought them to maintain the image required of a *Parrish Enterprises Ltd* executive. At least that's what he kept telling himself.

Other things remained the same. He still bought his socks and underwear from Tesco—the fancy silk ones didn't feel right—and he kept up his old gym membership.

Despite having access to the company's up-market, snot-nosed fitness centre, he preferred his sweaty old gym. It had taken years to find the right coach and mentor, and he wasn't about to risk losing his hard won edge. He did, however, pay extra to move the one-to-one training sessions into the back room of the *dojo*, away from prying eyes. Anyone following him to the gym would see an old style boxing club, complete with square ring and well-worn punching bags. He deserved some privacy. No one in "the firm" needed to know all his skills.

A life of relative riches could beguile and corrupt weaker men, but Freeman had a reason for temporarily crossing to the 'dark side', a reason that kept him honest, in his own way. Parrish's enticing life-style of luxury wouldn't change him, not one little bit.

One incident in particular brought his change of circumstances home in a real shock to the system. Early on a Monday morning, five months after he joined the firm, Parrish burst into his office. By that stage, Freeman had learned the man's moods and interpreted the glint in Parrish's eye to be one of mischief rather than malice.

"You'll never guess," he said, throwing the *Times Lifestyle Supplement* on Freeman's desk.

"Probably not, Mr Parrish. I read the *Guardian*," he said, picking up the glossy magazine, and turning the pages.

"Our old mucker, Luciano's coming to town."

The first name struck a chord, but Freeman couldn't add a surname or a face. "Luciano?"

"Wake up, boy. I'm talking about Luciano Montalbano, the cook with the butterfingered missus who don't got the Zinfandel Clasp no more."

Freeman kept his face immobile, but the temperature in the plush air-conditioned room seemed to plummet. He tried to work out what the evil midget wanted with the Italian chef this time. Hadn't they caused enough injury to the poor man?

"Oh right," he said. "That Luciano."

"Yeah, that one." Parrish pointed at the magazine. "Article on page seventeen says he's taking over the kitchen at the Eastbury Hotel, for a charity bash. Save the Children or Protect the Whales, or summat. Special invitation-only affair. It's hosted by that hairy Scotch cook off of the telly. You know the one I mean? Swears all the time."

Not an expert on fine dining, Freeman didn't have a clue, but nodded anyway and waited for Parrish to make his point.

Parrish thrust his hands into his pockets and rose onto the balls of his feet. "I've wangled us an invite."

"Us?"

"Yeah. The Executive Board and everyone what was in on the Zinfandel robbery, apart from Aldo, of course. That wouldn't go down too well. It seems that Unlucky Luciano and Aldo Pontini had a bit of a falling out. They don't speak to each other no more except through their lawyers." He chuckled. "Unlucky Luciano, get it?"

"Yes, Mr Parrish." Freeman managed a smile, but it didn't come easily.

"I crease myself up sometimes." He settled back onto his two-inch heels and scowled at Freeman's minimal response to his witticism. "Yeah, well, I figured it'd be a real hoot. We took his diamond. The least we can do is buy his food. An' it's for charity, so everyone wins. Meet us at the Eastbury at seven-thirty Wednesday night. You got some crumpet?"

"Not at the moment, sir."

The idea of socialising with Parrish and his group of ignorant thugs and yes-men turned Freeman's stomach, but he couldn't think of a legitimate reason to decline. He was still playing the newbie trying to ingratiate himself with the boss.

"Right," Parrish said, winking. "I'll book some tarts to keep us company."

Wednesday evening arrived and, despite the unease he'd felt since Parrish entered his office with the magazine, the outing wasn't a complete disaster. The food was sublime, the best he'd ever tasted. Parrish, although boisterous and cock-of-the-walk, was on his best behaviour and even reined in his potty mouth.

Parrish's "tarts" turned out to be high-class escorts who knew how to behave in polite company and which piece of cutlery to use for which course. Freeman followed their lead, Parrish didn't. The young woman assigned to Freeman—painfully slim, dyed blonde-hair, huge eyes, flawless skin, and a musical laugh—helped make the evening pass in a blur.

As the meal reached its conclusion, his tension lessened, until the waiter arrived with Freeman's portion of the bill—twelve-hundred quid. He had the same moment of stomach churning, heart-pounding, run-for-the-hills panic he'd suffered after opening Aldo Pontini's apparently empty safe. For a fleeting moment he considered calling for a defibrillator and then remembered the funds in his bank account. He had plenty to cover the extortionate bill.

That night he made three interesting discoveries.

First, having the victim of his first crime cook his dinner was upsetting, Freeman felt desperately sorry for Unlucky Luciano.

Second, Hutch's eyes never left him all evening. Freeman had the unpleasant impression that the big minder couldn't wait for him to screw up so his master would remove his muzzle. Freeman couldn't afford to let that happen, not yet.

The third discovery came later when he returned to his apartment to find that his escort was, in fact, a natural blonde.

———

IN EVERY RESPECT, Parrish kept his promises.

Freeman thoroughly enjoyed the legitimate side of his work. On his rounds, he toured the UK inspecting the corporate infrastructure, and monitoring and testing building security. He designed system upgrades and helped with their installation as and when necessary. He also conducted surreptitious security tests.

During his first week on the payroll, Parrish rented him a top-end workshop near Freeman's apartment and allowed him to kit it out with everything a security expert would need: hand and electric tools, lathes, infra-red and ultraviolet sensors, oscilloscopes, scanners, and bits of kit, the names of which most people couldn't even pronounce, let alone operate. His university workshop paled into insignificance by comparison. Whatever Freeman needed, Parrish would provide, as long as Freeman could make the business case for the outlay—for tax and accounting purposes. In his legitimate businesses, Parrish was scrupulous and transparent. Apart from the robberies in which he was involved, Freeman knew nothing about the other illegitimate aspects of Parrish's business empire, and was happy for things to remain that way.

In month two, on his second undercover visit to a high-end casino in Watford—*The Parrish Playhouse*—Freeman discovered a stock-control fraud involving the manager and his head barman. They were skimming thousands of pounds each week from the register.

Fearing the worst for the two men, Freeman sat on the information for more than a week. With mounting dread and being unable to think of an alternative, he presented the report to the following Monday meeting of the eight-man Executive Committee and waited for the eruption.

Each director read Freeman's three-page account and studied the invoice trail in silence. The hidden camera shots of cash entering back pockets were particularly damning. When he'd finished, Parrish rested his forearms on the boardroom table and spoke quietly. "Top notch report, Mr Freeman," he said and turned to the other directors. "Anyone have a problem with the evidence?"

No one spoke—most shook their heads.

Hutch, not an official member of the Board but always in attendance, coughed. "Would you like me to take care of things, Mr Parrish?"

"Nah, Hutch. This time I reckon we can go through the legal department. Must be seen to do our civic duty, right?"

Hutch frowned, perhaps in disappointment.

"Yes, Mr Parrish."

One or two of the more senior directors nodded in understanding. Freeman wanted to ask the obvious question but scratched at an itch on the side of his neck and kept his mouth closed.

"It's all about camouflage, son," Parrish explained, as though talking to a small child. "There ain't a single company in the leisure and entertainment industry as goes a whole year without a couple of employee disputes. We'll have the Old Bill do our work for us. Show the world that Digby Parrish abides by the rules and anybody taking food out of his mouth will feel the full force of the British judicial system." The speech extracted a number of smiles, a couple of titters, and one "hear, hear" from the assembly.

"And once those two numpties are banged up in one of Her Majesty's holiday camps," Parrish continued, "there ain't no telling what accident might befall them."

Hutch did the thing with his face that Freeman thought might be a grin, but could never be sure.

———

FREEMAN'S FIRST ACTUAL "OFF-BOOK" job—at a bonded warehouse in Tilbury Docks—took place three months after he joined the firm. They made away with a consignment of industrial diamonds from Amsterdam headed to a machine shop in Lancashire. Parrish led the raid and Freeman's tasks involved killing the alarm system and opening the vault—a ridiculously decrepit strongbox protected by a five-lever mortise lock that Freeman could have opened when aged eleven. The insurance value of the haul totalled £3.2 million, and netted Freeman the promised five-percent productivity bonus—a cool £160,000.

In September, Parrish sent Freeman to Liverpool with Adamovic to relieve a shop of a ruby-encrusted tiara and a collection of emerald engagement rings.

In December, he had two "off-book" jobs, one in Leeds, the other in Manchester. In February the following year, they undertook their first cross-border expedition. The team made off with nearly £1.5 million worth of diamonds from an exhibition in Cardiff's Millennium Stadium.

Two more jobs in the autumn, both in London and both successful, earned Freeman a total bonus for the year of £905,000.

Freeman saw more of the UK in those eighteen months than he had in his previous twenty-seven years.

In the summer and early autumn, Parrish stepped up a gear and organised four "business" trips to Scotland. The first three couldn't have gone better. They turned over two jewellery shops, one each in Glasgow and Aberdeen, and a museum in Edinburgh. The three operations netted a little under £3 million. Freeman's bonuses totalled close to £150,000.

The method of operation was simple enough.

Parrish would announce the upcoming job and deliver all the information Freeman needed to plan it apart from the strike date. He'd leave Freeman alone—Adamovic no longer acted as his constant companion—to work out the best means of entry and exit. Freeman sometimes had enough time to scout the target or build a specific tool for the task. On other occasions, he worked without notice and on the fly.

He much preferred working alone but sometimes needed an assistant to do the heavy lifting. Adamovic or one of the many other hired thugs would oblige, but not Hutch, who rarely strayed far from Parrish. Freeman often wondered what their relationship was based upon. It appeared to be more than just business, but they seemed an unlikely pair of friends or lovers.

The only times Parrish interfered was when the target haul

included diamonds. For those special tasks, Parrish would be all over the planning stage. He'd question, chivvy, offer suggestions, stand over Freeman while he worked, and generally act like an expectant mother nearing her delivery date.

On two occasions when Freeman took too long to find a safe point of entry, the Leeds and the first London job, Parrish became unbearable. He threatened to, "go in with a fucking army" if Freeman didn't, "pull his finger out of his arse and find another way." When diamonds entered the picture, Parrish's whole character changed.

Apart from the ten extramural jobs in eighteen months, Parrish left Freeman pretty well alone. Life was good, at least superficially.

———

FREEMAN'S carefully compartmentalised world fell apart when Parrish ordered a return trip to Edinburgh—the target, a high-end jewellery shop, *Throckmorton's Gems*, in the Old Town.

Although Parrish gave Freeman a generous three-week window to plan the job, he couldn't think of a sure-fire way to overcome an internal barrier that didn't involve a scalpel and bloodshed. Every other aspect of the job was a doddle. He tried to talk Parrish out of it, but the ultimatum came down from on high: "Sort it, or I send in the army with the shooters. End of story."

The answer came to Freeman during one of his insomniac nights as he sat through *Breakfast at Tiffany's*. The following morning he ran the idea past a sceptical Parrish.

"You can't be fucking serious," Parrish said, spluttering into his coffee.

Hutch handed him a napkin and stood back, not taking his eyes from Freeman, who suddenly understood what the tethered goat in *Jurassic Park* must have felt like.

"It'll work, Mr Parrish. I only need the owner, Andrew Morton, to open the door to the high-value area. After that, things will be golden. I can do the safe in minutes and the cabinets are easy."

"What you gonna do if there's customers?"

"I'll need help."

"What sort of help?" Parrish finished the coffee and pushed the cup and saucer away.

"Two men with baseball bats ought to be enough," Freeman said, and added, "It's a small shop. Exclusive. There won't be many people about and Morton only has one assistant, a middle-aged woman. There won't be any trouble."

Hutch's only contribution to the discussion was, "Baseball bats are of no use, Mr Parrish. They'll need shotguns."

"No!" Freeman said.

Hutch took a pace forward.

Freeman held his ground. "Use shotguns and I'm out of it. We had a deal, Mr Parrish. No violence, remember?"

"You was the one what suggested weapons, boy."

"Bats, not shotguns. I considered knockout gas or tranquiliser darts, but there's not enough control and this isn't *Mission Impossible.*"

He waited. Parrish and Hutch exchanged a look that Freeman couldn't interpret. He'd often thought that the two operated some form of telepathy.

"Well, Mr Parrish. Do we have a deal? No guns?"

Parrish took an age to make the decision.

"Nah. They'll go in with shotguns, but I'll make sure they're unloaded. Right?" Before Freeman could thank him, Parrish added, "But if anything goes wrong and you get caught, you're on your own. Get me? Cough to the filth and I'll let Hutch kill you slowly. Mention me as anything but your legit employer, and … well, let's just leave it at that for now, eh?"

"Yes, Mr Parrish," Freeman said. "Thank you."

"Shut the door on your way out."

Freeman left the office, worried, but confident he'd thought of everything.

Chapter Thirteen

DIGBY PARRIS
London, England

"WHATCHA RECKON, HUTCH?" Parrish asked, once they were alone.

Hutch took a seat, leaned forward, and their eyes met. Digby loved the raw power of the man, his smell, the way his muscles rippled beneath his shirt. With Hutch at his side, he could take on the world and win. He bet some people reckoned they was a gay couple, but the thought of touching another man in that way made Digby heave. Fucking poofs were a blasphemy and wanted wiping off the face of the earth. He were happy just having the big guy close by and guarding his back. In Digby's line of work, the comfort of feeling safe was a rare luxury.

"The way he shouted at you?" Hutch said. "Bugger's starting to get a little uppity. The smarmy toe-rag thinks he's calling the shots."

Parrish smirked. He could always rely on his main man to read the situation as well as he did himself. It was as though Hutch could see into his mind.

"Whatcha think I should do about him?"

As usual, Hutch thought for a little bit before answering.

"I'd like to slap him around a little, put him in his place. But it rather depends on how important he is to you."

Parrish scratched his todger. The fucking thing had been itching for days. If that whore he hired last weekend gave him crabs—or summat worse—he'd search her out, flay the skin off her back, and turn it into a fucking lampshade.

"Ordinarily, I'd let you loose on him, but he's got skills I need, for the moment. Wouldn't want him out of commission none, but I do want him put in his place."

Fuck. His dick was on fire. Nothing for it, he'd have to book into the clinic. Again.

Hutch raised his chin and smiled. The ice blue eyes caught fire.

"Did you have anything particular in mind, Mr Parrish?"

"Matter of fact, I do. I'm gonna show the fucking sod it's me who's the boss without breaking his valuable fingers. Go fetch 'Arry Bryce. He's knows the Scotch talent, an' the useless shit's been draggin' his arse lately. Could do with a little wake-up call of his own."

Hutch frowned.

"What's up?"

"Sorry, Mr Parrish. It's just that I'm a little uneasy. There's something off about Freeman. Something I really don't like."

"He done anything specific to piss you off or make you think he's cross-eyed?"

"No, not really… it's just that … well I don't like to say."

"Come on, Hutch. You an' me is friends. Spit it out."

Hutch's frown deepened and his mouth twisted into a grimace.

"I don't like the way he looks at me."

"What? You reckon he fancies you or summat? The background checks say he's straight."

"No, it's not that."

"Well? What the fuck's up?"

"Most people are too scared to look me in the eye, but he's not. In fact, he's too damned calm. I'm having trouble working him out.

I don't like it when people are unpredictable. It makes me a tad uncomfortable."

Parrish thought for a moment and then laughed.

"Nah, you got him wrong. Ever seen that movie, Rain Man? That's our safecracker, that is. He's one of them geniuses that don't got normal emotions. Nothing to worry about."

"I'm not worried, Digby, but I am going to keep watching him closely, if you don't mind."

"Course I don't, Hutch. It's what you're here for, among other things. I'll maybe reconsider Freeman's position after the *Throckmorton* job. Now, get me 'Arry Bryce."

Hutch took out his mobile.

"Yes, Mr Parrish."

Chapter Fourteen

MONDAY 27TH JUNE – *Evening*
Holton, Birmingham

JONES SIGNED and dated yet another overtime claim form, his twentieth of the day, and placed the file in the second "out" tray. The first tray, he reserved for case-related paperwork. He took the next form from the pile, read the name at the top, DS Charles H Pelham, and rubbed his hands together. Jones enjoyed reading the occasional work of fiction and often considered recommending that Pelham take an evening course in creative writing.

First day back at work after any sort of break was always a killer. He leaned back, covered his mouth with both hands to hide a yawn, and watched Phil dutifully ploughing through the national postings on the PNC. How he and the rest of the team could stare at computer or mobile phone screens for hours on end without going blind was beyond him. Jones struggled enough with reading tiny print on actual paper.

"Boss, did you see this notification?"

"Hardly. If it's important, you'll print it off, right?" Jones rubbed his eyes. At some stage, he'd succumb to the inevitability of reading glasses, but not just yet. "Who's it from?"

"Your mates in the National Crime Agency."

"Superintendent Knightly?"

Phil smiled and shook his head.

"Not exactly. One of their press officers has marked our cards. They've linked a series of unsolved jewel thefts to the same London team."

"Really?" Jones rested his forearms on the desk. "How many jobs?"

"Eighteen in the last twenty-seven months." Phil hit a key and the printer hummed into life. The smell of burning toner scoured Jones' oversensitive nostrils. "The notification doesn't give many details."

The printer spewed out three pages, but Jones wouldn't touch them until after they'd cooled and the unpleasant odour had time to dissipate.

Phil straightened. "Bloody hell, didn't read this part before."

"What's that?"

"The NCA reckons these boys have made off with twenty-six million, one-hundred-and-fifty thousand quid's worth of precious gems and rare metals so far. They have a particular fondness for diamonds, though."

"Twenty-six million?"

"Twenty-six, one-fifty, boss," Phil said, his smile growing wider. "Can't forget the small change."

"Any specific MO?"

Phil shook his head.

"Different methods, varied targets. They've hit jewellery shops, wholesalers, importers, designers' workshops, factories, and museums. Anything of value as long as it sparkles. High-tech security systems don't seem to faze them either. They must have at least one guy who knows his way around locks and top-end electronics."

"Anything else in the notice?"

"Not a lot. No forensics so far. They've struck in seven different police regions and none of the locals have come close to catching them. Operate all over the UK."

"Why haven't we heard of them before?" Jones asked. "I mean the media would be all over this in a heartbeat. For a start, they'd have given the gang a ridiculous name by now." Jones tried to think of something witty, but could only come up with *The Ice Bandits*. He kept it to himself.

"The NCA have only just linked the thefts. I'm guessing one of their forensic accountants spotted an association us poor plods missed, but they don't explain it in the notice."

"Keeping all us country bumpkins in the dark, eh?"

"As always. They have designated a rather catchy moniker to the gang, though. Wait for it … the JT1 Crew." Phil made a "ta-dah" sign, by throwing out his hands.

Jones grinned. "As in?" he asked, although he could probably give it a good guess.

"The gang is the NCA's top target in high-value robbery, so they called it, 'Jewel Thieves Number 1'. Original, eh?"

"Stunning. Must have taken them ages," Jones said, keeping his voice neutral. "Okay. What specific cases are the NCA linking them with?"

"They don't go into details. They're hosting a media conference this evening. Be on the nine o'clock news tonight I reckon. Juicy story like this will get lots of airplay. Might try and catch that if I can get a moment's peace at home."

"We haven't had any big jewellery robberies in the Midlands recently. Any reason we should be interested?"

Phil nodded and jerked a thumb at his screen. "It includes a list of potential high-value targets, one of which is down the road in Perry Bar."

"The Stafford Museum?"

"Exactly." Phil tapped the side of his nose with an index finger. "You should read tealeaves, boss."

"Any specific threat to the Rajmahl Collection, or are they guessing?"

"Nah, not really," said Phil, swivelling his chair and turning from the screen. "The prospect list is run on value alone." He passed Jones the cooled printout. "Includes the Crown Jewels in the Tower of London, Tiffany's, Harrods, a dozen jewellery shops in Hatton Garden, and Birmingham's very own Jewellery Quarter."

"Shooting in the dark then?"

"That's about the strength of it." Phil checked his watch. "Want me to ring the Stafford to arrange a security briefing?"

Jones considered the question for a moment before shaking his head.

"I'll have a chat with Dav Prasad from Robbery Prevention tomorrow. Wouldn't want to tread on his toes. Anyway, no one would have a pop at the Rajmahl Collection. No fence on the planet would buy the goods."

"Dunno 'bout that, boss. The *Mask of the Sultana* is worth twenty million on its own. Stunning piece of art, I reckon. Wouldn't mind taking Manda to see the bling up close, but tickets are too bloody expensive. It was a real coup for the museum to host the exhibition and they're milking it to bits. Made as big a splash as when King Tut's jewels did the rounds."

"Nothing to do with the Sultan of Rajmahl having bought the Stafford in 2008, I suppose?" Jones said. "Wouldn't surprise me to see him move the whole collection back to Rajmahl, buildings included. Remember what the Yanks did with London Bridge?"

"No boss, do tell."

"You are a such funny man, Philip." Jones checked the wall clock. "It's late enough. You might as well head off home. I'll do a few more timesheets and have an early night. I'm starting to see double."

Phil shook his head. "Thought I'd do a bit of revision first. My inspector's exams will be on me in no time. Can't get any reading done at home."

"Wife's mother visiting again?"

"How'd you guess?"

"Manda would never let you leave home with a tie that colour unless she was busy fending off her mother's parental support."

"Now who's being a funny man?"

———

THE OFFICE PHONE rang as Jones and Phil approached the staircase. Phil stood still for a moment and allowed his shoulders to sag. "Fancy leaving it, boss?" he asked. "It's been a long day."

Jones was sorely tempted but shook his head. "Better not. They'll be trying our mobiles in a sec."

Phil hurried to unlock the door and Jones sauntered along behind him. Long gone were the days when he'd rush to answer a phone call. He reached the office as Phil replaced the receiver and turned to face him.

"Well," Phil said, adding a theatrical sigh, "so much for an early night." He draped his jacket across the back of his chair.

"What's up?"

"They've found Kelvin Richardson, the suspect for the Post Office robbery. Apparently, it took four uniforms to stuff him into the back of a van. The custody sergeant needs him interviewed and booked."

Jones massaged his eyes with finger and thumb.

"You'd better get off home or you'll be here the rest of the night. I'll call Alex. It's her case and she'll want to be in on the interview."

"You sure? Don't want to feel like I'm running out on you."

"Alex and I'll be fine. With the evidence against him, I doubt we'll have much trouble getting him to cough to aggravated bodily harm."

"I really don't mind staying."

"On no you don't. Manda's expecting you back and I don't want her upset with me. She might stop inviting me over for Sunday lunch." He winked. "Anyway, Alex deserves the collar. She's shouldered most of the work and identified Richardson. She's met the victim's family, too."

"If you're sure," Phil said, grabbing the jacket and rushing to the door. "See you tomorrow. Call me back in if you need a hand."

Chapter Fifteen

MONDAY 27TH JUNE
Holton, Birmingham

JONES MET Alex half way to the interview suite on the ground floor. She pushed through the double doors, red-faced and breathing hard.

"Didn't take you long."

"Traffic is light," she said, brushing her hair out of her eyes. "Thank you for calling, boss. I've been eager to meet Kelvin Richardson."

She flashed a smile and followed Jones along the brightly lit corridor.

Jones lowered the inspection hatch on the interview room door. A uniformed constable—a broad-shouldered and slim-hipped individual whom Jones didn't recognise—stood over the prisoner, his back to the door. When Jones and Alex entered the room, the constable spun, fists raised. Alex gasped and jerked back.

"Stand down, Constable!" Jones barked, and flashed his warrant card.

The constable snapped to attention.

"Name?"

The man's eyes narrowed and he glanced at the prisoner.

"Your name, Constable. I know who he is," Jones said, jabbing a finger towards Richardson.

"Adeoye, sir."

Constable Adeoye sported a fresh black eye and couldn't meet Jones' intense stare. Jones forced down his immediate reaction. First impressions weren't always accurate, but things didn't look good for the constable who had positioned himself between Jones and Richardson as though trying to hide the prisoner from their prying eyes.

"Wait outside in the corridor for me please, Constable. I'll speak with you in a minute."

Adeoye hesitated and glanced first at the prisoner and then at Alex, who stood behind Jones' right shoulder.

"What are you waiting for, man? Get out!"

"Yes, sir." He took a final, glowering look at Richardson, and marched from the room.

Jones couldn't watch Adeoye leave. He closed his eyes for a moment to regain some composure and listened to the constable's boots squeaking on the polished floor of the corridor outside. The double stomp told him that Adeoye was standing-at-ease, parade ground fashion. Alex's heavy breathing and thinned lips showed that she'd made a similar assumption to Jones—the assumption that they'd interrupted Adeoye beating the prisoner.

The constable would wait, but the prisoner couldn't.

Interview Room B, the largest of three in the station, smelled of disinfectant, sweat, and vomit—a heady mix that played badly on Jones' sinuses.

Richardson, a huge and heavily muscled black man, engulfed the chair into which the arresting officers had poured him. According to the booking officer's handover briefing, a passing patrol had found Richardson living rough behind a disused boxing gym in the old city centre. The lab boys had taken Richardson's clothes for forensic examination and hygiene purposes and swapped them for an orange jumpsuit. A couple of sizes too small, it made Jones think of the Hulk in mid-transformation. At any moment, the man might rip open the seams and start turning green.

The left side of Richardson's face had sustained so much damage that swelling had closed the eye. Jones suspected a fractured cheekbone. A cut on the man's lower lip seeped blood. Head bowed, the big man flicked out his tongue to lick at the wound. His handcuffs, chained through a retaining clip bolted to the tabletop, restricted movement and made his fingers swell. Heavy-duty bolts secured the table to the floor. Richardson was going nowhere.

"Hello Kelvin. I'm Detective Chief Inspector Jones, and this is Detective Constable Olganski. We're here to question you about what happened in the Post Office last week. But before we move on to the interview, you look uncomfortable. Are you okay?"

Richardson squinted through his good eye and flashed an angry glare. "I's fine. Nothin' a matta wi' me. Innit."

"Well, I wouldn't enjoy being trussed up like that. If I take those cuffs off, will you promise to behave yourself?"

"Boss?" Alex whispered.

Jones raised a finger and shook his head.

"Come on, Kelvin. If you promise to stay calm, I'll remove the cuffs, and we can talk to each other like civilised human beings. Deal?"

Richardson nodded and held open his fists to extend the handcuffs.

"Constable Olganski, would you mind removing those bracelets, please?" He handed her the keys he'd taken from the desk sergeant.

Alex raised an eyebrow, but stepped forwards and did as Jones asked. While she did so, and with Richardson distracted, Jones slid his left hand into his jacket pocket and closed his fingers around the textured grip of his telescopic baton. No harm taking precautions.

Once released, Richardson sat up straight, stretched his arms out in front of a barrel chest, and rolled his shoulders. The joints in his neck cracked so loud that Jones grimaced. The prisoner took a huge breath.

"T'anks, man."

Jones removed his hand from the pocket but kept it close to the comforting truncheon.

"That's better. Can't have been pleasant for you, Kelvin. This furniture isn't designed for a man your size, I'm afraid. Sorry about that."

Jones shot a sideways glance at Alex who nodded that she understood his method.

"We're going to take this easy and I don't want you to get upset. In fact, I'm not even going to turn on the recorder until you're good and ready."

He approached the table but didn't stand too close. He didn't want to intimidate Richardson, assuming that was even possible.

"Now," he continued, "the swelling under your eye and the cut lip, did you receive them during the arrest?"

Richardson raised his head but didn't answer.

"You did kick up a fuss and sent one of my officers to hospital. We think you broke her arm. That wasn't nice. She was only doing her job."

Richardson shuffled in his chair. His eyes closed and he mumbled something.

"Sorry Kelvin, I didn't quite catch that."

"Sorry," he repeated. "Didn't mean nothin' by it. When the Po-Po gets me backed into a corner for no reason, I lose control. Self-defence, innit?"

"Well, that's all right for now. We'll discuss it later, but before we start the interview, I'm going to ask a doctor to look at your cheek and treat that cut on your lip." He nodded to Alex, who took out her mobile and dialled a number.

Richardson glowered at Jones through hooded eyes.

"It ain't nothin'. I's fine."

"No, you're not fine. I don't want anyone thinking we're not taking proper care of you. Once the doctor's checked you over, we'll start the interview. Is that okay, Kelvin?"

Richardson nodded this time and then rolled his shoulders again.

"T'anks."

"In the meantime, I imagine you must be thirsty. Would you like a drink of water?"

"Yes, please."

Two 'thanks' and a 'please'. Now we're getting somewhere.

Alex ended her call and closed her mobile.

"Dr Grey is in the building. He won't be long."

"That's a stroke of luck, eh Kelvin? We'll pop out and fetch that drink for you if you don't mind staying here for a moment. Detective Constable Olganski, could I have a word with you outside, please?"

Once in the corridor, Jones lowered his voice. "Fetch him a drink Alex, and keep him calm until the doc's finished the examination. If we interview him now, the CPS will tear our case apart."

Alex hurried off in the direction of the vending machines. Jones turned to Adeoye, who'd braced to attention the moment the interview room door opened. The man stood a good three inches taller than Jones, and about twice as wide—a match in size to Richardson.

"Stand easy, Constable Adeoye."

Adeoye stood at ease—feet shoulder width apart, hands clasped behind his back, chest out. His shoulders remained rigid and his eyes showed the fifty-yard stare of a well-drilled squaddie. Jones moved to stand in front of him, but Adeoye focused on a spot directly over Jones's head.

"Adeoye? Nigerian, right?"

"Brummie, sir. Born in Solihull, but my father's from a little village north of Lagos, sir."

His quiet voice stood out in sharp contrast to his bulk, and the accent was solid West Midlands.

"Why haven't I seen you before? I'd have remembered a man of your build."

"I transferred in from B Division last month, sir. This is my first week on lates."

"Relax constable, you're not on parade."

Adeoye's shoulders dropped a fraction, but his head didn't move.

"Army?" Jones asked.

Adeoye gave a flicker of recognition.

"Six years in the 2nd Parachute Regiment, sir. Is it that obvious?"

"'Fraid so, lad. So, you swapped one uniform for another?"

"Yes, sir."

Jones studied the man afresh. An imposing sight, he'd pressed his uniform jacket to military perfection. Its creases could slice through paper. His trousers, though, were less than pristine. They showed signs of recent wear and tear. Dust smudged the knees, and wrinkles softened the razor creases. Adeoye hadn't tried to brush himself down before taking on the guard duty, yet he'd paused to throw on a fresh jacket. Why? No senior officer would have called him to account for a few erroneous creases once they'd learned of his part in the struggle to arrest Richardson.

Sweat glistened on Adeoye's face, giving it the high gloss of polished ebony, and the temperature in the custody suite warranted a change to "shirt-sleeve order". Adeoye could have removed the uniform jacket without objection from either the custody sergeant or his watch commander.

Jones pointed to the bruise above Adeoye's right eye. "Did the prisoner do that?"

Adeoye paused. His eyes drew back into focus and he met Jones' challenge.

"No, sir. I … received an elbow in the face from a colleague during the arrest. A pure accident, sir."

"Put it in the incident report, and make sure the doc gives you the all clear after he's seen to the prisoner."

"Yes sir, will do, but is the medical exam strictly necessary? I've had worse injuries shaving."

"Do you often shave your eyebrow, Constable?"

The offhand comment earned Jones the flicker of a smile.

"No, sir."

"In your report, make sure you include the name of the officer who owned the elbow."

Adeoye frowned and hesitated again before speaking. "Sorry sir, but I didn't see who it was. Too much going on at the time."

"Yet you know it was an elbow and not, say … a knee?"

Constable Adeoye chewed his lower lip.

"Are we going to have a falling out, Constable Adeoye?"

"Excuse me, sir?"

"Cut the bull, son. Tell me how the prisoner received those injuries and who over-tightened his handcuffs."

Another hesitation and Adeoye's eyes flickered.

"Sorry, sir?"

"You heard me, Constable. Answer the question."

"The prisoner was injured during the arrest, sir."

"And if I leave you alone with him again, will his injuries worsen?"

Constable Adeoye stiffened. His head lowered enough for Jones to see the fire burning in his eyes.

"You've got it all wrong, sir. I would never—"

"Stand down, Constable." Jones kept his voice even and low.

Adeoye hesitated mid-bristle before relaxing. He lost a few inches of height as he returned to the stand-at-ease position.

"You aren't going back into that interview room until I can trust you. DC Olganski needs the protection and support of a reliable officer. Pass me your jacket." Jones held out his hand.

Adeoye blinked hard, but didn't move.

"Constable Adeoye, I won't ask again."

"But sir …"

Jones lifted his chin and stared the big man down. After a few seconds delay, Adeoye unbuttoned the jacket and slid it off his shoulders. He winced as he handed the jacket to Jones and stood to attention once more.

Two thin dark stripes ran diagonally along Adeoye's left shirt-sleeve, between shoulder and elbow. Another slashed across the side of his ribcage. The marks confirmed Jones had made a serious mistake.

"Constable Adeoye, please accept my apologies. When we arrived, you weren't threatening the prisoner were you? You were protecting him from the rest of your watch."

With obvious reluctance, Adeoye nodded.

"Constable Cook, the officer with the broken arm, she's well liked, sir. One of the guys is a bit … sweet on her. He lost his rag, but only for a moment. I had to step between him and Richardson."

Adeoye sucked air through his teeth and then reached across to rub an upper arm the size of a small tree trunk.

"Protecting a prisoner from the revenge of a fellow officer can't have been easy. Well done, lad. You're a credit to that uniform."

Adeoye blinked twice, ran a hand through his close-cropped hair, and took a deep breath. "Thank you, sir. How did you know about the …?"

His eyes dropped to the oil stains on his white shirt.

"I've seen the marks of a badly maintained telescopic truncheon before. Dirty oil. There'll have to be an investigation. I'm putting the officer who struck you and attacked the prisoner on a charge. I won't have that sort of thing taking place in my station."

Alex turned the corner at the end of the corridor. She carried two bottles of water in one hand and her mobile phone in the other. Jones held up his arm and she stopped out of earshot. Jones leaned closer to Adeoye.

"Things will be better for your friend if he talks to his watch commander before I make my report. Do I make myself clear, Constable Adeoye?"

"Crystal, sir. I'll have a word with him before we go off shift. Constable Pietersen's a good man. He'll be feeling guilty as all hell right now."

"Pietersen, eh? Okay, I expect him to do the right thing. Don't forget to have your injuries checked."

"No, sir, I won't."

Jones beckoned to Alex who arrived and shot Adeoye a questioning glance.

"Everything okay, boss?"

"It is now. Where's the quack?"

"Dr Grey is in the canteen. He said he'd be here after he finished his coffee and his Danish."

Did he now? Bloody civilians.

"Okay. You and Constable Adeoye keep an eye on our friend in there. Don't question him until I return from a bit of housekeeping, but make sure the recording equipment is ready for action. I won't be long."

Jones stormed along the hallway, burst through the double doors to the custody admin area, and stopped in front of the counter. A bearded sergeant slouched in his chair.

"I don't recognise you, Sergeant. Your name please," Jones asked in a voice as controlled as he could manage.

"And you are?"

"DCI Jones, head of the Serious Crime Unit." Jones flashed his warrant card at the man, who shuffled upright. "Now, can I have your name please?"

"Ogilvy, sir. I'm on secondment from Division 3."

"Interesting." Jones leaned forwards and placed his hands flat on the desk. "Now, I don't know how they behave in the third division, Sergeant Ogilvy, but here in the Premiership we know how to treat suspects in our care."

"Excuse me, sir?" The sergeant's jaw muscles bunched and he stared into the middle distance as Adeoye had done moments earlier. Jones could tell the man knew what was coming.

"Don't ever present me with an injured suspect until you've had him signed fit by a medic," Jones said, allowing his voice to increase in volume. "What the hell do you think you're playing at?"

The sergeant's eyes lowered.

"I didn't have the time. We had an officer on her way to hospital, and the prisoner was raving, sir."

"All the more reason for him to see a doctor then, isn't it? You bloody idiot!" Jones fixed Ogilvy with his most ferocious high-temperature glare. "I'll be keeping my eye on you in future, Sergeant Ogilvy. Don't let this happen again. Do I make myself clear?"

"Yes, sir. I mean, no, it won't, sir. Happen again, I mean."

Jones spun on his heel and returned to the interview suite in time to see Dr Grey enter Interview Room B.

Jones followed him inside.

———

WITHIN FIFTEEN MINUTES of entering the room, the doctor had treated Richardson's wounds, assessed him for concussion, and pronounced him fit for interview. A duty solicitor, an impossibly young man in a saggy grey suit and scuffed shoes, sat on a chair next to Richardson. The solicitor's presence resulted from the efficient work of the recently chastened Sergeant Ogilvy.

Alex powered up the brand new Digital Interview Recording system. According to Phil Cryer, and its vocal advocate and sponsor, Superintendent Peyton, the DIR recorded images and sounds of a quality acceptable to both the CPS and the Criminal Courts System. Jones, ever the sceptic, still took written notes and instructed his SCU subordinates to do the same.

In operation, the DIR remained silent and, in time, Jones almost forgot its existence.

"Okay, Kelvin. Now we've read you your rights, and the medic's declared you fit, we can start the interview. Have you anything to tell us about what happened in the Post Office on King Charles Street last Thursday?"

A small butterfly stitch held the cut on Richardson's lip together. His eyes focused on the half-empty plastic bottle cradled in his huge hands.

"I didn't do nothin'. Weren't there."

The acne-ridden solicitor remained silent, but stared at his client through timid eyes and hugged a fake leather briefcase tight to his chest—his battle shield.

"Well, that's not entirely true is it, Kelvin?" Jones nodded to Alex, who pressed a button on the remote control in her hand. An image appeared on the television screen standing on a trolley. The DIR had its own position in a recess, protected by a toughened glass sheet.

The film clip showed the unmistakeable figure of Richardson walking into the crowded Post Office.

After fifty-three seconds, the screen froze on the grainy image of Richardson's face. While the recording played, Jones never took his eyes from the prisoner. He waited a full minute before speaking.

"Do you have anything to add to your previous statement, Kelvin?"

Jones held his breath. The interview had reached a delicate stage. After seeing the evidence weighed against him, Richardson could react in a number of ways, one of them violent. As a precaution, Jones had left the door open a crack to allow Constable Adeoye ease of access. However, judging by the number needed to subdue Richardson during the arrest, he wondered whether he, Alex, and Adeoye would suffice. The baton in his jacket pocket became smaller and lighter with each passing second.

Richardson's reaction couldn't have been more unexpected. He dropped the water bottle on the table, buried his face in his hands, and broke down.

"I didn't mean ta do it. I couldn't help mesself. Saw the money an' took it."

Richardson pulled his hands away from his face to reveal cheeks streaked with tears. He looked little more than a large boy caught stealing sweets. Jones almost felt sorry for him until he remembered the police officer's broken arm and the hospitalised pensioner.

"How is da ol' guy?" Richardson asked.

He sniffled and Jones passed him a tissue from his pocket. Richardson blew his nose and sniffled again.

"Still in the hospital. He suffered a heart attack when he hit the floor."

Richardson folded as though someone had punched him in the stomach. He bent double, buried his face in his hands again, and let out a plaintive wail.

"Kelvin?" Jones waited for the man to look up. "I'm sorry, but we're going to charge you with the robbery and the attack on Mr"—he checked the victim's name in the file—"Arthur Crabtree. DC Olganski is going to read out the charges and after that, I'll have someone escort you to the cells. Is that clear, Kelvin? You can still make a statement if you wish."

Richardson nodded and leaned back, head lowered, and shoulders slumped.

Alex pushed a button on the DIR and the ten-inch screen on the unit split into two images. The upper half showed Richardson sitting behind the interview desk, the lower half displayed the words spoken by Alex as she read out the charges.

Jones stared in fascination as the speech recognition software within the device translated Alex's spoken words into text. A built-in laser printer would spew hard copy in A4 sheets later. He finally recognised the benefits of the DIR—nobody had to hand type statements any more. Maybe Peyton and Phil could convert him into a technophile after all, though he'd never allow himself to rely on digital recording without the written backup. He still maintained copious notes.

"Kelvin Dwayne Richardson, of no permanent address, I charge you with Assault Occasioning Actual Bodily Harm, contrary to Section 47, Offences against the Person Act 1861 …' Alex read from notes on the desk in front of her and continued to go through Richardson's charges.

A knock on the door made Jones spring to his feet, and fire flared in his belly. He signalled for Alex to stop. "For the benefit of the recording device," he said, "interview suspended at 21:29 for DCI Jones to leave the room."

Jones seethed. Whoever had the nerve to interrupt the interview better have a bloody good reason or they wouldn't survive the night.

Chapter Sixteen

MONDAY 27TH JUNE – *Late evening*
Holton, Birmingham

JONES JERKED OPENED the door to the officer-in-charge of the late shift, Inspector Jerry Sexton, but before Jones could chew him out, Sexton raised a hand. "Sorry to interrupt, sir, but this is important."

"What's wrong, Jerry?"

Sexton signalled for Jones to follow him along the corridor. Once far enough away from Constable Adeoye to speak privately, he continued. "I've been following the interview from the control room, sir."

Jones had forgotten that the DIR system had a central control hub where supervisors could follow the interviews. Although designed for monitoring and training purposes, it wasn't beyond the late watch to pass quiet times by following the progress of interrogations. They weren't above placing bets on the outcome either.

"Then you must know we're in the middle of charging the

beggar. What's wrong? Do you need another ten minutes delay to win the sweepstake?"

Sexton pulled back and placed a hand to his chest.

"DCI Jones," he whispered, "I'd never do that to you." A twinkle in the inspector's light brown eyes gave lie to the claim. "But this just arrived from the hospital, and I knew you'd want to read it."

He handed Jones the printout of an email.

"*Arthur Crabtree, admitted following an attack at the King Charles Street Post Office, died at 19:33, of complications following myocardial infarction.*"

Jones tugged at an earlobe and grimaced.

"Well, that's a crying shame for Mr Crabtree and his family, and it means we'll have to increase Richardson's charge to manslaughter."

"That's why I interrupted you, sir."

Jones knew there had to be a reason he liked Jerry Sexton so much. "Thanks, mate. You've saved us some paperwork. What time do you have on the sweep?"

Sexton shuffled his feet and looked away. "None of us were even close. Didn't think you'd take this long knowing the evidence against our Kelvin. We cancelled all the bets the moment you had to call in the medic. None of us spotted Richardson's injuries. Blood doesn't show up too well on the control monitors, seeing as they're black and white."

"You know unlicensed gambling is illegal, Inspector?"

"It's for charity, sir. You know that."

"Yeah, right."

"Actually, changing the subject, we were all dead impressed by the way you handled the interview. Keeping the suspect calm and making sure he received medical treatment is more than many would have done after he'd put young Cook in hospital."

Jones sighed.

"I've been doing this for a fair while."

"All the same, things could have turned nasty if Richardson had blown a gasket or collapsed from his injuries."

"Agreed."

"Now, David. If you don't mind, I'll have a quiet word with Sergeant Ogilvy. Bloody moron should have called the doctor immediately."

"It's all right, Jerry, I've already done that. You can consider him well and truly reprimanded. Hope he's learned his lesson."

———

"KELVIN," Jones said, after entering the interview room and retaking his chair. "I'm afraid I have some bad news …"

Before Jones had time to finish reading the hospital's email bulletin, Richardson screamed and dived sideways out of his seat. He fell to the floor, arms and legs flailing, and smashed the back of his head into the concrete again and again.

Alex threw herself on top of Richardson, but one of his arms caught her shoulder a glancing blow and knocked her against the wall. The door crashed open. Adeoye burst in and lunged at Kelvin, truncheon drawn. Jones scrambled to his feet, threw his arm out to stop Adeoye and hit a solid wall of muscle. It hurt.

"Stop!" Jones yelled. "Constable, go easy. I think he's having a seizure."

Adeoye held off, but Kelvin lay still and senseless on the grey floor. Alex sat in the corner against the joining walls, cradling her knee with both hands.

"Alex, are you hurt?"

"No, boss. I knocked my leg against the wall. I'll be fine."

She winced as Jones helped her stand.

"You sure?"

"Yes, boss."

"Take a seat for a minute, I'll ask the doc to check you over."

"Really, boss. I'm fine. *Skakad* … shaken, only."

"I was too slow. Sorry."

Jones squeezed her shoulder and she nodded. As for the young solicitor, he stood against the far wall hugging the briefcase to his chest. His eyes stared at Richardson and his mouth moved, but he made no sound.

Moments later, Jerry Sexton burst into the room with Dr Grey and a uniformed constable in tow. The medic stooped to work on his patient and Jones sent Adeoye and the other officer into the corridor. Jones heard Adeoye's deep voice explaining the situation to his mate.

Jones closed on the solicitor and kept his voice quiet but firm. "We have the whole incident recorded." He pointed to the DIR. "So I don't expect to see or hear a word about police brutality following the injury to our officer. Do I make myself clear?"

Pale and trembling, the solicitor was in no condition to argue. Jones helped him back to his seat. Alex recovered, but favouring her left leg, gave the solicitor the second water bottle they'd brought for Richardson. The young man had to hold it in both hands to prevent water spilling into his lap.

The kneeling medic, a middle-aged man with a comb-over, a belly to rival that of Charlie Pelham, and nicotine-stained fingers, glanced up at Jones. "He's out cold, but the heart rate is steady, breathing's strong, and pupils even and reactive. He should be okay, but it's a hospital job I'm afraid. He'll likely wake up with a fierce headache, but I don't think he's in immediate danger. Even so, I don't want to move him until the paramedics arrive. He might have a spinal injury."

Jones stared at the prone Richardson.

"A night in hospital before he goes down for manslaughter won't do him any harm."

Dr Grey brushed lint from the knees of his trousers and bent to reach for his medical bag, grunting with the effort. "Judging from his actions tonight, he's bound for a high-security ward at Broadmoor Hospital."

"Best place for the poor lad."

"Poor lad?" Jerry Sexton turned to Jones. "Bloody hell, sir. Are you forgetting that Richardson caused the death of an old man who did nothing more than collect his pension? And he broke a police officer's arm."

Jones lowered his voice and leaned closer to Sexton. "Yes, and if you'd seen the look on his face when I told him the man died, you'd know how devastated he was. He's ill, Jerry. See what he did to himself? No, he deserves our pity. Doesn't mean we shouldn't lock him up, though."

Jones stepped to one side as the shame-faced custody sergeant, Ogilvy, led a pair of paramedics to the doorway. They wheeled a stretcher between them and immediately set about fitting a neck brace and strapping Richardson onto a spinal board.

Minutes later, with Richardson on the stretcher, wrist hand-cuffed to a side rail, the room emptied. Jones, Alex, and Sexton looked on while Dr Grey took his leave and hurried off after the paramedics, the solicitor, and the two constables.

"Well, sir," Sexton said, after the stretcher and its entourage turned the corner, "if you don't mind, I'll go organise a guard detail at the hospital. Can't expect Adeoye and Greenbaum to stay with Richardson all night, can we now?"

"Right you are, Jerry. We still have all this paperwork to sort."

Sexton left and Jones turned to Alex. "How's that knee? Do you need to take some time?"

"No, boss. A bruise only. It'll be okay in the morning."

Jones studied Alex's eyes carefully. He wouldn't put it past her to tough it out as Adeoye had done. On the other hand, her skin colour, which had turned deathly pale immediately after the fall, had recovered to its normal healthy tan.

"You sure?"

Alex nodded and Jones saw something in her expression he hadn't seen before. What was it? Frustration?

"In that case, can you do the necessary, please?" Jones pointed into the interview room. "As soon as you've written and signed your injury report, get off home and rest that leg. Don't come in tomorrow if it's swollen."

"Boss," she said, eyeing the corridor to make sure they were alone, "if one of the men bumped his knee, would you make the same fuss?"

"Of course I would," he snapped, but the question made him think. He took a breath. "Damn it. Am I being an old chauvinist?"

Alex lifted an eyebrow.

"You aren't that old, boss."

Jones nodded.

That's put me in my place.

"Point taken, DC Olganski. I'll work on it, okay?"

"Thank you, sir."

Her embarrassed smile made him feel less of a berk and showed that he still had a lot to learn, despite all his age and experience.

Jones, you are a fossil.

He left Alex to close down the DIR unit. There was no need to sign or date evidence tapes since the closed-loop digital system operated with something called "double-redundancy" built into what the instruction manual called "hyper-secure servers".

Jones understood the individual words, if not the meaning.

Even though the IT firm that installed its digital architecture guaranteed the system as totally failsafe, Jones didn't believe a single word of it.

Chapter Seventeen

FRIDAY 18TH MARCH – *Sean Freeman*
Edinburgh, Scotland

FREEMAN, in the guise of John Devenish, visiting businessman, entered the hushed confines of *Throckmorton's Gems* on a dull morning with the delicious Angela Glennie draped on his arm.

Angela, the only bright thing he'd seen since crossing the border into a grey and damp Scotland, played her role to perfection. Dressed in a sleek skin-tight, dark blue dress, she was tall, elegant, and had smooth curves exactly where they needed to be. She was window dressing, brought along to distract—but what a distraction.

They'd met that morning when he briefed her on the role after recovering from the shock of seeing her in person. Her talent agency photo gallery, good as it was, simply didn't do her justice.

She owned hazel eyes that changed from light brown to pale green depending upon the background lighting. Right then, her irises were brown and studded with flecks of orange. Wide pupils betrayed her excitement in taking on the role he'd written for her.

Crisp and prim, the distinguished jeweller smelled money and pounced as soon as they crossed the threshold.

"Good morning, sir, madam. My name is Andrew Morton. Welcome to my establishment. May I be of assistance?"

Freeman stared down his nose at the man with the slicked back hair. Morton's waistcoat stretched tight around a wide belly. A heavy watch chain, without doubt twenty-four carat gold, drooped from a buttonhole, fed into one of the pockets, and glistened under the tastefully arranged spotlights. The same lights focused the customers' attention on shiny goods displayed under toughened glass cabinets and cast deep shadows in the lower-value section of the "establishment".

Ignoring Morton's overture, Freeman led Angela to the necklace displays. The moment they were close enough to see the goods and read the labels, she began tutting and sighing. She also threw out the occasional, "Oh dear," and added a headshake or two. It took her less than a minute to show enough displeasure to make the point.

"Sorry, darling," Freeman said, using the Home Counties accent he'd practised for the past few days and speaking loud enough for everyone in the shop to hear. "This really isn't good enough."

She sighed again. "What are we going to do?" she asked, making a passable impression of the late Audrey Hepburn, without delivering a pastiche. Her English accent was more than acceptable, too.

Three customers, an elderly couple and a middle-aged man, twitched their ears but studiously avoided staring.

Freeman returned to the counter. Morton still looked smug.

"May I be of assistance, sir?" her repeated.

"No thanks," Freeman said. "It seems we won't be staying." He flicked dismissive fingers towards the zirconium necklaces. "These … items … are not at all suitable. No, no. Not at all."

He turned to Angela.

"Sorry, my Angel," he said, cupping her elbow in his hand as support against the shock, "but I'm afraid that idiot concierge told us a bit of a porky pie. This isn't up to snuff, not at all."

Angela sighed. "Oh John, you insisted I leave the Cartier at home this trip and I simply *can't* turn up bare necked at the reception tonight. My Tory Burch simply *demands* something standout and glittery to counterbalance the design. I mean, the dress is *gorgeous*, but it needs something …"

Her hand snaked up to caress a naked throat. Such a lovely throat—pale, slender, and as flawless as the Zinfandel diamond he'd held for the briefest of moments.

"You're certain nothing here will do, Angel?"

"Absolutely not. We'll have to cancel."

Freeman was impressed. The girl had some acting chops and delivered her lines with conviction. The spoilt debutante sulk was a nice touch, and the plunging neckline of the clinging dress made sure nobody looked at him, not that it mattered too much. His mother wouldn't have recognised him in the rig he'd chosen. Dusky makeup and coloured contact lenses completed the disguise.

"Well, I didn't know we'd receive an invite to a grand opening, did I?" Freeman said, allowing his frown to deepen into a scowl. "Excuse me, Morton, but is this all you have to show us? The concierge at *The Atholl* assured us this was the finest jewellers in Scotland. I have to say, I expected a little more."

Morton's eyes widened in recognition. "Please forgive me, Mr Devenish," he gushed. "Alphonse *did* telephone ahead and explain your situation, but failed to describe you, sir." He leaned close and lowered his voice. "If I might be so bold, the front-of-house display items are for, shall we say, *general* consumption." He opened his hand and pointed to a heavy velvet curtain covering most of the wall behind the serving counter. "Our premier selection is through here. Please follow me, sir."

Freeman offered Angela the crook of his arm and they did as Morton suggested. Despite his planning, Freeman hadn't dared to hope it would be so easy. He reached into his trouser pocket and pressed the send button on his mobile.

Morton drew back the heavy curtain, pressed his right thumb to a small metal panel on the wall, and entered a combination into the keypad.

Freeman was in, and without the need for a scalpel.

With the gentle hum of a near silent electric motor, the bullet-resistant glass wall slid open to reveal a room half as large as the shop. It had far fewer items on display, but each was spectacular and protected by bullet-resistant glass cabinets. Although expected, the sight still made Freeman's heart flutter. The shining, prismatic glitters of seven million pounds worth of sapphires, rubies, and emeralds in the form of necklaces, bracelets, earrings, and tiaras would have intoxicated anyone who cared about such trinkets. He didn't—not much.

On his arm, Angela gasped.

Clearly pleased with the effect of his "grand reveal", Morton beamed and invited them to enter the sanctum sanctorum before him and signalled for his assistant, a slightly built woman in her fifties, to take his place front and centre.

Two seconds later and according to plan, the restrained tranquillity of Edinburgh's most exclusive purveyor of high-value jewellery descended into mayhem.

The front door crashed open. Two men—Tommy, tall and skinny, and Gordy, tall and stocky—entered and bolted the door behind them. Dressed in business suits, dark glasses, leather gloves, false moustaches, and blond wigs, each carried a sawn-off double-barrelled shotgun.

"Everybody down!" Tommy yelled in a high-pitched, strangled voice. He pointed the shotgun at the ceiling and pulled one of the two triggers. The muzzle barked fire and flashed light and punched a football-sized hole in the suspended ceiling. The decaying sound wave battered Freeman's eardrums, and the blast buffeted his face. The acrid stink of gunpowder stung his nostrils.

Angela and another woman screamed.

What the fuck's he doing?

This wasn't the plan. No shooting, he'd said.

Freeman clapped his hand across Angela's mouth.

"Shush. These bastards are serious."

He removed his hand. Angela stood wide-eyed, mouth open, and trembling. Urine rippled down her inner thighs and pooled on the plush carpet. She stared at him, disbelief and terror etched into her pallid face.

Morton scrambled towards a panic button on the inside wall beside the door, but was nowhere near fast enough. Freeman charged and sent Morton flying, but continued his forwards momentum and caught the jeweller before his head connected with a toughened glass cabinet. He lowered the old man to the floor gently, and leaned him against a cabinet pedestal.

"Sorry, Mr Morton," Freeman whispered, "but I can't let you lock yourself inside. There's no telling what these animals will do to the rest of us."

As Freeman stood, the crumpled jeweller groaned and buried his face in his hands.

Freeman needed to think of something—ad lib.

"Get down all of you. Do as they say," Freeman yelled as Gordy swung his weapon in a threatening arc.

In the far corner by the mantelpiece clocks, the elderly couple hit the carpet faster than Freeman imagined possible. The man positioned himself between his wife and the room, and covered her body with his. Freeman recognised bravery when he saw it and nodded.

The third customer, a grey-haired banker type, already prone, face kissing the carpet and eyelids closed, whimpered. The shop assistant hid behind the counter, covering her ears with trembling hands.

Tommy stepped forward. The shotgun bucked in his hands once more. A second ear-splitting roar had one of the cheap-side cabinets explode in a shower of shattered glass and inexpensive trinkets. Angela screamed again. Freeman grabbed her by the arm and pushed her to the floor next to the trembling Morton.

"Stay down, please!" He dropped to one knee beside her and whispered, "Wait here. I'll handle this."

While Gordy set about collecting Parrish's pre-ordered goods in Aladdin's cave, Freeman closed on Tommy, beckoning with his finger. The man, breathing hard, stepped forward.

"What are you fucking doing?" Freeman whispered.

Glassy-eyed and shaking, Tommy bared his teeth.

"Fuck off, arsehole."

"Abacus beansprout," Freeman whispered, adding a wink.

Tommy frowned.

"What's that?" he demanded, pushing his ear closer.

Freeman butted him in the nose and yanked the weapon from his hands. Tommy staggered backwards and Freeman jabbed him in the crotch with the butt of the shotgun. Tommy doubled over, gasping for breath.

Gordy, lost in his task of ransacking the goodies, had his back to them. With the shotgun raised, Freeman rushed him.

Chapter Eighteen

FRIDAY 18TH MARCH – *Angela Glennie*
Edinburgh, Scotland

THE CRAMPED BENCH seat inside the ambulance wasn't much of an improvement on the shop's carpet, and Angela Glennie couldn't stop trembling. The paramedic fussed for a few minutes, checking her pulse and shining a light in her eyes. Once he'd made sure she could follow his finger without falling off the bench, he asked the standard health questions. Did she have a headache, nausea, double vision?

Angela barely noticed the words, but managed to mumble, "I'm fine. I'll be okay," in response.

Her main concern was for John Devenish. He'd disappeared along with the robbers and she was absolutely terrified for his safety.

"What's your name, lass?"

The policeman, who'd introduced himself as Detective Inspector James Barrow, and confirmed it by showing her his ID card, had warm brown eyes; they were kind too. On any other day, Barrow might well have passed for a Scottish Geordie Clooney, including the greying temples and white flecked beard, but at that moment, tears blurred her vision, and she couldn't pull his features into proper focus. He gave her an encouraging smile and she cried. Why couldn't she control her emotions, or her quaking limbs?

Her legs smelled of dried urine, and she desperately needed a shower.

"Easy, miss," he said and touched her shoulder. "You're safe now. Can I have your name please?"

She sniffed and rubbed her eyes with the heels of her hands. In the reflection of the ambulance window, the subtle makeup she'd taken ages to apply that morning had smudged into dark patches.

She looked terrible and felt worse.

"M-My name's Angela Glennie … from the Royal Mile Talent Agency. I-I'm here on a gig."

Control left her and she burst into tears again. The green-clad paramedic, kneeling at her side, looked up at Barrow and shook his head.

"She's in shock, mate," he said. "Don't be pushing too hard, now."

Barrow squatted in front of her, supporting his weight by digging his elbows into his thighs. He grimaced as though his knees hurt. Angela appreciated his efforts to help her relax, but she had to fold her arms to stop them shaking and to keep from shivering.

"I understand this was a terrible ordeal for you, Ms Glennie." His quiet, rich tones soothed her a little. "I don't want to upset you, but we need to find these men. The other customers suggested you came in with one of them. Can you tell us anything? What's this about a gig?"

"You're wrong. You have it all wrong. Mr Devenish was—is—a hero. He stopped the robbery. You have to find him. He's in terrible danger."

"Really, miss?" Barrow said. His eyes turned in the direction of the shop. "The man you were with took on two men carrying loaded shotguns?"

"Yes, he did. He did?"

The doubt in Barrow's eyes told her everything.

She blew her nose on a tissue. "Why didn't they take anything then?" she asked.

"How do you know that?"

"Mr Morton told me nothing's missing. A-And they left one of the shotguns behind, didn't they? I saw it while waiting for you to arrive. Why would they do that?"

Barrow shook his head.

"No idea, miss."

She wiped her nose and blinked away the stinging tears.

"Where is he? Mr Devenish, I mean. He's hurt, isn't he?"

"We don't know yet."

She sniffled and used the tissue again.

"He was so brave. They must have taken him with them. Oh God, they'll kill him."

"Easy, miss."

Barrow touched her knee. She jerked it away and instantly regretted the action. Although only trying to comfort her, she needed him to listen. Mr Devenish was in danger. Why wouldn't the detective listen?

"Can you start at the beginning?" Barrow asked, keeping his voice steady and low. "You were here on a gig you say?"

The words tumbled out. "John Devenish is a client. He booked me for the morning."

"What for?"

Before answering, she swallowed and took a settling breath.

"He's part of an advanced location crew from Elstree Studios, scouting sets for an upcoming crime project. They're film studios, based in London," she added when Barrow looked confused. "Mr Devenish needed to keep his visit quiet." She sniffed again and took a deep, faltering breath. "He said that if word got out about the reason for his visit, the rental prices would steeple and cut the film's budget for extras. You know, walk-on parts for local talent, and the likes of me. He was lovely." She paused and called to the paramedic. "Do you have any water?"

The man reached into a compartment above her head and handed her a small plastic bottle.

"Sips only," he said. "Your stomach might be a little delicate right now."

She broke the seal and drank.

"Is Mr Morton okay? His breathing sounded ragged."

The paramedic nodded and wrinkled his nose.

"My colleagues in the other ambulance took him to hospital, but he's fine. Deep shock, but he'll recover after a good rest. We suspect he has a dislocated shoulder from the fall, but he should be okay. Probably keep him in overnight, man of his age. To be on the safe side."

"In your own time, miss," Barrow said.

Angela stared at the shop front through unfocused eyes.

"It all happened so quickly. Mr Devenish and I were going through the routine we'd rehearsed."

"Say again? What routine?" Barrow asked.

"Last evening, he sent the agency a script and director's notes by courier. I learned my part overnight. The package included a part payment—two hundred pounds in cash—and instructions to meet him at his hotel this morning, at nine-thirty. I had to dress like Audrey Hepburn from *Breakfast at Tiffany's*. Little black dress." She shrugged. "This blue one is the nearest thing I had, short of an evening gown. You know the film? *Tiffany's*, I mean? Audrey was iconic. Stunning."

Angela bit her lip. Why did she sound so scatter-brained?

Barrow nodded. "One of my wife's favourites. What hotel?"

"Sorry? Oh, yes. *The Atholl* on the Crescent. You know it?"

He nodded again.

"Impressive place. Love to stay the night, but that's not likely to happen on a policeman's salary." His attractive smile reassured her. "Did you go inside?"

"Yes. We met at the reception desk and waited while he paid his bill. After that, we ran through our lines in the breakfast room. He was a real professional. Covered all the usual stuff I'd expect from a director at an audition. You know, the basic plot, my character's motivation."

Barrow's knees cracked as he stood. "He actually stayed at the hotel?"

"Yes."

"Excellent. One moment, Ms Glennie, I need to get someone over there before they clean his room. And we'll need a description from you as soon as possible."

"If it helps find him, I'll do everything I can."

Barrow raised an eyebrow before turning his back. He tapped at the screen of his mobile and spoke quietly for a few minutes. By the time he ended the call and returned to the ambulance, Angela felt better. Drained, but loads better. At least she'd been able to control her movements well enough not to dribble water down her chin.

"Do you need to take Ms Glennie to hospital?" Barrow asked the paramedic.

"Yes, sir. She needs to see a doctor. Shock is a strange thing."

"If you don't mind, I'll accompany you and we can have a chat on the way. Would that be okay, Ms Glennie?"

"Call me Angela. Ms Glennie makes me sound like, so old."

The rear door of the ambulance slammed shut, blocking out the watery sunshine. Angela jumped, her heart skipped, and she was right back in the shop, reliving the sight of two armed men bursting in, waving shotguns. The crack of exploding cartridges and smell of gunpowder stayed fresh in her mind. Her ears still rang from the shots.

The engine fired up and the ambulance shook and rattled. Angela touched the cool plastic bottle to her forehead. Her heart rate finally slowed.

Barrow took the seat opposite and opened his notebook.

"Now, Angela. Tell me what happened in as much detail as you can remember. Start from the second you met this Devenish character at the hotel. What were your first impressions?"

"Don't know really. He's a wee bit above average height, maybe six feet tall. Average build, but fit-looking, trim waist, you know? Moved well. Graceful, almost like a dancer, but without the Armani suit I wouldn't have given him a second glance on the street, or in a nightclub."

"Nondescript?" Barrow suggested, making another note in his pad.

"Aye, nondescript. That's a sound word for him, but … I don't know. There was something behind the eyes. Don't know. Sadness? Loneliness?" She shook her head. "Maybe, I'm imagining it, y'know?"

"Possibly. Was there anything that grabbed your attention, or struck you as strange?"

"Not really, apart from his accent."

"Which was?"

"Well, posh English. Could have passed for an old-time BBC newsreader, y'know? They call it received pronunciation. We did a module on accents at college." She made a stab at replicating it for Barrow. "Struck me as rather strange, don't you know," she enunciated, and believed it a close match.

"Why? You said he was from London. Wouldn't you have expected him to sound English."

"No, it's not that. I expected a foreign accent. He had dark skin, like someone from the Mediterranean, y'know? His voice threw me for a moment." Angela shook her head. "Sorry, I must stop saying 'y'know'. Unnecessary repeated phrases are verbal tics. Understanding Characterisation, module three."

"The dark skin. Was it makeup d'ye think?"

"Could have been, but it looked pretty realistic to me. I mean, I do know my way around a makeup bag, and I didn't spot it."

Barrow smiled again. He had a wonderful way of making her feel at ease. He'd clearly interviewed the distressed before, and knew when to push and when to ease off. She liked him and wanted to help. She wanted to help Mr Devenish too.

"What happened when the armed men entered the shop?"

Angela put a hand to her mouth. "It happened so fast. Mr Devenish pushed Mr Morton and me to the floor and told us to stay down. I closed my eyes and started praying, y'know?"

Darn.

There it was again, the "y'know".

How embarrassing.

Barrow wrote in his notepad.

"What did you hear?"

"It sounded to me as though one of the men hit Mr Devenish. They had Glaswegian accents. Swore a lot and kept shouting that they had shotguns as though we couldn't see that for ourselves. Before they left, one of them told the other to "drag the moron" outside with them." Angela shuddered. "Oh God, that poor brave man. He's dead, isn't he? I know he's dead."

"We don't know anything for certain, Angela," Barrow answered. "I've issued a description of the getaway car. We have the details from a couple of shoppers in the street outside. It'll turn up soon. As for Mr Devenish," Barrow said, grimacing, "I'm not sure you heard what you think you heard, and I'd love a wee chat with him."

Angela made fists and straightened her back. "You don't believe me, do you? You think Mr Devenish is part of that gang, right?"

Barrow stared directly into her eyes.

"Ms Glennie, at this stage of the investigation, I'm keeping an open mind."

By the time the ambulance slowed for the turn into the Royal Infirmary, Barrow's gentle inquisition had extracted it all: sights, sounds, emotions, sensations. The cathartic effect was astonishing. Apart from the smell of her dried wee, Angela felt heaps better.

"You'll get a good picture of Mr Devenish from the CCTV at the shop and the hotel, won't you?" she asked.

Barrow sucked air through bared teeth. "'Fraid not, Miss. Both of those places are so damned exclusive, the clientele would never stand for it. The rich value their privacy. I'll need you to talk to a sketch artist, and go through some mug shots, if you wouldn't mind."

"Aye, of course. Like I said, I'll help any way I can."

As the ambulance squealed to a halt, Barrow barged through the rear door. Angela shielded her eyes from the sun. He climbed down to the road on stiff legs and turned to face her.

"You've been wonderfully brave, Ms Glennie. Take all the advice you get from the doctor and you'll feel better in no time. I'll have one of my officers contact you later this afternoon to take an official statement. In the meantime, if you think of anything, anything at all, don't hesitate to contact me."

He handed her his card, which she stuffed into a pocket in the clutch bag she forgot she still carried.

———

BARROW WAVED farewell to Angela Glennie as the paramedic led her through the automatic doors of A&E admissions. Once they'd entered the building, he beckoned to his driver, who'd followed the ambulance from the crime scene.

The front passenger seat of the Ford Mondeo was a damned sight more comfortable than the bench seat of the ambulance. Barrow leaned back against the head restraint and tried to rub the grit from his eyes.

"Where to, sir?"

"Back to the crime scene. Those arseholes terrified that poor wee girl and the others, and I want them found. You never know, forensics might find something."

"Ay, sir."

Constable Allen shifted into first and rolled out of the car park.

"Take your time, there's no need to rush. The CSIs will be ages yet, and I need time to think. Did you ask Control to check out the local traffic cams and any shop-front CCTVs?"

"Yes sir, but they've found nothing yet. Still, early days."

Barrow closed his eyes against the sun and listened to the sound of passing traffic. Internally, he sighed. Three months from retirement and he faced yet another violent crime he probably wouldn't solve.

Chapter Nineteen

FREEMAN TRAVELLED in the back of the stolen getaway car with the muzzle of Tommy's shotgun pressed into the nape of Gordy's neck. Tommy, in the front passenger's seat, moaned about his broken and bloodied nose all the way to the lock-up where they'd met to plan the job the previous afternoon. A dilapidated wreck of a place, but isolated and secure, it was the perfect setting to destroy the car and divvy up the spoils. Only there weren't any spoils to divide, since Freeman had forced Gordy to leave the shop empty handed.

Throughout the twenty-five minute drive, Gordy kept shooting him looks of pure malice through the rear view mirror.

"Mr Parrish is gonna tear your fuckin' arms off for this, wee man. Unless I kill you first, you fuckin' barmpot."

Freeman ground the barrel into the side of the big Scotsman's neck. "I wouldn't make me nervous if I were you, Gordy. I've no idea how light this gun's trigger action is. Pull up over there by the garage, but don't brake too hard or we might find out."

"Broke my fucking nose, he did, Gordy," Tommy whined. "Hit me in the bollocks too. Fucking hurts, it does."

"Shouldn't have come in blasting then, should you? Bloody idiots," Freeman said. "Quit your moaning and go open the doors. Don't do anything stupid or you'll be minus a big brother. Give him the car keys, Gordy."

Gordy handed them across, carefully.

"Gordy? Should I?"

Freeman leaned against the gun and forced Gordy's face into the steering wheel.

"Don't ask him, Tommy. I'm the one with the shotgun. I give the orders. Do it!"

Tommy limped to the garage, shuffling the keys with one hand while cupping his family jewels with the other. Freeman released the pressure and allowed Gordy to sit back.

"What the fuck was that shooting about?" Freeman demanded. "The guns were for show only. They weren't supposed to be loaded."

Gordy didn't answer.

Freeman flicked the gun butt and snapped the barrel against the side of the big man's head. A cut opened on the earlobe, dripping blood. Gordy barely flinched.

"Answer me."

"Fuck you, pal!" His yell reverberated through the car. "You're dead meat."

"Get out, but be careful. Don't fall over or do anything to make me nervous."

He shepherded Gordy, at a safe distance, into the abandoned garage and lined the brothers up side-by-side against the rear wall. Now what was he going to do? His one goal since Tommy let loose the first shot had been to get these bozos away from the shop without endangering the customers or Angela Glennie. Achieving that left him alone with two murderous thugs who were out for blood—his blood.

Gordy flexed his empty hands. His eyes searched the garage, no doubt looking for a weapon to replace the one Freeman made him leave at the shop.

"Why d'you use the gun, Tommy?"

"I was only …"

"Shut it, Tommy," Gordy growled. "Don't say nothing!"

Tommy cowered against the oil-stained wall that hosted a pinup calendar dated 2005. Ms July wore a doodled moustache and other inked additions that defined the intellect of the artist. Tommy's eyes glistened with tears. "But I didnae hurt nobody."

Freeman paused a heartbeat before responding. "Why'd you load the fucking things?"

"We work for Mr Parrish, not you," Gordy yelled as though the name-dropping would help his cause. "What's he gonna say when he learns you pulled us outta the shop?"

Freeman didn't have an answer, nor did he search for one. He had other things on his mind, like for instance, wondering how long it would take these two clowns to remember that Tommy had fired twice inside the shop before Freeman relieved him of the weapon. He now held two Scottish hard men at bay with nothing more than an empty shotgun.

Gordy was the one to watch, the leader. His eyes were alive, angry, and calculating. Tommy was the sheep.

Freeman's stomach churned and his hands were slick with sweat. He backed up a pace, keeping both men in view and out of reach.

Gordy slid a glance at his brother before returning his angry stare to Freeman.

"Who's gonna pay us our cut?"

"You're kidding, right? You ignored my orders, started shooting, and you still want payment?"

Tommy tilted his head, frowned, and then stared at the shotgun. Freeman could almost hear the cogs whirring.

Tommy waved an excited finger at the shotgun.

"Hey, Gordy …"

Shit!

Freeman lunged, pushed forward with his right arm, and pulled back with his left. The butt of the shotgun flipped up and connected with Tommy's nose. It exploded in a another shower of crimson. Tommy squealed and staggered backwards, his hands grabbing at his shattered face.

Freeman spun to face Gordy, who had dropped into an orthodox boxer's stance, shoulders rounded, leading with his left hand, and leaning back on his right leg.

"Empty, eh? Shoulda fuckin' known," Gordy said, backing off when he should have advanced. "I'm gonna enjoy this."

Freeman feinted left, then right, searching for an opening.

Gordy responded, matching Freeman's moves, eyes flicking between the shotgun and Freeman's face. His movements were fast and his guard stayed high. A boxer.

Tommy's howls cut through the silence. How long would he stay out of the dance?

Gordy smiled and shuffled closer.

"You're fuckin' toast, pal."

Freeman let go of the shotgun. Gordy's eyes followed its tumbling fall, his left hand lowered.

Freeman shuffled forward, and snapped a left jab at Gordy's throat. The blow connected with cartilage. Gordy coughed. Freeman followed up with a short right hook to the jaw. The shock-wave vibrated through Freeman's knuckles and into his forearm. Gordy's head whipped around. He staggered against a workbench, scrabbling at his throat. Freeman added a sweeping kick to the back of Gordy's left leg.

Freeman winced at the sharp crack Gordy's kneecaps made when they connected with the concrete and he bounced forward, pushing up a cloud of dust. He writhed on the floor, open-mouthed, gasping for air that wouldn't come.

Tommy shuffled forward, staring at his big brother. Freeman held up his left hand, index finger extended. His right hand throbbed and the fingers wouldn't respond to his commands. He feared at least one broken knuckle.

"Take one step towards me and I'll break your neck." Freeman spoke in a calm commanding voice, but he felt neither.

With blood streaming from his nose, adding to the dried claret from earlier, Tommy flinched. He stared at Gordy, who was making hideous wet choking sounds and, wide-eyed, mouthed the word "help".

Tommy made a move towards Freeman, but then changed his mind, and turned to stare at his brother.

"If I were you, son," Freeman said, "I'd be more worried about him than me."

Keeping his eyes on both men, he stooped to pick up the fallen shotgun, swung it hard, and smashed the stock on the concrete. It shattered. Brown and white splinters scattered over the floor.

Tommy's Neanderthal brow ridges almost hid his eyes. Comic confusion etched the face of a fool.

"I'd get him some ice. It'll help reduce the swelling," Freeman added, backing towards the double doors, sliding his feet, and feeling for trip hazards. Surprise had worked in his favour the first time, but he had no illusions. A concerted attack by these two would likely see him in the hospital, or a mortuary.

Time to go.

Freeman reached the garage doors and opened one with a back kick. He turned and sprinted to the hire car, desperate to be clear of the place before hurling up his breakfast.

Chapter Twenty

FRIDAY 18TH MARCH – *Sean Freeman*
Edinburgh to London

SURPRISINGLY, Freeman made it out of Edinburgh without throwing up and without interference from the boys in blue.

He found it hard to concentrate on driving. His mind was a scrambled mess of fractured sights and sounds: gunshots, screams, flying glass, blood erupting from Tommy's nose—twice—Gordy flapping on the garage floor struggling to breathe, and Angela Glennie's beautiful, but terrified face.

At thirty-three miles from the border, Freeman screamed and punched the upholstered roof of the hired BMW. He regretted it the moment his fist landed when the blow reactivated the throbbing, stabbing pain in his knuckles.

"Jesus, what a fucking god-awful mess!" he shouted at the windscreen.

As the big BMW cranked out the miles and England slowly drew nearer, Freeman asked the questions he'd been putting off since the disaster in the shop.

What the hell was he going to do now?

Should he run and hide or stay and face Parrish's inevitable rage?

No, running was out of the question. Parrish would find him, and he had John Freeman to consider.

He had to tough it out.

Freeman eased up on the throttle. A speeding ticket wouldn't do him any good, and it wasn't as though he wanted to reach London any sooner than absolutely necessary.

He stuck his hand through the open window to let the flowing air work its chilling magic on the bruised knuckles. Ice would help, but he wasn't about to stop and buy some until he'd left Scotland far behind.

Parrish would have learned about the aborted robbery by now; the story was all over the news. The radio headlines sounded like something out of a bad 1960s newsreel:

Jewel Robbery foiled by have-a-go-hero.
Police in Scotland are looking for a Mr John Devenish, who single-handedly foiled an armed robbery. In a statement issued by Detective Inspector Barrow of the …

BBC RADIO NEWS repeated the story every half hour or so. They even ran a thirty-second interview with Angela Glennie, who sang the praises of the missing film producer who, she said, saved the lives of four customers and the shop staff.

She sounded wonderful over the airwaves. Her warm Scottish accent melted through the car's speakers and worked to sooth Freeman's ragged nerves. He could have listened to her for hours. The message she delivered sounded good too.

If Angela Glennie had survived her ordeal well enough, he couldn't say the same for Andrew Morton. The reporters had been unable to interview him due to "medical complications resulting from a fall". Freeman hoped the old chap was just playing for sympathy or a big insurance pay-out.

On the other hand, maybe he could use Morton's "medical complications" as a defence. He'd have to think on it.

Everything had gone so bloody well until the Moron Brothers rolled up and Tommy started shooting.

Why the hell did he do it?

Freeman hadn't hired the brothers. That was down to Parrish, or more likely one of his lackeys. Could he use that fact in his defence? He added another idea to his "to be worked on" pile.

Given the Moron Brothers worked for Parrish, had Parrish sanctioned the use of loaded weapons, and if so why?

Freeman tried to find the answer, but nothing made sense. He'd always known Parrish's original promise of no violence was a crock of shit, but he'd buried the thought deep, not wanting to dwell on the negative when everything had been going so well.

Through the windscreen, black clouds, laden with rain, rumbled up from the English side of the border, as though warning him of the storm awaiting him in London.

"Yeah, that's right Sean, 'Beware the Ides of March'!" he cackled, and cursed himself for being a fanciful idiot.

Within minutes, the clouds blocked out the sun and the first spots of rain hit the windscreen. The slipstream caught the drops and caused tracks of their runoff to form crazy paving patterns until the humidity sensors activated the wiper motors.

Crazy paving. Madness.

What about using Tommy's madness?

The skinny nut-job's behaviour in *Throckmorton's Gems*—glazed eyes, high-pitched ranting, shaking hands—suggested a major loss of control. Maybe he could use that, too.

The big Beemer's engine purred and the wheels rolled over the tarmac. The road surface hummed beneath the tyres, interrupted by the irregular bumps and thumps as cracks and potholes stressed the suspension. The metronomic sweep-thump of the wipers calmed him and gave him the ability to think.

With three ideas to work on before he reached London, he at least had hope.

———

FREEMAN SHIFTED INTO FIFTH, and then into fourth, turned left at a small roundabout, and the A1 morphed into the A1167. He'd taken the scenic route to avoid any potential roadblocks on the main roads, and to delay his return to London. He'd also switched off his mobile to avoid Parrish's inevitable ranting and to give himself time to flesh out his defence.

He passed through the cold, grey town of Berwick-upon-Tweed, in a slow blur of half-noticed shops, junctions, and traffic lights. When he picked up the A1 again he opened up the throttle, but kept the speed five-miles-per-hour beneath the limit.

At Wetherby Services he stopped to refuel.

Before filling the tank, he parked up for a coffee and stared into the black liquid for three minutes before taking the first small sip. It did nothing but scald his tongue.

Unable to delay the inevitable any further, he hit the power button on his mobile. Seven missed calls, all from Parrish, no messages.

A young family at the next table, father, mother, and baby in a stroller, laughed and cooed. Their happiness did nothing to lighten Freeman's mood. Other travellers in various stages of fatigue carried out their business. Would he ever be that carefree again?

He hit the number and waited. Parrish answered halfway through the first ring.

"Where are you?"

Freeman told him.

"You've been following the news, Mr Parrish?"

"'Course."

"You know it wasn't my fault, don't you?"

"Whose fault was it then?"

"The Jock fuckups and whoever hired them," he said without hesitation.

"Yeah. That's what I thought you'd say."

"It's true, Mr Parrish. My plan worked perfectly. I was in the back room and ready to take the stuff when they came in and started shoo—"

"Not over the phone, dickhead!" Parrish paused for a scary moment before adding, "How long you gonna be?"

"Six, maybe seven hours. Friday evening traffic's a balls-ache."

"Come straight to the office."

He sounded calm enough, but over the phone it was impossible to tell.

"Yes, Mr Parrish." Freeman hesitated, but had to ask. "Are we cool?"

"Icy. Be here by nine o'clock, or don't come at all. Get my drift?"

"Yes, Mr Parrish. I'll be there."

Freeman disconnected the call. His fingers shook. He finished the coffee in two long gulps, ordered another one to go—large, double strength—and bought a bag of ice cubes for his hand.

He spent the following six hours in the car with one hand on the wheel, the other hand wrapped in an ice blanket, and his mind churning through his limited options.

Chapter Twenty-One

London, England

THE OFFICES of *Parrish Enterprises Ltd*, one-half of Centre Tower's eighth floor, were deserted, the partitioned cubicles dark. The corridors, lit by subdued emergency lighting, echoed to his footfalls. He marched towards the boardroom with the eager tread of a jungle celeb approaching a bush-tucker trial.

Although his stomach churned, the sweat pooled under his arms and down his back, and his heart raced, he tried to present the picture of a confident yet apologetic employee. It was a tough ask when all he really wanted to do was turn tail and make like the Roadrunner.

Pausing at the closed boardroom door long enough to wipe his face with a tissue, he took a breath and knocked.

"Get in here, Freeman," Parrish bellowed.

He shook the cramp out of his good hand before entering. The doorframe, which incorporated an electronic signal scanner, bleeped. Freeman made a show of removing the mobile from his pocket. He backed into the hall, deposited the phone on the designated table outside the door, and returned to the room. This time, the doorframe remained silent.

Parrish sat in his usual position at the head of the oiled teak table. Hutch and Adamovic flanked him. A third man, Harry Bryce, the HR Director he'd seen in boardroom meetings and recognised as the crossword guy from the *Crown & Cushion*, occupied the chair on Parrish's left, facing the entrance.

Freeman tensed when he saw Bryce's destroyed face—black eye, bruised cheek, cut lip, bloodied nose.

How many more bloody noses today?

Bryce cradled his right hand against his chest to protect three dislocated or broken fingers. He trembled, and whistled with each breath, suggesting a cracked nose and a shattered dental plate.

As Freeman stepped further into the room, Adamovic made sure he could see the shiny black automatic held in a relaxed right fist. Although pointed at the floor, the gun's presence hung heavy in the room. Hutch stared at him, sneered, and then dropped a giant paw on the beaten man's shoulder. When a hand the size of a dinner plate touched his jacket, the old man crumpled and let out a muffled squeal.

"What's going on, Mr Parrish?" Freeman asked, and nodded towards the injured man.

"Shut up and sit." Parrish pointed to the chair opposite the broken Director of Human Resources.

Freeman shook his head.

"I'd rather stand if you don't mind, Mr Parrish. I've been sitting in the car for hours."

The last thing he wanted to do was lower his sight line and increase his vulnerability.

Adamovic twitched. The revolver's muzzle lifted a centimetre or two and turned towards Freeman. He took the hint, and the chair.

"This is your first lesson in boardroom discipline, shit-for-brains." Parrish pointed to his left. "Old 'Arry fucked up big time. Hired those two Jock morons and lost me that load of very nice rocks."

Hutch squeezed Bryce's shoulder. The old man's scream turned Freeman's guts into knotted ropes. He gritted his teeth and wiped his hands along his thighs to avoid making fists. Sweat dripped from his forehead into his eyes. He blinked away the sting.

"Stop!" he shouted. "The fuckup was my fault. I should have come up with a better plan."

Adamovic raised the pistol and aimed it at Freeman's chest.

Parrish jerked his thumb and Hutch relaxed his hold. Bryce's scream reduced to a pitiful whimper.

"But 'Arry's in charge of hiring and firing. He recommended the Jocks in the first place and I told them to follow your instructions. Now, either 'Arry fucked up, or I did. Do you think I'm a fuckup, Hutch?"

Hutch shook his big, square head.

"No, Mr Parrish. You don't make mistakes. Harry here's the fuckup, and so is he." The blond monster stared at Freeman.

Freeman lowered his eyes to stare at Bryce's deformed fingers. Anxiety turned to white-hot anger, but Adamovic and the gun made him powerless to act.

"Possibly," Parrish conceded. "But 'Arry chose the Jocks and it seems the job went south because of them." He locked eyes on Freeman. "It's like this, son. We all need to take responsibility for our actions. Think of poor old 'Arry as your whipping boy. I can't afford to have Hutch break your fingers, or to have Adamovic blow off one of your kneecaps. Oh no, you're too valuable … for the moment. What you need to remember, is that you now have a black mark on your record. There ain't no sideways promotions or demotions in this organisation, only terminations of contract. You get my drift, son?"

Not trusting himself to speak, Freeman lowered his head and nodded. His right hand throbbed, reminding him of the consequences of violence. Bryce's battered face and quaking body confirmed the point.

Parrish broke the short silence. "Okay, message delivered. Mr Adamovic, take poor 'Arry to hospital and get him patched up. He seems to have had a terrible fall. And leave the shooter here. You won't need it with 'Arry."

Adamovic gave the pistol to Parrish, who put it on the far side of the table, well out of Freeman's reach. Adamovic then helped Bryce from the room, handling the beaten man with surprising gentleness.

As for Freeman, he felt guilty as hell. He'd shifted the blame onto the man who hired the Moron Brothers with no consideration for the consequences. It had been relatively easy when he didn't know the individual concerned, but seeing the result of his cowardice drove his guilt home. He didn't like himself very much at that point, not one little bit. But he liked Parrish even less.

He couldn't look at Hutch, the coward who beat up an old man, for fear of losing control altogether. The fight in the Edinburgh lockup had ended well, but he'd already pushed his luck that day and couldn't take any more risks. And in any case, what chance would he have against the big bastard and the psycho with the shooter?

Eyes on the prize, Sean. Eyes on the prize.

Hutch moved closer to Parrish, the bodyguard returning to his appointed place.

"What happened at Morton's?" Parrish demanded. "Every detail."

Freeman launched into the explanation without hesitation.

"I made it inside with the expensive stuff and the Scottish morons arrived, pumping shot into the ceiling. The owner, Morton, looked like he was about to croak. Heart attack, I think. Sorry, Mr Parrish, but I had to deal with the Jocks on the fly so people didn't get hurt."

"Who gives a flying fuck about some old git's dodgy strawberry? You fucked the job and I'm out of pocket."

"I'm really sorry, Mr Parrish."

Again, he lowered his eyes in deference before raising them again. He needed to keep his guard high and couldn't do it without looking up. Every nerve in his body screamed for action, but he stayed quiet.

Parrish stared at him, stone-faced. The blue-grey eyes behind the wire-rimmed glasses were dead, no emotion, no light.

"Fuck up again and I'll kill your father."

Freeman shut his eyes, clenched his jaw, and stopped breathing. He made sure Parrish could see terror in his every twitch and shiver.

"And then," Parrish continued, "I'll send Hutch to Brisbane to pay a visit to your kid sister."

At the mention of his name, Hutch straightened. The thin half-smile cracked his face.

"You wouldn't mind a little trip to the Antipodes, would you, Hutch?"

"No, Mr Parrish, not in the slightest. I understand it's nice and warm down there this time of year."

"You're going to kill Becky?" Freeman's voice turned reed thin. He struggled to force the words through a constricted throat. He needed Parrish to see his fear. It was the only thing he could think of that might appease the psychopath.

"No, son, but by the time Hutch finishes with her, she'll wish he had. You like 'em tall and blonde, don't you, Hutch?"

"Tell you the truth, Mr Parrish, I'm not really all that fussed. Tall, short, blonde, brunette, they all scream as loud in the end."

Freeman wanted to leap across the table and find out how tough Hutch really was. The scar tissue around the thug's left eye suggested a weakness he might target, but such a futile action would ruin everything. Parrish smiled, his hand rested on the table, drumming fingers millimetres away from the automatic. Freeman closed his eyes and lowered his head in defeat.

Parrish breathed in through his nose, sighed out the air, and rubbed his hands together. "Right. Now we understand each other a lot better, let's get back to business, eh?" He flicked his fingers at Hutch, who crossed to the hospitality table in the far corner. "I'll have a coffee. Sean, you want one?"

"No thanks, Mr Parrish. I'm good." At that moment, coffee would have had the same effect on his stomach as battery acid.

"Suit yourself, son." Parrish said, his voice business-as-usual. "I reckon your aborted mission cost me a couple of million quid this afternoon. Nah, let's be generous and call it one-and-a-half mil. You're gonna work it off. I'm withholding your future bonus pot until you've cleared the debt. Shouldn't take more than a year. Agreed?"

Freeman couldn't wrap his mind around the way Parrish was able to chop and change. He'd just watched a man being beaten to a pulp and had threatened to kill and maim Freeman's family. Now he dropped into a discussion about the company bonus scheme as though it was a normal part of running a business in the modern world.

"Whatever you reckon is fair, Mr Parrish."

"I should fucking well think so." Parrish slurped his coffee. "Right, next order of business. What d'you make of Leeds during your last visit?"

As though he'd snapped his fingers to magic away the evil, Parrish launched into an outline discussion of their next job, a jewel importer in Oakwood, Leeds.

Despite nodding and mumbling something relevant whenever Parrish paused to ask a question, the only sound Freeman really heard was Harry Bryce's scream pulsing through the teak panelled boardroom. Half an hour later, Parrish dismissed him and he hurried from the room.

———

"WELL, HUTCH?" Parrish asked. "Whatcha think?"

"I think you were wrong, Digby." Hutch grinned.

"Really? When was I wrong?"

"When you said he was like the Rain Man. He may be a savant when it comes to locks and electronics, but he's no emotional cripple."

"Why d'you say that?"

"I have no idea how he bested the Scottish brothers, I'll have to find out, but he nearly soiled his trousers when he saw what I did to Harry. And when you threatened his family, I thought he was going to cry."

"And that makes him what? A coward?"

"No. Normal." Hutch smiled. "I can handle 'normal'."

"You happy now then?"

"Yes, Mr Parrish. I'm happy enough. Still don't trust him though."

Parrish sniffed. "Me neither. I don't trust nobody but me and you. Make sure Adamovic and the others keep close tabs on him."

Chapter Twenty-Two

The City, London

UNABLE TO FORCE SLEEP, Freeman threw back the covers, wrapped himself up against the cold, and sat on the balcony to await the dawn's arrival. The apartment offered a spectacular view of the river and London's lights, which never dimmed, but the architectural beauty, both new and old, which he would normally find entertaining, left him cold.

A fat pigeon landed on his balcony's handrail, puffed its feathers, and started preening.

What next, Sean?

The questions, plans, and answers rolled around in his head. They ebbed and flowed in time with the growing river traffic.

As night bled into morning, Harry Bryce's battered, pain-filled face wouldn't leave him alone, but that wasn't all. Another face kept working its way onto the screen in his head—the face of a young woman, a young Scottish woman with dark brown hair, hazel eyes, and a knockout smile.

147

"Fuck's sake Sean, don't go there," he said. The pigeon stopped mid-preen, looked up, but didn't answer.

By seven o'clock, Freeman could think no more. Leaving the cold morning to carry on without him, he slid the balcony doors closed, kicked off his slippers, and switched on the fifty-six inch, smart, full-HD TV. He selected BBC News 24, but muted the sound after five minutes. Neither the state of the UK economy, nor the platitudes of the Chancellor of the Exchequer, a slap-faced, chinless man with a smarmy grin and a plummy accent, held any interest.

Freeman padded, barefoot, into the kitchen enjoying the under floor heating, filled the percolator, and nearly dropped the coffee grounds into the sink when Angela's face brightened the screen. He ran into the lounge and fumbled with the remote, taking an age to find and release the mute button.

The rolling tickertape banner read, *Shootout in Edinburgh's most exclusive jewellery store.* Freeman leaned forward on the couch, elbows on knees, and increased the volume.

Angela dissolved into footage of police in Day-Glo tabards standing behind incident tape outside *Throckmorton's Gems*, and then returned to the studio for a face-to-camera shot of the news anchor. After a two-minute review of the events, Angela reappeared. Freeman barely took in what she said at first. The memory of her lying face down on the plush carpet, exposed, vulnerable, and trembling under his touch, returned to haunt him.

Oh for Pete's sake.

At that moment, Freeman was lost and he knew it.

How had he allowed Angela Glennie to infect his mind so deeply? He barely knew the girl and she'd never want to know him, not after what he'd done.

On the other hand, she did think him a hero.

No, Sean. Don't go there.

The interviewer had collared her on the steps of the Gayfield Square Police Station, Edinburgh—an imposing backdrop to any on-screen appearance. A couple of nervous-looking men stood behind her, one in plain clothes, and the other in a fancy police uniform—polished buttons, medal ribbons, and pips on the epaulettes.

Clearly a recording, the early evening sun highlighted the lighter flecks in Angela's hair. She wore a modest white blouse, top button undone. A tiny gold heart at her throat flashed as she answered the reporter's questions with the relaxed certainty of a pro. Freeman hit the record button. He didn't want to miss another word.

"I understand you were in the shop at the time of the robbery, Ms Glennie," the journo said.

"Yes." She blushed prettily and cast her eyes down. Freeman felt a stab of guilt at her discomfort. "I was there when the two men burst in and started firing shotguns."

"How did you feel at the time?" the reporter asked, clearly a founding member of the "let's ask stupid questions" club.

"I was terrified, obviously," she answered. Her fingers played with the heart.

"I'm sure you must have been. My sources tell me you were with Mr Devenish, the man who tackled the robbers?"

"Yes. The police got it completely wrong to begin with," she answered, her voice firm. "They thought Mr Devenish was part of the gang. Complete nonsense, of course, but I put them right."

She glanced at the cops before smiling at the reporter.

"Go on girl, you tell 'em," Freeman said to the TV.

"He was … fantastic. So brave," Angela continued. A slight catch in her voice tripped Freeman's heart. "Saved us all. I mean, he foiled a robbery for heaven's sake."

"You're certain an unarmed man took on two robbers carrying shotguns?" the incredulous reporter asked.

The camera zoomed in close. Angela didn't flinch. "Yes, that's exactly what I'm saying. Mr Devenish deserves a medal and a reward."

Reward? Now there's a thought.

For a fleeting moment, he wondered how he'd claim it?

"Has anyone heard from this Mr Devenish since the alleged robbery?"

Angela tilted her head and jutted out her jaw.

Any moment now, she'll be wagging her finger or tapping her foot.

"There's nothing 'alleged' about it," she said, with a voice that allowed no argument. "When two men rush into a jewellery store with saw-off shotguns and start shooting they aren't exactly trying to jump the queue."

Freeman laughed.

"Atta girl, Angela, you tell her."

He hadn't felt so happy in a long while. Years.

Angela spoke again. "To tell you the truth, I'm really worried for his safety. I mean, nobody has seen or heard from him since he chased the men from the shop. There's no telling what might have happened to him."

The journalist thanked Angela and then thrust her microphone under the uniformed officer's nose. "Chief Superintendent Argyle, what steps are the police taking to find these men?"

Argyle smiled with as much conviction as a man selling used cars from a backstreet lot.

"We are in the early stages of a difficult and ongoing investigation. I have put my most experienced officer, Detective Inspector Barrow, in charge." Argyle indicated the plain-clothed man standing at his side.

Way to pass the steaming hot turd, matey.

"But we are unable to comment further since this is an ongoing investigation. I would just like to say that armed robbery is a very serious offence and one that Police Scotland will investigate to the utmost extent."

Freeman blocked out the naff drivel as the TV hack tried pumping the bland Chief Superintendent for information. For his part, Argyle sidestepped the inquisition with the athletic grace of an octogenarian leaning on a Zimmer frame. The studio director must have decided that Angela offered a better visual treat than either the tired police officers or the dowdy reporter, and the camera panned back to her for the wrap-up.

Freeman replayed the recording and froze the picture on a close-up of Angela staring daggers at the journo.

God, she's gorgeous. Fire in her belly and diamonds in her eyes.

Although Angela's face dominated the screen, Inspector Barrow's grey hair showed in its fuzzy top corner. An idea formed and Freeman did what he always did when that happened—he studied it from all angles, made a plan, tried beating it to a pulp with a mental hammer, and thought about it some more. The clock on the TV screen ticked over thirty-five minutes before he made a considered move.

The laptop fired into life when his fingers touched the keypad. He hit the combination of keys Corky had hardwired into its operating system. The bespoke, high-security browser opened up and the camera flickered on. Corky, never away from his operations centre, an airy penthouse somewhere in the world where the sun always shone, gave Freeman the benefit of his crooked half-smile. "Hi there, you old toss pot," he said, smiling.

"Hi, Corky. You've lost weight."

"Yeah. Bought a treadmill. Wassup?"

"Nothing much. Busy?"

Corky shrugged. "Nothing Corky can't put off to help his best friend in the whole wide world. Whatcha want and how soon?"

"Detective Inspector Barrow, Police Scotland. Give me everything you can find, full bio, service record, personnel file if you can get it, and I want it yesterday."

Corky did what he usually did when given a task. He blinked hard to commit the information to memory, nodded, and broke the connection without saying another word. Freeman placed the laptop in hibernation mode and spent a few minutes staring at Angela Glennie's picture on the TV before walking to the kitchen to make a breakfast of toast and tea.

He'd given Corky what, for him, amounted to a simple task and could do nothing but wait.

Ninety-seven minutes later, the laptop double-beeped. Freeman hit the keys again and Corky reappeared.

"That didn't take long."

"Piece of piss. The cops couldn't build a decent firewall unless they hired someone like Corky. Oh, wait, they did hire him, but didn't think to ask about the backdoor Corky added to the spec.

Dozy idiots. Barrow's file's in the service folder. Don't print it off. Delete it when read. I know you'll remember the details."

Corky ended the session. Despite the extraordinarily secure satellite interface between Freeman's state-of-the-art laptop and the comms system in Corky's HQ, the little man rarely spent long in direct communication—a security measure he'd learned from Freeman, back in the day.

Freeman read the comprehensive file on DI Barrow—which included the detective's personnel file—and confirmed his plan of attack. He launched the notepad and started typing.

John Devenish Esq,
Address withheld,
19th March

MS ANGELA GLENNIE,

c/o The Royal Mile Talent Agency
Royal Mile,
Edinburgh E12 8XZ

DEAR ANGEL(A),

After yesterday's events, I thought you needed an explanation, and I simply had to let you know what happened after I left Throckmorton's.

First of all, I'm fine. No broken bones (bruised knuckles only).

Don't really know what came over me. I'm normally a safety conscious bloke, but when those thugs started shooting, I snapped. My old army training took over.

In my experience, most thieves are cowards and bullies at heart and those shotgun-wielding morons were no different. The moment I faced them down, they scarpered. I gave chase, but they had a car waiting and I lost them. The reason I didn't return to face the police is that I wasn't supposed to be in Edinburgh. My boss would have had a 'Connery' if she knew I was 'off reservation' like that. No excuses, she'd have fired my sorry arse the moment I returned to the office.

To cap it all, my insurance cover doesn't allow me to act without the express permission of the board. Insurers can be right bastards, can't they? Eh? Bloody vampires the lot of them (excuse the language). And they're in charge of a broke system.

I laid awake last night in my Brighton flat, imagining what you must think of me for running out on you like that.

Oh yeah, while I remember, you were fantastic on the news this morning. In fact, when you appeared up on the screen, it made my day. Thankfully, you looked unharmed by the ordeal and for that, I am truly relieved. Indeed, I give praise to the Lord that He delivered you from the evil unscathed.

By the way, thanks so much for speaking up for me. I couldn't believe the police actually suspected me of being part of the gang. Me a jewel thief? Imagine that!

Please show the redoubtable Detective Inspector Barrow this letter and give him my apologies, but I am unable to make a statement. I hope I haven't broke any laws.

Please think kindly of me.

Yours truly,

JR Devenish

FREEMAN READ and reread the letter, deleted the crass reference to 'praising the Lord', and grinned at the wordiness. With the obscuring references—he'd never served in the army or lived in Brighton—it would do nicely. He wondered whether Barrow would understand the clue, but decided he couldn't make it any more obvious in case one of Parrish's police lackeys accessed the letter. According to Barrow's police file, he appeared bright enough, but official records didn't tell the whole story and could be deceptive.

He hit the "print" tab, fired the letter through the cheap inkjet printer and, after dragging on a pair of surgical gloves, folded it into a self-seal envelope.

The stationery bore the watermark of The Rampart Inn, Stoke, stolen during an earlier "away day" trip, and would tell the police nothing. Before leaving the Rampart, Freeman had removed the linen from the bed and had sanitised the room with a liberal application of odourless spray-bleach. The aerosol's trace-evidence-killing magic and the anti-static cloths he used in conjunction with the bleach were as essential a part of his luggage as his underwear and shaving kit. He'd done the same thing at *The Atholl* in Edinburgh, and in every other hotel and guest room he stayed in since joining Parrish's firm. In his new life, it paid to be careful.

After lunch, he hopped the tube to Acton, found a sub-Post Office after a twenty-minute saunter in the sunshine, and posted the envelope first-class. From there, he visited Harry Bryce in his hospital bed and spent the rest of the afternoon getting to know even more about both the unfortunate Human Resources Director, and *Parrish Enterprises Ltd.*

Chapter Twenty-Three

Birmingham, England

DETECTIVE SERGEANT PHIL CRYER'S excitement mounted as he changed gear and slowed to approach the crime scene. Double murders didn't happen every day in Birmingham, and he was going to be leading the investigation, at least until the boss turned up to do his thing.

It wasn't as though he'd grown callous. After all, two people had died which was a desperate shame, but he'd joined David Jones' Serious Crime Unit for this very reason, and he was going to make the most of the opportunity. The fact that Manda's mother still infested his home and Manda had backache-induced insomnia made the early morning call a godsend rather than a chore.

Finding the route to the scene wasn't a problem. He'd scanned a Birmingham street map when he first moved to the city. As a result, he'd never need the services of a GPS.

Two thirds of the way along Erskine Street, the flashing blue lights and the milling reflective tabards gave him all the warning he needed. He pulled his Ford to a halt at the temporary *Police Stop* sign and left it parked in the middle of the road. The first on-scene had diverted local traffic around this immediate stretch of road, and he had no need to find a real parking space.

Yellow and black crime scene tape held back a small crowd of sleep-deprived onlookers. Some still wore their dressing gowns and slippers. What these people hoped to see at that time in the morning was beyond him. Couldn't they think of anything better to do than gawp at the facade of a Victorian town house?

Breakfast, for instance?

His stomach rumbled at the thought of a full English breakfast at the canteen later. For the past month, Manda's latest health kick had restricted him to a single breakfast bowl of muesli or porridge. Good-oh. What full-grown man could survive on that rabbit food until lunch?

Looking on the bright side, at least the crowd would provide a target for the canvassers, which he planned to organise the minute he'd taken control of the scene.

Phil flashed his warrant card at a uniformed constable he didn't recognise in the mêlée of people jostling for a better look and ducked under the tape. The constable made a note of his name, rank, and time of arrival, and jotted the information on the form attached to his clipboard. Standard Operating Protocol required a dedicated incident officer to maintain a list of anyone attending the crime scene.

Phil stood still for a moment to absorb the scene—a trick he'd learned from the boss. Time to steady the nerves, reset the inner clock, and tune into the vibe of the place.

Three storeys tall and in the middle of an unbroken terrace stretching for a hundred metres on either side, number 163 Erskine Street was an impressive building. The pile of stones and bricks topped with slates would be worth a mint. It turned his little semi-detached home into a hovel by comparison. Still, if he wanted a big house and a bigger bank balance, he wouldn't have joined the police. He'd have used his particular set of skills to make money, on a TV game show for example—or as a card counter in Vegas.

Three stone steps led up to a covered portico with twin columns either side of a six-panelled black door. The door stood wide open, but not in welcome. Hardly in welcome.

Phil climbed the steps and met an ashen-faced Wash at the threshold. The young detective, the SCU's newest member, shook his head slowly and breathed through an open mouth.

"Morning, Phil. Hope you haven't had your breakfast yet. Pretty ugly in there."

"The call said two bodies?"

After an obvious gulp, Wash nodded.

"A man and a woman, both naked. Looks like they may have been disturbed doing the naughty."

"The naughty?" Phil asked, cocking an eyebrow.

"Sex, Phil. I reckon they were, you know, doing the vertical mamba, having it away, hiding the purple salami." He made a hip level fist pump to hide the action from the onlookers.

Phil shook his head. "Let's keep this professional, shall we, Detective Constable?"

"Sorry, Sarge."

Wash had the grace to look suitably embarrassed, and Phil moved on. "Any signs of a break-in?"

Wash shook his head. "Not so far." He leaned against one of the columns and took another deep breath. "SOCOs just moved in and kicked me out of the house. Can't say I'm disappointed, though. Blood and guts all over the place. Looks like a chuffing abattoir. The male victim is lying on the first-floor landing, belly slashed wide open. We found the woman in bed with her throat cut … and other, more intimate damage. The photo gallery in the front room suggests they're probably husband and wife. And the homeowners."

From his elevated position on the stoop, Phil took time to check the police vehicles lining the street. A tell-tale white and yellow Range Rover of the West Midlands Crime Lab, parked three spaces down from his Ford, concerned him.

Please, no.

"Who's up there?" He held his breath, praying it wasn't Ghastly.

"Don't worry, Sarge, it's the night shift. Mr Prendergast's not around. In any case, didn't you hear? Ghastly's pulled another sickie. Claiming work-related stress, but it's more likely cock-up-related guilt. Geordie Saunders' team is up there, thank fuck."

"Don't let the boss hear you talking like that about a colleague. He'll be here soon."

"The boss is too generous. We all know Ghastly's an accident waiting to happen on the brink of a disaster. At least we won't have to work around the pony-tailed fruitcake tonight. Like treading on eggshells when he's about. Never seen anyone with his experience so spooked at a crime scene. Makes me seem like a veteran."

"How long they likely to be?"

"Geordie reckons another couple of hours at lease. Loads to do up there. They've called in the day shift, but they won't be here for an hour. The ME's already pronounced. Liver temp puts the estimated time of death between two and three-thirty. It ties in well with the 9-9-9 call, which was registered at two-seventeen."

Wash tapped the screen of his palm tablet.

"Who called it in?"

"Anonymous. A woman. Said she heard screaming. Left the address and hung up."

"Anyone trying to trace the call?"

"Control say it was made on a prepaid mobile. Untraceable."

"Burner phone?"

"Dunno, Sarge. Could be."

"Hope not, or we might be talking professional hit."

"Really? Here?"

Phil studied the old terraced house again. It could be Victorian, perhaps even Georgian. The boss would tell him which. Architecture wasn't Phil's bag. "The caller's either the killer, which is unlikely, or an immediate neighbour." He pointed to the houses either side of the crime scene. "And I'm betting on a neighbour."

"What makes you think that?"

Phil paused a little, trying to make certain of his guesswork.

"Those walls are stone, not brick and, judging by the window recesses, nearly a metre thick. Nice retrofitted double-glazed panels too. Unless the front door or windows were open during the killings, the sound wouldn't have travelled far. I doubt it'd have made it as far as the pavement." He paused as Wash nodded in considered agreement. "Which room is the woman's body in?"

Wash pointed at a sash window. First floor, to the left of the front door. "That's the one. See the blood splatter on the glass? The drapes were already open, but the windows were closed when we arrived."

"In that case," he said, "I'm betting our anonymous caller is in number 161. And I can see a curtain twitch, so we won't be waking her."

"You're sounding more like the boss every day."

"Thanks. I'll take that as a compliment."

"That was the intention."

"I'll go have a chat with her. You take a couple of uniforms. Question the crowd and interview the neighbours in 165."

"Do you want me to call in Alex and Charlie?"

"Nah, not yet. We'll leave that decision to the old man. Hope he doesn't hang about. I'm starving. Could do with some breakfast. Manda's put me on restricted rations again."

"That reminds me. How's she doing?"

"Blooming."

Wash smirked.

"Won't be long now 'til you're up to your eyeballs in nappies and baby vomit and falling asleep at work."

"Thank you, Detective Constable Washington. Your concern for my wellbeing is most appreciated," he said, arching an eyebrow but failing to intimidate the grinning eejit, who'd clearly recovered from the shock of seeing a pair of mutilated corpses. "Start canvassing the locals."

"Certainly, Sarge. I'm right on it."

Chapter Twenty-Four

SUNDAY 3RD^H JULY – *DS Phil Cryer*
Erskine Street, Birmingham

PHIL STEPPED out through the neighbour's front door, closed it gently behind him, and walked straight into the first question from his recently arrived and tired-looking boss.

"What's this about a burner phone?"

From David's thoughtful frown, Phil could tell the same thoughts were running through the boss' head as had run through his own at the first mention of an untraceable mobile.

"Nothing sinister, boss. It belongs to the neighbour, Mrs Gladys Shuttleworth." He pointed over his shoulder to the door through which he'd just emerged. "Turns out the son bought the phone for her. She uses it for emergencies if she can't reach the landline. Wears it on a chain around her neck unless she's in bed."

"She heard shouting through those walls?"

"Yep. The old dear may be a bit unsteady on her pins on account of her arthritis, but she's got the hearing of a bat. I tested her by whispering and she told me to stop being so rude."

Jones smiled, as Phil had done at the time. "As in, 'it's rude to whisper in public, young man'?"

"Yep. You've got it, boss. She used to be headmistress at the local secondary school, when it was still a Grammar. Her mind's a razor. In fact, I rather liked the old battle-axe."

"What did she have to say for herself? Why didn't she give her name to the emergency operator?"

"Accident. She pressed the disconnect button by mistake and thought she might cause a fuss by redialling 9-9-9. You should see her hands, boss. Fingers gnarled and arthritic. I'm amazed she managed to make the call in the first place."

"Fair enough. Exactly what did she hear?"

"She wrote the words down, but they don't help much. Just a load of expletives and a high-pitched scream cut short."

"Too much to ask for a name or an accent?"

"Actually, she can do one better than that. She might have seen the killer."

David scratched his earlobe.

"That was lucky. How often does that happen?"

They both knew that finding a lucid eyewitness didn't always guarantee a break in a case, but it sometimes helped.

"At least, she saw *a* guy running down the street a couple of seconds after the scream ended. Look, you can still see her curtains twitching." Phil pointed towards Mrs Shuttleworth's bedroom and waved. A frail, distorted hand returned his greeting. "The old dear has a high-backed armchair in the window. Loves to watch the world pass her by. Bit of an insomniac too, as it happens, which is lucky for us."

"What are her eyes like?"

"Wears reading glasses, but her distance vision's as good as her hearing. I asked her to read the registration numbers on the parked cars. Eyesight's better than mine."

Phil smiled, but David didn't return it.

"Description?"

"Unfortunately, she only caught him from the back, didn't see his face. The suspect is short, between five-seven and five-nine.

Stocky or fat. One or the other, she couldn't be sure. Dark hair, thinning on top. So long and wispy at the back, it overlapped his shirt collar. He wore a light-coloured summer jacket, dark trousers. Mrs Shuttleworth can't tell us the actual colour because of the street-lights, which are yellow, by the way."

The lights had gone out at six-thirty, ten minutes before the boss' arrival. A pale orange sun was already showing its optimistic head over the Birmingham skyline. Wispy clouds striped the sky and held out the promise of a warm summer's day to come. Another scorcher on the cards and they'd be spending it knocking on doors and waiting for forensics results. His stomach rumbled again. Maybe they could send one of the uniforms on a coffee run.

"Are the SOCOs still up there?" David asked, nodding towards the house of death.

"Geordie Saunders' team. He's already uploaded preliminary photos to the server if you're interested."

"Of course. Work your magic with that pill-thing."

"It's a tablet, boss. As you damned well know."

The boss grimaced again and stepped to Phil's side to view the photos on the eight-inch screen. They rubbed shoulders, or they would have done but for the fact that Phil stood a good eight centimetres taller than the boss. David's shoulder barely reached the middle of Phil's upper arm.

David himself cut a slim, almost ascetic figure. Anyone passing him in the street might have mistaken him for bank manager, or a librarian.

Phil scrolled through the photos and David leaned in, squinting hard. He wondered whether the old man needed reading glasses. If so, Phil wouldn't be the one to suggest it.

"Hang on, what's that?" David said, wagging a finger over the screen.

The picture showed the first-floor landing, harshly lit from behind by one of the SOCO's halogen arc lamps. He was pointing to a dark patch on a cream-coloured wall leading to the bedroom, not the puddle of blood on the carpet beneath the smashed hall mirror. "Definitely not dark enough for blood. Zoom in for me."

Phil spread forefinger and thumb over the image and centred the detail to the middle of the little screen. "Agreed. Too light for blood. What do you reckon it is?"

"Not sure. The ME says the killer caught the couple in the middle of the act, right?"

"That's the way Wash described it to me. I arrived after the SOCOs, so I haven't been inside yet."

Phil almost smirked at the old man's reluctance to use a less delicate description, unlike young Wash. David could be a sensitive soul at times. Phil ran through a few synonyms for copulation in his head that definitely wouldn't make his incident report.

"Yes, boss. Looks as though they were killed shortly after having sexual congress. Sad, but according to Geordie they'd finished, so at least they went out after a bit of a high." He lowered his voice for the last part of the statement.

"Not funny, Philip."

"Sorry, boss. Gallows humour."

"Gallows? What on earth do you know about that? We banned capital punishment decades before you were born, lad. Let's lay off the sick humour until we're out of the public eye, eh?"

David glanced towards the camera flashes coming from the local media hacks who jostled and heckled at the edge of the growing crowd. Any moment now, Phil expected them to start yelling their absurd questions. Not that he was worried. When the inevitable happened, David would handle the media intervention with his usual aplomb. The boss had his own tried and tested way to handle media intervention—usually, by ignoring them completely.

No doubt about it, David Jones was a law unto himself. In time, Phil would develop his own approach, but for the present, he'd follow the boss' lead.

"That's why I whispered, boss."

David turned his back to the throng and spoke as quietly as Phil had. "Wouldn't put it past those beggars to point a mic at us or have a lipreader on the payroll."

"Paranoid much, sir?"

This time, David did smile in response.

"Did Geordie analyse that mark yet?"

"Don't think so, sir. His team concentrated on the bedroom and bathroom first. Why?"

The glint in Jones' eye told Phil that the dark patch meant something. He enlarged the area of the picture and turned the screen to landscape, searching for anything that might have caused the discolouration. A spilled drink, or a pot plant knocked from a stand? Nope. Nothing in the photo could have made the mark, yet the boss was interested. Very interested.

"Do you happen to have Geordie's number in your phone?"

"One minute." Phil dialled the number from memory and handed the phone across. "You have something, don't you?"

"A squat peeping tom, spying on a pair of young lovers? Yep. If I'm right, I might know the sick little scrote. He's never hurt anybody before, though. Would much rather run and hide, but there's always a first time. If it's the person I'm thinking about, the victim must have backed him into a corner." He held up a hand and spoke into the mobile. "Hello, Geordie? DCI Jones here ... Yes, I'm outside the front door right now ... Yes thanks, I understand you're short-handed ... Do the best you can, but don't rush things. Tell me, the stain on the wall beside the bedroom door, have you tested it yet? ... Seminal fluid? ... Thought so." A grim smile cracked his face as he nodded at Phil. "Can you tell whether there's any sperm present?"

Jones grunted a couple of times while Geordie Saunders no doubt delivered an eloquent explanation of the process required to determine the presence or absence of spermatozoa in a sample of seminal fluid. Outside of a laboratory and without the aid of a microscope it would not be possible. Phil knew the answer to that one, as did the boss, but he allowed Geordie his moment in the limelight.

"I understand," David said, at last. "I know you're on nights, but I don't suppose you could stick the sample under the 'scope before you clock off, could you? ... Thanks, Geordie. Much appreciated. Phil and I'll be up in a minute." He ended the call and slipped the mobile into his jacket pocket.

Phil sighed and held out his hand. "Excuse me, boss?"

"Yes, Phil?"

"Can I have my phone back please?"

He frowned.

"Huh?"

"You just nicked my phone," he said, grinning.

"I did? Bloody hell. Sorry Phil, mind's on other things." He dropped a hand into the pocket and fished out two identical, police issue mobiles. "Darn it, which one's yours?"

Phil retrieved the one with the slightly faded call buttons. Jones nodded and scratched at his chin. "Of course, yours is forever clamped to your ear. You youngsters will have the damned things surgically implanted next."

"Actually, there's a research programme at MIT—the Massachusetts Institute of Technol—"

"I know what MIT stands for, Philip!"

"Yes, of course you do, sorry. Anyway, there are a few teams at MIT investigating that very issue. Right now, they're making good progress with nanotech and graphene—"

"Oh God, spare me the details."

"Okay, so tell me about the call to Geordie. Why the interest in semen and sperm?"

"Geordie is going to analyse the sample the moment he gets back to the lab, but I'll be surprised if he finds any sperm present. Not if I'm right about the killer's identity."

"You going to keep it to yourself, or let your second-in-command know?" Using his unofficial title still had the power to raise goose bumps.

"During any of your trawls through the sexual offenders archive, did you ever come across the name Albert Erwin Pope, aka 'Alby'?"

"Nope. But, then again, I haven't had time to read them all. At least, not yet."

"That's a surprise. His casefile is pretty hefty. If I'm right, Alby's the pervert we're looking for."

"Bloody hell, boss. Do you know every villain in Birmingham?"

David tilted his head to one side.

"Seems that way, eh? Most of the old lags around here have crossed my path over the years. It's the young upstarts and the incomers that slip past me."

"Why are you interested in the sperm count?"

"Alby Pope fires blanks. Sick little creep claims it's one of the reasons he's a watcher not a doer. I've sent him down a total of four times in the past twenty years. Each time he goes away, he signs up for counselling and laps up the pills they give him, promises to be a good boy in future. Then, the moment he makes his release date, all bets are off. The little armpit stops taking his meds and gets up to his old tricks." He pointed at the tablet. "Do you want to see if the PNC has an up-to-date address for our little friend? He might still be at his mother's place. Edgecombe, if my memory's up to scratch. Soon as you've done that, we'll take a trip over there and see if we can't pick him up."

As Phil started tapping on the screen, the boss wandered over to Wash who still hadn't finished interviewing the gawkers.

Chapter Twenty-Five

Holton, Birmingham

RYAN WASHINGTON TRIED to drown out the background noise of the canteen, which thrummed and rattled with the feeding frenzy of lunchtime at a primary school. Sixty-odd police officers and civilian support staff shovelled hot food into hungry mouths or waited in line for service. Snippets of conversation and the occasional raucous laughter rose above the background hubbub. Someone behind the serving hatch dropped a glass. It shattered loudly on the tile floor. The immature among the group—the majority—greeted the noise with a cheer and a round of applause, reinforcing the scholastic vibe. Sometimes, Wash despaired of his fellow officers, but at least they weren't embittered, world-weary old sods like Charlie Pelham.

The racket died to a dull rumble, low enough for Wash to hear Charlie's self-pitying moans. "I keep telling you Wash, the old man's losing it. I'm the senior sergeant on the team. I should have replaced Big Jock McDougall. It's my bloody turn. Passed my OSPREs seven fuckin' years ago. The old man's deliberately blocking my promotion, and he won't tell me why."

Wash could have given Pelham a hint, loads of hints, but he wouldn't have listened, and if he did, Wash would have made his life even tougher.

Pelham tapped the table with the handle of his fork. "I got time served, and a list of collars as long as your arm."

Wash nodded a reluctant agreement, but wondered when Charlie had last added to the famed list.

"You look at my arrest record. It's double what Phil 'Memory Man' Cryer's got."

"Well," Wash said, "Phil's isn't bad considering he's only been a detective for a couple of years."

Pelham sat up and stabbed a pile of chips with the fork. "And that's my fuckin' point, son. A DC for four years, a DS for two, and he's already acting second-in-command of the squad."

"Unit," Wash corrected.

"Huh?"

"It's the Serious Crime *Unit*. I don't want to be associated with anything in the West Midlands called the Serious Crime Squad, not after what those arseholes got up to."

Pelham threw out a hand.

"Nah, bollocks. One or two bad apples don't spoil the record of a damned fine bunch of coppers."

"What?" Wash couldn't let that one drop, not even for the sake of harmony. "You mean the same guys who beat confessions out of the Birmingham Six? The Squad responsible for more injustices than any other crime team outside of the Met? Are they the cops you're defending, Sarge?"

Wash couldn't take any more of Pelham's apologist support for the SCS, a Squad disbanded back in the '90s after decades of corruption. Their team, the SCU, had emerged from under the dark shadow of their predecessors after years of spotless detection, thanks largely to the impeccable work of one DCI David Jones.

Pelham ignored Wash's attack.

"Yeah, bloody fast-tracked superstars, fresh from university with their fucking degrees in sociology and criminal psychology, and not knowing diddlysquat about real policework. The only way to learn about being a copper is by feeling collars, old son. You listen to Charlie Pelham, the voice of experience. I know what I'm talking about, and don't you forget it."

He paused his lecture long enough to stuff the chips into his face. Wash leaned away in preparation for the inevitable spray of half-chewed potato.

"An' I tell you another thing for nothing. The boss and Alex are interrogating that deviant, Alby Pope, right now, ain't they?"

"Yes. And your point is?"

"My point, DC Washington, is there ain't no way Alex should be anywhere near Alby Pope. The little fucker's got a thing for blondes, especially big ones, if you know what I mean." Pelham moved both hands in front of his chest in a gesture that was both unnecessary and downright sexist.

Wash ground teeth and wondered what long-term damage he'd do to his career if he were to land one on Pelham's fat nose. Damage would probably end up being terminal. He averted his eyes and tried not to listen.

Charlie continued after pausing to swallow. A gobbet of chip fat slid down his chin. He wiped it away with the back of his hand. "She'll drive little Alby potty. Mark my words, that bloody murderer is gonna blow a gasket being in a room with her for more than five minutes."

"That's why the boss chose her as his wingman." Wash hated it when Pelham dissed the old man like this and the constant drip-drip torture was getting worse.

Pelham's mouth opened in a loud guffaw. Wash averted his eyes from the bits of half-masticated food. "Wing*man's* right enough. She's a fine looking woman is our Alex, but it's a crying shame she bats for the other side. Bloody waste of a good woman, if you see what I mean." He issued a lascivious wink, which Wash couldn't ignore.

"Charlie, that's enough. She's a workmate for fuck's sake."

"Mind your language, Detective Constable Washington. Remember who you're talking to."

Wash moved fast to change the subject and deflect the growing tension.

"And what's wrong with fast-tracking graduates? I went to university, remember?"

"Yeah, but you did engineering. Subject fit for a real man. You weren't no *'ologist'*." Pelham sucked up the last piece of sausage, giving Wash a brief respite from the verbal assault.

Wash's phone, which sat on the table next to his empty plate, buzzed. He grabbed it as though it were the final lifebelt on the Titanic and checked the caller ID: Comms Room.

"DC Washington, Serious Crime Unit," he said.

"Ah, there you are, Constable. There's a new job for the glorious SCU." Sergeant Hoyte's clipped and plumy tones were a massive relief after being on the receiving end of Charlie's ill-educated Cockney rant. "DCI Jones is indisposed and Phil Cryer is taking a personal day, so you and Charlie Pelham win the prize. Check your emails for the case number and details. I've updated the call log and associated information into the database. It's a nasty one. Three patrol cars on scene and the ambulances have just arrived. Two male casualties at *Green & Sons* …"

While Sergeant Hoyte gave him an outline of the incident, Wash took the access information from his inbox on the tablet and plugged it into the search screen on the PNC. As he read, the canteen faded to silence.

"Charlie, we've landed the big one."

He looked up to see an empty chair. Pelham leaned against the serving counter five metres away, pudding bowl in hand, rabbiting to one of the civilian support staff—a plump brunette wearing a skirt six centimetres shorter than her legs deserved. Well, maybe ten centimetres too short. Pelham, the daft sap, stood tall, sucking in his gut, no doubt trying to entertain her with one of his war stories. Her body language, leaning in close and facing him square on, suggested that she enjoyed his attention.

Wash couldn't believe anyone with working eyes and ears could fancy Charlie Pelham. Took all sorts, he supposed, and made his way to the counter. As he approached, Pelham turned his back and continued his spiel. This was the one where Pelham disarmed a bank robber single-handedly. Wash had heard him spout the same rubbish a thousand times, and on each retelling, Pelham added another little embellishment. This time he'd included a hostage. The woman gasped, "Oh Charlie, that's wonderful." She touched his chest. "But I gotta go now or I'll be late back from lunch."

Pelham hitched up his trousers with his free hand, making sure not to spill his custard. "You tell that officious prick in the admin office you were helping Detective Sergeant Pelham with his enquiries. That'll shut the bugger right up."

She giggled and made her way to the exit, making sure to exaggerate the hip sway. Pelham relaxed his belly, held up his hand to silence Wash, and studied the woman's rear until the double doors closed behind her.

"Fucking hell, mate. Did you see that? I'm in there. Ripe for the taking. Be ever so grateful I spent the time on her. Won't expect no *cordon bleu* meal before it neither. Quick knee trembler behind the chippie's gonna do for that one. You mark my words, son."

Wash shuddered at the mental image and wondered what Charlie's wife would do if someone let her know about his extra-curricular activities. He pushed the tempting thought away and made the announcement.

"We've had a call from Control. Someone's turned over the Digbeth branch of *Green & Sons*. Sounds nasty. Couple of victims hospitalised. Blood all over the place, apparently. This'll make the national news. C'mon, it's our chance to lead the investigation."

Pelham sniffed, stared at the contents of his pudding bowl, and reached out to the canteen of cutlery behind him. He didn't need to look—the hand found the right compartment as though drawn to the dessert spoon by a magnet.

"Uniforms cordoned off the scene?"

Wash nodded.

"Yeah. Three patrol cars arrived within minutes, but the blaggers were long gone by that time. Don't have any more details yet."

Pelham heaved himself away from the wall and walked his bowl back to their table.

"What about SOCO?" he asked, without turning his head.

"Five minutes out from the scene."

Pelham took his seat and dug into his pudding.

"Well then," he said, "there ain't no need to rush is there? It's a twenty-minute drive to Digbeth this time of day. I don't have to waste my treacle tart."

"Bloody hell, Charlie," Wash said, keeping his voice low despite wanting to scream and yank the fat bugger out of his chair. "The bastards are getting further away."

Pelham vacuumed up a spoonful and made a smacking sound with his lips.

"Cool head, sunshine. The buggers are well away by now, and the SOCOs won't let us into the shop for hours. All we'll be doing is cooling our heels on the pavement. Who's in charge on scene?"

"Sergeant Doland. He's supervising the crowds and setting up the street canvass."

Pelham nodded. "Excellent. Vic Doland's a good bloke. He'll keep the place tidy for us. No need to panic, Wash."

"I'll fetch our jackets from the office and meet you at the car."

"All right, lad. Knock yourself out. I'll be along in a minute. Don't leave without me."

Wash slammed through the canteen doors and kicked at a waste bin in the hallway. It crashed against the wall and toppled over, spilling its contents of plastic cups and used serviettes over the floor. He stooped to tidy the mess. What had he done in a previous life to deserve this purgatory? He'd never build a decent career if he didn't get out from under Pelham's shadow.

"Inspector Charlie Pelham, Second-in-command of the West Midlands SCU?" he muttered as he stomped towards the staircase. "God save us all."

Chapter Twenty-Six

TUESDAY 5TH JULY - RYAN 'WASH' *Washington*
Holton, Birmingham

WASH SAT IN THE CAR, and he stewed.

He gripped the steering wheel of his Ford Focus with both hands and twisted the leather hard, wishing his fingers were around Charlie Pelham's throat. He'd been waiting ten minutes and bugger still hadn't deigned to show his face. He'd give the lazy fat sod another sixty seconds and then he'd bugger off, alone.

Before he had time to add to the thought, Pelham rolled through the double doors and sauntered down the steps. Wash flicked the switch to activate the blues, but Pelham ignored the hurry-up and shook hands with a passing uniformed sergeant, a large woman with formidable hips.

"Fuck's sake, Charlie," Wash said under his breath. "One day, I'm going to throttle you and take my time doing it."

Pelham patted the woman's shoulder and studied her well-upholstered rear end as she climbed the steps. Wash was amazed he'd shown such restraint. He wouldn't have been surprised if

Pelham had tapped her on the backside, but even he wasn't daft enough to do that in full view of the surveillance cameras. What was it with Charlie Pelham and big women?

"Come on, Charlie." Wash called.

Pelham dropped into the car, which sagged on stressed springs.

"Hold your water, Wash. Give us a chance to strap on my seatbelt and watch the luscious Annabelle strut her funky stuff. She's a goer you know. Reckon I'm in there. Remember her striptease at last year's Christmas party? Magnificent arse. Like two giant marshmallows fighting in a pillowcase."

Wash clenched his teeth, threw the car into first, and raced out of the car park, wheels spinning. He hit the sirens before easing up at the junction onto City Road, dropped into second when the oncoming traffic parted, and screamed towards the city centre. He pushed the Ford towards the tachometer redline. Pelham took hold of the passenger's grab-strap.

"Fuck's sake, Wash. What's the rush? You trying to get us killed?"

"Control received the emergency call at twelve-twenty-seven." He pointed to the digital clock on the plastic dashboard. "Look at the time now. We should have been on scene half an hour ago, but you're too busy chatting up the other ranks."

"Behave yourself, Wash." Pelham's self-satisfied smile nearly caused Wash to hit the central reservation. He tweaked the steering wheel, avoided a bollard by a whisker, and regained control of the vehicle, but not his temper.

"As a matter of fact, Detective Constable Washington, while you was fetching the car, I were doing some police work," Pelham said, releasing the strap. He made a sucking sound with his tongue, stuck a finger into his mouth, and started digging at some food stuck between his teeth. "You got any dental floss? There's a bit of meat stuck. Driving me nuts."

Wash wasn't in the mood to watch Pelham work the remnants of his dinner from inside his face with a length of white tape.

"No, Sarge," he lied. "You used the last of it yesterday. What were you saying about real police work?" He activated the sirens again before negotiating a roundabout. Once on the ring road, a dual carriageway, he mashed the throttle into the floor panel.

With the finger still in his mouth, Pelham answered. "I called Control and registered us as the active team. So everything's hunky-dory, well … sort of."

"Hell, Charlie. Don't like the sound of that 'sort of'. What's wrong?"

Pelham wiped the wet finger on his trouser leg. "Nothing for you to fret over, and fuck-all we can do 'bout it anyway. Have a guess who's leading the forensics team?"

Wash signalled left, yanked on the handbrake, and slid the Ford sideways into the turn. "Don't bloody tell me, Reg Prendergast?"

In the canteen, Wash doubted the day could get any worse, but it just had.

"Yep," said Pelham, and shook his head. "Ghastly's back from sick leave. He's there right now working the scene with his finger-print powder and little cotton buds."

"Christ's sake. He's not on his own is he?" Wash slammed on the brakes as a Renault Clio pulled out from a side road. A quick blast on his horn forced the terrified driver to pull over and allow him to squeeze between the car and an oncoming truck.

"Bill Harrap's with him," said Pelham, reaching for the strap again as Wash negotiated yet another mini-roundabout, "but Pat Elliott's on another shout, so Ghastly's doing some of the heavy lifting for a change."

He flinched as Wash missed clipping a white van by the thickness of a coat of body paint.

"Detective Constable Washington, if you crash and kill us both with your reckless driving I'll bloody murder you. Slow the fuck down. That's an order."

Wash eased off the revs, dropped the speed to a sedate twenty-miles-per-hour over the speed limit, and relaxed when the next right marked their final turn. "Sorry, Charlie. I'm too keen." He nearly added, 'and I forgot you were such a bloody wuss', but thought better of it.

He carried out the manoeuvre. Two hundred metres later, he

pulled the car into a tyre-squealing halt behind one of three patrol cars. He turned off the blues.

"Bloody fool," Pelham grumbled, wrestling with his seatbelt.

Wash jumped from the car and studied an area he knew well, having grown up within five miles of the crime scene. Standing within the Bull Ring and Inner City Regeneration Zone, Purser Street, like many in this part of town, had received the benefit of a non-surgical facelift, courtesy of part-EU funding. The gleaming frontages, unbroken windows, and shiny paintwork, were a long way from the beaten and battered streets of his childhood, but the recently applied yellow "Police Incident – Do Not Pass" tape brought a sense of the past howling back. The authorities could paint the woodwork and sandblast the stone and brick facades, but the underlying stench of age and corruption remained. This was hardly Birmingham's famed Jewellery Quarter.

As he and a puffing Charlie Pelham approached an inconspic-uous shop, spectators, held back by the tape and a uniformed constable, turned. Some raised mobiles and took pictures. Wash lowered his head and shouldered his way through the ghouls. Behind him, Pelham raised his hand for silence and spoke in a stage whisper to a hack reporter from the Chronicle, a local rag long rumoured to be going out of business at any moment.

The reporter, 'Old' Luke Wilson, named after his fashion sense —trilby hat and sports jacket complete with leather elbow patches—rather than his actual age, held up a digital recorder. "Can you tell us anything, Detective Sergeant Pelham?"

"We're in the early stages of a serious investigation, Mr Wilson. No doubt we'll be issuing a statement in due course. We'll leave no stone unturned in our hunt for the perpetrators of this heinous crime. Will that do?"

Pelham grinned and winked at Wash, who sighed and shook his head.

The constable on guard raised the tape. They scooted under-neath, and crossed into the relative tranquillity of the preparation area where they leaned against a wall to pull on plastic shoe covers and nitrile gloves.

"Bloody embarrassing for Old Luke to get here before us," Wash said, making a point not to glower at his sergeant. "How'd he do that, Charlie?"

"Dunno." Pelham nodded towards the three-rows-deep crowd pressing against the flimsy barrier. "Some of them great unwashed call the press first and the police second. That's the problem with twenty-four-hour news, lad. Everyone wants his name on the telly and in print. And Wilson's prob'ly bought hisself a police scanner."

He grunted as the shoe cover ripped and he had to grab another from the box on the pavement.

The SOCOs had rigged a canvas screen in front of the shop, using self-standing poles and guy ropes anchored with weights. It stretched in an unbroken 'U' from the pavement to the road and spanned most of the shop's frontage, leaving a narrow opening for access.

Wash peeked around the side and pursed his lips in preparation for a whistle he never blew.

"Bloody hell, Charlie. It's an abattoir in there. Worse than the mess Alby Pope left behind at Erskine Street."

Tracks of arterial spray decorated the inside of the shop's plate glass window. Footprints in blood, three sets, led from the open glass door to the edge of the pavement, reducing in definition as they went. Flies crawled over each print. Yellow numbers—indexed for scaling purposes—paralleled each footmark. Wash guessed it showed the handiwork of Bill Harrap rather than Reg Prendergast, but chided himself for being too hard on the man. As the boss kept saying, even Ghastly deserved the benefit of any doubt. He did— but only once.

Wash allowed himself a grim smile. Despite his gruff and wizened exterior, David Jones could be a bit of a wag at times. Fair but firm, unless you crossed him, or created a mess in his personal space. Do that and you'd face the ultimate in withering fallout.

The dependable Vic Doland issued quiet instructions to a young constable, whose pale skin and shaking hands suggested that he'd been unfortunate enough to catch a view inside the shop. Pelham stood tall, but the top of his head still only reached Doland's shoulder.

"What you got for me then, Vic?"

Doland up-nodded in greeting and jerked a thumb towards the jewellery shop, beckoning Pelham and Wash to follow. "Charlie, Wash, how you doing this fine summer's afternoon?"

"Control said two persons reported injured. Both dead?" asked Pelham, quickening his usual lacklustre delivery.

Wash's heart fluttered. This would be his first murder as one of the lead investigators.

"Surprisingly, no," Doland answered. He raised his shoulders in a tiny shrug. "At least not yet. One of the victims, name of Colonel Frederick Winterbourne, *Green and Sons'* Chief Security Officer, lost a load of blood." Doland pointed to the footprints and the window splatter. "Most of this here claret used to belong to him."

Wash studied the dark red pools on the shop floor and wondered how anyone could lose that much blood and still live.

"What'd he do to deserve that?"

Doland answered. "Refused to give up the combination to his security box."

Pelham nodded as though he knew what had happened. It took Wash a little longer to work it out.

"Christ," he whispered. "By 'security box', you mean one of those metal attaché cases couriers handcuff to their wrists?"

Doland nodded and made a face—a cross between someone sucking a lemon and a patient suffering from haemorrhoids.

"The bastards cut off the Colonel's hand with a hacksaw," he said, lowering his voice and hiding his mouth with a hand.

"Bloody hell," said Pelham, showing some rare empathy. "Keep that information quiet, understand?"

"Of course. None of my people will let that particular nugget slip out."

Wash swallowed hard. "Why didn't he bleed out?"

"The Colonel was damned lucky. See that young lass in the back of my car?" Doland pointed to a patrol vehicle. A small figure— brown hair tied in a ponytail, glasses, white school blouse buttoned up to the top, school tie missing—sat in the back with a mobile phone pressed to her ear. A police officer, whom Wash recognised as the delectable PC Susan Blakelock, had a protective arm draped around the girl's shoulders.

"Corrine Chambers," Doland continued. "Brave lass. Used her school tie as a tourniquet, and then dialled 9-9-9. She's only sixteen. Saved the Colonel's life. No doubt about that. Deserves an honour of some kind."

"Have you taken a statement?" asked Pelham.

"Name and contact details only. She's a bit shaken. PC Blake-lock's looking after her. She'll go gently on the lass. Her father should be here any moment." Doland opened his hands in a shrug. "The paramedics wanted to take her with them, but she refused. Said she had to talk to a detective, but needed to see her dad first."

Pelham sucked in his gut, and rearranged his shirttails. "You reckon the lass saw summat important?"

Doland nodded.

"Yep, but I'd wait for her father to arrive. Be on the safe side, eh?"

"I agree with Sergeant Doland, Charlie," Wash said, the glint in Pelham's eyes telling him the fat sod wasn't listening. "We should wait for her dad. I mean, it can't have been easy on the kid dealing with all that blood."

Pelham sniffed, and looked down his nose at the two of them.

"Time's a-wasting, and we need a description," he said, and strode to the car.

Wash followed him closely.

As Pelham approached, he rotated his hand at the wrist in a "wind down the window" motion. PC Blakelock looked at Doland for permission before leaning across the girl and pressing the button. The window rolled down and the girl, a mere child with clear skin and a trembling lower lip, turned big brown eyes on Pelham. She edged closer to PC Blakelock as Pelham grabbed the handle and yanked open the door.

Dark splodges stained the front of the girl's blouse. Larger patches showed around the cuffs and lower sleeves. A clear plastic bag, half-full of red-stained alcohol wipes and used paper towels rested in the footwell at her feet. That the girl wasn't a total wreck said a great deal for her spirit. Wash hoped nightmares wouldn't haunt Corrine Chambers' future dreams.

Pelham grabbed hold of the doorsill, grunted as he bent at the knees, and pushed his head towards the girl.

"Hello, Miss Chambers. Connie, isn't it? I'm Detective Sergeant Pelham. Do you mind if we have a little chat?"

He used his "telephone voice", and the accent moved all the way from London's East End to Billericay's Estuary Essex.

This wasn't right. Wash wanted to intervene and judging by the way Susan Blakelock compressed her lips, she felt the same way.

"Corrine," said the girl. "My name's Corinne not Connie. Warrant card, please."

"Excuse me?"

"I asked for your warrant card," she said, speaking more slowly.

Pelham straightened his back and forced a laugh.

"Of course you did. My mistake. I should have shown you this first." He flashed his ID at her and was about to withdraw it when Corrine held out her hand. With obvious reluctance, Pelham passed it over. The schoolgirl studied the wallet a full minute before handing it back.

"Thank you. I now know who to complain about when my father arrives."

Wash relaxed. The girl was a complete natural. He folded his arms and risked a glance at Doland, who turned his head and hid a smile by scratching at his earlobe.

"Badge number 6-9-8-9," Corinne said. "I'll remember that."

The skin around Pelham's collar glowed bright red, but he continued.

"I have to say, miss, you did a marvellous job in the shop. Saved that poor man's life and that's the truth. Using your tie showed great initiative. Have you ever considered training to become a nurse?"

Corrine Chambers faced forward and tucked in her chin. "Sergeant Pelham, you are a sexist, you know that? I happen to have a provisional acceptance for medical school at Guys University Hospital, dependent upon my A-level results." She turned cold eyes on him. "I will attain four A-stars. I'll speak to the other officer, not you." She pointed at Wash and then clutched the handkerchief in her lap.

Wash suppressed a grin. Vic Doland walked away shaking his head.

Pelham stood and grunted when his knees creaked. He turned his back to the girl and leaned close to Wash.

"See what you can get out of her," he whispered, and muttered, "bloody brat" before reaching for a cigarette and striding back towards the shop of gore.

Wash smiled at Corrine and gave her a surreptitious thumbs-up.

"Nice one, lass. He can be a bit full-on, but he means well," he lied.

He squatted in the same manner as Pelham had done, but kept his distance. Corinne worried away at the cotton handkerchief with trembling fingers. Despite her outward show of strength, the premature exposure to her future life as a doctor had clearly shaken the girl more than she cared to admit.

"He has halitosis and bromhidrosis."

Wash frowned. "Brom-what?"

"Bromhidrosis. The technical term for BO," she said. "Don't know how you can stand to work with him."

"You get used to it." Again, he lied.

If he carried on like this, Wash would need a trip to the confessional, and a nose job.

Corinne turned her shoulders and faced him. Her eyes, although puffy, were bright. "I suppose you'd like a description of the robbers and their getaway car?"

"You're kidding? You have that information?"

She nodded and wiped her nose with the hard-worked hankie.

"I told Susan everything I saw and showed her the picture I took on my phone." She held up the mobile for Wash to see the screen.

Corrine tilted her head towards PC Blakelock, who tapped her personal radio. "I forwarded the information to Control five minutes before you and Sergeant Pelham arrived," she said.

"And you didn't think to tell us this earlier?"

Blakelock's smile faded a little. "I thought about it, but, well … you know." Her frown and sideways glance at Pelham told Wash exactly what she thought of the man's interpersonal skills. "The description and photo is now on the system. I thought it important to notify Control so they could alert the patrol cars. I was about to tell Sergeant Doland."

"Fair enough," Wash said. "I don't have a problem with that. Corinne, would you mind telling me exactly what you saw and did? But only if it's not too upsetting. We can wait for your father if you prefer."

"No, no. It's okay," she said, and took a deep, stuttering breath before making a verbal statement.

Chapter Twenty-Seven

Digbeth, Birmingham

"SO, LET'S GET THIS STRAIGHT," Pelham said, through his bulbous blue-veined nose, "according to little miss trainee doctor over there, we're looking for two males, around six feet tall, average weight, wearing business suits and Mickey Mouse facemasks. Is that right so far?"

Wash nodded and peered through the cloud of blue smoke hanging around Pelham's fat head.

"And they drove off in a dark blue BMW Five series," Pelham continued. "And you got all that from the memory of a traumatised schoolgirl?"

Wash nodded.

"Yes, Sarge."

"Shame she didn't manage to take down the licence number, eh?"

"That's just it, Charlie. I've kept the best until last." Wash smiled

183

and held up his tablet. "She took a photo on her mobile. Every patrol car in the region is on the lookout."

Pelham stared at the blurred image on the screen—the rear of a dark saloon. "Okay, let's see where it turns up after they torch it, shall we?" He sniffed. "Won't do us no good. Let's hope Ghastly and Bill Harrap come up with some decent forensics."

"Never satisfied, are you, Charlie," Wash mumbled and reached into his pocket for a cigarette of his own. No matter how often he'd tried to give up, working with Pelham made it impossible. The prick would destroy the good intentions of a saint.

Pelham drew on his fag and turned to Sergeant Doland. "Vic, what about the shop manager? Why didn't he do nothing for the Colonel?"

Doland made the pained face again.

"The man's name is Joachim Albrecht. We found him lying on the floor behind the serving counter with the back of his head caved in. Still alive, but only just. They took him to Queen Elizabeth's in the same ambulance as the Colonel. The medic didn't look too optimistic about the jeweller's chances, but said the old soldier should survive. They took the hand with them in a cool box, you know, like the ones you'd take on a picnic. They're going to try sewing it back on. Microsurgery, eh? Like something out of a science fiction movie."

All the time he talked, Doland scanned the street, the protective father hen monitoring his family of chicks. Six uniformed officers, working individually and with clipboards in hand, stopped pedestrians or entered other premises in search of eyewitnesses and viable CCTV footage.

Pelham shrugged. "Good luck to the Colonel. Don't envy him the rehab. Did you call the shop owners?"

Doland nodded. "There's an emergency contact number registered at the station. The Regional Director's on his way. Bloke called Mainwaring."

"Regional Director, you say?" Pelham asked. He took a final draw on his fag, dropped it on the pavement, and stamped it out. He flicked the stub into the gutter with his foot, leaned in, and cupped his hands against the shop window to shield his eyes from the sun's glare. "What a mess. Any witnesses apart from the schoolgirl?"

Doland checked the crowd behind Pelham and lowered his voice. "Not a one. At least no one who's prepared to come forward. Control's looking at the traffic cams, but that one's facing the wrong direction." He pointed at a traffic light camera, some fifty metres distant. "I'm hoping some of the local shops will have surveillance, but I reckon the lassie's photo is going to be our best shot."

Wash scanned the street, looking for banks with outside ATMs, which all had built-in security cameras, but found none. "Any surveillance inside the shop, Sergeant Doland?"

"I took a quick shufti from the doorway before the SOCOs arrived. Two security cameras, but there's spray-paint on both lenses. Not sure what you'll get from any recordings. You'll have to ask Mainwaring when he arrives.

"Will do, Vic," Pelham said. "What's his ETA?"

Doland stared over Pelham's shoulder. "I bet that's him now."

A sleek black Audi R8 Spyder, with the paintwork gleaming and the soft top down, growled to a stop behind Wash's Ford, which looked drab and dowdy by comparison. Wash salivated at the masterpiece of German engineering. A broad-shouldered, sharp-suited man in his late thirties or early forties climbed out. He stood with one hand grasping the car's reinforced windscreen mounting and the other clamped over his open mouth. After a moment, he shook himself free of his apparent trance, and reached into the passenger compartment. When he straightened again, he was carrying a small silver briefcase. He transferred the case from his right to his left hand and searched the crowd near the sightscreen.

His eyes alighted on the nearest police uniform. "Sergeant Doland?" he called, and stepped towards Wash's group. His free hand trailed along the Audi's sleek bodywork for longer than seemed necessary to Wash, although he'd have probably done the self-same thing if he owned such a gorgeous hunk of machinery. Whether he'd have done it under the same circumstances was a different matter.

Pelham advanced to meet the new arrival.

"Mr Mainwaring?"

The man nodded, but his eyes locked onto the canvas screens that hid his business. "Yes, yes." The fingers that had caressed the Audi combed through a head of thick and wavy salt and pepper hair. "Rod Mainwaring, Regional Director, *Green & Sons*."

He didn't offer his hand.

Mainwaring's restrained public school voice lacked emotion and immediately grated on Wash's proletarian nerves.

"Detective Sergeant Pelham, in charge of this investigation."

Mainwaring frowned and shook his head slowly.

"This is terrible," he whispered, but the eyes scanning the street were shrewd, calculating, and emotionless. Wash wondered what the calculations told him. How much trade they were losing due to the closedown? How could he bump up the insurance claim?

"Do you know what happened yet?" Mainwaring asked.

"Early days, sir," Pelham responded. "We've only just arrived. Is there a back entrance to the shop with an office where we could chat in private?"

"Yes, of course. Follow me."

Mainwaring led them at a brisk pace, fifty metres along Purser Street. Wash extended his stride to match Mainwaring's speed. Pelham had to jogtrot alongside to keep up. They made two right turns and entered a shaded, litter-strewn access road. The left side of the avenue ran parallel to a footpath. A rusted chain-link fence—holed and in sad disrepair—offered little security.

No one spoke until Mainwaring stopped at the rear of his shop. He pulled out a set of keys and tutted at the overfilled wheelie bins marked with the *Green & Sons* company logos.

"Bloody contractors. We pay a fortune for rubbish collection and they're always late. Place is an utter shambles."

The Regional Director found the correct key and pushed it into the lock first time, fingers steady. He covered the security keypad with one hand and punched in the six-digit code with the other before tensing and turning to face Wash and Pelham.

"Good Lord," he said. "How callous that must have sounded."

Mainwaring combed his hair into place with his fingers again. "Forgive me, but this episode has knocked me for … well, I'm all over the place. Colonel Winterbourne, Freddie, is a friend of mine. I really ought to be with him at the hospital, but the company must come … well, you know."

"We understand, sir." Wash spoke for Pelham, who was still struggling to catch his breath. "We won't keep you long, but the sooner we know what the raiders made off with the better."

Mainwaring's eyes lost focus for a moment. "Gosh. Has anyone spoken to Eleanor? Freddie's wife? I mean, does she know?"

"No, sir. We know nothing of the Colonel or his family," Pelham gasped and wiped his forehead with a handkerchief. "Now sir, would you mind?"

Wash had a hard time believing Mainwaring's abrupt change in attitude. The words were right, and spoken with the correct degree of emotion, but the man's cold eyes revealed nothing. Mainwaring redialled the security code, which had timed out during the brief discussion, and turned the handle. He opened the door and they entered a dimly lit stockroom.

A second door led to the shop via a narrow corridor.

The iron-rich stink of coagulating blood punched Wash in the nose. Flies buzzed around his head. The drone mixed with the sporadic sound of a flashgun popping and squealing as it recharged. Bill Harrap was hard at work photographing the scene. Another sound, less distinct and bubbling below the others, told him that Ghastly was there too, chuntering to himself as he always did when working a scene.

A door marked 'Private' gave access to the office.

Wash followed Mainwaring and Pelham into a small, overstuffed room. Approximately three metres wide and five deep, a large glass panel dominated the left-hand wall and allowed an unrestricted view of the shop, as seen from behind the serving counter. Blood, flies, SOCOs, and a load of broken display cabinets dominated the view.

The office was sparsely furnished. A wooden desk faced the door and a row of six metal filing cabinets stood guard against the right-hand wall. Two chairs, one behind the desk, the other in front, told Wash that he'd be standing in the doorway looking down. His premonition proved valid as Mainwaring slid behind the desk and took the upholstered chair. He laid his briefcase on the desktop and indicated that Pelham should take the visitor's seat. Pelham dropped into it like a sack of coal hitting a cellar floor. The chair bounced and squealed in protest.

Green & Sons' Regional Director studied Ghastly and Bill Harrap's activities through the window for a moment. From what Wash could make out through the spy screen, very little stock remained in the shop.

"One-way mirror," Mainwaring said, indicating the glass with a tilt of the head. "Bullet resistant too, but didn't do poor Freddie or Joachim much good." Mainwaring wrung his hands, raised his shoulders to his ears, and let them fall as though they were too heavy to hold up any longer. "So much blood in there … What happened? Were guns involved?"

"We don't exactly know yet, sir," Pelham answered, noncommittally. "As I said outside, our investigation is at a very early stage."

"Sergeant Pelham," Mainwaring said, a studied frown creasing his tanned forehead. "I saw an item on the news the other night about a national gang of jewel thieves … JT something-or-other. You don't think they were responsible for this, do you?"

Pelham paused for a moment and looked through the glass again, brows knitted. "Too early to say, but it is a possibility."

Wash closed his eyes and bit his tongue. What was Pelham playing at? He shouldn't be speculating at this stage of an investigation. That's how rumours got started.

Mainwaring put a hand over his mouth. It seemed to be his default reaction to shock. "Gosh. That's awful. How can I help?"

"First thing you can do is give us a copy of the security video for the time of the robbery and as far back as you keep the tape."

"That won't be a problem, but I shall have to contact the data centre. Our live system feeds straight into the company's server hub. I believe we keep the data for a fortnight or so, but you'll have to ask Freddie." He frowned. "Oh dear, that was unforgivable. I really don't know what we're going to do without his guiding hand on our tiller." He lowered his head to bite a thumbnail. "But you can see from the screen that the system no longer seems to be working." He pointed at the wall above and to the left of Wash's head where a pair of CCTV monitors displayed nothing but blackness.

"Spray paint on the camera lenses," Pelham said.

"Oh I say," Mainwaring responded, and bit the nail again. "That's rather annoying. Those cameras are quite expensive. Only installed a few months ago. Wonder whether they're still under warranty?"

"The moments before they applied the paint might prove useful, Mr Mainwaring," Pelham said. "There is one more thing, sir. How soon can you give us an inventory of the missing articles?"

Mainwaring smiled and opened the metal case. "Ah, now there I *can* help you, Sergeant." He took out a manila folder and slid it across the desk. "Here's a printout of the stock held as of closing time last night. We operate an excellent EPOS system. That's electronic point-of-sale, don't you know. I have asked our stock control department to run a special audit of today's sales, which they will email to me shortly. After that, I will need access to the SFA."

"The what?" Pelham asked.

"My apologies. I mean the Sales Facilitation Area." Mainwaring paused and took in Pelham's blank look. "The shop floor," he said, pointing through the one-way glass.

Pelham turned to Wash and gave him a look that said, "Is this guy taking the piss?", or something very similar.

"I have a team of auditors on standby at head office," Mainwaring continued. "The moment you allow us access to the SFA, I'll call them in."

Pelham sat up straight. "Nah," he said. "That ain't going to happen for a while, Mr Mainwaring. The forensics officers will be here for hours and will take any remaining stock to the lab for analysis. Best we can do is to provide you with photos and a receipt for what we take away. I assume you can work from them?"

Mainwaring paused before answering. "I suppose that will have to do. You'll give us a crime number for our insurance claim?"

"DC Washington, give the man his crime number," Pelham said, and snapped his fingers as a chivvy up.

Wash prayed for Pelham's chair to collapse under its enormous load, but wrote the information taken from the screen of his tablet into Mainwaring's proffered notebook.

"Once you have the information, how long will the audit take, sir?" he asked, trying to keep his voice calm and steady.

"A couple of hours, no more."

"Mind telling me where the safe is, sir, and whether it's been opened?" Pelham asked.

Mainwaring broke out a smug grin. "Certainly, Sergeant. I'm leaning on it." He patted the table with the palm of his left hand. "This is a small branch of *Green & Sons*, and doesn't usually hold many individual pieces above the minimum insurance value for overnight vault storage. I checked the safe's security tab the moment I sat in this chair. It is locked and shows no sign of having been interfered with."

Wash edged forward from his position in the doorway.

"Would you mind opening the safe and confirming that its contents are intact?" he asked.

Pelham sat up straighter and placed his hands flat on the table, mirroring Mainwaring's gesture. "Good idea, Constable. Well, sir?"

The Regional Director shook his head. "Not possible I'm afraid. The online security system changes the combination of each shop's safe or vault and only the individual manager, the chief security officer, and the mainframe has access. So you see it's impossible for this safe to have been opened by anyone other than poor Freddie or Mr Albrecht, the manager."

"Both of whom are now in hospital and incommunicado."

"Precisely," he answered through another wintery smile.

"Can you interrogate the security system and get the combination?" Pelham's voice rose in volume.

Apart from when he was chasing his latest romantic target Wash had never seen him so worked.

Mainwaring shook his head again. "I'm afraid not. I don't have security clearance."

"Who does? Freddie and Mr Albright?"

"That's correct?"

"What about Mr Green or his son?" Wash asked.

Mainwaring broke out the insufferable, superior smile again.

"Oh dear, you know nothing about our company, do you."

Not yet mate, but I bloody will do, soon enough.

"You see, there is no Mr Green. The founder, Alfonse Grün, died in 1965. His only son, Helmut, passed away in 1989, leaving a widow who married a chap called Frederick Winterbourne. Colonel Winterbourne. Understand now?"

Pelham raised his chins. "And he didn't change the company name?"

"That's right, for continuity. In a small but growing family concern, continuity is paramount." He crossed his arms to signal that this part of the conversation had ended. "Is there anything else you need?"

"When will we be able to access the safe?" Wash asked.

Mainwaring scratched his chin. "Not until eight o'clock tomorrow morning, when the combination is changed."

"Can't you advance the change protocol? We need to be certain nothing's been taken."

"I'll call our IT Director, see what she can suggest."

"Thank you, sir," grunted Pelham, struggling to his feet. "I think that's all for now. Would you mind stepping out of the building? We'll call you when you can return."

"What's that? You're throwing me out of my own premises?"

"For the present, sir. We'll be as quick as we can."

"But what about security?"

"We're the police, sir. We ain't gonna rob the place or leave it unguarded."

Mainwaring bristled and his hands bunched into fists on top of the desk. The sounds of Ghastly's mumbles and Bill Harrap's photo shoot bled into the quiet office. Neither Pelham nor Wash wilted under the Regional Director's glare.

"Very well," Mainwaring barked, and exploded from his chair, slamming the briefcase shut with a force that shook the desk lamp.

"Make sure to let me know the moment my people and I can enter. I shall be in my car."

He sidestepped around the desk, but Wash blocked the man's exit. "There is one thing more, Mr Mainwaring."

"Yes?"

"What was in the Colonel's courier's box?"

Mainwaring took a pace back. Colour drained from his face. "I have no idea."

"Really? That surprises me. I was under the impression that people who trade in high-priced jewellery were rather keen on stock control."

"Don't be so damned impertinent, man. What I meant to say was, I know exactly what Freddy left the office with this morning, but I'm not sure what remained in the attaché case when he arrived here. This may have been his first delivery today, his last, or anything in between. Freddy didn't tell anyone his itinerary. Security reasons, don't you know."

He sniffed.

Yes, I know. I also know that you are a pompous gobshite.

Mainwaring leaned towards Wash and tried an intimidating chin thrust. Wash stared him down and refused to step aside.

"So?" he asked.

"What do you mean, 'So'?"

"What was the value of the stock in Colonel Winterbourne's attaché case when he left your head office?"

Mainwaring turned to Pelham, who batted back the man's intense stare with one of his own.

"Freddie left with seventeen diamond rings, a number of sapphire brooches, and a ruby necklace," he said, in a voice so low that Wash had to lean closer to hear the words more clearly. Mainwaring swallowed. "They had an insured value of one-hundred-and-thirty-three thousand pounds."

"Christ almighty," Pelham said, and closed his eyes for a moment.

Wash's scalp tingled. This didn't feel right. "Why don't you use a security firm?"

"We do. In fact, we use a number of methods to transport the merchandise, and we randomise the usage. Freddie's the boss and is in charge of security. You'll have to ask him to defend his strategy. Now, if you don't mind, I need to contact our insurers to confirm that they both knew about, and agreed to, Freddie's transportation protocols. For all I know, we're not even covered for this loss. Is that all? Can I leave now, please?"

Pelham pursed his lips. "Stand aside, Detective Constable. Allow Mr Mainwaring to go about his lawful business."

Wash turned sideways, and said, "Take the back door please sir, and mind how you go."

Mainwaring brushed past Wash and slammed the door behind him.

"Arrogant prick," Pelham said, loud enough for the departing Mainwaring to have heard.

For once, Wash agreed with his senior partner's considered assessment.

"Sales Facilitation Area, my arse! Did you hear that bullshit?"

"Didn't show much compassion for the injured Colonel, did he? The sod were more worried about the damage to the bloody CCTV cameras. Flash git with his poncey car."

Pelham stopped talking for a moment and turned to stare through the one-way glass.

"Jesus, what's old Ghastly up to? Look at him standing there like a lemon while Bill Harrap does all the work."

I know exactly how he feels, you lazy fat git.

Wash stepped forward to join Pelham and caught a close up view of the carnage in the shop for the first time.

Silver, red, and the purple of the velvet-lined shelves dominated the colour palette. White light from the surviving spotlights reflected back from the shards of glass and pools of blood.

"Looks like something out of an 'orror movie," Pelham said.

Again, Wash had to agree.

The shelves and cases near the front, the ones containing cheap watches, earrings, and bangles, remained untouched. The ones closest to the sales counter were broken and empty.

While Bill Harrap—identified by his stocky shape and chewing jaw—made busy with a camera and notepad, Reg Prendergast—he of the stooped shoulders and bottle-bottom spectacles—stood still and stared at the floor. Although the hood attached to the one-piece paper suit hid the grey ponytail, and a paper dust mask covered most of the man's face, Wash would have recognised the skinny, twitchy Ghastly anywhere.

Wash would never understand or agree with the injustice of a system that allowed Ghastly to make team leader ahead of people with the calibre of Bill Harrap and his mate, Patrick Elliott. It didn't seem fair, but given the red stuff Prendergast currently studied, and the method of its extraction, office politics seemed like small potatoes by comparison.

As Wash watched, Ghastly jumped to attention and yelled at Harrap, although the man stood less than a metre away. "I want loads of shots of this area. And watch where you're standing, man! Don't disturb the evidence."

Harrap scowled, but held his tongue.

The boss considered Bill Harrap and Pat Elliott, two of the best Scenes of Crime Officers in the region, but bad leadership could disturb even the most professional of operations. Wash slid a sideways glance at Pelham, who stood watching the SOCOs at work and checking the time on his mobile.

"Bloody man's not only useless, he's a bully," Pelham said, without lowering his voice.

"What's wrong, Charlie?"

"Fed up with standing out here scratching my arse. Good job we didn't bust a gut getting here in the first place, eh? How long did the schoolgirl say the gang were in here?"

"Three minutes, no more."

Pelham nodded and spoke almost to himself. "In and out with the choice goods and poor Freddie's attaché case in less than five minutes. Pretty slick operation despite all that blood."

"What do you mean?"

"Even though the place looks a mess, those evil bastards knew exactly what they was doing," Pelham said, scratching his ear with one hand and swatting away a fly with the other. His ability to multi-task never ceased to impress.

"A professional team you reckon?"

"Yep," Pelham answered, adding a wink. "Left all the crap and only bothered with the expensive stock. I reckon they staged the smash and grab to put us off track."

"You don't think they could read the price tags on the shelves then?"

Pelham gave Wash something that his father would have called an "old fashioned" look, which incorporated an arched eyebrow and a sneer. "This has all the hallmarks of that flash national mob, the JT1 Crew."

"You're talking about that press conference by the NCA. The one Mainwaring mentioned, right?"

"Don't be dense, man," Pelham said, and waved a hand towards the shop. "This has robbery their signature written all over it."

"Are you serious?" Wash struggled to keep his cool. "Charlie, we can't link every jewellery store robbery in the country to the same bloody team."

"Of course not. But think about it. They disabled the security system and made off with the expensive gear. They also targeted the Colonel's delivery, so they must have been following him. This sounds like serious planning to me, not the work of opportunist thieves."

The light shining from his normally lacklustre eyes showed Wash that Pelham could see his credentials for the vacant inspector's post improving by the second.

Wash tried another tack.

"Are you sure? I mean, isn't this place a bit low rent for the JT1 boys?" he asked. "They normally target bigger shops. Think about it. According to the NCA, JT1's last job netted over a million quid."

"Slimmer pickings in here in Birmingham."

"Bollocks, Sarge. You ever visited the Jewellery Quarter? Knock over any shop in that square mile and you'll net millions. This place is small potatoes."

"So what? These buggers are new to the area. Outsiders. Don't know nothing about the city. This is the JT1 Crew. I'm certain of it. And we're going to nail the bastards." Pelham scratched his nose. "Vicious sods and they're only going to get more violent. They used shotguns in Edinburgh, didn't they?" He lowered his voice again. "I'm surprised they didn't blow the Colonel's hand off. Would have been a lot quicker than the 'acksaw."

"Not funny, Charlie."

"Weren't meant to be, son," Pelham said. A wicked smile creased his face. "I'm going to have a word with Vic Doland, see if his Woodentops have come up with anything. You hang about here for a bit. Make sure Ghastly don't fall over and fuck up the scene. Or perhaps you could offer him a hand?" He chuckled.

"Fuck's sake, Charlie!"

"Gallows humour, son. If you don't laugh, you cry."

Wash watched Pelham leave through the back and waited a minute before following.

Pelham turned left into Purser Street. Wash hurried to close the gap and stopped at the corner. He peered around the wall and studied his sergeant's actions. Pelham made a brief stop at the barrier tape, said a few words to Luke Wilson, the reporter, and stood directly in front of Ghastly as the Senior SOCO exited the shop and headed towards his Range Rover.

After he'd allowed Ghastly to pass, Pelham met a newly arrived Ford in police livery as it disgorged a worried-looking man in a business suit. On the man's appearance, Corrine Chambers jumped out the patrol car and raced into his arms. Wash smiled. The tiny girl, barely five feet tall, disappeared into her father's embrace.

Wash took the mobile from his pocket and dialled. Typically, the call went straight to voicemail.

"Boss," he said, although he knew the chances of David Jones being prepared, or able, to operate the call retrieval system were as likely as Charlie Pelham going on a diet and swearing off whisky and wild women. "It's Wash. I'm at a robbery scene in Digbeth." He read the crime number from his tablet. "Can you call me when you receive this message? It's urgent. Cheers."

He ended the call and dialled Alex's number, with the same result.

Twenty metres away, Pelham crossed his arms and waited for father and daughter to separate. Luke Wilson hovered in the background.

Wash called the control room. "DC Ryan Washington, badge number 9573."

"Morning, Constable, Inspector Wilkie here." The Chief Communications Officer rarely dropped the formal call signatures; he had to be alone in the comms room.

"I need DCI Jones to call me."

"What's wrong? Has the old boy forgotten to charge his mobile again?"

"No idea what you mean, sir. Last I heard he and DC Olganski were interviewing Alby Pope. Would you mind asking him to call me, please? It's important."

Wash ended the call and stepped out onto the Purser Street pavement. He couldn't see Pelham anywhere. Worse still, Luke Wilson had disappeared.

Chapter Twenty-Eight

TUESDAY 5TH JULY – *Early afternoon*
Holton, Birmingham

BY THE TIME Jones and Alex left Pope in the interview room guarded by the two constables, the little murderer had returned to his nail-biting, nibbling worst. In the corridor, Jones ran a hand through his hair. "Nicely done, Alex. Don't know how you could hold his hands like that without vomiting."

"Wasn't easy, boss. I wanted to tear him apart for what he did to Mr and Mrs Al Karem, but that's not what we do in England, *ja?*"

"No, Alex. Not anymore."

She took out another wet wipe. "Tonight, I'll need a long, hot shower, but first I need to go and wash my hands properly."

"Don't blame you," Jones said and gave her a rueful smile. "Don't blame you one little bit."

"DCI Jones?"

A constable approached from the direction of the main reception area. He looked young enough still to be at school, but then again, so did most of the people Jones worked with these days. Well, maybe some of them might make undergraduates. He suddenly felt every one of his fifty-odd years.

"Yes, Constable …?"

"Porterhouse, sir. A call came in for you at reception."

"From whom?"

"DC Washington, sir. He's asking you to contact him on his mobile. Said it was urgent, sir."

"Is it now? Why didn't he call me himself?"

Porterhouse opened his mouth, but no words emerged.

"Come on lad, spit it out."

"Sorry sir, but he said your mobile went through to voicemail. He thinks you may have switched off your phone when in the interview room."

"You mean he said I might have forgotten to charge the battery again?"

"No, sir. That's what Inspector Wilkie said … sorry sir, I mean …." Deep red splodges blossomed on the constable's acne-marked cheeks.

Jones took pity on the youngster. The lad would soon toughen up after a few months on the beat. "I know what you mean, son. Okay, message delivered. Thank you."

Porterhouse made a swift about-turn and hurried back to the security of the reception desk where Inspector Wilkie would no doubt be laughing into his coffee mug at the lad's discomfort.

Alex smiled. "The poor boy was terrified of you, boss. Someone's been filling his ears with tales of your ferocity. Would you like to borrow my phone?"

"Yes please."

Jones reached for her offered mobile. His phone's battery had, indeed, died the previous evening and he'd forgotten to hook it up to the home charger again. It currently rested on a desk in the office —on charge.

Alex had opened hers to Ryan Washington's number in the contacts list. All Jones had to do was press the call button, which he managed with the silky ease of a consummate professional. It didn't take long for the detective constable to answer.

"What do you have for me, Ryan?"

"Hi, boss. Sorry to disturb and thanks for getting back to me so fast. We've had a jewellers shop turned over." He had to shout over the background noise of heavy traffic. "It's pretty bad, boss. Two victims in intensive care. One's really in a bad way. We could do with your help."

"Okay, give me the address."

"We're on Digbeth High Street, *Green & Sons*."

"Yes. I know the place. I need to pop up to the office first, but I'll be there soon as I can. Is Phil with you?"

"No boss, he's taken Manda for her scan."

"Oh, right. Yes, of course. I forgot."

"I'm here with Charlie, sir. Which is why I called you. I think you need to get over here, pronto. That reporter, Luke Wilson's been hanging around, and Charlie's, well, he's being Charlie. You understand?"

"Yes, Ryan, I do. Say no more."

Jones ended the call and passed the phone back.

"Alex, stay with your new best friend and keep at least one of those constables with you at all times. Alby's acting up and … well, you know. I want you safe."

"I can handle Alby Pope, boss. He's small."

Jones nodded. "I'm sure that's what Mr Al Karem thought, too. Take care, understand?"

"Yes, boss."

"Good. When Pope's medic arrives, follow procedure. On my way out, I'll send an inspector down to help with the booking forms."

Alex stiffened. "I can manage the paperwork, boss."

"I know Alex, but this is a double murder. Procedure demands a senior officer attend the booking interview. It's no reflection on your competence."

"Yes, boss," she said, trying to hide her disappointment by turning to face the interview room.

Jones placed a light hand on her shoulder. "You did a great job in there, Alex. I won't forget it."

"Thanks, boss." She straightened and gave him the sort of smile that would have had Alby Pope melting into a puddle on the floor.

"I'm going to see what Charlie's been up to, and I'm also going to tell the custody sergeant to have the cleaners fumigate that bloody room when you're done. Stinks so much in there, I nearly hurled."

"Yes, boss. Me too."

Chapter Twenty-Nine

TUESDAY 5TH JULY – *Early afternoon*
Digbeth, Birmingham

JONES ENTERED the blood-spattered premises of *Green & Sons* and took in the crime scene in an extended, slow sweep. Flies, drawn from miles away by the scent of blood and other matter, buzzed and flowed in frenzied waves. He prepared himself for the onslaught. Flies were only flies after all, even though they fed and walked on faeces.

Filthy creatures.

He swatted one away from his face, managed not to shudder, and forced his mind to concentrate on the scene.

The SOCOs were gone, but had left the place in a terrible state. Fingerprint powder, yellow evidence markers, and foot trays littered the floor. Reg Prendergast's sloppy ways showed in the detritus, but Jones was surprised Bill Harrap hadn't taken his equipment or tidied the place as was his standard operating procedure.

"Afternoon Charlie, Ryan," he said, nodding to each in turn.

Pelham, who'd been facing away from the door when Jones

entered, pirouetted, and nearly toppled over. His face turned to toasted cheese, both in colour and texture. He shot Ryan a fearsome scowl before recovering some composure. "Watcha, boss. Thought you was busy with that pervert, Alby Pope. We've got everything under control here."

Ryan nodded. "Hi sir, I'll go see how the search team's getting along."

"No, wait there a moment, Wash. I need a full briefing. Broad brush report please, Charlie."

"Yeah, right. Sorry, boss. We've only just gained access to the scene. Ghastly took bloody ages and then buggered off and left us with this pigsty. As for the gang, I've issued Control with a good description. They've alerted the traffic patrols to stop and search all dark blue BMW 5 Series on a 2014 plate. They have the registration number, too. If the car's still on the road, we'll find it, but"—he wrinkled his mouth—"they've had nearly three hours to switch motors."

Jones nodded. "Yes, I heard the broadcast on the way over. How did you find the description? I understand the victims are in no condition to give statements."

"Yeah, the vics are in a bad way—"

"Vic-*tims*," Jones corrected. He'd bludgeon some respect into Pelham or remove him from the SCU altogether. Either way, he'd had more than enough nonsense from a man with the experience to know better. "Did you find witnesses or security footage?"

"Yeah, right, victims," Pelham continued. "Didn't find no film yet, but Sergeant Doland has uniformed teams searching for useful CCTV. Should be some good stuff on the street. The area's full to overflowing with shops and offices. Did you notice that posh wine bar across the street? One of Vic Doland's girls is over there now asking if they've got surveillance."

"By 'one of Vic Doland's girls', I take it you mean a female police officer?" Jones lowered his voice to a growl. "If you're delib-erately trying to annoy me DS Pelham, it's working."

"Don't mean nothing by it, boss. All that political correctness bollocks gets in the way of building good working relationships."

Wash stared hard at Jones as if to say, "See what I have to put up with every day?".

Jones resolved to send Pelham on the next available sexual harassment training course, but shelved the thought for the moment.

"A witness then?" he asked.

"Wash spoke to the schoolgirl what saved the Colonel from bleeding out."

Pelham gave a rundown on Corinne Chambers' actions, her statement, and the photo she'd taken of the getaway car.

"Good witness, Ryan?" Jones asked. "Reliable?"

"One of the best I've ever talked to, boss. Her memory's almost as impressive as Phil's."

"Really? That good, eh?"

Wash nodded. "Not far off."

"I'd like a chat with the lass myself at some stage."

"You'll be lucky," Pelham said. "She's a bit uppity. Took a bit of a shine to our Wash though, since the two of the are pretty near the same age."

Always taking the mick.

"Where is she now?" Jones addressed the question to Wash who looked ready to explode.

"Her father took her to hospital for a check-up. She did come into contact with blood, after all," Ryan answered. "She kicked up a heck of a fuss. Wanted him to take her home so she could tweet her friends."

"Fair enough," Jones said, as though he understood and condoned the youngster's need to send her every thought and action into cyberspace. "As you have her trust, perhaps you can arrange a formal interview as soon as she feels up to it. Any point in putting her in a room with a sketch artist?"

"Not really. Even I can come up with a reasonable likeness of Mickey Mouse. Might struggle with Goofy though," Wash said, adding a wry grin. "She's promised to visit the station with her parents tomorrow morning to make a formal statement."

"Excellent. I wish everyone was as public spirited. So what

happened? Looks like Saturday night at Hockley after closing time." He stared down at the blood, treacle-like, dark, and mottled.

Pelham read from his notebook. "Most of that claret's from Colonel Frederick Winterbourne. He's *Green & Sons'* head honcho. Arrived with a metal attaché case full of stock a little before eleven o'clock this morning. Seconds later, two white blokes"—he raised a hand to forestall Jones reprimand—"sorry, boss. I mean, two IC1 males entered the premises and removed the Colonel's left hand with an 'acksaw, before, or after they knocked the manager over the head. Then they nicked a load of sparklies from the cabinets, and had it away on their toes. Didn't touch the safe. Whole thing took less than five minutes." He closed the notepad and stuffed it in his inner jacket pocket. "Real professional operation. I reckon it has to be that national mob, the JT1 Crew. Precious little doubt about it." Pelham allowed a smug grin to puff up his cheeks.

"Ryan," Jones said, keeping his tone steady. "Would you mind checking on the progress of the street canvass? Sergeant Doland was about to debrief his troops when I arrived. They might have come up with something of interest."

Ryan clearly catching the harshness in Jones' tone, headed for the exit without saying a word. He jumped over the bloody footprints and nearly collided with Bill Harrap.

"Careful, Wash. These suits are expensive, mate," Harrap said, tugging at his cheap disposable coverall.

The young detective managed a quick apology, but didn't hang around any longer than necessary.

"Mr Harrap," Jones said. "I wondered when you'd be back to collect your stuff."

Harrap stopped chewing his gum for a moment. "Mr Jones. Sorry 'bout that, sir. Mr Prendergast needed me to drive him back to the lab to start the analysis. Wouldn't let me tidy up first, but I'm afraid I do need to take a few more blood smears."

"More?"

"There was a bit of an … accident, but there's no probs."

"Accident? Is Mr Prendergast okay?"

"Yeah. Had a bit of a fall. Don't know how serious yet, but he's in good hands. Pat's looking after him." Harrap gave Pelham a furtive glance, before adding, "The old trouble, you know?"

Jones understood what exactly the Australian meant and a sense of sadness threatened to engulf him. He understood the effects of mental illness—he'd seen example enough in his life and some of it from the inside. "I understand, Bill. Let me know how he is the moment you have any news, right?"

"Right-oh," he said, tapping a gloved finger to his temple in salute.

"How long will you be?"

"Five minutes for the samples and fifteen to tidy up. It'll give you a chance to get some fresh air. It's a bit rank in here, but doesn't bother me much. Aussies are used to the odd blowie or two."

"Blowie?"

"Blowflies, sir."

Jones moved further into the shop to allow Harrap room to work and signalled to Pelham. "Is there an office out back?"

Pelham led the way.

Once alone with Pelham, Jones couldn't hold back his anger any longer.

"Come on, Charlie, out with it. What the hell's the matter with you?"

"Don't know what you mean, boss," Pelham answered, his demeanour as slovenly as always.

Jones took a breath before laying into the useless article. "Point one. Don't you ever refer to Reg Prendergast as 'Ghastly'. He's as much a member of this team as you are, and deserves our respect and support. Do I make myself clear?" Pelham studied a spot on the floor. "Point two. You've had a face like soggy lettuce from the moment I walked in. What's that all about?"

Pelham straightened and stared past Jones to the doorway, no doubt checking for prying eyes and ears.

"Off the record?"

"If you like." Jones leaned against a counter, after making sure it was clear of trace evidence and SOCO equipment. The glass was cool through his light summer jacket.

"This is my case, boss." A vein popped out at Pelham's temple and his face turned a darker shade of red. "You come barging in here taking over. It ain't right. I have everything under control and would have briefed you this evening after we'd wrapped up here. Yeah, and while we're on that subject, you've been blocking my promotion since Jock left. And now look what's happened. The second I land a big case, you muscle in on the action." He paused for breath. "I'm a good detective and you damn well know it."

Jones counted to five before responding. He couldn't control himself long enough to make it all the way to ten.

"You finished?"

Pelham nodded and took a pace back. As Jones had done, he took care not to step on any evidence. At least he knew how to behave at the locus of a crime scene.

"I would have left you to it, Charlie. You *do* know what you're doing and when you put your mind to it, you can be a decent detective. But you're lazy and I can't trust you anymore."

"What?" Pelham's jowls wobbled. "That's bloody rubbish."

"Before I left the station, Ian Wilkie called me over and showed me something on the Internet."

Pelham frowned. "So?"

"In quiet moments Wilko likes to keep abreast of local news. He considers it part of his remit as a community police officer. Did you know the Evening Chronicle has a website where they post snippets of stories in advance of their published editions?"

"Since when was you interested in the internet, boss?" Pelham swallowed and his frown deepened. "And anyway, what about it?"

"You know the headline they're running with tonight?" Jones took a scrap of paper from his pocket and showed Pelham his note:

Diamond Geezers!
The JT1 Crew hit Digbeth Jewellery Store.

"ANYTHING TO SAY about how the Chronicle received their information, Charlie?"

Pelham hesitated before leaning forward and trying to go on the offensive.

"Yeah, I told 'em. Nothing wrong with that, is there? We need to warn the public not to approach. Using the media is our best chance of catching these buggers." He pointed through the one-way glass at the stained flooring and the smashed glass counters. "Look at that place. We were seconds away from this being a murder investigation." He counted off the points with his fingers. "I had good descriptions of the gang and the getaway car. We know it's the JT1 and if we get ahead of this we can stick a finger in the eye of the National Crime Agency and their overfunded Robbery Task Force. Look boss, I made a judgment call that going to the press was the right thing to do. As officer-in-charge, that's my prerogative."

"But what if you're wrong, Charlie? What if this has nothing to do with JT1? You might have just screwed up big time."

"What?"

"Come on, man. Look at the place." Jones pointed through the one-way glass as Pelham had done. "I doubt this shop stocks any single item worth more than, what, a couple of grand?"

He singled out a glass case beside the service counter, smashed and empty, a torn poster advertised the shop's star buy of the week —a diamond necklace on sale for *£999.99 - 33% off RRP*.

"See what I mean?" he added. "JT1 doesn't knock over places that bother with price tags. For God's sake, they made off with the best part of two-and-a-half-million pounds worth in the first Edinburgh job."

"You've been speaking to Wash," Pelham said, his protruding lower lip showing the petulance of a spoiled child.

"What d'you mean?"

"He said pretty much the same thing earlier. Is he reporting to you behind my back?"

"Never mind about that. What did he say?"

"He thought the same as you. That this mightn't be the JT1 crew."

"And you chose to ignore him?"

"But I—"

"You've never heard of copycats?" Jones said, shaking his head. "Ryan Washington's a bright police officer or I wouldn't have chosen him for the team. You should listen to him more often. And there's another thing you overlooked."

"What's that?"

"The JT1 have a cracksmith, don't they? According to the file, he's one of the best the NCA has ever hunted. This person opens safes, disables state-of-the-art security system in seconds, leaves no forensic trace. Leaps tall buildings in a single bound. A criminal superman, right?"

"And?" Pelham frowned, clearly not making the connection.

"Think about it, man. Why did the blaggers need to hack off the Colonel's hand? Why didn't they ask Superman to open the cuffs instead? He could have done it in seconds without all the flaming gore."

The distended vein at Pelham's temple looked ready to burst. A tear of sweat rolled from his woolly sideburn and soaked into his shirt collar.

"Fuck," he said and winced. "Should have thought of that. I … sorry, boss."

"We'll talk about it later." Jones paused for thought. "How much did they get away with?"

"Don't know exactly," Pelham mumbled, easing his weight from one foot to the other. "I haven't let the Regional Director, bloke called Mainwaring, do a stock take yet. He's out front in that flash Audi, waiting to call in his team of auditors. He did reckon the attaché case might have contained over one-hundred-and-thirty grand worth of gear. Gave me a list, which I've added to the report."

"What'd you make of this Mainwaring character?"

"Honest opinion?"

"Of course."

"He's a smarmy, self-satisfied git. More worried about the loss of his stock and damage to the shop than the injury to his colleagues."

Bill Harrap tapped on the glass partition and waved a gloved hand. "All finished, Mr Jones. I'll start packing up now."

"Thanks, Bill," Jones called. "Need a hand with your equipment?"

"That'd be good. It'd save me a couple of trips to the car."

"Charlie?" Jones nodded his head towards the shop.

Pelham hesitated, frowned, and said, "Oh, yeah. Right. I'm on it, boss."

"After that, take a lead on the canvassing. I want a report and all the CCTV footage you can find by close of play."

Pelham chewed at his lower lip and hesitated again before hurrying out of the office and entering the shop area where he grabbed a couple of small boxes. "Where you parked, Bill?"

"Follow me, mate," Harrap called, "but don't hurt your back or nothing."

Jones followed Pelham, picked up a heavy lighting unit, taking care not to singe his hair on the crinkling-hot halogen lamp—he'd done the same thing often enough in the past—and carried it through to the SOCO's Range Rover. He passed it to an empty-handed Pelham, who staggered under the weight.

Ryan and Vic Doland stood near the canvas screen, talking quietly. Jones joined them.

"Afternoon Victor, mind if I borrow young Ryan for a moment?"

Doland grinned. "So long as I can have him back later, undamaged and fully house trained, Chief Inspector."

"Can't promise the potty training."

"Very funny, boss," Ryan said, showing a gentle scowl.

"Which one's Mainwaring?"

Wash pointed to a car parked behind one of the patrol vehicles. "Arrogant sod in the Spyder. Like me to introduce you?"

"Why not? Let's see what he says now he's had time to stew in the sun for a while."

Before they reached the sports car, Mainwaring jumped out and waited for them, tapping his foot on the tarmac.

"'Bout bloody time," he shouted, chest pumped out, nostrils

flared as though he could smell the shop from where he stood in the open air. "I've been here ages waiting for you lot to let me in. What's taking so long? I have a business to run."

Ryan shot Jones a quick glance before answering.

"Excuse me, Mr Mainwaring. Won't be too much longer. This is Detective Chief Inspector Jones. He's taken over the investigation."

Mainwaring, three inches taller than Jones, tried to intimidate him by leaning close. Jones gave no ground, but cast his eyes slowly over the man, head to toe and back again. He took in the hand-made leather loafers, the smart lightweight suit trousers, and the cream coloured silk shirt and tie. The man dressed to impress, but should have worn a jacket to hide the dark sweat patches under his arms.

"You're in charge of this shambles, Jones?"

"Good afternoon, sir. Please follow me."

"Where to?"

"I'd like a little chat in private, if you don't mind. It'll be cooler in the back office. Mind how you go on the blood. It can be a little slippery."

Chapter Thirty

Digbeth, Birmingham

JONES CHECKED the reflection in the shop windows to make sure Mainwaring followed and stopped inside the doorway to allow him to lead the way through the shop.

Mainwaring didn't hesitate, rubberneck, or wrinkle his nose against the pungent tang of stale blood, but hopped athletically over the largest puddle, and made his way through the gap in the service counter. He entered the back room, where he took the seat behind the desk and signalled, rather grandly, for Jones to take the other.

Jones stood with his arms folded. He said nothing and waited. Ryan stood in the doorway, silent.

Mainwaring grew restless. He turned his head to stare through the glass and into the shop.

"Horrible," he muttered.

"What is, sir?" Jones asked.

"The mess. Poor Freddie. Losing a hand. Must have been a terrifying ordeal."

"And who might Freddie be, sir?"

"Colonel Frederick Winterbourne, Freddie, the company's MD and CSO."

"CSO?"

"Chief Security Officer. Really, Chief Inspector, I've already explained this to your juniors. Don't you people talk to each other?"

"Forgive me, Mr Mainwaring. I've just arrived and was keen to give you access to the site as soon as possible."

Mainwaring leaned back and stared down his nose at Jones.

"Ah, well. In that case, good. Finally a man who understands commerce."

"I do try, sir." Jones resorted to deadpan, and kept his tone flat. "You were saying about your boss, Freddie?"

"Yes. I don't know how he's going to cope, poor man. Will he recover, d'you think? To lose a hand at his age, and with a hacksaw." He shook his head. "Absolutely too awful to contemplate. How could anybody do such a thing? Gosh, I have no idea what he must be going through."

Jones pursed his lips and studied the man for a moment before speaking. "As I understand it, sir, he's in surgery and will be for many more hours. I hope to interview him as soon as he regains consciousness from the anaesthetic."

"Good God, man, do you have to?" Mainwaring plucked a ball-point pen from a caddy on the desk, and started to twiddle it between finger and thumb. "Can't it wait until he's had a chance to recover a little? I mean, he'll take some time to recuperate at his age. I wouldn't want you to hamper his healing process. He'll be morti-fied when he realises what he's lost. His handicap will suffer, for a start."

"Handicap? You think he'll be worried about his golf swing?"

"Yes, Detective Chief Inspector. He plays off three, don't you know. Captain of his golf club these past five years. Very proud of his achievement. No idea what he'll do if he can't play a round at the weekends."

Jones glanced at Ryan, whose disbelief showed in his curled upper lip and barely perceptible headshake.

"A terrible shock for the Colonel and his family, I'm sure," Jones said. "Have you had a chance to talk with Mrs Winterbourne, sir?"

Mainwaring's eyes shifted from Jones to Wash and back again. "No. Eleanor, I mean, Mrs Winterbourne's not answering her mobile. She might still be at her country club. They have a strict no mobile phones policy in the treatment suite. I sent one of my staff around to speak to her in person. Didn't think this sort of information should come over the club's intercom."

"Quite so. Very sensitive of you, sir." Jones rubbed his hands together. "Well, sir, that's all I need from you for the moment. Please carry on. Oh, and I'd appreciate an inventory of the missing stock and an insurance valuation as soon as you can provide one. Detective Constable Washington, let's leave this good man to carry on with his work, shall we? Mustn't stand in the way of commerce."

Jones turned and signalled for Ryan to leave ahead of him.

"Chief Inspector?"

Jones stopped and looked behind him. "Yes, sir?"

"What about the mess in there? Who's going to clean it up?"

Cheeky bugger.

Jones smiled when he wanted to jab the officious git in the eye with the ballpoint he still twiddled between his manicured fingers.

"You'll find a list of specialist cleaning firms in the Yellow Pages or on the Internet. I'm sure your insurance company will cover the cost. Good day to you, sir."

He ushered Ryan through the door before self-control deserted him. Once outside, he found a position where Mainwaring couldn't see them.

"You're right Wash. He is an arrogant arsehole. And I'll bet this month's salary he's a jewel thief too."

"What? Are you serious?"

"Deadly," Jones said, and pointed at Ryan's tablet. "You can search the Internet on that thing, right? I mean, you have a signal here?"

"Yes, boss. What are you looking for?"

"Can you find a photo of Colonel and Mrs Winterbourne? There's bound to be one online somewhere. If there's no photo of them on the *Green & Sons* website, there'll be one from the golf club. I've never known a golf club captain to shy away from anything that looks like publicity."

"Gut feeling, or have you twigged something, boss?" Ryan asked, without looking up from the tablet screen.

"Bit of both, Ryan. How's that search going?"

Ryan smiled at the screen, his baby.

"Didn't take long. The Chronicle's running a big story tonight and has a photo of Mr and Mrs Winterbourne. And you're right, it's a shot of last year's end of season award ceremony at the Harbairn Golf and Country Club. Wanna look?"

"No, no. Let me guess. The Colonel's in his mid- to late-sixties, grey-haired, but distinguished and tanned after all that golf. Mrs Winterbourne, Eleanor, is much younger with fading glamour model looks. How close am I?"

"Bang on, both counts. How d'you know? Have you seen the photo before?"

"Nope," Jones answered. "Think about it, Wash. You saw what I saw."

"Hell boss, I don't know, unless …" A light came on behind the young detective's eyes. "The blood."

Jones grinned. "What about the blood?"

He loved it when junior officers had the nous to work things out for themselves. He also enjoyed being proved right when he selected Wash for the SCU ahead of dozens of other, more experienced applicants.

"It didn't faze Mainwaring, did it?"

"Go on." Jones nodded encouragement.

"Most civilians would puke at all that gore, wrinkle their nose up at the very least, but Mainwaring didn't bat an eye. In fact, he only mentioned it when you stood over him in the office. Either he's a cold fish, or he's used to seeing the red stuff. Reckon he's ex-military, or a butcher?"

"Could be, but there's more to it."

"What else have I missed?"

"You're friends with Manda Cryer, and Alex's wife, Julie. You've met Charlie's wife too, right?"

Ryan frowned. "Of course, but I don't see what you're getting at."

"Any idea where they are right now? Or would you know what gym they use, if any?"

Ryan turned away and searched the road for Pelham, talking to a tall woman who carried a shopping bag. They were facing the crime scene and Pelham jotted notes on a clipboard.

"Charlie's wife in a gym? Are you serious?" Ryan grinned. "But I take your point. I wouldn't have a clue where Manda is right now. Julie neither."

"Yet Mainwaring knows the Colonel's wife well enough to tell us why he can't reach her."

"You reckon Mainwaring and the boss' wife are doing the nasty? Yeah, he strikes me as the sort to play around. But it's a bit circumstantial."

"Agreed, and it comes under the heading, interesting, not suspicious," Jones said.

"But you've got more, right boss?"

Jones pointed to the tablet.

"Any mention of a hacksaw in the article? Or anywhere else in the public domain?"

"Hang on a sec. I'll expand the search." He swiped the screen a couple of times before lowering it and tapping his temple with an index finger. "Bloody hell. I'm an idiot. How did Mainwaring know about the hacksaw?"

"That's what I was wondering. Did either you or Charlie mention it during your earlier interview?"

Ryan looked up at the sky as if for inspiration before shaking his head.

"No, I was with Charlie from the moment Mainwaring arrived and started throwing his weight around. Neither of us said one word about a hacksaw. And Bill Harrap had already boxed it up by the time Mainwaring arrived. No way he could have seen it."

"So how'd Mainwaring learn that particular detail?"

"He's been alone in his car for a while. Could've phoned the hospital I suppose."

Jones shook his head. "They might have mentioned microsurgery and the hand, but the hacksaw? Doubt it. Not over the phone and definitely not to a non-relative."

"Good point. Want me to call Queen Elizabeth's? See whether Mainwaring's checked in on his boss."

"Please, and carry on with your internet search. I'll have a quick word with Charlie. I think we might be able to use his relationship with the local media."

"What's your plan, boss?"

Jones scratched his chin. He needed a shave.

"Don't have one yet Ryan, but I'm working on it. Keep searching. I'll be back in a mo."

Jones took a few paces towards Pelham before the detective noticed his approach. He signalled for Pelham to join him and Ryan, and returned to Ryan's side, making sure Mainwaring still couldn't see them through the shop window.

Pelham's shoulders slouched and he made heavy weather of his approach. A crowd of sightseers blocked the pavement and he had to step into the road to pass them. Jones beckoned him again and Pelham increased his pace.

"Yes, boss?" he called when still ten metres away.

Jones raised a finger to his lips and then pointed at the canvas barrier hiding most of the *Green & Sons'* shop front. Pelham's reluctant frown became one of inquisition.

"What's up?" he asked when the three of them were close enough to talk quietly yet still hear each other above the din of gawkers and the rumble of traffic.

"When you spoke to Wilson—"

"Boss, I gave you my reasons for that and I apologised. Are you still gonna give me a hard time?"

"Shut up and listen, man," Jones barked. "Did you tell Wilson about the hacksaw?"

Pelham gave him a pained look.

"Course not. What d'you take me for? I'd never release that sort of detail. Why?"

Jones explained his suspicions, in part to enlighten Pelham, and in part to work through any gaps in his logic. When he'd finished, Pelham asked to see the photograph of the Colonel and his wife. He took the tablet from Wash and studied it for a full minute before speaking.

"Wash, what year did Mainwaring say the Colonel married the heiress to the *Green & Sons* fortune? 1989, weren't it?"

"That's right, '89. Why?"

"Well, look at this picture of Eleanor Winterbourne. How old she look to you?"

"Dunno, difficult to say. Mid-thirties?"

Jones looked at the photo for the first time. His wild-arsed guess hadn't been far off. The young Mrs Winterbourne, blonde, blue-eyed, pocket supermodel looks, couldn't have been older than about forty unless the photographer's airbrush had worked a particular magic.

"If she's forty now," Jones said, "she'd only have been in her teens in 1989."

Pelham shook his head.

"Nah. She ain't forty. No bloody way."

"Ryan, check the DVLA. Let's see what her driving licence says."

Pelham smiled. "I see what you're getting at. You reckon the first Mrs Winterbourne pegged it and the horny old Colonel bagged himself a trophy wife. She gets tired of screwing a wrinkly, and makes eyes at the smarmy git in the flash Audi. They play hide the chipolata while Colonel Blimp plays golf of a Sunday morning."

"Keep going, Charlie," Jones said. "You have such a wonderful turn of phrase," he added dryly.

"Yeah. The evil sod, Mainwaring, was laughing at us. Wouldn't surprise me if he didn't hack the poor bugger's hand off himself. Oh fuck!" Pelham half-turned and raised his face to the sky.

"What's wrong, Charlie?"

"Just remembered. It were Mainwaring who first mentioned the

JT1 Crew. He fed me the bait and I swallowed the fucking hook. The bastard."

"Boss," Wash said, interrupting Pelham's verbal self-flagellation. "Eleanor Winterbourne is thirty-six. In 1989, she'd have been in primary school."

Pelham punched his left palm with his right first. "Right, let's go arrest Mr Smartarse, shall we?"

"On what charge?" Jones asked. "Sleeping with the boss' wife? It may be morally wrong, but it's hardly illegal. And we're only guessing about that."

"Why don't you let me sweat it out the bastard?" Pelham asked. "Prissy little arsewipe won't last long in an interview room."

Jones shook his head emphatically.

"No, that won't work. He'll hire an expensive lawyer and give us nothing but 'no comment'. I want him caught with the Colonel's attaché case in his manicured mitt. I've a better idea."

"What's that?"

"We'll use your friend in the local press."

Jones stared at the gleaming black Audi and remembered the haughty, silk-shirted Regional Director leaning against the windscreen.

I'm coming for you, Mainwaring.

Chapter Thirty-One

WEDNESDAY 6TH JULY – *Sean Freeman*
The City, London

THE FOUR SHORT months since Edinburgh had fried Freeman's brains. So much had happened, he didn't know whether to throw himself from Blackfriars Bridge, buy a machinegun and take his chances at *Parrish Enterprises Ltd*, or join the French Foreign Legion.

Week after week, Parrish had piled on the pressure, ordering so many "off book" jobs that Freeman found it almost impossible to maintain a professional detachment. Parrish slowly, inexorably, dragged him into the darker, messier jobs. After Edinburgh, he'd had no option. The only thing keeping him sane—his light shining in the dark—lived a seven-hour drive away. Too bloody far away, but at least he'd found someone with whom he could spend time— maybe the rest of his life.

Pack it in, you soppy bugger. Now's not the time.

The pressure mounted on all sides.

Adamovic rarely left him alone, and every time Hutch looked sideways at him—which was often—he salivated like a predator waiting for its latest prey to present itself, to expose his throat. Freeman needed a way out before Parrish decided he'd outlived his usefulness.

His exit strategy, developed before he'd even met Parrish, was set and ready to initiate, missed one vital ingredient.

Freeman found it, or at least thought he had, while watching a police press conference on the BBC News Channel. The missing component appeared in the middle-aged and most unlikely form of DCI David Jones, a slim almost gaunt man with wavy grey hair, a soft West Midlands accent, and intelligent eyes. Freeman wouldn't know for sure until Corky came back with the deep dive information. Trouble was, the little internet goblin still hadn't turned up with the goods yet.

In the six hours since he'd first seen the *Green & Sons'* press conference, with its continual references to the so-called "JT1 Crew", Freeman hadn't been able to sit still. For the first time ever, Corky had let him down. A task that should have taken his go-to man no more than a couple of hours, had dragged into the night.

The "contract" had started well enough.

As usual, the self-proclaimed "*World's greatest information acquisition specialist*" had responded to his call instantly, and, when he did, Freeman nearly fell out of his chair. Clean-shaven, and with neatly trimmed hair, Corky had never been so presentable. Only the multiple earrings spoiled the new image.

"Bloody hell, Corky. Going to a wedding?"

Corky's embarrassed smile and reddening cheeks told Freeman his wild-arsed guess hadn't been that far off. Corky's next words struck Freeman dumb for a moment.

"Corky's got a date in a couple hours."

"Jeez, mate," he managed, eventually. "Who is he and when am I going to meet him?"

"Whatcha mean 'he'? It's a woman. A real live woman. Beautiful she is, too. So stop taking the piss or Corky won't be answering your calls no more."

Freeman continued smiling but let the matter drop and placed his request.

Before Corky signed off, he did something that tilted Freeman's world even further; he waved and said, "Laters."

Freeman's response, "Who are you and what have you done with the real Corky?" landed on a blank screen.

Unable to sit at his favourite spot on the balcony due to the howling wind and rain pulsing in from the direction of the estuary, Freeman paced his lounge and shot dark looks at his silent laptop each time he turned at the end of a length.

"Come on, Corky. What the bloody hell's taking so long?"

The digital clock on his mobile ticked away the minutes with stultifying, mind-numbing pace. 01:16.

After four hours, Corky still hadn't called.

A bowl of muesli tasted of cardboard, the hot and sweet coffee did nothing to improve his mood, and the regular news bulletins had pared the *Butchery in Birmingham* item to a two-minute review. DCI Jones' appearance barely made it past the editor's shears.

The digital age came to Freeman's rescue; he found an uncut version of the press conference on the Net, and watched it three times while waiting for Corky's report.

Something about Jones' behaviour on the podium and his responses to the hail of questions hadn't felt right. Uncomfortable in front of the cameras, the DCI wasn't the smooth mouthpiece the police would normally drag out to allay public fears. That role belonged to the chesty blonde at Jones' side, Veronica Poole. She scowled each time the middle-aged cop refused to confirm that their prime suspects were indeed the "notorious JT1 Crew", which one young journo in a cloth cap and tartan sports jacket insisted on calling, "Diamond Geezers".

The moment Freeman heard about the *Green & Sons* robbery, his immediate thoughts turned to Parrish. Had the runt-sized psychopath carried out one of his lowbrow smash and grab efforts? A five-minute read of the *Green & Sons* website knocked that idea on the head. The regional jewellery chain was nothing but a down-market retailer selling cheap tat to the masses. Parrish wouldn't have wasted his sweat on the rubbish they sold.

The information generated a question.

If Freeman had ruled out Parrish, and, by default, the JT1 Crew so easily, why hadn't DCI Jones and the West Midlands Police done the same thing? The veteran cop didn't look stupid. How many stupid people reached and maintained the rank of Detective Chief Inspector these days?

No, Jones had something else on his mind and Freeman's inquisitive nature wanted the answer.

He poured yet another mug of rich-roast and walked it to the lounge. The laptop bleeped.

About bloody time.

He hit "receive" and a frowning Corky appeared on the screen. Sun beat through the windows behind him. Where was his base of operations these days, Australia? Or was the well-lit backdrop a computer-generated special effect? With Corky, nobody could ever tell.

"What's up, mate? Did she dump you already?"

Corky's frown deepened. "Shut the hell up. Corky missed his date thanks to your DCI-freaking-Jones."

Freeman jerked. A drop of coffee spilled onto the laminate floor. His senses started tingling.

"What d'you say?"

"DCI David Jones is the modern equivalent of a chuffin' ghost."

"Really? Can't you find anything on him?"

"Nah, it's not that. I got all the usual stuff; police personnel file, commendations, arrest record. That's the biggest part of the file, by the way. The man's put away loads of nasty beggars in his time. Had a hand in closing the West Midlands Serious Crime Squad back in the nineties, too. Wouldn't mess with him if you know what's best for you, mate."

"No intentions of it. Looks like you've found plenty, so what's the problem?"

Corky grimaced into the lens and gave a strong impression of a man suffering acute constipation.

"It's more what Corky ain't found. Got his home address, the bank account they send his payroll to, the garage what works on his car, inside leg measurement, but …" He sighed and shook his head.

"Don't keep me waiting, Corky. What's the 'but'?"

"This particular Dibble don't have an electronic footprint. Least not one Corky can find. The bloke don't go online, don't use his work mobile for nothing other than phone calls even though the thing's Internet enabled. Far as Corky can tell, he don't have a personal mobile, rarely accesses his work emails, and when he does, his typing speed's the same as a fruit bat. He don't have a computer or a Wi-Fi connection at home. Don't bank online neither."

Freeman nodded.

"So, our DCI's a Luddite?"

"Might agree with you, if Corky knew what a Luddite was," Corky said, adding a grim smile. "Don't know what you have in mind for him, mate, but Corky wouldn't trust a guy he couldn't follow online."

Freeman took his turn to frown.

"What's your impression? Is he bent? As a cop, I mean."

Behind the blue-tinted lenses, Corky's eyes widened.

"God no. The bugger's as clean as any Dibble Corky's ever researched. Never had as much as a parking ticket. Don't have that many citizen complaints against him neither. Much lower than the national police average. In fact, the geezer's so clean he probably squeaks. He lives well within his means, and that can't be easy. Have you seen what they pay DCIs in the UK? Sixty grand a year for all them hours he works. Criminal."

"You'll keep digging though?"

Corky nodded. "Of course Corky's gonna keep diggin', but only after he's apologised to Bryony for blowing her off. It'll cost Corky big time in grovelling, but she's worth it."

"Thanks mate, I owe you."

"Yeah, too right you bloody do," he said, and dropped the connection, ending the longest conversation they'd had since a face-to-face meet when they buried Corky's mother.

He stared at the blank screen, weighing up his options before breaking protocol and printing the Jones file—all eighty-four close-typed pages of it.

While reading, his excitement rose.

He read the report twice before passing it through the shredder and burning the little strips of paper in the kitchen sink.

As Corky had said, DCI David Aaron Jones did appear to be an honest cop. Was Jones the one? Was Jones the missing component?

He moved on to the next step of his nocturnal investigation. No point in trying to get to sleep, it was far too late, and he had no time to waste.

The laptop came in handy again. Apart from the special video-conferencing portal, Corky had installed a number of other bespoke and highly effective applications. Freeman opened one and spent an hour and a half scouring the West Midlands Police Service sector of the Police National Computer.

Once finished, he scrubbed the laptop's hard drive with a high-powered magnet; Corky and he had an old school method of staying in touch involving snail mail and a one-time-only cipher.

The results of his PNC research had been promising, but he needed certainty. Sending the message to DCI Barrow hadn't worked, would Jones prove more intelligent?

Just how bright are you DCI Jones?

He needed a test. Two minutes were long enough to come up with an idea, but building the device in the workshop he'd created in one of the spare bedrooms took a little longer.

As the sun brightened the eastern skyline, he made the most important decision of his life so far.

Go for it.

He placed two phone calls. During the first, made on his land-line, he left a cryptic message on Parrish's voicemail. "Off to Birmingham. Museum visit. Back tomorrow." Parrish would understand what it meant.

The second call, made on his burner phone, was to a very special woman living north of the border. He left another message. Angela wasn't a morning person. He'd catch her later.

After a swift change into motorcycle leathers, he double-locked the door to his flat and headed to the basement garage. The big black Triumph, a recent—and very fast—addition to his lifestyle, stood waiting.

Chapter Thirty-Two

WEDNESDAY 6TH JULY – *Early morning*
Holton, Birmingham

JONES STARED through his office window and took in the dark, grey morning. The forecasted thunderstorm had shattered the mini heatwave. He'd beaten the deluge by seconds and inwardly thanked his eternal insomnia for forcing him into work early.

The elation that always accompanied the successful completion of a case had yet to fade. Nothing could dampen his mood, not even the weather or the drive to work in the borrowed BMW.

Jones' mind turned to the regular dance he had with Sam Tallon, a man he'd known since buying his beloved Rover from new, back in the mid-80s. It was the same every time he took the old dear in for its ever-more expensive and exhaustive annual service.

Tallon, a magician with a socket wrench, would spend thirty-minutes tutting and sighing and trying to convince him to sell the "museum piece" and buy a new car.

"This was state of the art when I sold it to you, Mr Jones, but you

226

just can't get the parts these days." … "This thing went out when Noah first put up his umbrella." … "It's no wonder Rover went out of business. Get yourself a nice new BMW, Mr Jones. They're much less hassle. Easy to work on too, if they ever go wrong, which is rarely."

Tallon would usually follow the remarks with a gap-toothed grin and end up diving under the bonnet to say he'd finish the work by the end of the day. Jones would take the courtesy car, almost always a spanking new BMW, and hate every mile he drove in it on principal.

They'd been playing the game for years, but Jones loved his old Rover, and hated the idea of change. Always had.

Outside his office window, the lashing rain, driven at forty-five degrees from the vertical by the gusting wind, and hammering into the car park below in watery explosions, didn't matter. He still smiled.

Sheet lightning lit the sky twice and the office lights flickered before holding firm. He considered belting out a chorus of *Oh What a Beautiful Morning*, but decided the night shift might take offence and call for a policeman.

Oh dear, Jones. Cut it out.

He faced the room, sipped his tea, and soaked in the quiet, taking a moment's pause before plunging into the day. He placed his mug on the coaster he'd bought on his single, heart-breaking trip to Australia in '97, but even that memory, and the years of guilt he'd lived with since, couldn't kill the mood completely.

The mess on Phil's desk caught his eye. Unable to stop himself, Jones hurried over, straightened the pile of files, and dropped the ballpoint pen into the desk caddy. Phil tried his best to keep their shared office as neat as Jones would like it, but he didn't seem to notice the chaos he left behind.

He returned to his side of the office, the tidy side, sat behind his pristine desk, and stared at the buff-coloured folder he'd collected from the reception desk on his way in. It contained the interim report from Section 14, West Midlands Police Service's covert surveillance unit—the "obbo" team. He already knew what the file contained, but, as lead investigator, he needed to read and sign it for the record.

He grinned again.

Rarely had a plan worked so well.

The previous night's national evening news, and all the bulletins since, had led with the *Green & Sons* robbery. The bloodletting had lent a salacious edge to the story, guaranteeing it top spot. Each news channel attributed the bloody crime to the JT1 Crew, and quoted "sources close to the police investigation", which of course, meant Charlie Pelham. The story also included a brief review of all the crimes attributed to the gang dating back more than eighteen months.

The story broke so early into the investigation that the Deputy Chief Constable and Veronica "Ronnie" Poole, the West Midlands Police Press Officer, a perennially harassed-looking civilian, had to arrange a hurried press conference. Before the briefing, which Ronnie insisted Jones attend, she'd pulled him to one side and given him the evil eye. She demanded to know why he'd usurped her authority by talking to the press, which went contrary to standard operating procedure, and "Pissed off the DCC, big fucking time." Off camera, the petite and photogenic blonde wasn't averse to using a colourful turn of phrase. Jones found it off-putting. To him, the unnecessary use of foul language was the reserve of the young, and the poorly educated.

Jones had allowed Ronnie to rant away, taking full responsibility for Pelham's so-called blunder. He ate the humble pie—the taste of which he usually hated, but managed to stomach on this occasion. Her reaction would be even worse once she discovered he'd used the press leak as a ploy to flush out Mainwaring, but he could live with the woman's future anger.

As the most senior police officer present at the conference, Jones had faced the bulk of the inquisition. He mumbled a few hackneyed phrases, but avoided the "no stone unturned" and "heinous crime" clichés. He sidestepped each mention of the JT1 Crew and its growing crime spree—he'd never let anyone catch him in a delib-erate lie—but did agree that "certain aspects" of the crime led his investigation in a "particular direction". Old Luke Wilson had been there trying to coin his "Diamond Geezers" tagline, but nobody else took up the baton.

One bright spark in the back row asked whether Jones had called on the NCA for assistance. "Not yet," he answered, and stepped from the podium to an artillery salvo of flashing lights and yelled questions, leaving the diminutive but photogenic Ronnie to handle the wrap up alone.

Digital and local news channels carried the press conference live, while the terrestrial and national stations repeated an edited version throughout the night. The morning press led with gory headlines. Jones' particular favourite, *Butchery in Birmingham*, actually made him cringe.

Well before the madness, and before he left Digbeth, Jones had tasked the obbo unit—supervised by a fired-up Charlie Pelham—to follow Mainwaring everywhere he went. Before Jones left *Green & Sons* for his appointment with Ronnie, he'd offered two-to-one odds to Pelham and Wash against the surveillance operation lasting beyond midnight. Neither took his bet.

Jones reached for the obbo report and the accompanying still photos, and started reading. This part of the paperwork trail, he loved. He skimmed through the file header details and homed in on the good stuff:

18:23 - MR RODNEY MAINWARING, *Regional Director of Green & Sons (Sub#1), delivers audit and estimated losses to DS Pelham outside the shop.*

18:26 - Sub#1 secures the premises, drives to Queen Elizabeth Hospital— no stops. Spends twenty-three minutes apparently comforting a woman later iden-tified as Mrs Eleanor Winterbourne (Sub#2).

Colonel Winterbourne is still in surgery. Mr Albrecht, the shop manager, still unconscious.

18:49 - Sub#1 leaves Queen Elizabeth's hospital and drives directly to his home outside Tamworth, half an hour northeast of Birmingham. Keeps to all speed limits, obeys all road signs.

19:33 - Arrives home, parks car in driveway, facing out.

JONES PRÉCISED the next part of the report. The obbo team used a parabolic microphone and picked up Mainwaring's laughter as he watched Jones' apparent discomfort during the press conference. Jones particularly enjoyed that part.

20:20 - SUB#1 *makes phone call.*

A NOTE in the report's margin read, "*No phone tap in place. A transcript of Sub#1's side of the conversation is being prepared.*"

20:25 - SUB#1 *leaves house. Meets a man (Sub#3), later identified as Sub#1's younger brother, Rupert Mainwaring, in the Warwickshire Arms public house, five minutes from his home.*

THE REST of the account followed in the same vein, but Jones loved every word.

The report covered the following two hours in minute detail. The upshot was that two members of the surveillance team, posing as a married couple, followed the Mainwaring brothers into the pub and worked their way close enough to eavesdrop on an increasingly celebratory discussion. It included much backslapping and ribaldry.

At eleven o'clock, the worse for five pints of beer and whisky chasers each, the brothers poured out of the pub. Charlie Pelham ordered their arrest immediately after Rupert handed Rodney a silver attaché case he'd taken from the boot of his car, a late model Renault Megane. Rupert tried to run, but Ryan downed him with a rugby-style ankle tap. Jones would love to have seen it, but the incident occurred out of shot of the surveillance camera. No doubt,

Ryan would describe it in infinite detail when he arrived at work in an hour or so.

During his brother's abortive escape attempt, Rodney Mainwaring tried to bluster his way out of what he thought was a drink driving charge, unwilling or unable to believe he'd been the victim of a police sting.

Jones wished he could have been there in person to see the expression on Rodney Mainwaring's supercilious face, but had to make do with the recorded images. He did have the pleasure of being present when Pelham and Ryan—the new Dynamic Duo—booked the brothers and locked them in separate holding cells to marinate overnight. Neither man would be interrogated until they had sobered up, giving the team plenty of opportunity to move the investigation forward.

A locksmith contracted to the West Midlands Police opened the attaché case in the forensics lab, watched by the team, Bill Harrap, and Patrick Elliot. They found the Colonel's complete inventory of goods, all one-hundred-and-thirty-three-thousand pounds worth of it. Another sack in the boot of the Megane contained the sundry items taken from the shop's cabinets and a pair of Mickey Mouse facemasks.

To cap everything off, blood spatter on the attaché case matched blood from the scene, and the hospital sample taken from Colonel Winterbourne. The evidence against the Mainwaring brothers was as strong as any case Jones had seen in years. They didn't need a confession, but Jones expected one from the terrified and babbling Rupert, who seemed the brother more likely to break under questioning. As Bill Harrap announced at a little after two o'clock in the morning, "Job's a ripper."

As for Eleanor Winterbourne, she left the hospital at eleven o'clock and a second team tailed her to the family home, Green Mansion. She spent the night dialling the elder Mainwaring's phone number. They would deal with her later, but Jones gave Section 14 instructions to arrest her the moment she made any move to abscond. She could visit the hospital only, but if she headed anywhere else, the second obbo team would pounce.

Jones finished reading the report, initialled each page, and signed and dated the table at the foot of the top sheet. He placed the file in the first "out" tray and released a contented sigh. He'd promised Pelham and Ryan first shot at interviewing young Rupert, but that wouldn't happen for an hour or so. They'd leave Rodney to stew for a little while longer.

With time to kill before the team's arrival and the start of the interrogations, Jones' mind began to wander. A list of 'what ifs' built in his head. He took a pad from his top drawer and jotted notes.

1. *What if the Colonel doesn't survive surgery?*
2. *Up the charges to murder*
3. *Play young Rupert off against Rodney*
4. *Is Eleanor guilty of nothing more than adultery?*
5. *Unlikely, but keep an open mind*
6. *Confirm her alibi for the time of the robbery—she may have been driving the getaway car, (fanciful—Corrine Chambers didn't mention a third robber)*
7. *Was the Colonel in on the robbery and did Mainwaring double-cross him, leaving him for dead in the expectations of taking both the wife and control of the company?*
8. *Why would the Colonel steal stock from his own company?*
9. *Insurance fraud?*
10. *Check the state of the company's finances*
11. *Why did the Colonel schlep around town with a briefcase full of stock?*
12. *Check how many times he's done this before*
13. *If first time—suspicious*
14. *Did the Colonel have adequate insurance cover to use the attaché case?*
15. *Talk to the company accountant and insurance broker*
16. *Check the company's insurance contract*
17. *Was the company over-insured?*
18. *Phone robbery division for an independent valuation of the stolen goods*

19. *Confirm Mainwaring's valuation*
20. *Stock control? Is that an issue?*
21. *Are the stolen jewels real?*
22. *Is the company viable?*
23. *The Digbeth shop looked rundown—is it profitable?*
24. *Search for any criminal reports related to Green & Sons*

JONES MADE a few more comments and noted the number of times he'd written the word "insurance" and "broker", but, no matter how long he stared at the pages, answers wouldn't come. He'd pass the notes to Pelham and Ryan for their follow-up investigations and see whether they couldn't fill in some of the blanks.

With nothing better to do until the team arrived, Jones stared at the stack of files filling his "in" tray. The dark green ones at the top of the pile drew his interest. Their colour set them apart from the others and designated them as external memos and files. He pulled out the first one and read the label, handwritten by Phil: *Notification #5/JT1/July, National Crime Agency.*

Jones' senses tingled. This had to be some kind of karma. He'd used the JT1 Crew to help close the *Green & Sons* case. Maybe fate wanted him to learn more about them. He opened the three-inch thick file and started reading.

Chapter Thirty-Three

WEDNESDAY 6TH JULY – *Early morning*
Holton, Birmingham

AS JONES CONTINUED READING the NCA file on the JT1 Crew, the building slowly came to life around him, filling his head with loud conversation, banging doors, and stomping feet.

Why can't police officers walk quietly?

By the time Phil had hustled in, bedraggled, and hung his coat on the radiator behind the door, jones had made even more notes.

Rainwater dripping from Phil's coat turned the beige carpet below the coat hooks into a muddy brown. He stomped to his desk, dropped into his chair, swivelled to face his computer station, and hit the power button. The silence was angry and palpable.

"Morning, Philip."

The DS took a moment to reply.

"Morning, boss," he mumbled, without turning from the screen.

Jones tried again.

"Lovely day."

"Got soaked crossing the car park."

"It'll brighten up later. Fancy a coffee? I'm off on a canteen run."

C'mon Philip, that ought to do it.

Phil swivelled in his chair to face Jones, the slight furrow on his brow an ounce of muscle tension away from a full-blown scowl.

Any second now.

"Bloody hell, boss," he opened.

And here we go.

"I take one personal day, one day, and you close two huge cases! A double murder and an attempted murder. Makes me feel kind of redundant."

"First off, Alex won Alby Pope's confession. I had little to do with it."

"Yeah, right. I believe you. And second?"

"Oh yes. Things started motoring on the jewellery robbery and … well, you know how it goes." Jones opened his hands in apology. "Didn't have time to contact you until it was too late. Middle of the night by the time we wrapped it up."

"Never stopped you before. If I had a fiver for every time you woke me—"

"Hang on a minute. You told me yourself, Manda isn't sleeping well. It wasn't an emergency, and I decided to let you rest. Family comes first, right?"

That's got him.

"Yeah, well, fair enough, but imagine how I felt seeing you at that news conference last night. Manda asked why I wasn't up on the platform beside you. She asked whether I'd upset you. You should have given me a bell … Oh, never mind. What was that about a canteen run?"

"Yes. My shout. I imagine you want to know what happened?"

Phil stood and reached for his extra-large Aston Villa mug and made a "you're kidding" face.

"Don't be daft, boss. I read the PNC file before leaving home. Nice catch with the Mainwaring boys, by the way. I'm guessing it was you who thought of using the JT1 Crew as part of the scam after Charlie's cock up, right?"

Jones shrugged.

"Some things don't reach the PNC. So what did you think of my TV performance?" He reached for his jacket.

"Dreadful, but Ronnie was on fine form. Did she give you a bollocking for the press leak?"

"Tried to, but I can't take her seriously when she totters around on those four-inch heels. Your Manda gives me worse tongue-lashings when I don't finish my greens."

Phil broke out a rueful smile. "Tell me about it. You did let Ronnie know that Charlie spoke to the Chronicle without your permission, right?"

"And have that slip of a woman think I can't control my team? Not likely." Jones stabbed his pen into his desk caddy and stood.

"Did she teach you all those clichés? 'Diligent police work', 'acting on intelligence gathered at the scene', 'arrest imminent'. I mean, you were *so* embarrassing."

Phil mugged a grin during the final sentence.

"Right, Philip, for that performance review, I've changed my mind. You're buying breakfast. Oh, second thoughts, I'll still pay if you can help me with something."

Jones opened the office door and allowed his sergeant to leave first.

"What's that?"

"Tell me what you know about the workings of the UK business insurance sector." Jones closed and locked the office behind them. "I'll give you until the canteen to collect your thoughts."

"Don't need that long, boss," Phil said with all the smugness of the super-confident, and led the way along the corridor toward the lifts and the stairwell.

Jones' grin widened—it was great to have his "Memory Man" back on-side.

"By the way, Manda says you're looking far too peaky these days. Reckons it's down to lack of sleep and not having a good woman to take care of you." His eyes widened as Jones took in a sharp breath in preparation of delivering a mild rebuke. "Hang on, boss. Before you jump down my throat, don't shoot the messenger."

"Please tell Mrs Cryer to mind her own …" Jones shook his head. "Strike that. Tell Manda thanks very much for caring, but I'm fine, and looking forward to her next invite. I haven't seen Jamie for ages. She'll forget about me before too long."

"What? Jamie forget her Uncle David?" Phil shook his head. "Villa's gonna win the title before that happens."

At the end of the corridor, Jones pushed through the fire doors and took the stairs. Phil pressed the call button and waited for the lift.

———

SAFELY INSTALLED at their customary table near the double doors overlooking the makeshift patio, Jones and Phil relaxed. The rain had slowed to a light drizzle and even though the garden tables and chairs ran with water, three sad souls took advantage of the only place set aside for smokers. They sat, huddled under a dripping sun umbrella. Blue smoke hung in a cloud around their heads, the lee of the building preventing any air movement and subsequent smoke dispersal.

Jones nodded at them. "They look like they're having fun. The joys of smoking, eh?"

Phil glanced at the group. A faraway light softened the focus in his eyes. "Filthy habit. Manda made me give up as the price for us dating. A price worth paying, I might add. Don't have any vices these days, apart from food."

He put the huge mug of coffee down on the table and vacuumed up the doughnut—iced and with coloured sprinkles—while Jones stared in awe at the man's appetite. Manda would have provided a solid breakfast before he left for work and less than one hour later, he was vacuuming up almost as many calories as Jones consumed in the average day.

"Enjoy that?"

Phil smacked his lips and wiped them with a paper napkin before crumpling it into a ball and tossing it, basketball like, into a nearby bin. It swished in without touching the rim. "Sure did. Have to take my opportunities. In this job, we never know when we'll be able to snatch a bite."

"Better watch out or we'll have a second Charlie Pelham on the team." Jones stared at Phil's stomach.

"Ouch. That wasn't nice."

"Payback for the televised clichés snub."

"I was joking."

"I wasn't."

Jones took his turn to wink and stole another sip of tea while waiting for Phil to recover from the jibe.

"Now you've finished your second breakfast," he said, "enthral me with the complexities of the UK insurance business. I'll try not to yawn."

"And then you'll tell me why you're interested?"

"You haven't guessed?" Jones asked.

"Judging by the colour of the file you were reading when I arrived, you're taking a real interest in the JT1 Crew."

"Bingo. I'll make a detective of you yet," Jones said. "Give me a few years, though. Right then, off you go."

Jones leaned back and prepared to be impressed.

Phil drained the Villa mug. "Basically, the insurance game is all down to spreading the risk. Initially, it works the same way as household insurance. You cover your potential losses with an insurance company who charges a premium. The moment the risk exceeds an individual insurance company's ability to cover the loss in comfort, they spread the risk by sub-contracting to a re-insurer. Usually, they go through reinsurance brokers, who act as sort of middlemen and take a commission for arranging the deal."

Jones pulled his earlobe.

"So, how's that work from a *Green & Sons* perspective?"

Phil paused for a moment before answering.

"They own and run nine shops in the Midlands and insure each shop for damage to buildings, third party liability, and lost, damaged, or stolen stock."

"Fair enough. They pay premiums for each shop, like I do with my home contents insurance?"

"Not quite. They'll have a group insurance and a total liability running into millions of pounds. Let's say someone targets *Green &* *Sons* and knocks over each shop at the same time, unlikely I know, but if that did happen, their insurance company would be liable for millions in pay-outs. That's when the re-insurers come into play. And these re-insurers spread the bets, depending on the size of the risk and their ability to cover it comfortably."

"And each time they share the load, someone has a finger in the pie, right?"

"Too right," Phil answered. "The original insurer pays a premium to the reinsurance company and a commission to the rein-surance broker for putting the two insurance companies together. Oh, by the way, this has nothing to do with the insured business, in this case, *Green & Sons.* They'll only deal with the first insurance company. But in the end, it's always the customers who shell out the coin."

"Okay, let's keep on topic." Jones interrupted. "You've read the NCA files on the JT1 Crew. Don't suppose you saw a link between the robberies and the insurance or reinsurance companies?"

"None."

"What about the brokers?"

"Nah," Phil answered, playing with the empty mug.

"None of the robberies involved the same jewellery companies, insurers, or re-insurers. The broking houses and reinsurance brokers are pretty diverse, too."

"Damn it, there has to be a connection somewhere. How and why is this gang targeting those particular businesses? How are they getting their information?"

"No idea," Phil said, eyeing the serving counter. Probably trying to decide whether to snaffle another pastry.

"Me neither, but the NCA found a link, so it has to be there somewhere."

"Why d'you keep mentioning the brokers?"

Jones tried to rub the stiffness out of his neck.

"Not sure, Phil. I read something this morning that stood out as weird. Can't explain it. Damned annoying. By the way, thanks for the printout."

"Only takes the push of a button, boss. You could learn to do it yourself."

"Yeah, well, thanks anyway. Wish I knew what the NCA had left out of their attachment. They're not telling us everything."

"Why don't you ask your mate, Superintendent Knightly? He owes you a favour or two."

Jones shook his head.

"Things don't work like that in real life. He'll probably say it's operationally sensitive and I don't need to know. It's not our case anyway. I'll think on it some more." He stood. "Come on, Detective Sergeant, time to start work. Charlie's going to be in soon and I want to brief him before he interviews the Mainwaring brothers."

Phil's eyes popped. "You're letting Charlie take the lead?"

"Why not? He was responsible for breaking the case."

"Unintentionally."

"Perhaps, but I might have been leaning on him a bit hard recently. I've seen him in the interview room a few times and he knows what he's doing. When he can be bothered. And young Ryan will be there to keep him in order."

"Shouldn't it be the other way around?"

"In an ideal world Phil, yes."

———

JONES LED Phil into the SCU briefing room to find that Ryan and Alex had already beaten them in.

"Any sign of Charlie?" Jones asked.

Ryan shook his head. "Sorry boss, not seen him yet."

Jones checked the wall clock: 08:20. No one really expected Pelham to arrive for ten minutes, but there was always a first time.

"Never mind, he can catch up. Let's get going. Alex, what's the state of play with Alby Pope?"

Before she could answer, Pelham ambled through the door. He had a carryout cup of coffee in one hand with the lid still in place, a folded newspaper under his arm, and wore a smug grin. Phil's expression, wide-eyed surprise, probably matched Jones' own—it was far too early for him to break out his poker face.

"Morning all," Pelham said. "Lovely day." He plopped down in his chair. "Just had an interesting chat with the Super." He paused, giving the information a chance to sink in.

"You did?" Jones asked.

"It ain't like that, boss. I weren't going over your head or nothing," Pelham said. "He buttonholed me on the way in. Wanted me to pass on a message."

He took the lid off his coffee and slurped.

"Which was?" Phil asked.

"He wanted to congratulate us on breaking the *Green & Sons* case so quick. The Chief Constable were cock-a-hoop."

"Excuse me, Charlie," Alex said. "Cock-a-hoop?"

Pelham's grin didn't falter. "Means he were overjoyed, Alex. The Chief thought we was the dog's bollo—"

"Okay, Charlie, we get the message," Jones interrupted.

"Jumping the gun a little, aren't you?" said Phil. "We haven't charged them yet."

Pelham shook his head. "Foregone conclusion, matey. Custody sergeant told me Rupert Mainwaring screamed through the night begging someone to take his statement. All the while, big brother, Rodney, was trying to calm him down from the next cell." He paused long enough to attack his drink again before adding, "Seems like poor little Rupert don't like small spaces."

Ryan stood.

"Where you going, DC Washington?" Pelham asked, eyes half closed.

"Thought we could read Rupert his rights."

Pelham waved him back to his seat.

"Another ten minutes won't matter. Rupert can simmer in his own juices for a little longer," he said, then spoke to Jones. "What d'you reckon, boss?"

"You're in charge of the interviews, Charlie. I'll leave the decisions up to you."

"Right you are. I'll finish my coffee and then we'll take a little stroll down to the custody suite. What we gonna chat about?"

Phil answered for Jones. "Alex was going to brief us on how she got Alby Pope to cough for double murder."

Pelham spluttered into his coffee. "You what?"

Alex stood this time. "Phil is giving me too much credit, I think," she said. "I did nothing but follow instructions from the boss, and Mr Pope collapsed into heaps."

"Collapsed in a heap, did he?" Ryan asked. "Give us the gory details. You tell me your story and I'll tell you ours."

Before Alex could respond, strident alarms shook the room. Three long blasts followed by two short signalled a bomb threat. An intercom announcement cut through the bells.

"Evacuate the building. This is not a drill!"

Chapter Thirty-Four

Holton, Birmingham

PELHAM JUMPED to his feet and screamed, "Out, everybody out, now!" He sprinted to the door and left the room at a speed Jones thought him incapable of achieving.

The alarms changed to an ululating wail, interspersed with the repeated announcement that this was not a drill.

Ryan and Alex, standing, exchanged glances before turning to Jones for instructions.

"Rear exit. Use the stairs," Jones answered, loud but calm. "When you reach the car park, make sure everyone stays well clear of the building."

They hesitated.

"Go on, move!"

While Alex, Ryan, and Phil turned left at the doorway, Jones peeled right, heading towards the staircase at the front of the build-ing. He opened each door along the corridor, checking for stragglers.

Although no one could have slept through the siren's howl, Jones couldn't ignore a lifetime's role of responsibility. A shadow at his shoulder caused him to turn.

"Where in the hell are you going, boss?" Phil shouted above the raucous din. "The rear exit's the other way."

"Pity's sake, Philip. Why can't you ever follow orders?"

Phil shook his head. "I'll help you search."

Without waiting for his response, Phil checked the rooms on the left side of the building, leaving the other side to Jones. Working together, it took seconds to confirm the eighth floor was clear. They made the main staircase and cleared the seventh floor before a sudden thought flipped Jones' stomach. He stopped dead and grabbed Phil by the arm.

"Have you seen Helen Ambridge this morning?" he yelled.

"Yes," Phil answered, breathing hard. "We arrived together. Shared the lift. Oh Christ." Phil's eyes widened as the implications hit home.

"Where's her office?"

"Sixth floor."

"Bloody hell, what bright spark housed her up there? Hurry."

From a dead start, Jones reached the stairwell first and took the stairs two at a time. Phil's heavy footsteps sounded over the noise of the alarms. The racket in the confined space drove through Jones' head with the force of a rusty metal spike. He covered his left ear and used his free hand to grab the banister for balance. They careened down the two flights and half-landing, and crashed through the double fire doors to the sixth floor.

Phil whooped in air with shuddering gasps. "Room 648!" he yelled, pointing down the hall.

Furthest away. Had to be!

The door was unlocked and the room empty.

"She must have been somewhere else when the alarms went off. Do you think she got out?" Phil shouted, leaning a hand against the doorjamb to catch his breath.

"She could be anywhere. Who's the Senior Health & Safety Officer?"

Phil made a bitter face between gasps. "Superintendent Peyton."

"Bloody hell. Who put him in charge?" Jones cut a hand through the air. "Nope, never mind. We'll clear this floor and make our way down to the ground."

They searched each room on the floor while retracing their steps to the fire exit. Inspector Wilkie, clipboard in hand, met them at the head of the stairs.

"Ian," Jones called, "Helen Ambridge?"

"No problems. I issued her with an emergency key to override the service lift. She just called from the car park to tell me she's safe."

Phil shot a Jones a look that said, "Now he tells us".

"You've checked upstairs?" Wilkie called.

"Yes," Phil shouted. "Eight and seven are all clear. So's this one."

"Great," Wilkie said, and ticked three boxes on his form. "The building's empty. Let's get moving."

The three jogged down the stairs, Wilkie and Phil abreast, and Jones a couple of steps behind. At each half-floor landing, the tall windows gave Jones an excellent view of the car park and the shift sergeants marshalling their troops to a safe distance. The sun had broken through the cloud and reflected in the puddles. Helen, in her wheelchair, was with a group of civilians looking up at the building. A pocket of individuals in white lab coats showed Jones that the forensics people had reacted well to the emergency.

The custody sergeant and two of his officers had corralled their prisoners, the brothers Mainwaring included, into a makeshift pound in a far corner of the car park. Rupert Mainwaring stood with his hands over his ears, shoulders bowed and shaking. Rodney faced his brother, but had his back to Jones.

Wonder what Rodney's thinking right now?

Once they'd reached the ground floor, Jones clapped Wilkie on the back. "Excellent work, Ian," he shouted. "We'll make a first class Health and Safety Officer of you yet."

"You have to give me a frontal lobotomy first and dial up my jobsworth gene to eleven."

Whatever the situation, Jones could usually rely on Ian Wilkie's acerbic wit to raise a smile. "Can you do something about the noise?"

Wilkie spoke into his radio. A second later, the alarms cut, leaving Jones' ears ringing—annoying, but a huge relief after the cacophony.

"Thank you, sir," said Phil, finally managing to speak.

Jones had never seen him so flushed. Sweat plastered the blond hair to his forehead in pointed ringlets. Damp patches darkened the shirt at his armpits and made his love handles more pronounced as the cotton clung to his skin.

For the first time since leaving the briefing room, Jones remembered his missing jacket, left on the hanger behind his office door; it held his keys, wallet, and mobile phone. His whole life carried in a single piece of clothing. If the bomb threat proved to be real, and the building blew, he'd have a hard time finding his spare keys in the building site he called home.

Nice one Jones, great set of priorities. Bang on.

He grimaced at his inadvertent use of the word "bang".

"Ian, what spiked the alarms?" Jones asked.

"You're never going to believe it," Wilkie said, and coughed in embarrassment.

"Try me."

"Oh no, sir. Come with me. You'll have to see for yourself."

Chapter Thirty-Five

Holton, Birmingham

INSPECTOR WILKIE hurriedly led the way through the double fire doors and headed for the main reception desk. The foyer, empty except for the uniformed desk sergeant and an ashen-faced constable, echoed to their footsteps.

Sergeant Featherstone stood beside a young constable, who sat at the reception desk with his left hand partway inside a brown parcel the size and shape of a shoebox. The young man's free hand, clamped over the wrist of the other, kept the package steady. Sweat dripped from the tip of his nose onto his desk blotter. Featherstone had an arm around the youngster's shoulder, propping him against his chair.

As Jones approached, the sergeant's eyes swivelled, but his head stayed still. The constable, young, slim, dark-haired, and close to tears, didn't react to their appearance. Jones closed on the tableau and recognised the young man from the interview suite the previous day.

"Morning, Feathers," Jones said, keeping his voice low and steady. "Playing pickpocket dip are we, Constable Porterhouse?"

He held up an arm to hold back Phil and Wilkie before approaching the desk.

"This ain't funny, sir," Feathers whispered, his face as pale as his young charge. "Please don't make us laugh."

The constable's chin trembled, dimples formed.

"I-I'm sorry, sir," he croaked. "Didn't realise it was a bomb until it started ticking when I opened it."

The young man couldn't tear his eyes from the manila package. He even blinked slowly.

Jones moved around to the front of the oak reception desk and rested a gentle hand on the surface, making sure the constable could see how steady it was. Jones needed to show calm, despite having had first-hand knowledge of what a parcel bomb could do to an unprotected body—he'd lived through the darkest days of the IRA bombing campaign.

"What's your first name, Constable?"

"S-sorry, sir?"

"Your first name, lad."

"Gareth, sir." The boy raised his head an inch. His Adam's apple, standing proud in a slim throat, bobbed once.

"Judging by your accent, I'd say you're from South Wales. Am I right?"

"Swansea, sir. Born and bred."

His eyes flicked up and met Jones' steady gaze for a second. They were blue and filled with tears.

"Swansea, eh? I spent a summer near there about twenty-five years before you were born. Pentowyn. Ever been?"

"Y-Yes, sir. My family used to have a caravan. We'd spend the summer holidays near there. Bit of a dive now though. Only the old folk visit these days." The chin dimpled again. "What's happening, sir?"

"Don't worry, lad. Help's on the way."

"Th-The courier looked genuine, sir. He had all the proper

documentation and everything," Porterhouse said, plaintive and clearly terrified.

"Okay son, we'll talk about that in a minute." Jones reached across to touch the young man's shoulder, but thought better of the idea. He nodded encouragement to Feathers, and the older man returned the gesture. "You two hang on here a minute, I'll be right back. Don't go anywhere now, will you."

"Very funny, sir. We'll still be here," Feathers said, his mouth twisted into an ironic smile. Still keeping hold of Porterhouse, he used his free hand to push his black-framed glasses back up to the bridge of his shiny nose.

Jones turned away, ushered Wilkie and Phil to the far corner of the foyer and they huddled into a tight group, speaking quietly. "You've called the Army Bomb Squad?"

"On their way, sir," Wilkie whispered, and checked his watch. "It'll take them at least another forty minutes to get here from Chetwynd Barracks."

"That long? They're on this side of Nottingham."

"The M42'll be chocka this time of day."

Where isn't.

"Okay," Jones said through a sigh. "We'll have to keep things calm until they arrive."

"You're the senior officer present, sir. What are your orders?"

"I am? Where's the Brass?"

"London. The Prime Minister summoned every Chief and Deputy Chief Constable in the country to attend a security meeting, COBRA. You know what they're like. Not much advance notice."

"Why wasn't I told?"

"They sent the senior officers an email last night. You should have picked it up on your mobile this morning."

"Damn emails. What's wrong with paper memos or telephone calls? Where's the Super?"

"Went with them," said Wilkie, keeping a straight face.

Despite the tension, Phil smiled. "Trust Duggie to wheedle his way onto a boozy junket. Looks like you're in charge, boss."

"Wonderful." Jones brushed his hair back using both hands. "Ian, the building's clear, right?"

"Definitely," Wilkie said, and showed him the clipboard. "Checked the rest of it myself."

"Okay. You and Phil get outside and set up a perimeter no closer than fifty metres from this side of the building. Close the roads, too. There's no telling how powerful that bomb could be. If it is a bomb." Phil opened his mouth, but Jones silenced him with raised hand. "No Phil, not this time. I need you outside. Go."

With obvious reluctance and a look that could splinter granite, Phil followed Wilkie through the main exit. Jones returned to the front desk.

"Sergeant Featherstone, thank you for your efforts, but you can leave now. Standing there like that, you're making the place look untidy."

"Oh no you don't, sir," Featherstone said, taking care to shake his head slowly. "You're not bullying me like you did your sergeant. Constable Porterhouse is my responsibility. I'm stopping right here."

The steel glint in Featherstone's eyes forced Jones to back down. "Right you are, Sergeant. We'll have a word about your insubordination in the pub later." Jones winked although he'd never felt less confident in his life. His watch read 08:53. They had ages to wait for the bomb squad.

He needed to keep the young constable's mind occupied.

"Gareth, tell me what happened when you took receipt of this happy little gift. Start from the top."

"Um … I-I …"

"Take your time, son. There's no rush."

Porterhouse took a shallow breath. "A motorcycle courier pressed the main door buzzer at about ten past eight. Sergeant Featherstone wouldn't buzz him in 'cause he was still wearing his helmet, so I went to the door to vet him. I checked his credentials, sir. I really did." Porterhouse's hand twitched as he looked up.

"Easy Gareth, I believe you. What happened next?"

"A-As I said, his ID looked real. It said he was a member of the official courier's service. The papers are over there." He turned his sweat-bathed head to his left slightly, but kept the rest of his body stock still.

"We'll get to the paperwork later. Carry on."

"I made him take his helmet off before I'd open the door."

"Excellent. We'll have him on the main security cameras. No need to describe him. Keep going."

"I reread the papers and escorted him into the lobby. Then he handed me the package."

"Did he take it from a bag?"

Porterhouse screwed his eyes shut. "Yes ... he had one of those orange reflective sacks slung over his shoulder."

Jones nodded.

"Interesting. Did he seem worried to you? Sweaty face? Shifty eyes? That sort of thing?"

"No, sir. He was dead calm. Jokey even. Said he'd have gotten here sooner but had a bit of trouble with his bike. Said he'd like to drop-kick the thing into touch and buy himself a new one, but his tosser of a boss wouldn't stump up a loan. He didn't seem worried at all and waved the parcel around without a care. That's why I accepted it and signed his receipt."

With the package upside-down, Jones couldn't read the label. "Who's it addressed to?"

"You, sir. DCI D A Jones, Serious Crime Unit."

Jones stiffened.

"D *A* Jones? Are you certain?"

As far as Jones was concerned, very few people knew his middle initial. He never used it, and hated the name it represented, Aaron.

"Yes, sir."

"And you opened it?"

"Yes, sir. Standard procedure with parcels, according to Sergeant Featherstone." He shuddered.

Another tear of sweat dropped from his nose.

"I messed up, didn't I? Put everybody in danger." Porterhouse's eyes implored Jones to pull him out of this mess.

Jones leaned over the desk. The ticking from within the package was loud enough to drive through the remaining tinnitus generated by the alarms.

How many bombers use mechanical timers these days?

Phil would know, but this wasn't the time to ask.

"Listen to me, Constable Porterhouse," he said, forcing a smile. "You might just have saved many lives."

The youngster's face contorted in confusion. "Really?"

Jones lowered a steadying hand on Porterhouse's wrist. "Most people faced with this situation would have yanked their hand out of the bag and tried to run. That alone might have set the thing off. You did well, son. Really well. I'm proud of you, and so is the gruff old sergeant beside you. Isn't that right, Sergeant?"

"Yes, sir. Most definitely, sir."

Constable Porterhouse's proud smile took a couple of years from his age. He should have been wearing a school blazer, not a police uniform.

Featherstone grimaced and dug a fist into his lower back. "Sorry, Gareth. My old back's killing me. Mind if I rest my bones?" He slid into the chair next to Porterhouse, and eased out a contented groan. "That's better. Much more comfy."

"Is the box vibrating? Or warm?" Jones asked.

"Not vibrating, sir. Didn't get as far as opening it, though. My fingers are touching the cardboard, but it isn't warm. I am though."

"Not surprised. Won't be long now. I'd fetch you a drink of water but I don't want to risk nudging you."

"I understand, sir. I might throw it up anyway. And I wouldn't want to wet myself," he said, and cracked out another brave smile.

No doubt about it, the lad had spirit.

"Can you tell me exactly what the courier said, word for word?"

"I'll try." His forehead crinkled in concentration. "I opened by asking him for his ID. He had it hanging from a cord around his neck, *JC Davidoff, Bonded Courier Service, Birmingham.* I double-checked his name with the registered list. That's when he made the joke about his initials. 'That's me,' he said, 'JC, Jesus Christ. At least that's what my dear old Dad used to say when slapping the back of my head'." Porterhouse licked dry lips before continuing. "Then he mentioned the delay caused by his bike. He said, what was it? Oh yes, 'Bloody bike's a liability. I had to pull up on the hard shoulder and reseat the HT leads, put me behind time so I opened the throttle'. Then he pointed to the security camera and said, 'Hope I haven't broke any laws'."

"What sort of accent did he have?"

"Difficult to say. My dad would have called him 'plummy' like, you know. Why, is it important?"

"Might be, Gareth. I'm impressed. You have a good memory and an eye for detail. It wouldn't surprise me to see you as a detective in a few ... Hang on a minute, what was that again?"

Jones stood up straight. The information rotated into place with the smooth click of a safe's combination lock. His heart rate raced, and the warning mechanism in his head eased back from "nuclear alert", to "heavy traffic on the way home from work".

"He definitely used the phrase, '*broke* any laws'?"

"Yes, sir."

"You're sure he didn't say 'broken'?"

"No, sir. That's exactly what he said. I remember thinking it was bad grammar." He swallowed. "You see, I'm doing English 'A' level at evening classes and know my grammar. It stood out, because apart from that one cock ... I mean, apart from the blunder, he spoke like a bit of a toff. Like I told you."

Jones took a moment to consider the new information. Did he have enough to gamble the lives of these men? He could wait for the bomb squad but then he'd have to cede control and anything could happen. They'd probably destroy the package with a controlled explosion. Jones couldn't allow that—he'd never learn the message sent by JC Davidoff.

"If you'll excuse me, Constable, I've had enough of this nonsense."

He reached out for the package.

"Sir!"

"David!"

Porterhouse and Featherstone yelled in unison.

Jones silenced them with a cold stare and a flick of the head.

With a surety and calm born of confidence, Jones grabbed the package with both hands and held it steady.

"Constable Porterhouse, remove your hand."

The youngster didn't move. Featherstone tensed, his face wrinkled into a silent question aimed directly at Jones.

"Constable Porterhouse, consider this an order. Remove your hand from the package. Do it slowly but do it now."

Porterhouse shot a sideways look at Featherstone, who nodded. "Do as you're told, son. The DCI knows what he's doing." The doubt in Featherstone's eyes told Jones he wanted to add "I hope", but didn't dare.

The constable closed his eyes as he moved his left arm. The wrist, sodden with sweat, showed first, and then came the pale, shuddering hand. The ticking seemed to increase as they held their collective breath. With his hand finally free of the bag, Porterhouse let out a half sob, half cry and slumped back in his chair. Featherstone took him by the shoulders.

"Sergeant Featherstone, take the lad away and give him a cold drink," Jones said, his grip still firm on the package, heart battering against his ribcage. "Constable Porterhouse?"

"Yes, sir?" he answered, colour flooding back into his youthful face.

"Come talk to me before the end of your shift. We need to arrange a time for me to stand you to a steak supper."

The constable closed his eyes and shook his head at the joke he'd probably heard a million times.

"Thank you, sir," he said, his voice firmer than it had been moments earlier.

"Now, you two can leave me alone with this message."

"Message, sir?" Porterhouse asked.

"I think so."

But won't be sure until I open the bloody thing.

"Feathers?" Jones called.

"Yes, sir?"

"Make sure Phil Cryer stays out there. He'll want to come rushing to the rescue once he hears I'm still inside."

"Will do, sir."

The two hurried towards the door, the burly old sergeant supporting an unsteady Constable Porterhouse.

Once the double doors had swung closed, Jones released the package. It tilted and settled lower on its left side. Jones squeezed his eyes closed, held his breath, and waited to be proven wrong.

The padded bag, in all its yellow glory, remained stubbornly and reassuringly intact.

Jones shuffled around to the other side of the reception desk, and slid into Porterhouse's warm, damp chair.

Wailing sirens broke the relative silence. The Bomb Squad!

Damn, they're early.

Seconds passed, and the wailing grew loud enough to drown out the ticking.

Inside the envelope, as Porterhouse described, rested a rectangular box, pink in colour, and made of thin cardboard. Tiny lettering in the corner drew Jones' attention. He leaned forwards to read it, sniffed, and recognised the smell immediately.

"Oh for God's sake. You have to be kidding!"

The sirens fell silent.

Jones pulled open the left-hand desk drawer, removed a pair of scissors, and working with extreme caution, eased the blades towards the padded envelope.

The front doors whipped open. A man in the uniform of a captain in the British Army Royal Logistics Corps, Explosive Ordnance Disposal Regiment, filled the doorway.

"Stop what you're doing, you damned fool!"

"Stand down, Captain," said Jones, and slid the open scissors through the edges of the brown paper envelope. "I think you've had a wasted trip."

The box stopped ticking.

Jones stopped breathing.

Chapter Thirty-Six

Holton, Birmingham

"A BOX of doughnuts and an alarm clock!" the captain said, hands on hips. "How d'you know it wasn't a bomb?"

Jones collapsed against the back of the chair and stared at the contents through the clear plastic window in the doughnut box, praying his trembling hands wouldn't give him away. His stomach churned.

Don't throw up, Jones. Do not throw up!

"Suspected," he managed to say, "but I didn't know for certain."

The prayer worked as well as they always did. The skin on his face cooled and his stomach lurched. He raised a hand to his mouth, rushed as nonchalantly as he could to the toilets located behind the reception desk, and vomited into the nearest pan. The world grew silent apart from the fading tinnitus and the puke splashing into the water. He took a short breath before another pulse hit and he vomited again.

Jones leaned against the side panel of the stall until the heat returned to his face, the sweat cooled at his scalp, and his heart rate settled to something near its normal steady beat. Recovering quickly, he splashed cold water on his face, and dried off with a paper towel taken from a dispenser he'd normally avoid with greater enthusiasm than an invitation to a stag night at a bordello. He rinsed out his mouth with water from the fountain, dabbed his lips with his clean handkerchief, and felt ready to return to the world.

The soldier—mid-forties, sandy coloured hair, weather-beaten face—stood guard over the box. He waited for Jones to return to his seat before making the formal introductions.

"Captain Williams, EODR," he said, offering his hand, which Jones shook firmly. "You'll be DCI Jones then?"

Jones nodded.

"Feeling better?"

"Yes thanks," Jones said, unable to meet the man's eyes. "Sorry. That was a little embarrassing."

"No need to apologise, Chief Inspector. Happens to me all the time. Never trust a bomb disposal engineer who has no fear. Usually means he has no brains, either." He pointed at the former suspected package. "Opening that was bloody impetuous, but I guess you had your reasons?"

"I had certain … well, let's call them clues, that made me suspect it wasn't dangerous."

"You risked your life on a suspicion?"

"Isn't that what you do all the time in your job?"

"Suspicion and years of training."

"Me too." Jones smiled weakly and rubbed his face hard to reawaken some feeling.

"These clues," Williams said, "care to elaborate?"

Jones shook his head and smiled. "One of them was the smell of fresh-baked doughnuts. I mean, sending doughnuts to a police station. The courier was taking the mick. Sorry, 'fraid I can't tell you anything more. This is part of an ongoing police investigation. But," he added after seeing a flash of annoyance flare in the officer's eyes, "I'll call you with an explanation as soon we've cleared the case. Deal?"

"I'll hold you to that, Chief Inspector."

"You can rely on me to keep my word, Captain Williams. Tell me one thing though. How did you get here so fast? We weren't expecting you for another hour or so."

Williams frowned. "We received your first emergency call at oh-seven-thirty-two. When the second call came in, we were already on our way."

"There were two emergency calls?"

"Yes, Chief Inspector."

"The cheeky bugger," Jones said, adding a grim smile.

"Sorry?"

"You received the first call forty minutes before the courier delivered the doughnuts."

The new information tallied with Jones' developing view of JC Davidoff. The man was toying with him, taunting him, making it personal. If he wanted Jones' interest, his ploy worked better than a charm.

"Talking about doughnuts, Chief Inspector, I don't suppose I can take them to my men. We missed breakfast."

"Sorry, Captain. That's evidence and there's no telling what they might contain. Those little delights are going straight to the lab for analysis, but our canteen serves some moderately acceptable grub. Tell the staff to put it on Superintendent Peyton's account. He'll be delighted to treat you. How many in your team?"

"Five."

"Excellent. I can recommend the full English breakfast with all the trimmings. To die for," he said, adding a wink to his encouraging smile.

"On behalf of my men, I thank you, Chief Inspector, and your Superintendent."

"It's my pleasure. Sorry to have interrupted your day."

Williams shook his head.

"No need to apologise. We're all getting home safe after a bomb shout. In my book, that's an excellent result."

———

JONES' whole team sat around the SCU conference table together with Sergeant Featherstone and Constable Porterhouse. Few strangers received an invite to the Unit's lair, and Porterhouse's stiff-shouldered, glassy-eyed demeanour showed the expected awe. Each of them held a cup, apart from Porterhouse, who chugged from a bottle of cola.

After the morning's exploits, Jones' tea was nectar.

In front of Porterhouse lay a packet of crisps, roast beef flavour. Two minutes earlier, Jones had dropped the packet in front of the lad, saying, "Here's your steak dinner lad, I'm not made of money." The table erupted with the release of tension and Porterhouse flushed bright red. He opened the bag and offered it around.

Only Pelham accepted. He grabbed a quarter of the bag's contents and started munching. Between bites, he said, "That soldier bloke nearly had kittens. We could all see the back of his neck turn dark purple when you ordered him to stand down."

Jones scratched the tip of his nose. "He did look a tad miffed, eh? Can't blame him really. He'd just spent an hour racing through traffic, preparing to tackle a terrorist bomb. When he arrives, some idiot copper tells him to hang on a moment while he attacks the suspect package with a pair of scissors. Hardly going to endear myself to the poor chap, was I?"

Porterhouse sat at attention, staring straight ahead. The crisp packet on the table in front of him untouched since Pelham's attack.

"Constable Porterhouse," Jones said, "I'm adding a commenda-tion in your record. You reacted well today, lad."

The youngster blushed again as Ryan and Phil, sitting on either side in an honour guard, clapped him so hard on either shoulder Jones feared for his physical safety.

"Go along with Sergeant Featherstone and write up your inci-dent report. Then make an appointment with the counsellor. Delayed shock can be crippling."

Porterhouse looked to his sergeant, who gave an almost imper-ceptible "don't argue with a senior officer" headshake. The young-ster snapped to attention, gave a crisp parade ground salute and turned towards the door, clearly desperate to leave the group and tell his story to anyone who'd listen. Feathers waved goodbye and escorted his charge from the room.

"One moment, Constable Porterhouse," Phil called.

The boy stopped so suddenly he might have walked into a brick wall. He turned about-face. He looked more terrified than when he thought his hand rested on a bomb. Phil pointed to the crisps. "Forgotten something, Meat?"

Porterhouse blinked. "Meat?"

"What else are we going to call a bloke with your surname?"

"Right. Thank you Sergeant," he said, "but I'm not really all that hungry. Please help yourself."

Feathers and the lad left the room. Phil picked up the packet, tipped the remaining crisps into his mouth, and washed them down with his coffee. Pelham seemed a tad miffed at missing out on a second mouthful.

"Boss, how'd you know the package was this JC Davidoff, or rather, John Devenish's idea of a joke?" Ryan asked.

"Doubt it was a joke," Jones answered. "The bugger was sending us a message."

He leaned over to a side table and pulled a green plastic evidence tray onto the desk.

The tray contained the doughnut box, wrapping paper, the doughnuts, the alarm clock, and a printed note, which held the words, *Go for broke. Regards, JR Devenish Esq.*

Alex spoke next.

"Before we do anything else, boss, will you please tell us why you thought the package wasn't dangerous?"

Jones studied her and the rest of his team. What could he tell them that made sense? Could he tell them that a warning mechanism lodged somewhere deep inside his head told him when things did and didn't make sense? Could he call it a "gut feeling", or would they lose respect for a man they thought sensible and reliable?

He pushed back his chair and made his way to the window. A pale sun glowed through a thin sheet of high cloud. British summer had returned in all its amiable and gentle glory. He turned his back to the glass. The morning's activities had changed his shoulder muscles into slabs of cement. This time, the sun's warmth did nothing to ease the cramp.

"Hope I haven't broke any laws," he announced.

They stared back, faces blank.

Phil was the first to speak. "Come again, boss?"

Jones crossed his arms and repeated his words, adding, "It's what the courier said to young Porterhouse. What's wrong with that saying? Alex, you have the best command of English grammar here. Speak up."

Alex frowned. "It should be, 'broken' not 'broke'."

"Exactly."

"What you getting at, boss?" Phil asked.

"Phil, the letter John Devenish wrote after the second Edinburgh job? Remind me what he said about the Scottish detective … Barrow, wasn't it?"

"Right, just a mo." Phil closed his eyes and thought for half a second. "It said, 'Please show the redoubtable Detective Inspector Barrow this letter and give him my apologies, but I am unable to make a statement. I hope I haven't broke any laws'. Bloody hell, boss, you remembered that? I'm impressed."

"I only read the file this morning. Thought it stood out a bit, but the rest of the letter wasn't exactly high prose. Ryan, do you mind?" He pointed to the computer on the spare desk.

Ryan scooted over to the empty chair and started working the keyboard. "Printing it off now, boss."

Alex reached across to the printer and distributed a copy to each member of the team except Phil, who didn't need one. Jones gave them all time to read. Pelham took longer than the others.

"Anyone spoke to this DI Barrow geezer?" Pelham asked. When nobody responded, he added, "I'll give him a bell." He reached for his desk phone.

"Charlie," said Jones. "Don't forget about the Mainwaring brothers."

"I won't boss, but they're in with their lawyers now. I've booked the first interview for one-thirty."

Jones waved him on and Pelham pressed the button for the switchboard operator.

"Hullo Diane, Charlie Pelham here, love. Can you find me a number for the Police HQ in Edinburgh? Yeah, that's right, Scotland. I'll wait."

Jones addressed the rest of his team. "Anyone had a chance to examine the evidence?"

Alex answered. "The note is printed on cheap copier paper and by an inkjet printer. The laboratory may be able to tell us more, but they can't compare it with the original he sent to DI Barrow. The NCA has that one."

"Presumably, the Edinburgh Police Labs and the NCA analysed the original note. What did the results say?" Jones asked.

"Dunno," Phil responded, "I can't access the NCA database. You were going to talk with Superintendent Knightly, remember."

"Let's hold off on that for a moment. I'd rather work with what we have here before we bring the Glory Boys in. They'll want to take over. After all, Devenish, or whatever his real name is, did approach us."

"You, boss. Not us," Ryan said. "The package was addressed to you in person, remember."

Alex cleared her throat. "Might I ask a question, boss? In fact, two questions."

"Fire away."

"First, why did this man, Devenish, send the clock to you?"

"I'd like an answer to that, too," Jones answered. "And the second question?"

"Why make it appear to be a bomb?"

While Jones struggled for an answer, Pelham slammed the phone down and shouted, "Scotch idiot."

"Charlie? What's up?" Jones prayed Pelham hadn't just added fuel to the Scottish desire for independence.

"The bloody Jock I just spoke to is a moron," Pelham said, swivelling his chair to face the group. "It turns out that DI Barrow retired a few weeks ago. The moron I spoke to, a bloody civilian from the HR department wouldn't give me his contact number.

Wouldn't put me through to his successor, neither. Obstructionist Scotch git."

"How've you left it?" Phil asked, before Jones had the chance to say anything.

"Mrs Jobsworth said the best she could do were to call Barrow and ask him to give us a bell."

"Charlie, that should be *Ms* Jobsworth, I think?" Alex asked, smiling.

Pelham raised both hands in surrender.

"Sorry Alex, my mistake. Boss, if you don't need us, mind if I take Wash off to the canteen and brief him on how we're going to tackle little Rupert Mainwaring?"

"Sounds like a good idea," Jones conceded.

Pelham and Ryan left the room with Pelham saying, "C'mon Wash, let's go cram in some calories so we got the strength to knock some heads together."

Ryan gave the room a shrug as he opened the door for Pelham and followed him out.

Chapter Thirty-Seven

"ALEX," said Jones, after the door had closed behind Pelham and the keen Ryan. "Find anything interesting on the packaging?"

"Nothing on the envelope, boss," she answered, and tucked an errant lock of wavy blonde hair behind her ear. She held up the box, sealed in its clear plastic evidence bag. "But we do know where Devenish bought the doughnuts. The address of the bakery is on the box. Would you like me to go to the shop and interview the baker?"

"Yes please, right after you take this stuff down to the lab. Ask Pat Elliott to put a rush on the analysis. Leave the clock though. I'll walk it down after I've had a closer look."

A frown crossed Alex's face, and her eyes lowered to the evidence tray.

"What's wrong?" Jones asked.

"After what happened yesterday with Mr Prendergast, they're

understaffed, I think. Wouldn't it be better to give the evidence to the evening shift?"

"Perhaps, but I want it processed today. And anyway," Jones said, lowering his voice, "Elliott and Harrap have been carrying poor old Reg for months. They'll probably be more efficient without his … assistance." As soon as he said the words, the guilt hit and Jones wished he'd kept his thoughts to himself. "Keep that between the three of us. Okay, Alex?"

"Of course, boss." She made a zip-the-lip gesture and added a little wink.

Jones winced inwardly. When he was a junior officer, his superiors would never have allowed him to act in such a familiar way, but, in truth, he preferred the less formal approach. A relaxed atmosphere allowed the creative juices to flow. As long as the Unit maintained the hierarchy, he encouraged the banter. What he wouldn't condone was the kind of direct insubordination that Charlie Pelham had exhibited more than once over the past few months.

Alex took the evidence, leaving Jones and Phil alone in the big room. After a few moments, Phil broke the silence. "I have to ask the question again, boss. What's Devenish playing at, sending you stuff like this?"

Jones thought for a moment. "Don't know for certain. A bomb scare gave him plenty of time to lose himself and that motorbike. We had other things on our minds at the time than setting up roadblocks."

"No, I meant why not send the package through the post?"

"Good question. The method certainly concentrated our minds on the issue. Maybe he wanted to wind me up. Send a challenge. Show me how smart he was? Who knows?"

"But why the note and this cheap piece of crap?"

Phil held up the clock—a plain plastic rectangle, white, with a circular face, thin black hands, and roman numerals. He rotated it and studied the back, an indented brass key the only feature. He turned the key anticlockwise and the clock started ticking again, louder than Jones thought it should have done for such a small timepiece. The relevance was obvious. Devenish had rigged it to be loud enough for Porterhouse, or whoever, to hear above the noise of a busy police station.

"Hang on a moment," said Jones and held out his gloved hand. "Let me see that, please."

Phil passed the clock across the desk.

It was heavier than Jones expected, no doubt due to the mechanism that added volume to the ticking. He held it up to the light streaming through the window and angled it so he could see along the line of the back. The little brass key stood slightly proud of the surface and rotated anticlockwise in time with the ticking. "So that's how he did it."

"Did what, boss?" Phil squinted along the edge of the clock as Jones had done.

"I wondered how Devenish arranged to have the clock start ticking the moment young Porterhouse started to open it and not before." Jones touched his index finger to the centre of the key and the ticking stopped with the lightest pressure. "A bit old school, but it works. All Devenish needed to do was hand Porterhouse the box with the address side up and the back of the clock would press against the bottom of the box—"

Phil finished the sentence. "And when Porterhouse turned the package over to open it, 'tick-tock'." He sneered and shook his head. "It's a bit hit-and-miss, isn't it?"

"You think?"

"Well, yeah." Phil screwed up his lips again. "What we know about Devenish—if he is the leader of the JT1 Crew—is that he's a mechanical and electronics genius. Why use this cheap piece of tat? Why not use an electronic timer?"

"Electronic timers don't make a noise and he wanted to stop us opening the box long enough to make his getaway?"

Phil raised a bellwether finger. "But you can programme electronic timers to tick if you want them to."

"You can? Didn't think of that. Perhaps Devenish had another reason. Maybe he's trying to tell us something other than how smart he is."

"You could be right." Phil's raised eyebrow and wrinkled nose told Jones he wasn't convinced. "The bugger could just be a nut-job who likes pissing off the police."

Jones turned the clock over and examined the face. The hands were set to twelve o'clock. Despite the loud ticking, the large hand didn't move and the clock had no sweep hand. The manufacturer's name inscribed on the face read, *Brooker Clocks, London*, only there was something wrong with the second 'o' on the *Brooker*. It was darker than the first.

"Just a moment," he said.

Jones put down the clock, opened one of the drawers on the cabinet behind him, and fished out a magnifying glass. He focused the lens on the nameplate. A diagonal line cut through the second 'ø'.

"What the hell?" He handed the clock and glass to Phil. "Take a close look at the name. Tell me what you see."

"Nothing … ah, wait a minute, there's a mark on the second 'o' in Brøøker's. It's too neat to be a scratch. It looks like a forward slash. Any idea what it means?"

Jones smiled. "You know what, Philip? I really think I might do. What did the note say?"

"Go for broke."

"And the message to Porterhouse?"

"Er … 'hope I haven't broke any laws'."

"And what were we talking about this morning in the canteen?"

"Insurance. Oh no," he said and slapped a hand to his forehead. "So bloody obvious. He's telling us the JT1 Crew gets their information from broking houses or brokers, right?"

Jones hiked his right eyebrow. "Could be."

"But why tell us something the NCA and all the other forces will have already checked out? Like I said, he's a nut job."

The phone on Pelham's desk buzzed, interrupting Jones' thoughts. Nearer to the phone than Jones, Phil answered.

"Holton SCU, DS Cryer speaking … Ah, DI Barrow, thanks for getting back to us so quickly." Jones pointed to his ear and Phil nodded. "Excuse me, sir. Do you mind if I put you on speaker-phone? … One moment." He hit a button on the handset.

"DI Barrow? This is DCI Jones."

"I'm no' DI Barrow any more, sir. Just plain old Mr Barrow since I retired. Although I prefer 'Jimmy'."

"Retired, eh?" The thought of his own impending retirement sent the blood sluicing into Jones' shoes. "How's it going?"

"Retirement?" The disembodied voice was animated. "Oh it's fantastic, man. Love it. My garden's never been prettier, an' the wife loves me being under her feet all day. An' if ye believe that, you're no' much of a detective." After a slight pause, Barrow added, "Why d'ye think I phoned you back so quick? I'm climbing the walls here, man."

Phil smiled into his hand at Jones' worried frown. He knew well enough what Jones thought about the prospect of retirement—they'd discussed the matter often enough.

Barrow continued. "I understand ye want to talk with me about John Devenish, the so-called have-a-go hero?" The disdain with which Barrow spoke the words made it clear he felt the same way about press hyperbole as Jones did. Already, he liked the Scotsman immensely. "You're thinking about the letter he sent the wee lass, Angela Glennie?"

"Exactly," Jones answered. "What did you make of it?"

"If you don't mind ma language, I thought it a crock of shite. For my money, Devenish was in it up to his eyeballs, but I couldn't prove a thing." He coughed. "At first, I thought Morton, the shop owner, would discover a missing solitaire diamond or some such. Then I reckoned the robbers had a falling out and aborted the job, but nothing came of it. We did the usual stuff, ye know. SOCOs swept the shop, ran a house-to-house, checked the CCTV, but came up wi' nothing. Suffered the usual media brouhaha, and then the letter arrived. We analysed it, of course. Searched for Devenish, but found nothing. Couldn't find the two shotgun carriers either. The ground might as well have swallowed the buggers whole. We found the getaway car in a disused lockup. Torched and useless. A dead end all around."

"Who's handling the case now?"

Barrow cleared his throat and Jones could sense the man's annoyance, even down the phone line. Phil could too, judging by his knowing glance.

"I'm afraid," said Barrow at last, "the moment the NCA found a link between this case, and all the others, my former boss shunted the whole file across to them. Couldn't get shot of the case fast enough. It's now languishing in the 'pending file', if you see what I mean."

Jones understood exactly.

The "pending file" meant that the current investigating officer had shifted the case away from his "active" pile and over to archive —a neat way of massaging the crime numbers.

"Yes, Jimmy. I know exactly."

"So," Barrow said. "How can I help you?"

"The final paragraph in the letter Devenish sent to Angela Glennie mentions you."

"Aye."

"What did you make of it?"

"Apart from the wee shite calling me 'redoubtable', you mean? Not a lot. I thought he was taunting me, y'know? Is there something you'd like to tell me?"

"Love to, Jimmy, but …"

"Aye," he said. "Ah know. Ongoing investigation. Will you call me when you *can* talk about it?"

"I promise. Give your personal contact numbers to DS Cryer and we'll be in touch. And thanks a lot for your time."

"Don't worry 'bout it, sir. I've got plenty o' that on my hands."

I bet you have.

While Phil took Barrow's details, Jones ran through the information in his head one more time. Everything led back to the NCA and their investigation, but he couldn't bring himself to contact Knightly just yet. Something held him back. He hoped it wasn't pride, but wouldn't rule that out completely.

Phil replaced the handset. "Helpful bloke. Felt a bit sorry for him though. Didn't sound as though retirement suited him too much, eh?"

Jones tried to detect a slight taunt in Phil's tone, but decided he was being too sensitive to the whole end-of-working-life situation and let it pass.

Phil continued. "Interesting he feels the same way as you do about Devenish."

"What d'you mean? I haven't told you what I think of Devenish."

Phil grinned. "Nah. But you think he's part of the JT1 mob, and I agree."

"Perhaps. Doesn't answer the main question though. Why'd he contact me?"

"Maybe he wanted to make sure his crew wasn't blamed for the *Green & Sons* butchery."

"But what difference would that have made to him? Since the Edinburgh job, their signature's turned more and more violent. The last three jobs on their jacket included firearms. Why take the risk of sending us this message? I don't like mysteries."

"Yes you do."

Jones reached for his mobile.

"Who're you calling?"

"Superintendent Knightly. I've changed my mind. It's about time we pooled our resources."

Jones tried to sound happy, but inside he was disappointed. His mood deepened to annoyance and then anger when the man on the NCA switchboard put him on hold for five minutes and said the Super was unavailable and would return his call "in due course".

He closed the connection and simmered for a few moments before moving on with the rest of his day, which included a search for a man on a big black motorbike. Within two hours of searching through traffic camera footage, he and Phil lost count of the number of suspect motorbikes they'd seen criss-crossing Birmingham's city centre.

At half past five, his mobile chirruped. He didn't recognise the number. "Jones here."

"Hullo there, Mr Jones, it's me, Sam, Sam Tallon."

"Hi, Sam. I'd almost forgotten about you. We've been a little distracted today."

"Yeah, I heard about the bomb scare. It's been on the news all afternoon. Are you okay? Is this a bad time?"

"No, no. What's up?"

"Your car's ready."

"Excellent. You can take back that piece of overpriced German engineering. Can't stand all those bells and whistles. Give me my old Rover any day."

"I know, I know. Are you still at the station?"

"Yes, I'm still here."

"Excellent. Thirty minutes suit you?"

"Okay, Sam. Anything unusual?" The annual service on a car of the Rover's vintage always threw up some queries and unexpected costs, but Sam didn't usually offer a delivery service.

"Nothing I couldn't fix."

"Oh dear. Expensive?"

"Not really. Nothing you can't expect with an old bucket of bolts, Mr Jones."

"Sam, how many times do I have to tell—"

"Yeah, yeah, I know. You're happy with the old dog. I ain't trying to sell you a new motor. Be with you in half an hour."

Before Jones had a chance to say anything else, Sam ended the call, leaving Jones to worry what the old mechanic had found wrong with the Rover this time. He took a deep breath and resigned himself to another unpleasantly exorbitant bill.

Chapter Thirty-Eight

THURSDAY 7TH JULY – *Evening*
Holton, Birmingham

IT HAD BEEN a long day fraught with tension and ending with an unsuccessful search for Devenish and his bloody motorbike.

Jones dropped heavily into the warm cocoon that was his beloved Rover. He draped the carefully folded jacket on the passenger seat, and leaned his head against the headrest for a minute to prepare for the drive home. Long days and short nights had taken their toll and exhaustion hit hard. On other days, he'd sleep in the office, but today, he needed to go home. For various reasons, he needed to maintain his semi-regular routine.

Ignition on, windows lowered. The leather seat squeaked in welcome as he made himself even more comfortable. He reversed out of his designated parking spot, arm along the back of the passenger chair, aching back reacting against the twist, and took a route that was so familiar the car might almost have found its own way home.

The Aston Expressway—normally a misnomer—was less busy

than usual, and Jones suffered none of the usual early evening jams. The minute he reached the dual carriageway, he hit the power button on the radio: BBC Radio 4. He caught the end of the evening news and reached the M6 junction during the weather forecast—tomorrow promised light rain with extended sunny periods.

Something to look forwards to.

Jones made good time and was well into the following programme—a current affairs discussion on the right to die—by the time he made the exit onto the M54 westbound. The broadcast didn't generate much interest, but he kept the radio on for company and out of habit. Maintaining his standard drive-home routine.

With the urban lights no more than a dwindling glow in his rear view mirror, the radio voices dissolved into regular bursts of static—white noise. Jones sighed. He didn't normally lose signal here, and never on a clear night. Thunderstorms could interfere with reception, but long-wave broadcasts were usually pretty reliable. He pressed a button to change to the nearest digital channel, but the white noise continued with the same rhythmic pulsing. He frowned, turned down the annoying sound, and concentrated on the engine note.

The engine coughed once and juddered before catching and returning to its standard pleasant hum. He eased the pressure on the throttle and dropped the speed to a cautious forty-five, hoping to nurse the old dear back to the cottage rather than wait on the hard shoulder for an hour for the breakdown service. He spent a nervous ten miles in the slow lane until the sign for Exit 6 gave him some relief. The engine coughed once more, but recovered again as he turned the car right and joined the deeply potholed A5223. The Rover's suspension coped well with all but the deepest crevices as Jones carried out his twice-daily hazard-avoidance routine.

Damned tank track.

At least the cool breeze wafting through the open windows had the power to refresh. That, together with his concern for the car, removed any chance he'd fall asleep at the wheel.

He and his beloved mechanical beast made the ten miles to

Much Wenlock without further incident, but the engine finally cut out completely when they were still five miles from home.

"Damn it!"

The car had enough momentum to roll into a lay-by, where Jones yanked up the handbrake without pressing the ratchet release button—his concession to the building anger. The hazard warning lights still worked, but that was all.

Jones retrieved his jacket and draped it over his knees, smoothing out the creases that had formed in the sleeves.

"Good evening, DCI Jones."

"Bloody hell!" Jones' heart tried to escape via his throat. He snapped his head to the left expecting to see someone leaning in through the open passenger window—nothing.

"Who's that?" Jones called, scrambling for the door handle.

The central locking buzz-clicked and the electric windows rolled upwards, but stopped before reaching the doorframe, leaving a two-inch air gap.

"Hello," the disembodied voice answered, coming from the radio. "Now you're safely stopped, mind if we have a little chat?"

Jones peered through the windscreen and each window in turn, searching the area around the lay-by. Late dusk lowered the visibility, but it was still bright enough to see that the road and the hedgerows on either side appeared empty. Apart from the voice, the only other sound came from the crinkling of superhot metal as the engine cooled.

"Where are you?" Jones demanded.

"Can't you tell? I'm speaking through your radio," the smoothly modulated voice answered.

"Don't be so bloody ridiculous, I know that," Jones answered, "but I'm guessing you're out there in the dark somewhere, watching me, right?"

"Touché, Mr Jones." The voice was male, well spoken, English, but with no detectable accent. Jones put him in his late twenties or early thirties. "Or can I call you David?"

"You can call me DCI Jones," he answered, fingering the slightly reassuring bulk of the telescopic truncheon in his jacket pocket. It would take very little effort to smash one of the part-open windows and escape. Not that he intended anything of the sort.

Jones' mind ticked over at the same pace as the cooling engine. If the man on the radio, presumably John Devenish, had wanted him dead, he could have run him off the road or planted a real bomb. No, the jewel thief wanted something from Jones. He sat back and let Devenish play out his game.

"Of course. You give very few people the honour of calling you David. Perhaps one day you'll think I've earned the accolade."

"Doubt it. Who the hell are you?"

"Oh come on," the voice chided. "A detective with your reputation, and a valid one given your record, would have already worked that out. Please don't try to play me, DCI Jones. It would be a waste of your time and would hamper what I hope will grow into a useful partnership."

"Partnership? I doubt that very much."

"You know who I am, don't you," the voice continued. "Come on take a guess. Go for *broke*."

"John Devenish."

"Correct. Although that's not my real name, as you'll already have gathered."

"I have," Jones answered and sank back into his seat. He might as well try to make himself comfortable. He didn't appear to be going anywhere for a while and was keen to learn more about his adversary. Like, for example, what the bloody hell was the jewel thief up to? "But as well as being a captive audience, you have me at another disadvantage."

"Really?"

"You have my real name, but I don't have yours. Care to redress the balance?"

"In a sec, Mr Jones."

"Why the histrionics with the bomb scare? And why this nonsense with the car? You could have called in at the station for a chat."

"And risk arrest before I could tell you my story and ask for your help? Not likely."

"What? You send a hoax bomb, destroy my car, kidnap me, and you still expect my help?"

"Yes please."

"Are you mad?"

"Some might think that, but I hope not."

The central locking system clicked, the passenger door opened, and a dark figure appeared in the frame. He bent at the waist and popped his head into the car, an apologetic smile on his youthful face.

"Good evening, DCI Jones, I'm Sean Freeman, aka John Devenish. It's grand to meet you at last. Mind if I join you?"

He slid into the passenger seat and thrust out a hand.

Chapter Thirty-Nine

THURSDAY 7TH JULY – *Late evening*
Near Much Wenlock, Shropshire

"SEAN FREEMAN? ANOTHER PSEUDONYM?" asked Jones, refusing the offered hand.

"Not this time. It's my real name. You'll notice I'm not wearing gloves?"

Jones nodded and watched the man calling himself Sean Freeman press both palms onto the windscreen. The heat from his skin formed mist on the cooling glass.

"There's my calling card. You'll find my fingerprints on the AFIS database."

"For an old crime you didn't commit?"

"No. I used to be a member of the Guild of Master Locksmiths. They take biometric measurements for elimination purposes at crime scenes. You'd be surprised how many locksmiths the police suspect of being criminals, Mr Jones … or maybe you wouldn't."

Jones prided himself on having a half-decent poker face. He'd won many a pot at the irregular games with colleagues, but it clearly failed him as he felt his jaw drop. Any number of scenarios popped into his head, the most striking being that he faced a lunatic who didn't mind giving away his identity because he didn't intend to leave Jones alive to tell the tale.

Strangely enough, the most worrying option also seemed the least likely. Freeman could have arrived armed, but instead sat in the passenger's seat empty-handed, wearing a thin, tight-fitting top that covered no firearm-shaped bulge. All that separated them was a raised handbrake lever.

Jones took a moment to study his passenger, who did the same in return.

Above average height, possibly five-eleven, six feet judging from the way he filled the seat, and athletically built, Freeman had an interesting face, strong but not striking. He'd blend easily into any European crowd. Muddy blond hair trimmed short, blue eyes, surprisingly open and honest. Thin lips sat above a clean-shaven, strong chin. Here was a pleasant, if unremarkable man in his early thirties. His clothing was burglar chic—dark blue long-sleeved shirt, black jeans, black trainers.

"Okay," Jones said at length. "You have my undivided attention. What now?"

"Now, I tell you a story."

Jones arched an eyebrow. "What then?"

Freeman pursed his lips before answering. "Then, DCI Jones, you can decide whether to arrest me right away, or help me catch the bastards responsible for these jewel thefts."

"Assuming you're not that man, of course."

"Oh, I am involved, but not in all the robberies, and certainly none of the violent ones. There you have my first confession. And, by the way, I had nothing to do with the one at *Green & Sons*."

"I know. We closed that case this afternoon."

"Really?"

Freeman looked surprised and distracted. His eyes alternated between scanning the area around the car as though he suspected the hedgerows to explode with armed officers, and flicking to the clock on the dashboard. At the same time, he picked at the seams of his jeans with manicured fingers, and tapped the footwell carpet with a jittery right foot.

"I'd have thought you'd have seen the item on the evening news."

Freeman shook his head. "I've been a shade busy today. Why?"

"The *Green & Sons* case. We made some arrests this afternoon."

"Did you?" Freeman pulled the focus on his eyes to register Jones. "Inside job, right?"

"How'd you guess?"

He sniffed and took a break from rubbing his jeans and started scratching his chin. "Seemed too much like a setup to me. Who did it? The trophy wife and the regional manager?"

"More or less," Jones answered, trying not to sound surprised at Freeman's depth of knowledge regarding the case.

"I'd check out the owner too, despite the hand thing. Their business is tottering on the brink of bankruptcy. They've been trying to offload the Digbeth shop for years. Wouldn't surprise me to learn that the whole thing's part of an insurance scam."

Jones tilted his head and looked at Freeman sideways. "Have you hacked into the database and read the case file?"

Freeman's eyebrows shot up. "Bloody hell. Am I right? Just throwing some guesswork at you."

Jones didn't know what to make of Freeman's claim, but he didn't press the point. "So, you have something to tell me?"

"Yep. Are you prepared to listen?"

"I'm all ears." Jones crossed his arms and twisted to face Freeman, but the steering wheel made the position uncomfortable. "This isn't going to work, is it?"

"What? Sitting in the car for any length of time?"

"Exactly. Plays havoc with my lower back."

"Can't you think of this as a stakeout?"

"Now you're being daft. We're not in America and I'm no longer a kid. Why don't you un-zap my car so we can do this thing in a civilised manner?"

"What? So you can accelerate to warp-factor nine and drive me straight to jail?"

Jones shook his head slowly. Despite the strangeness of the situation, he was beginning to like the villain who had shown no hint of menace, so far. In fact, the worst accusation Jones could level at the man was that he seemed distracted. Freeman's quiet and uncertain demeanour could of course, be an act. The man had demonstrated a keen sense of the dramatic with the day's activities, but Jones trusted his own instincts as he had with the false bomb. They weren't infallible, but in this case he'd take the risk.

"Nope," he said, "so I can drive home. I'm gasping for a cuppa. You have my word I won't arrest you until after you finish telling your tale."

Freeman stared into Jones' eyes before nodding. "Your word's good enough for me, Mr Jones." He secured his seatbelt and leaned his head back against the seat restraint. "As for the tea, don't tell me … loose leaf, not teabags?"

"Have you been searching through my rubbish bins?"

"Now who's being daft? I know you bag up your personal stuff and take it to Holton station for disposal. I'd say that was standard operating practise for a senior police officer serious about his privacy. Am I correct?"

"More or less." Jones wasn't about to give the thief any free background information. Freeman didn't need to know the real reason for the added caution Jones took over disposing of his rubbish.

Jones loosened his tie, undid the top shirt button, and pressed the window button. To his surprise, the glass descended. He snapped a sideways look at Freeman, who raised his open hands, palms forward. "I reactivated the car the moment I sat down. Feel free to fire her up. I'll remove the electronics package I installed when we get to your place. Won't take but a minute."

Jones turned the ignition key. The engine purred into life—and it purred smoothly. The car's high beams exploded the gloom. So far, Freeman had lived up to his word. Jones would take him at face value, at least for the moment.

"So," Jones said, "answer my question about the electronics.

Why do it this way?" He pointed towards the engine compartment before checking his mirrors and pulling back onto the quiet road.

"How else could I demonstrate my skills? After all, anyone can *claim* to be a member of the notorious JT1 Crew." He pressed his hands together and drew them to his lips as though in prayer. "Hell, that sounded rather pompous, didn't it? Look, to be honest, I'd have preferred to do this from a thousand miles away, by satellite phone or Internet video feed, but you don't use anything like that, do you?"

"Correct. Big Brother isn't watching me."

Not much.

"Your aversion to modern technology is a real pain in my backside."

Jones increased speed, but kept below the limit; he didn't want to spook his new friend. He ignored the first turning that led to his lane and headed for the second, a mile further along.

Freeman turned his shoulders to face Jones. "I hope you're taking Stoneway, DCI Jones, and not leading us around the houses."

Test answered, Freeman clearly knew the local area. "I tend to use Stoneway on the homeward journey and Birch Lane on the way out, makes for a nice little circuit. I do like to mix things up. One of my little foibles. You know the area?"

"I took a scout around this afternoon."

"Have you been inside my house?"

"No."

"Why don't I believe you?"

"I'm no liar, Mr Jones. Not really. Tell the odd fib now and again, but only if I have to."

Jones changed gear and cut into Stoneway, slowing to negotiate what was nothing more than a deeply rutted farm track. Despite what he told Freeman, he rarely used this route for fear of damaging the Rover's aging suspension.

Since he'd last used Stoneway, his farmer neighbour had filled some of the worse potholes with rubble, but it did little to improve the going.

Freeman reached for the grab strap above his head and shook his head. "DCI Jones, you really do need to relax. I know it must be difficult for you to trust someone you must consider as nothing but a common thief—"

"I doubt there's much 'common' about you, Freeman." Jones grimaced as the rear wheels lost traction and the back of the car jagged left. He dropped down into first gear, reduced the revs, and regained control. "You'll have to forgive an old man his set ways. I need to feel you out, as it were. Can't help it after all my years in the job."

"Okay, fair enough. I didn't break into your home for two reasons. First, because I know about your particular … what shall we call it, skill set? You'd have noticed anything moved or missing. I expect you already know what kind of aftershave I'm using. I didn't want to risk warning you of my interest until we had this chat."

"And the second reason?"

"You won't believe me."

"Try me." Jones risked a quick glance at his passenger, whose rueful smile seemed genuine.

"I don't like breaking into private homes. Too intrusive and rarely profitable."

The track levelled out and merged into the slightly better surfaced Birch Lane. The last dregs of twilight gave Jones enough light to see the land and his garden stretched out below. A motorcycle rested on its prop stand in front of his garden gate. Freeman had pointed the bike facing uphill for a quick getaway.

"Triumph Tiger 800 XC," Jones muttered, half to himself.

Freeman looked Jones up and down. A frown creased his forehead. "You know your bikes. A closet Hell's Angel back in the day?"

"No chance. Can't stand the things. I scraped more than enough bikers off the tarmac in my days as a traffic officer. Death traps, the lot of them. We identified that machine from the surveillance cameras at Police HQ." Jones pulled up alongside the motorbike. "No wonder we couldn't find it if you've been here all afternoon."

"Not quite all afternoon," Freeman said, "but a good part of it."

"You didn't answer my earlier question. Why the bomb threat?"

"It was the only thing I could think of to deliver my message and still have enough time to scarper. But, I imagine you've already gathered that, right?"

Jones nodded.

"There was another reason, though."

"Go on."

"It was a test."

"Really. Do tell."

"Well," Freeman said, his eyes scanning the surroundings. "If you'd allowed the bomb squad to destroy the package, I'd have known you weren't as sharp as your file suggested."

"And in that case?"

"I'd have tried to find another police officer to hear my story."

"Why d'you call the bomb squad?"

"I didn't want to disrupt the work of the West Midlands Police for a moment longer than absolutely necessary. I'm a responsible citizen."

Jones snorted. "Sure you are." He cut the engine and removed the key. He manipulated one of the house keys to point out from between his fingers and hid his hand behind his thigh. "What now?"

The pivotal moment had arrived. If Freeman had lied to lure him home ... well, the answer to that was obvious.

"Please relax, Chief Inspector. There's no need for alarm. Keys only have one legitimate use." He pointed to Jones's hand. "I'd hate to have to hurt you. I only resort to violence when there's no other choice."

"What happened in Edinburgh?"

"Huh?"

"Those two thugs with the shotguns. Where'd they disappear to?"

Freeman tensed. His hands stiffened. "You think I topped 'em?"

"They've still not surfaced."

"Last I saw of them was in a garage in Edinburgh. Both were alive, but neither was feeling particularly chipper. And that's Gospel."

"Really?"

"You have to believe me or I might just as well bugger off now and try this alone."

"Try what alone?"

"Try to bury a man called DB Parrish," Freeman answered quietly. "Sorry, Mr Jones, it's a long story."

Jones read the analogue clock on the dashboard. 20:55.

"Okay. I'll give you until eleven o'clock before slapping on the handcuffs. That enough time?"

Judging by the latent power coiled into the man sitting next to him, Jones doubted he'd be able to do anything more than wave goodbye should Freeman decide to wander away. On the other hand, he needed to take the lead, if only for the sake of appearances. On top of that, there was something else about the man, something behind the eyes, a vulnerability and sadness that made Jones want him to be honest, at least as far as that went.

Freeman pinched his lower lip. "It'll have to be enough, won't it?"

Jones opened the door and levered his aching bones out of the car. Behind him, Freeman slid from the passenger seat and stood in a silent, fluid motion.

"Better get started on your tale while I make us that cuppa."

Jones had to review his earlier estimations. Freeman stood three and a half inches taller than Jones, and was far more strongly built.

Freeman leaned forward, rested his forearms on the roof of the car, and studied the cottage. "Do you have any coffee?" he asked.

Jones shook his head. "Don't drink the stuff. It's either tea or water." He wasn't about to offer alcohol to a man he didn't trust.

Freeman wrinkled his nose. "Water it is then. I never could acquire a taste for tea."

"Philistine," said Jones, adding what he hoped was a disarming smile. The levity surprised him.

Freeman received his jibe well and released another boyish grin. Enigma? Chameleon? Jones couldn't tell, not yet.

Jones sidestepped the motorbike and hurried down the path to open the front door. He beckoned Freeman to follow, but not before sniffing the air inside the hall. He found no change in ambience and no lingering fragrance of Freeman's spicy aftershave. Freeman had only been wrong once so far that night—Jones had no idea what brand name to give the man's cologne. Perhaps he'd told the truth about not entering the cottage.

"Come through to the kitchen and start talking while I fill the kettle. But before you start, explain how you did that thing with my car."

Freeman pulled a chair out from under the kitchen table and placed it in the far corner, facing into the room, back to the wall. He stretched out his legs.

"I'm afraid that was fairly simple. Those old Rovers are a piece of piss ... sorry, piece of cake to break into and work on. Basic electronic ignition that's easy to piggyback a transmitter-receiver relay into the circuit. I operated it through the remote control box of a model aeroplane. You noticed that it interfered with the car's radio signal?"

Jones nodded and decanted the used leaves from the teapot into a strainer and tapped them into the compost bin.

"That was a bit careless of you. I'd have thought you'd be able to include a suppressor into the system to dampen the interference."

"That was intentional, Mr Jones, as was the intermittent engine misfire. I wanted you to concentrate and drive slowly. The last thing I wanted on my conscience was for you to get hurt in a crash."

"When did you do this?"

"This afternoon, when the car was in the garage for a service."

Jones stiffened. "I'm going to kill that mechanic. How much did you pay him?"

"Don't blame Sam Tallon, Mr Jones. He knows nothing about my visit. I did the work when he was called out on a breakdown, just before he returned the car to you."

"A hoax breakdown call, I imagine?"

"That's right, Mr Jones. No doubt about it, I'm a terrible man, but I did need him away from the garage for at least half an hour."

Jones filled the pot and replaced the lid without stirring the makings. Stirring came later—after the tea had drawn.

"Sure you won't have one?"

"No thanks, water's fine."

Jones filled a tumbler with tap water, handed it across, and then carried the pot and his extra-large mug and a jug of milk to the table and sat opposite Freeman.

"Ready when you are."

Freeman's eyes lost focus for a moment before flicking up and to the right, the sign of a man searching his long-term memory rather than accessing his imagination. Alternatively, Freeman might be a gifted liar or someone who had read a textbook on neuro-linguistic programming, as Jones had done, once or twice.

"Okay, where to start." Freeman took a long drink. "My father was a locksmith, owned a shop a few miles from here. All you need to know for now is that I've been making keys and opening locks since before I started pre-school. Some might say I was a natural, but I worked hard on my skills. Nothing worth having ever came easy. Don't you agree?"

"I do."

Freeman drained half the water and stared at the remaining liquid for a moment before setting the glass on the table. His use of the coaster earned him significant Brownie points.

"A little over two years ago, I was working in a jewellery shop in London, a pretentious place near Golders Green called *Archibald and Daughter*. One morning, a customer named Digby Parrish entered and asked me to make him a special key …"

Chapter Forty

THURSDAY 7TH JULY — *Late evening*
Near Much Wenlock, Shropshire

TWO-AND-A-HALF HOURS LATER, after Freeman had talked more or less non-stop since they'd entered the cottage, he asked. "Well, Mr Jones. What do you think?"

"It's an old story," said Jones. "A man seduced by easy money finds himself mixed up with people he can't control. I don't see what I can do for you."

"I haven't quite finished yet, but what do you think so far?"

Shortly after finishing his second cuppa and a round of cheese sandwiches each, with Freeman accepting a glass of milk, semi-skimmed, Jones had moved them into the lounge. They recorded what turned out to be a detailed confession on the compact digital device Freeman had brought along for the job.

"Well?" Freeman asked.

"As I said, you tell a good story, Mr Freeman. How much is true?"

"All of it. Listen, the way I see it, this all boils down to gut instinct. Do you believe me, Mr Jones? And will you help?"

"Can't answer that yet. First thing is, you are a thief, and I can't let you get away with that. I'm a policeman, and I'm not in the habit of allowing criminals to go free."

"Yep, I understand. It's part of our deal. You help me and I'll come quietly. You have my whole story on that recorder and it won't take you long to verify what I've said. Before I leave tonight, I'll sign a statement if you need one. You also have my trace forensics all over the cottage and your car. There's no way I'll run. I have nowhere to go."

"What makes you think I'll let you leave?"

"Let me go and I'll set up Digby Parrish for you to catch him in the act."

"How?"

"I know the next target."

Now we're getting somewhere.

"Which is?"

"Oh no." Freeman jumped to his feet and started pacing the room, wearing more holes into his threadbare carpet. "I can't tell you that until I have your word to let me go. If you arrest me now, Parrish will abort the job and I won't have any leverage."

Jones watched Freeman pace and considered his response. He wanted to trust the young cracksmith, who, if Jones were to believe his story, only joined Parrish's firm to help a terminally ill father—a laudable act and one he'd have Phil confirm as soon as possible. On the other hand, Freeman could be trying to sell him a lemon. He needed more time and more information before he could make a decision. "Are you prepared to answer a few questions?"

"If I can. You've been patient enough. I could see you've been desperate to drag out the thumbscrews since I started talking."

"Not a bit of it." Jones stood. "Not my style. I leave that to my subordinates. My DS, Phil Cryer, is a dab hand at the third degree."

"The what?"

"Bloody hell, man. How old are you?"

"Twenty-eight next birthday," Freeman answered without hesitation.

Jones took the fast response as evidence of honesty. "Oh dear," he said, shaking his head in forced patience. "How very young you are. Never heard of the third degree, eh? Don't worry. It's not important."

Freeman stopped pacing and returned Jones' steady stare.

"Why now?" Jones asked.

"Excuse me?"

"Why are you coming forward now? You could have done this any time over the past two years."

A shadow clouded Freeman's face and he looked away.

"John Freeman passed away two weeks ago."

"Oh. I'm sorry for your loss, but hang on a minute." Jones felt his brow knit and made a conscious effort to relax his facial muscles. "With your father gone, Digby Parrish has lost his hold over you, unless you're worried about your sister."

Freeman's wry smile returned. "No, Mr Jones. I don't have a sister. Never did."

"What?"

"There are ways to falsify a back story. In the spy game it's called building a legend."

"What? Are you telling me you're a spy?"

"No. I'm a locksmith and a thief. I didn't lie to you, but I'll explain it all after you've taken down Parrish and Hutch. Do we have a deal?"

Jones hesitated again. Freeman told a convincing tale, but was holding something back. Jones could see it in the young man's twitchy movements and in his desperate eyes. "Why don't you come to the station and give a statement? We can run with the case in the official way. I have contacts in the National Crime Agency who owe me some favours. With their help and your inside knowledge, we could make a case in a matter of weeks."

Freeman closed his eyes. His lower lip trembled. "That's just it, Mr Jones. I don't have weeks. As I said, I'm afraid I haven't finished my story."

Jones tried to remain calm, but his patience wore precious thin.

"The whole story, you said. Give it. If I learn you've been hiding anything, my help's out of the question."

Freeman slumped into his chair, and stared at his trembling hands.

"The other day, Parrish told me he'd sanctioned the shotgun attack in Edinburgh. He set me up to bind me into his fucking team. You see, John Freeman took a turn for the worse last Christmas and Parrish must have thought I was going to split when he died. It was only a matter of time, he was really ill." He stared at Jones. "When those Scottish morons arrived at Morton's shop with shotguns blasting, I had to act to prevent collateral damage. Parrish said he was okay about my intervention. Laid the blame on poor Harry Bryce, but I know better now."

Freeman shuffled in his chair and rubbed his hands on the cushions. Jones let the sacrilege slide.

"It gets worse, Mr Jones."

Of course it does.

"Keep going."

"A couple of days after I aborted the job, I went back to Edinburgh to find out how Angela Glennie was coping with the aftermath."

Jones smacked the arm of his chair. "You did what? Bloody idiot."

"Don't you think I know that now?" Freeman snapped. "I didn't intend for us to actually meet. Only wanted to check that she was okay … you know, from a distance."

"So what happened? She recognised you, right?

Freeman up-nodded.

"I couldn't believe it, like."

For the first time, Freeman's smooth Home Counties accent slipped into a charmless West Midlands drawl.

There's that chameleon thing again.

"I mean," he continued, "I was in disguise when we met the first time. Didn't think there was a chance in hell she'd recognise me, like, but she took one look and rushed across the road to talk to me, and …"

"Cupid's arrow struck?" Jones could feel Freeman's pain. He could probably predict the next chapter of the story, but didn't intend to pre-empt the jewel thief's words. He still treated this as a police interview, despite the location, and despite the fact that Freeman had turned off the recorder.

"Keep going, Mr Freeman."

"My dad was 'Mr Freeman'. I'm 'Sean' to my friends, and 'Freeman' to everyone else." He raised an eyebrow and paused. Jones didn't respond, but rolled his hand forwards as a signal for Freeman to continue.

"To cut a long story short, we've grown to know each other rather well since last March." Freeman flushed and Jones sighed. "This is going to sound like a bad romance novel, but we … oh crap, you can guess what happened."

"Okay, I get the picture. Love bloomed, etcetera, etcetera."

"You're a cynic, Mr Jones."

"Probably."

"Never been in love?"

"No," Jones lied.

"Not even when you were my age?"

"The topic is you, Freeman, not me. What does Ms Glennie think of your chosen career?"

"She knows nothing about that side of my life. She still thinks I produce independent films. If she knew I was a thief, she'd run a mile. Things were going great with us until that meeting with Parrish two days ago."

"Don't tell me. He had you followed and is using Ms Glennie as leverage?"

The jewel thief nodded. "I was being careful, but fuck … sorry, but yes, you're right. I'm scared for her. To be honest, I don't care about me, but she has nothing to do with this."

"What does Parrish want from you next?"

"Are you going to help me or not?"

"I can't promise anything. Not without more information."

Freeman took a moment before answering. "You've heard of the Rajmahl Exhibition?"

It was Jones' turn to slump back into his chair. He crossed his arms. "Oh for pity's sake. He wants you to steal some of the best-protected artefacts in the country outside of the Tower of London? Is he mad?"

"Probably, but he has inside knowledge."

"An insurance broker?"

Freeman smiled again, but this one was sad.

"So, you *did* work out my clues."

"It wasn't difficult, but you haven't suggested anything we didn't think of ourselves. Even so, we can't find a pattern or a single link to all the robberies."

Freeman shot forward in his chair.

"But that's just the point, Mr Jones. There is no single broker. There can't be, the targets have been too diverse. Parrish has a huge network on his payroll, or under his thumb. It's the only way he can be getting so much valid information. And he knows the precise layout to the Stafford Museum."

"Okay, I believe you. When's this going down?"

"No idea. Parrish never says until the last moment. But I know he's going in armed."

"Hell! Give me the details and I'll arrange a reception committee. Easy enough to spike someone's guns if you know they're coming."

"No you can't do that. If the police suddenly show up or the security setup at the Stafford Museum changes, Parrish will abort."

"So? We'll keep him under surveillance until the next job."

"No, that won't work!"

"Why not?"

Freeman's shoulders sagged and he rubbed his face.

"There's something else I haven't told you."

The warning mechanism in Jones' head, which had activated the moment the car radio started playing up, belted out a claxon wail. "What?"

"I can't contact Angela. She's disappeared."

"What? Come again?" Jones demanded.

"I haven't spoken to Angela since yesterday morning. She's not answering her mobile." Freeman breathed the words.

"That doesn't mean anything. Could she be at an audition?"

"No," Freeman answered, making fists. "When we're apart, we speak two or three times a day, either by phone or video link. I've called and called, but her phone goes straight to voicemail. I talked to her agent this morning and he's pissed at her for missing a job. She's never done that before."

Freeman finished his statement teary-eyed and with both hands gripping the arms of the chair as though to stop himself falling to the floor.

Here was Jones' answer. No wonder Freeman had been so jumpy. This news changed everything. He stood and approached Freeman, looked down in sympathy at the broken young man.

"I am going to help you," he said, and dropped a hand onto the man's shoulder. Freeman's deltoid muscle bunched and he raised his head to meet Jones' stare.

"Really?"

"Yes, but our agreement still holds. Once we bag this Parrish character and find your girlfriend, you're going away for a long time. And if I find you've been lying to me, the deal's off. Understand?"

"Yes. I'm going nowhere until Angela's safe." Freeman's eyes glistened under the glow from the wall lights. He appeared close to losing control. "What happens next?" he asked.

"Wait there a moment. I need to call my sergeant. Won't be long."

"What?" Freeman braced his hands on the arms of the chair as though about to push off and head for the door.

"Easy, lad." Jones pushed down on Freeman's shoulder. "Don't worry. You can trust him, he's a good man." He turned to face the hallway door. "Phil," he called. "You can come in now!"

The door opened and Phil Cryer edged into the room. "Evening, boss."

Chapter Forty-One

FRIDAY 8TH JULY – *Early morning*
Near Much Wenlock, Shropshire

"YOU BASTARD!"

Freeman shook off Jones' hand, and in one flowing movement sprang forward and took up what Jones recognised as first defence position, Japanese martial arts, possibly aikido. He stood poised, left foot ahead of right, knees bent, arms forward, hands open and fingers relaxed. His breathing came hard and fast, and his eyes swept the room.

"Jumpy isn't he, boss?" Phil asked. He closed the door and leaned his considerable bulk against it.

"Relax, Freeman," Jones said, holding up his hands to mirror Freeman's fighting stance. "The only way out of the room is through this door, and that means you'll have to go through us. I have little doubt you can take me apart. After all, I'm a frail old man, but Phil isn't. You could try the window, but they're locked and triple-glazed. You're not getting out that way. Let's just take it easy, eh?"

Freeman's breathing slowed. He flexed his fingers, but didn't lower his arms. "What's going on, Mr Jones?" he asked, his low voice barely carrying the distance between them.

Phil folded his arms but stayed put, not taking his eyes from Freeman. "I was wondering when you were going to announce my presence, boss. It's chilly in that hallway, and I've been bursting for a pee for the past half hour.

"What's happening?" Freeman asked with more urgency.

"You going to tell him, boss?"

Jones waited a few moments before answering—he judged that Freeman needed time for his nerves to settle.

"Mr Freeman," he said, the moment the man relaxed his shoulders a fraction, "are we going to stand here posturing all night, or shall we start working to find your girlfriend?"

"How?" asked Freeman, pointing at Phil.

Jones shook his head. "Oh come on now, you didn't think I'd fall for the old car tampering ploy did you?" He returned to his chair and indicated that Freeman and Phil should also sit.

"What?" Freeman asked without moving from his position in the corner, apparently feeling safer for having his back defended by two solid stone walls.

"My mechanic, Sam Tallon, and I go back a long way. He knows better than to return my car without double-checking everything first." Jones crossed his legs as a signal for Freeman to relax. "Sam spotted your little modification and showed it to me when he delivered the car to the station. Then I called my sergeant and another of my colleagues who loves engines and electronics. They added a few minor modifications to your equipment." He paused. "At this point, I suppose formal introductions are in order. Detective Sergeant Philip Cryer, meet Sean Freeman, aka John Devenish."

Phil said, "How do," flashed his warrant card, and returned it to his hip pocket.

Freeman said nothing, but the taut cables in his neck eased off a touch more.

"Okay," Jones said. "Phil, you know what I'm like with technology, you take up the story."

Phil winced and waggled his head.

"Could do, boss, but I wasn't kidding about needing the loo. Are you cool now, Mr Freeman?"

"You're not going to lock me up?"

"I gave you my word," Jones said, and again pointed Freeman to the chair.

This time Freeman accepted the offer, but leaned forward, hands resting on knees, primed for instant action.

"Okay Phil, quick as you like, please."

Phil ducked out of the room with the speed of a commuter late for the last bus home.

"Okay," Jones said, "time's short so I'll tell it the best way I can. From what I understand, Sam and my men left your device in position and reverse-engineered your radio frequencies, or something. Don't know how they did it, but I leave all that clever stuff to others. I'm just an old-fashioned copper, brought up on landlines and police radios." He shrugged. "It turns out that the minute you started transmitting messages to my car, they were able to trace the signal back to you."

"Clever buggers. Is that why you didn't kick up too much of a fuss when I introduced myself?"

"More or less. After all your messages and clues, the false bomb, I guessed you were going to try to contact me face-to-face. Didn't know why though, but I'm glad you reached out." Jones removed the comms pickup from his ear and showed it to Freeman. "Phil's been in contact with me since I left the station. He said you were controlling the car from here, which is a damned cheek, by the way. I kept schtum in case you were listening in."

Freeman shook his head slowly. "That detour down Stoneway rather than Birch Lane wasn't just to test my local knowledge?"

Jones shook his head.

"Not only that. I risked my poor old car's suspension to give Phil time to get into position. He's the only other person on the planet I'd trust with my front door key."

The door opened.

"Wow," Phil said, grinning. "Didn't know you cared, boss."

Worry lines etched into Freeman's face showed where his thoughts lay. "What are we going to do about Angela?"

"We need to handle this carefully. Before you arrived, I'd never heard of a Digby Parrish. He's not on my patch. What about you, Phil. Name familiar?"

"I've heard of *Parrish Enterprises* of course, but know nothing about the management board. We need access to the PNC. Digby Parrish is a Londoner you say, Mr Freeman?"

"Just Freeman, or Sean," the man said, glancing at Jones. "And yep, North London born and bred. The bloody scumbag's bound to have a record, unless he's paid off all of your colleagues in the Smoke."

"What'd you say?" Phil bridled, and took a half pace forward.

"No offence meant, Mr Cryer, but I've heard Digby boast about how he's Teflon-coated and has loads of people on his payroll. Police, Customs & Excise men, prison guards, reporters. Told me he plays golf some weekends with a High Court judge. I can't trust anyone. That's why I took so long to come forward, but Angela's disappearance has forced my hand. You're the only one I can rely on, Mr Jones. And you vouch for Mr Cryer, so I'll go along with that."

The pleading, searching look in Freeman's eyes convinced Jones of the man's fear and vulnerability.

"Before I can do anything," Jones said, "you need to tell me exactly what Parrish said about Ms Glennie, and why he's taken her now."

"I told you about the Stafford Museum, right? Basically, I told Parrish he was mental. The Stafford might as well be Fort Knox." Freeman rubbed his face with both hands before climbing out of the chair and standing in front of Jones, eyes glistening and puffy. "That's when he told me he knew about Angela and me. He didn't threaten her directly, he never does, but he's taken her, Mr Jones. The bastard's going to kill her if I don't do what he wants. You have to help us, Mr Jones. Please."

Jones turned to Phil. "What do you think, Phil? Want to get the ball rolling on this one? It might mean an all-nighter."

"No worries boss, who needs sleep?" He turned to leave.

"Where you going?" Freeman asked.

"Back to base. I need secure access to the PNC and certain other search engines. I want to see what we have on Digby Parrish. I also need to do it without calling attention to myself—in case Parrish isn't telling porkies about his paid network."

Freeman looked from Jones to Phil, and then back to Jones. "I don't like the idea of too many people learning about this. Parrish can't know I've spoken to you or Angela's dead. Why don't you have Internet here?"

Phil snorted. "Don't go there."

"I mean," the thief continued, "who doesn't have the Internet these days?"

"As I said earlier, you could have knocked on my door and invited yourself in for a chat any time."

Freeman sighed and looked up as though searching for inspiration in the ceiling joists.

"Oh really. Now why didn't I think of that?" he said, his voice laden with sarcasm. "You mean stroll up to a cop's house and hand myself over? Yeah, right. Like that was going to happen."

"I would have listened to your story."

"Perhaps, but I couldn't take the risk. For all I know, you have an arsenal hidden away in here and would have blown my head off before I had the chance to open my mouth."

"You have a lot to learn about the boss, Freeman," Phil said, and winked at Jones.

Some of Jones' inner tension subsided. Clearly, Freeman hadn't been able to learn everything about him from trawling the Internet. Freeman might well have hacked the local police servers and accessed his personnel records, but he clearly hadn't interpreted the findings very well. If Freeman had done so, the man would have learned that Jones refused to apply for a firearms certification every year until he reached the age limit for the induction course. Perhaps the reasons for Jones' hatred of firearms, and his other secrets, were still safe.

"Better get off, Phil."

"Okay boss, I'll see you later. And while I'm at it, I'll call the guys in for an early start. We'll need to do some serious planning. Seven o'clock suit you?"

"Sounds good." Jones waved him off.

Freeman stepped forward, hand outstretched. "Mr Cryer. Thanks for everything. Angela doesn't deserve any of this."

Phil shook the man's hand briefly. "We'll do what we can for her. I promise you that."

Jones listened as Phil clomped down the hall dialling the plink plonk numbers on his mobile. He opened the front door and said, "Hi Manda, I'm on my way. How you feeling?" The door closed on the rest of the conversation.

"Tell me what you know of Parrish's plans for the Stafford," Jones asked.

Freeman turned to face the window, head lowered. "Can't tell you much at the moment. He's a cautious bastard. All I know is the exhibition closes next week and I'm guessing he's set the job for this weekend."

"So," said Jones, standing. "We've less than two full days. Not much time to organise a reception committee."

"Long enough for Angela, Mr Jones. Can't bear to think how she's feeling right now."

Chapter Forty-Two

UNSHAVEN AND CRUMPLED after a full night's research, Phil turned from studying his computer monitor. "Do you trust him, boss?"

Jones thought for a minute before answering. Could he really trust a man under as much pressure as Freeman?

"Good question. I should say no, but my sense is he's a decent sort at heart. You saw how grateful he was when we agreed to help. Hope he doesn't prove me wrong. How much of his story can you verify?"

"Most of it. I've gone through his immediate history and accessed his educational record, schools, university. National insurance and tax records check out. All seems above board. His father, John Freeman, was definitely a locksmith. Suffered a massive stroke six years ago and spent five years in St Margaret's coma hospice. Died on Thursday, June 25th, in a convalescent home, just as

Freeman said. Want me to go back any further, check out his mother and grandparents?"

"Perhaps later, when we're building the court case," Jones said without concentrating. "I'm happy enough for now."

"What do you reckon to Freeman putting his hands up and coming quietly once this weekend's over?"

"Remains to be seen. What do we know about *Parrish Enterprises?*"

"Leisure conglomerate. Keeps a low profile and pays its taxes on time. Bars, casinos, strip clubs, hotels, that kind of thing. Most of the premises are licensed to provide alcohol, food, and gambling. Freeman appeared on the website as SVP of Corporate Security eighteen months ago. It all checks out so far, but I can't go any further than the published annual accounts, which show good turnover and healthy profits."

"Why not?"

"There's a flag on the PNC file and you'll never guess who's flying it."

"The NCA?"

"Bingo," Phil said, his lopsided smile returning to grace the morning. "Want me to respond to the flag?"

"Hell no. Can't risk Parrish learning we're looking at a flag on his name. You remember what Freeman said about his being Teflon-coated. We need to keep this quiet. Angela Glennie's life's in danger. We need to go in the back door, but …"

"But Superintendent Knightly didn't return your call yet?"

"Correct. Tell you the truth I'm fed up with his one-sided attitude to friendship. Thinking of cutting him from my Christmas card list."

"You don't send Christmas cards."

"Quite," Jones shot back. "Doesn't mean I can't have a list though. I wonder how early the Super arrives at work. Let's find out, shall we?"

As he reached for the desk phone, it rang, and Jones picked up the handset. "Jones here … Ah, Brian, thanks for getting back to me. I was about to give you a call. Mind if I put you on speaker? DS Cryer needs to hear this."

He hit the speaker button and mouthed, "Superintendent Knightly."

"…how is the sergeant?"

"I'm fine thank you, sir," Phil answered.

"Good, good. And you, David?"

"Yep, okay, but time's against us."

"Really? Looks as though I have an apology to make. I was out of the country when you called yesterday. My assistant left the message on my internal voicemail, bloody idiot. I only picked it up five minutes ago. I told him to contact me immediately the next time you tried to get in touch. So, how can I help the country's finest detective?"

Jones ignored the compliment.

"What can you tell me about *Parrish Enterprises Ltd.*?"

"Nothing." The response came quickly. Too quickly.

"Really? There's an NCA flag on the file."

"We're a big organisation, David. Growing all the time. What's your interest?"

"Are you stonewalling me, Brian?"

Knightly didn't answer for a moment.

"Chief Inspector Jones, please don't take that tone with me. I'm inclined to ask around the office, but not until you tell me why."

Jones didn't like the way the tone of the conversation had changed. Knightly's defensive attitude ran contrary to his normal demeanour. He considered making the call private, but he needed Phil's counsel.

"Excuse me, sir. I have information that the owner of the company, one Digby Parrish, might have graduated from robbery to abduction. I need your help."

"Okay, Chief Inspector," Knightly said. "Give me what you have and I'll see what I can do."

Jones outlined the situation and arranged for Phil to send the NCA links to the anonymised PNC file he'd created overnight. They spoke for five more minutes and ended the call with an agreement to video conference that afternoon.

"That was strange," Phil said once Jones had replaced the handset.

"Yep. I think the Super knows more than he's letting on."

"Do you trust him?"

Jones smiled. "Philip, I met Brian Knightly back in '73. We've worked together off and on ever since. I trust him as much as I trust you—with my life."

"Thanks, boss."

"You're welcome."

"So why was he being so evasive?"

"No idea. I suspect he'll tell me when he can."

Phil checked his watch. "Time for breakfast before we brief the troops?"

"Blimey, Philip, don't you ever think of anything but your stomach?"

"It has been known."

———

THE WHOLE TEAM, minus Charlie Pelham who was halfway to Edinburgh, gathered in the SCU briefing room for the video conference.

Alex and Wash had returned from touring the Stafford Museum undercover, armed with a bagful of brochures and a patron's-eye overview of the existing security arrangements. The brochures showed a luxurious building, containing row upon row of oak display cabinets standing on plum-coloured carpets linked by parquet flooring. Lit by subtle spots and hidden strips, the museum gave the impression of an expensively appointed Victorian mansion.

Jones had also dragged in his go-to man from the Armed Response Unit. Inspector Giles Danforth—tall, powerfully built with broad shoulders, bulging biceps, and Popeye forearms—wore a dark blue polo shirt with the letters ARU embroidered on the breast. Jones had known the ex-soldier for the best part of a decade and considered him one of the best officers with whom he had ever served. He would trust Giles Danforth with the lives of his team any day of any week.

Phil pecked at a keypad and the large TV, dragged in on a metal trolley from the comms room, flickered into coloured life. The round, grey-bearded face of Superintendent Knightly appeared on the screen, sitting behind his London desk. An attractive blonde woman in her late-thirties sat to Knightly's left. Jones recognised her as Knightly's trusted, and highly skilled, second-in-command.

"Chief Inspector Jones, good to see you." Knightly opened, his senior rank allowing him to take the lead, at least initially. "You've met Inspector Eldritch. She's more familiar with the Parrish case than I am."

After Jones had introduced his team, Knightly continued.

"What have you learned since we last spoke?"

"Not a lot, sir."

Jones gave an overview, which amounted to precious little. He rounded off by offering the single nugget. "The only thing else to add is that I heard from Sean Freeman an hour ago. He was frantic, but held himself together long enough to tell me the raid's set for four o'clock Sunday morning."

Knightly traded glances with Eldritch, who nodded and pointed to a file on the desk in front of her.

"Makes sense," Knightly said. "Empty roads and the security guards at their most tired. Doesn't give us much time to organise a reception committee, though."

Knightly started fiddling with his beard. Jones recognised the man's poker "tell".

The old boy's embarrassed. Wants to say something.

"Are you able to tell me why you're watching Parrish, sir?"

Knightly glanced to his left again. "Yes ... we've had an obbo on him for the past three weeks following an anonymous tip. We've a tap on his phone too. He's mentioned the Stafford a couple of times, but we didn't realise he considered himself strong enough to target the Rajmahl Collection."

Phil jotted a note and passed it to Jones, who struggled to read the semi-legible scrawl.

No wonder we couldn't find much on Parrish.
NCA keeps their intel in-house—bloody Prima Donnas.

JONES NODDED and leaned closer to the desk microphone. "It's a shame we didn't know about Parrish and his link with JT1 before now, sir. I think we need to talk about sharing our information more freely. We are all on the same side after all, and the West Midlands *is* my patch."

The Super closed his eyes for a moment before responding.

"Sorry, Chief Inspector, but we've had some very serious operations go tits-up due to information seepage. Our standard operating procedure is to keep the information to ourselves during the early stages of an investigation, and that's all I can say on the matter. However, I do have permission to allow you access to this case file now. You should have the codes."

"DC Washington," said Jones. "Do the business, please. Allow access for everyone in the unit and send an email. I'll have a hard copy." Ryan moved to the computer desk. "It would be nice for us to know as much as the NCA does about our joint target," he added without lowering his voice.

"Yes, well, we should discuss the details of the operation before getting side-tracked." Knightly checked the time on his wristwatch. "We have less than sixty hours to plan a joint operation. What do you have on the museum itself?"

Phil cleared his throat before answering.

"The Stafford beefed up security when they announced the Rajmahl Exhibition. They hired two extra security men per shift and installed new electronic countermeasures. Usual stuff, heat sensors, motion detectors, infrared alarms, but they only cover the most sensitive display areas. Apparently, would have cost too much to wire the whole place. Despite that, Parrish would need artillery to break into the vault—"

"Our latest intel," Knightly interrupted, poker-faced, "is that Parrish has access to explosives."

Ryan, standing by the printer, gave out a low whistle.

Giles spoke for the first time. "If they're going in old school, smash and grab style, why do they need Freeman?"

Before Jones could avoid answering the question, a phone rang on Knightly's desk. He held up a hand, "Excuse me one moment please."

During the short interlude, the skin on Knightly's face not hidden by his beard or glasses, changed from pale pink to tomato red. A moment later, he replaced the handset, glanced at Eldritch, and turned his attention back to the screen, frowning.

"Sorry about that Chief Inspector, but I've just been told our surveillance team has lost Parrish." He placed an elbow on the desk in front of him and toyed with his beard again. "He gave them the slip an hour ago. Hutch and Adamovic are missing too."

Jones wanted to say something curt, but managed to hold himself in check.

Alex cleared her throat. "Can I ask a question, boss?"

Jones pointed to the microphone. "Feel free."

"Inspector Eldritch, was there any mention of Angela Glennie during the telephone tap?"

Eldritch shuffled the papers on the desk in front of her. "Not directly," she answered, "but yesterday morning at … eleven-twenty three, Parrish received a call from someone using a burner phone. The conversation lasted seventeen seconds. No introductions. The caller, who had a Scottish accent, possibly Glaswegian, said, 'No trouble with the collection. The package will be with you overnight'. Parrish replied … 'Good. Make sure the merchandise is undamaged.' Then the call ended. We didn't know what it meant at the time and assumed it was related to a drugs shipment."

Jones glanced at Phil, whose deep frown gave away his thoughts. Jones addressed his next words to Eldritch. "So we work on the assumption that the 'package' refers to Angela Glennie, and that

Parrish has her tucked away somewhere, possibly in England. Damn. Freeman was right to be scared. Any idea where they might be holding her?"

Eldritch shook her head. "None I'm afraid, Chief Inspector. The call was too short for a trace."

"In that case," Jones said, "the safest thing for Ms Glennie is to intercept Parrish's mob at the Stafford. Parrish isn't above murdering witnesses, but his hired muscle might be more reluctant, especially when we have them on toast for armed robbery."

Knightly nodded his agreement.

"Good idea. There's a schematic of the architect's blueprints for the museum on our server. You'll also find an overlay of the new electronic security measures they installed for the exhibition."

From his desk, Ryan called out, "Yep, got them. I can put it up on the big screen any time you like, boss."

"Excellent," said Jones. "How did you manage to get hold of that stuff at such short notice, sir?"

Knightly played with his beard again and glanced sideways at Eldritch.

Here it comes.

"The museum trustees contacted us for a risk assessment when the Sultan of Rajmahl first agreed to sponsor the exhibition. Inspector Eldritch and a colleague visited the Stafford early last year and gave them input in terms of security modifications."

Bloody knew it!

Jones couldn't let it slide. "Let me get this straight, Superintendent Knightly, sir. You came to Birmingham without notifying us first?" He stared into the camera above the screen, trying to make his point without raising his voice. "This is way beyond the remit of the NCA. You're supposed to liaise with the local police. If we'd known you had the architect's drawings and security plans, it would have saved us hours of work this morning."

The twin vertical lines on Knightly's forehead deepened. "Point taken, Chief Inspector, but there were … operational exigencies."

"Which were?" Despite the situation, Jones wasn't prepared to let the matter drop. If he were alone with Knightly, he'd be banging fists on tables at this point.

"The trustees specifically asked us to keep a low profile. They were aware of the spate of unsolved jewel robberies and called us in for a risk assessment. We needed to limit the number of people involved to 'need to know'."

"And we didn't 'need to know'. Is that it, Superintendent?"

"I have already apologised, Chief Inspector. Shall we move on now?"

Jones added this factor to his list of grievances for later discussion. "Ryan, put up the plans now, please."

The schematic—white lines, dimensions, and lettering on a dark blue background—replaced Knightly and Eldritch on the TV. The two officers were relegated to a small rectangle at the top right-hand corner of the screen.

The title, *Stafford Museum of Middle Eastern Culture – Ground Floor*, appeared at the top, underlined in bold. Other script, date, and copyright details followed below.

Jones studied the plans while Alex, at Jones' command, took them through a guided tour based on her morning's visit. Ryan used the computer cursor as a pointer to follow Alex's route. She started with the entrance: double doors with a metal detector, kiosk, and two static guards. An anteroom-cum-reception area acted as a filtering point. Visitors entered on the left of a roped barrier and exited on the right. Jones augmented the map tour with pictures from the brochure.

When Alex reached the chamber holding the Rajmahl Crown Jewels, Eldritch added some details to which Alex and Wash, as paying guests, would not have been aware.

"During opening times," Eldritch said, "the collection is protected by the latest electronic security system, a package we recommended and installed by a firm we vetted. Apart from the pressure and thermal sensors, signals from CCTV monitors stream into a computerised imaging system. If any of the display pieces move by as much as three millimetres, it sends an alarm to the central security desk in the lobby and the guards can activate the security barriers." She paused for a moment before lighting up the screen with a smile, and adding, "That will lock the whole building up tighter than the Super's wallet."

Ryan lost control of the cursor for a moment, clearly enraptured by the woman's dimples, or something. Jones had to admit that Eldritch did fill the inset screen rather nicely. He also appreciated the joke, as did Knightly, who was renowned for his generosity, especially when his team had earned a good conviction.

"There is something else you should know," Eldritch continued. "Once the museum closes to the public, the guards move the *Face of the Sultana*, the collection's most valuable single item, to the museum's vault."

"Really?" Jones asked, and opened the museum brochure to the centre page spread. He studied the picture once again, and this time read the blurb. Solid gold, twenty-four carat, with sapphires for eyes, pearls for teeth, and a diamond-encrusted tiara, it was the life-sized face of the original Sultan of Rajmahl's first wife. According to the hyperbolic text, the tenth century object was an "unfathomably beautiful work from ancient Persia, whose true origins are lost in the mists of time".

To Jones, the piece of nicely crafted metal looked a tad garish, and the face, being too perfect and symmetrical, unrealistic.

"Yes," Eldritch answered. "The insurance company insisted on the added precautions due to its value. Alone, the *Face* is insured for fifty-five million pounds."

Again, Ryan whistled.

The moment Jones heard the words "insurance company", his old friend the warning mechanism in his head, screamed out the alarm. He could tell from the way Phil tensed, that he felt the same way. They shared a look that confirmed Jones' interpretation.

"Where and how secure is this vault?" Phil asked the question before Jones had the chance to do so.

"It's on the ground floor adjacent to the main exhibition hall," Eldritch answered.

Wash followed the Inspector's directions and moved the cursor from the main chamber, through one door into a corridor marked as three metres wide and thirty long. This led in a straight line to the rear exit and allowed access to the museum's archive, restoration, and storage rooms via half a dozen doors. Three pairs of double fire doors, both sets locked and alarmed and located at ten-metre intervals, prevented direct access between the exhibition areas and the rear chamber, marked on the plans as "Goods Receiving Bay".

With only one way through into the rest of the building, the bay, twelve-metres wide and ten-metres deep, acted as a secure area for receiving and dispatching exhibits.

The vault itself was a rectangular room, four-metres by three-metres, and situated between the exhibition hall and the first set of fire doors. The vault's single opening was in the access corridor. It had walls of one-metre thick concrete, reinforced with steel mesh, and embedded with vibration sensors. Another smaller square abutted the rear wall of the vault.

"What's that small square?" Jones asked. It had no key on the plans, and, from its size and shape, could have been a service shaft.

Knightly fielded the question. "That's another of the museum's treasures, an antique safe. The security guards lock the *Face* inside a safe, inside a vault, and the vault itself is on a time lock. The lock won't open before eight o'clock in the morning, on weekdays and Saturdays, and nine o'clock on Sundays. The *Face* is as secure as anything I've seen in the UK outside of the Bank of England."

A safe inside a safe?

Jones saw it as clear as day. He saw Parrish's whole plan. The other robberies had been little more than preludes to the big one, dress rehearsals.

"The safe inside the vault, sir, it wouldn't be a Miles & Archer, Monarch 1908, by any chance?"

Jones would have bet big money on the answer.

"How could you possibly know that, David?" Knightly turned to Eldritch, who shook her head and shrugged as though to say, "I didn't tell him".

"You didn't read the whole report of my conversation with Freeman, did you, sir."

"No. As you can imagine, there's been a bit of a flap on since we talked this morning. What have we missed?"

Ryan and Alex exchanged knowing glances. Phil studied his fingernails.

Jones summarised his report, covering Parrish's initial approach to Freeman.

After Jones finished, Knightly chipped in with, "The Sultan of Rajmahl donated his Monarch to the Stafford when he bought the museum four years ago. This explains why Parrish recruited Freeman in the first place."

"You know what this means, don't you sir?" Jones asked.

Knightly nodded. "Parrish has been planning this robbery since *before* the insurance company insisted the *Face* be kept overnight in the Monarch."

"Exactly," said Jones. "And after we've found Angela Glennie, I think the NCA ought to investigate the UK insurance industry." He looked at Phil who hid his smirk by lowering his head and removing lint from his shirtsleeve.

Chapter Forty-Three

FRIDAY 8TH JULY – *Afternoon*
Holton, Birmingham

JONES ALLOWED the murmur of his team to die before continuing. "This also goes to confirm Freeman's position as almost a victim in all this. He's been leaving clues ever since the second Edinburgh job, but we've been too dim to pick up on them."

"You mean the 'broke/broken/broker' messages?" Eldritch asked, whose pained expression showed that she'd finally twigged their meaning. She answered her own question. "So we have to conclude that Parrish has been manipulating the insurance market. But how? One of the first things we investigated was the possibility of insurance fraud, but we found no pattern. We vetted thousands of insurance people. Nothing jumped out at us."

"That's the beauty of Parrish's operation. He never uses the same source more than once or twice. He hits different towns, uses different methods, and hires different personnel. The only consistent factors are the high-value of the goods stolen, and Sean Freeman."

Knightly frowned and rolled his hand forward to move on the

discussion. "Did Freeman tell you how they plan to tackle the Stafford job?"

Jones hesitated. Freeman hadn't wanted to reveal his plan, but, after Phil had left the cottage, Jones had insisted and threatened to remove his support. Freeman relented and had begged him to keep the method secret, but Jones had only agreed not to include the detail in his report. He weighed the need for secrecy against operational necessity.

"Okay, this is 'need to know'. Superintendent Knightly, do you vouch for your people?"

Knightly straightened, "Of course."

"Who else is in that room with you?"

"Just me, Inspector Eldritch, and the AV operator," the Superintendent answered, pointing over the top of the screen.

Jones rubbed his chin and looked at Phil, the only person he'd told so far. Phil shrugged, and shook his head.

Thanks Phil, great help.

"Would you mind asking the operator to leave please, sir?"

"Really, David, is that absolutely necessary?"

"Yes, sir. 'Need to know'. I gave my word."

"Oh, very well," Knightly said, and waved at someone behind the camera. The picture on the screen vibrated for a moment. Seconds later, Knightly nodded for Jones to continue.

"Okay. Please don't take any notes. I don't trust anyone outside these two rooms, and I know your memory's almost as good as DS Cryer's."

"No need for the soft soap, Chief Inspector," Knightly said. "Carry on."

Jones continued. "Initially, Parrish wanted Freeman to hide in the museum after they closed the place for the night, but he discounted that option."

"Why?" The question came from Eldritch.

"The museum security system counts the punters both in and out. They'd soon twig if anyone stayed behind after 'lights out', and the movement and thermal sensors would pick him up at some stage."

"So what's he going to do?" Knightly asked.

"He says he's found another way inside. Didn't tell me what, but if he says there's a way, I believe him."

"What happens if he does manage to break in?" Eldritch asked the question this time.

"He's supposed to disable the surveillance, open the rear doors, and unlock the internal barriers between the goods loading bay and the vault. After that, Parrish will give Freeman half an hour to crack the Monarch. If he fails, they're going to use a shaped explosive charge."

"What? That's preposterous. They're more likely to damage the *Face* than get hold of it."

"Freeman's confident he can open the Monarch. After all, he does have the key."

"But he doesn't have the combination," Knightly added.

Jones leaned forward, eager to move the meeting forward. "I doubt that'll worry a man with Freeman's skills. Let's assume he can do what he claims and discuss our response."

"What do you suggest?" Knightly asked, deferring to Jones as the man on the ground.

"I recommend we take them before they enter the building. It's a maze inside the museum and they'll have explosives and half a dozen potential hostages. Things could become complicated."

Knightly looked at Eldritch, who dipped her head in agreement.

"Okay, that makes sense," he said. "You'll have armed officers on hand?"

"Inspector Danforth will be in charge of the operation until such time as we have Parrish and his crew in custody." Jones turned to Giles. "You can take over here, Inspector."

Jones left the armed part of the operation entirely in Giles' hands. Using the architect's plans and an aerial photo of the museum and its grounds, he discussed the takedown with Inspector Eldritch. Both seemed to talk the same language when it came to lines of fire, tactics, and weaponry, and Jones was happy to let them talk uninterrupted.

While the inspectors worked out the details, Jones spoke with

Knightly on a separate line. "Brian," he opened, "I'm worried about Angela Glennie. Knowing Parrish's methods, she's in real danger. Any suggestions?"

"Not really. We can't search hard or contact the media without letting Parrish know we're onto him. Sean Freeman's position is tenuous too. There aren't many people in Parrish's organisation privy to the job details. If we go in now, Parrish is bound to suspect Freeman as the leak. Best we can do is keep a watch on as many of Parrish's known addresses as we can and hope someone screws up enough to give us the girl's location. We'll keep up the phone taps, but with Parrish in the wind, I'm not optimistic."

"I don't like this one little bit. The poor girl must be terrified. She doesn't know anything about Freeman's professional life. The pressure's building on him too. He must be near hysterical. I hope he can keep things together until we finish this thing."

Jones couldn't bring himself to say it aloud, but he couldn't shake the feeling that Angela Glennie was already dead.

Chapter Forty-Four

Holton, Birmingham

AFTER TWO HOURS of discussing and planning as best they could, Jones stood to dismiss his team. "Okay people, thanks for your time. We'll meet back here tomorrow at midday for the pre-match briefing. Meanwhile, go home and have a good rest."

As the detectives dispersed with a clatter of chairs and a murmur of excited voices, Giles closed on Jones. "I've confirmed the arrangements with DI Eldritch. Bright spark that one. She has a good grasp of weapons and tactics. Not bad looking either, eh?" he said, adding a double eyebrow hitch and an encouraging nod.

Jones tidied his papers, placed them in a folder, and stuck the folder under his arm.

"Really, Giles? Hadn't noticed."

Giles gave him an old-fashioned look.

"No, of course not. Anyway, we'll have snipers in position covering the museum car park. Six should be enough since the sight lines are pretty decent. Apart from the snipers, I'll allocate three teams of two for the building, and the NCA will match our numbers. We'll have more than enough firepower. Parrish never goes in with more than three men, plus Freeman, who'll give us no trouble, I hope."

"If I've read the lad correctly, he's only interested in saving Angela Glennie," Jones said. "But I've been wrong about people before. Don't take anything for granted. Treat him the same way you treat the others until you're sure he's under guard."

Giles's expression remained stony. "You know me, David. I never take chances."

"Just thought I'd mention it. How will you use the three teams?"

"One for each entrance, front and back, and another for the side street in case any of the blaggers give us the slip. Sound good?"

"You're the one with the tactical knowledge, Giles. I'm happy to be guided by you."

"Twelve men then, you got it." He touched his right index finger to his forehead, said, "See you tomorrow for the muster," and turned to leave. He reached half way to the door before he stopped and returned. "Damn it, what's wrong with my memory? Beth's been harping on at me to invite you to dinner for ages. "

"Excellent, thank you," Jones said, managing to summon up the required amount of enthusiasm. The last time he'd visited the Danforths, Beth and Giles had smothered him with gratitude for a minor service he'd provided way back in 2008. Giles, an army reservist, had been on tour in Afghanistan, and Jones had dealt with a neighbour with an unhealthy interest in vulnerable military wives. A sick sod, who, thanks to Jones and the man's attempted escape, currently showed a dodgy set of National Health dentures whenever he felt moved to smile, which wouldn't have been often inside prison.

"Weekend after next?" Giles prompted.

"Fantastic, can't wait," he said, dredging up a smile. Life hadn't blessed Beth with Manda Cryer's gift in the kitchen, but at least she wouldn't invite a "girlfriend to balance the numbers". Jones's guilt at his churlishness made him wince.

Ungrateful bugger, Jones. They're good people.

———

JONES SPENT the hours after the conference call sorting out the paperwork for the operation, briefing the DCC and a mithering, penny-pinching Superintendent Peyton, and organising release forms for the ARU. The NCA agreed to form a backup presence outside the Stafford and were booked to arrive on Saturday evening in plenty of time to help set up the operation.

He spent another hour staring at the architect's blueprints, with Phil Cryer acting as a sounding board. At one point, when tired eyes and desperation turned the drawings into wavy squares and the writing into hieroglyphics, he asked Phil whether he'd forgotten anything.

"If you have, I can't see it, boss."

"Let's go through it one more time from the start. I can't help thinking I've missed something obvious."

At a little after five-fifteen, Charlie Pelham called from Edinburgh to give Jones a progress report. He hadn't heard Pelham so animated in years.

"Jimmy Barrow met me at the Waverley train station at midday. He's a good bloke, boss. Knows his way around the city and happy to help us bypass the locals. Been acting as my taxi driver too. Between you an' me, he loves the idea of helping us 'wee Sassenachs'." Pelham's attempted Scottish accent made Jones' ears bleed. "Beautiful place, Edinburgh, but it's been pissing down all afternoon."

"Angela Glennie?"

"Oh yeah, right."

Pelham hacked out a wet cough without covering the mouthpiece, during which, Jones closed his eyes and tried not to picture the follow up action.

He continued.

"So we went to the Royal Mile Talent Agency first. Right backstreet dive it is. Her agent, a sweet little gay bloke called Angus, confirmed that he hadn't seen or heard from Glennie since she left work Tuesday night. I got a recent picture of her too. A real looker.

318

Although fuck knows what she looks like now after being with Parrish for—"

"Is that unusual?"

"What?"

"Damn it, Charlie, stick to the point. Is it unusual for Angela Glennie not to turn up for work?"

"Yeah. Little Angus called her, and I quote, 'my most reliable rising star'. Bit pretentious considering the guy ain't exactly dealing with Hollywood A-listers. More like extras and look-alikes. Anyhow, he considered it were unusual, especially since she missed an audition Wednesday afternoon. He were most upset, but more at the loss of his commission, I'm guessing. Anyway, we drew a blank there, so Jimmy drove me 'round to her place. Landlady owns the flat below. She weren't helpful until I flashed my warrant card and swore her to secrecy. Eventually, she let us borrow the spare keys to Glennie's gaff."

"Anything interesting inside?" Jones asked. He could sense where this was going.

"Nothing, boss. Didn't take long to search. The place is little more than a bedsit. No signs of a struggle. Couldn't tell whether there was any clothes missing or nothing. We come up blank, boss. Nada, zilch."

"Okay, Charlie. I get the message."

Jones was about to end the call when Pelham spoke again. "Why'd you send me up here, boss? Been a complete waste of time. The locals could have handled this. Or maybe Jimmy could have done it alone. I mean, I made up for the *Green & Sons* cock up, didn't I? We charged the Mainwaring brothers for robbery and attempted murder, and Eleanor Winterbourne for complicity. Ain't I forgiven?"

"I couldn't trust this to a stranger, Charlie. Needed to send an experienced senior officer to fly under the radar," Jones answered, only half-lying. "Stay up there overnight and pump DI Barrow for all the information he has on the Edinburgh robberies. Ask about the two thugs with the shotguns, too, and check whether he had any suspects that didn't make the official file. I'll sign your expenses chit, but don't go overboard. B&B, not a hotel, and I'm not paying for you to have a night on the tiles, right?"

"Yes, boss. See you Monday morning."

Jones disconnected the call without telling Pelham about the operation. He didn't need to hear the useless article moaning about being side-lined again.

By six-thirty, Jones called time on the day and sent Phil home. He stayed an extra hour trying to memorise the layout of the museum's ground floor—just in case.

Chapter Forty-Five

FRIDAY 8TH JULY – *Evening*
Near Much Wenlock, Shropshire

JONES REACHED HOME WITHOUT INTERRUPTION. He threw a precooked frozen meal in the oven and had a long hot soak in the tub while it cooked. He normally preferred a shower, but the pressure of the previous few days had seeped into his bones and left his muscles both tense and twitchy. His neck ached so much he could barely turn his head.

By the time the searing bathwater had worked its temporary magic, Caravan's *Cunning Stunts* had reached its storming crescendo and had signed off with the pleasantly lyrical acoustic guitar piece.

He threw on a dressing gown and ambled downstairs. The kitchen welcomed him with the tantalizing aroma of hot shepherd's pie, which went down nicely with a glass of a half-decent *Côtes du Rhône*. He spent the rest of the evening listening to his growing CD collection. He bought the cheap CD player and a few emergency recordings after his turntable finally gave up the ghost following nearly three decades of stalwart service. The sound from the new electronic format was too clean and too pure, and not a patch on his LPs. He missed the hiss and clicks, and 'life' of analogue recordings, and would replace the turntable the moment he finished restoring the cottage—always assuming they were still being manufactured at such a distant time.

He carried the NCA file on Digby Parrish to bed and read for an hour until his drooping lids and unfocused eyes made him stop. The alarm clock on his bedside table registered 01:13 when he finally turned off the reading light.

Jones dreamed for the first time in months—fragments of real and imagined memories.

DIGBY PARRISH STANDING *in front of a woman bound to a kitchen chair … the massive Hutch behind the chair, smiling … holding the woman … stopping her and the chair from falling. Parrish swinging his fists … Angela Glennie, bruised and bloodied. Each blow landing with a sickening metallic ring.*

Metallic ring?

Only it wasn't a dark haired Angela in the chair, it was a redhead. A slim, beautiful, auburn-haired woman with a rounded, protruding belly … Siân!

Oh God, Siân.

THE PHONE'S shrill bell rang. Incessant, aggressive, it rang in time with Parrish's punches and battered through Jones' dream. The landline in the hall!

Damn it.

The orange numerals on the alarm clock glowed 02:43. Nobody rang his landline in the middle of the night, not even salesmen. Cold hands clutched at Jones' guts. He threw back the quilt and pulled the dressing gown from the back of the bedroom door, dragging it on as he stumbled down the stairs in the dark.

He reached the downstairs hallway at a dead run, used his shoulder as a buffer to stop his head hitting the wall, and snatched up the handset.

"Jones here," he said, breathing hard. "This had better be good."

"Mr Jones, it's me, Sean Freeman. Thank God you're home!"

Freeman's words were rushed but whispered. The sting of excitement and fear hit Jones hard. His racing heart pumped adrenaline-fuelled blood through his system. He tried to quiet his heavy breathing.

Freeman continued. "Parrish, he's called it forward. We're going in tonight … I mean, right now."

"Easy, son. Slow down. Talk me through it again."

"You need to listen, Mr Jones. I can't speak for long. Parrish called the job for tonight. I'm outside the museum right now!"

"You're what!"

"This is the first chance I've had to call you. Adamovic has been up my arse all evening, but I managed to give him the slip without him knowing I did it on purpose. Trouble is, he knows where I'm supposed to be, so he'll be here any minute. The plan's the same as before, but one day early. Get your people in place by four thirty and you'll still catch us … Fuck, there's a car coming. I've got to go."

"Freeman? Freeman!"

The line fell silent. Jones tapped out Phil's number from memory. He picked up the call after five rings.

"Phil, it's me."

"Boss? You all right? You sound breathless."

"Listen Phil, don't have time to explain. The Stafford job's on for tonight. Get the team to the station. You need to be ready by the time I get there. Meet me in the foyer, and don't forget to call Giles."

Six minutes later, Jones was in the Rover, bouncing up Birch Lane with the throttle jammed to the floor, the engine screaming, and driving as though the road surface was the smooth tarmac of a recently laid motorway.

Chapter Forty-Six

SATURDAY 9TH JULY – *Sean Freeman*

Night time vigil

A COOL BREEZE hushed in from the west, bringing with it the damp smell of promised rain and the rumble of distant motorway traffic. City lights, orange, yellow, red, and white, lent a colourful backdrop to the scene and formed deep shadows, one of which Sean Freeman found particularly useful.

Standing between Freeman and his target was a double-bonded brick wall, Victorian, solid, one-and-a-half metres tall. Black wrought iron railings topped with vicious-looking spikes mounted atop the wall looked impressive, but added little in terms of security. The paltry fortifications hid a car park and a row of buildings that didn't look too imposing from the back.

The rear aspect wasn't a patch on the grand Victorian and Georgian facades on display out front for the punters. The people who built these mausoleums weren't to know that urban sprawl would overtake their city in times to come. What would once have been magnificent rear gardens backing onto the river, had been parcelled up over the years and sold to developers. The target building itself was still magnificent, but Freeman wasn't there to admire the architecture, fine though it was.

He'd been leaning against the rough oak tree for the best part of an hour—waiting, watching. The building and grounds had been silent since his arrival. The empty car park was dark—no movement-activated lights had flared despite the five rocks he'd lobbed over the wall since his arrival. None of his daylight observations had shown security lights, but he had to make sure before committing himself to the most dangerous job he'd ever attempted. Given the choice, he wouldn't be within a fifty mile radius of the place, but the situation had forced his hand. If Angela and he were to have any future, Parrish had to go away, and for a very long time.

Freeman had no idea what to expect inside, but the odds were good that the guards would be dozing, if not actually asleep at such a late hour. At least, that was the hope on which he gambled his life.

He pulled the black woollen hat down on his head to cover his pale ears and took a deep, calming breath. The first part, outside in the open, was the most exposed and perhaps most dangerous of the whole process.

Silence surrounded him, oppressive and scary. The tree bark against which he rested was rough and comforting through his thin top. He threw a final rock, the biggest yet, and received the same silent and dark response. Freeman closed his eyes and prayed for the first time in forever.

If anything went wrong ... no he couldn't think that way, he needed all his wits. He had to concentrate on his part of the job—the rest was up to DCI Jones.

Angela and Freeman's lives rested on Jones, on luck, and on Freeman's ability to crack a safe that should have been unbreakable without a plasma torch or a thermite lance.

Ready, Sean?

Enough light spilled from the surrounding buildings for him not to need vision enhancement—such were the challenges of being in the centre of a city that never slept. He peeled himself away from the dark security of the tree, darted across the lawn, and thumped against the brick wall, heart racing, breathing shallow and rapid. He peered over the brickwork, climbed the railings, and dropped to the concrete on the other side, silent and sure.

Clinging to deeper shadows inside the wall, he reached the rear of the building and found the back doors. Double height and width, they were a legacy of times past when the wealthy Victorian owners used the rear entrance to receive private patrons in horse-drawn carriages.

Glad to be moving at last, his fears melted away as the work took precedence. Inactivity was the killer. This was what he did, what he was born to do. Having to rely on the actions of others crippled him, but here, leaning against the brick wall looking up, Freeman was in his element.

He studied his target entry point.

People who had grown up with technology often showed blind faith in its infallibility, and Freeman used that against them. Any security system made by man had its flaws. Part of Freeman's skill was to identify those flaws and design a workaround. He had yet to fail and he couldn't afford to start now.

The only certain way to make a building secure is to create a bank vault and exclude windows, but who wants to live in a building without windows? Buildings, be they offices, houses, or museums, needed light. Artificial would do at a pinch, but people prefer natural light and views, and for that, windows were essential. Windows were always, without exception, the best point of access for the thoughtful burglar, and Freeman considered himself as such a creature.

The toilet window on the first floor seemed perfect.

He slipped the dark rucksack from his shoulders and removed a bundle of small diameter cylindrical carbon-fibre rods. One of the strongest and lightest materials available, carbon-fibre had other useful properties—it was neither magnetic nor sonorous, nor did it show up on thermal or infrared sensors.

It took him forty seconds to assemble the ridged pole by slotting together each of the dozen stepped bars. He planted the wider end into the ground below the window, rested the tip against the windowsill, and shimmied up the pole as easy as you like—he'd been practising the skill for months. In his line of work, he never knew when it would be handy to play circus monkey.

With feet crossed and scissor-locked onto one of the pole's ridges, and the heavy backpack tugging on his shoulders, Freeman removed a small black box from his pocket. He placed it on the sill below the window catch and pressed the "activate" button. The device emitted a quiet hum. An LED display scrolled through the search programme he'd written specifically for the task. Thirty-five seconds later, the amber light turned green.

He paused to check for sound and movement behind the glass.

Nothing.

Next, from the bag, he removed a pair of modified compasses complete with suction cup and diamond-tipped trammel bar. With the time-served tool of the burglar's art, he removed a perfect circle from the frosted glass. The glasscutter might have arrived on the Ark, but it worked and Freeman wasn't about to change it for a modern laser scalpel.

A gust of wind ruffled his shirt and chilled his back. Sweat soaked into the rib of his woollen hat and dripped into his eyes. Muscles burned with effort. His crossed legs began to tremble as fatigue attacked. It wouldn't be long before they cramped up and he'd lose grip on the pole.

Next came the moment of dread. Would the signal jammer do its job? The green digits held constant, showing that the transponder signal hadn't modulated. The window sensor should be inactive.

Wouldn't take long to find out.

Come on Sean. Get on with it.

Hands steady, Freeman removed the circle of glass from the compasses and stuffed them into his pocket. Then he reached inside the hole with slow, careful fingers, grabbed the handle, and tugged upwards.

The lock clicked open.

He paused, both deafened and relieved by the powerful silence.

Either the sensor jammer worked, or a silent alarm had sent armed guards rushing to his perch.

Freeman pushed and the sash window slid upwards.

Silence.

He wriggled through the opening and paused, waist balanced on the ledge to listen.

An ambulance siren wailed in the background, the Doppler undulation showing its rapid movement along a fast road—there was little traffic to impede its progress so early in the morning. His heart rate spiked and slowed with the mobile sound of the ambulance.

He slithered into a room that smelled of pine freshness, planted his feet on smooth tiles, and pulled the carbon pole up behind him, disconnecting each segment as he went and placing it on the floor. It wouldn't do him any favours to leave the pole outside as a signal to any passing guard.

After two minutes sitting on the toilet seat waiting for his hammering heart and heavy breathing to slow, and his muscles to relax, he recovered enough to continue.

Taking care not to break the silence, he stowed the rods in their compartment at the side of the pack, and fixed the glass circle back into place with clear tape. From the outside, to anyone playing a torch over the window it would look undamaged—at least that was the plan.

Stage One complete. Time for Stage Two.

His penlight reflected back from the shiny ceramic and chrome bathroom fittings. Black marble tiles with white and pink veins screamed opulence if not taste. He removed the woollen hat and pressed his right ear to the cool door. Few sounds transmitted through the thick wooden panel.

The old building creaked and groaned, which was okay by him. Any noise that masked his progress was good noise. Door open, he followed a route memorised from building plans and one earlier visit.

Fifteen paces along the hall, keeping close to the walls to avoid creaking floorboards, had him reach the head of the landing. He descended the wide staircase, leaning heavily on the banister handrail to lighten the load placed on potentially squeaky treads.

The ground floor made without problem, he paused again.

Don't rush, Sean.

The floor, oak parquet in a herringbone pattern, showed the patina of age and countless feet, but gave off the aroma and shine of a recent polish. The smell of stale cigar smoke hung heavy in the air. The place reeked of old money and exclusivity.

Oak display cabinets with bevelled glass panels showed the trappings of opulence to all who had the privilege of entering this expensive palace of affluence.

Everything—everything—depended on the next few minutes. Sweat ran down his cheeks; he wiped them dry with the woollen hat.

Freeman crossed the anteroom and hurried along the hall to the rear doors. His crepe-soled shoes barely made a sound, but his heart surely pounded loud enough to wake every guard in the place, or trip the acoustic alarms. After first oiling the pair of heavy bolts, he slid them open.

The pick gun made easy work of both five-lever mortise locks. Three gentle pumps of the trigger, a quick jiggle-turn in each lock, and he'd converted the fortress into an open house, the double doors no longer a barrier to entry or exit.

Two more locked internal doors and a safe to open, and his work for Digby Parrish would be over—one way or another.

A quick about-face, twenty paces towards the next set of double doors, repeat the process with the pick gun, and he was through to the front of the house and past the main staircase. He reached the reception rooms where the security equipment protected the items of real value—the special stuff.

The time on his wind-up analogue wristwatch—a digital wouldn't suffice—read, 04:13.

Parrish and his men would be arriving at the museum any moment now. Would DCI Jones be in place? Would his sirens and blue flashing lights wake the neighbourhood?

Please, God, let him be ready.

Freeman placed a bare hand on the upper panel of the target door. He could almost sense the hum of electronics—thermal, infrared, and movement sensors. Any human setting foot inside that room would set off a bank of alarms that no one could sleep through.

This was why Freeman earned the big bucks.

Yeah, right.

When talking to him about the art of opening locks, his father had a saying: "Don't use a sledgehammer to crack a nut." That was fine for most cases, but sometimes the blunderbuss approach was the most efficient method. Given time, Freeman could overcome the suite of sensors scanning the cavernous rooms beyond the door, but time was a luxury he didn't currently have.

He reached into the backpack for his magic weapon—his version of a blunderbuss. A black box, twenty-four centimetres square, it had a small clear plastic bowl on the front face the shape of a satellite dish.

Freeman placed the box on the floor in front of the door and pointed the dish towards the treasure room. He unwound a three-core lead, plugged it into the nearest electrical socket, and pressed the button.

The LED display counted the charge from zero to one hundred.

Freeman didn't want to be close to the device when the capacitor reached full charge in about thirty seconds. He jogged to the rear doors, dropped into a foetal position in the corner, his back to the blunderbuss, and watched the sweep hand on his Timex count down the seconds.

He'd done his bit and could do no more. Everything else depended on DCI David Aaron Jones.

Chapter Forty-Seven

Holton, Birmingham

JONES TURNED into the Holton Police HQ car park, jammed his foot on the brake pedal, and pulled the Rover to a screeching stop alongside his parking spot. The back end jagged under the sideways loading and the acrid smell of burnt rubber hanging in the air stung Jones' nostrils.

The Rover's flashing blues had made big holes in the sporadic early morning traffic and his usual one-hour potter had taken less than thirty-five minutes. All the way from home, visions of a missed crime and a dead Angela Glennie had washed unbidden through his racing mind.

The car park stood ghostly empty. Few vehicles showed under the floodlights' fluorescent glow. Phil was standing at the top of the entrance steps, waiting. Ryan paced in the background, smoking one of his foul-smelling roll-ups. There was no sign of Alex.

Jones pulled on his game face. His troops needed to see him in control when, in reality, his nerves were shredded. He leapt from the car, leaving it parked diagonally and taking up two spaces; he tried to ignore the parallel black arcs left on the tarmac by his overworked rear tyres.

Phil met him half way up the steps, his worried frown visible in the half dark.

"Bloody hell, boss," he said, raising his arm and throwing an obvious glance at his wristwatch. "That was quick. Didn't know your old Rover could reach speed limit let alone break it."

Jones smiled, enjoying Phil's tension breaker.

"Morning, Philip," he answered in a voice more controlled than he expected. "Everything set?"

Phil's glum expression had Jones' internal warning mechanism fire off a rapid double-blast.

"Inspector Danforth's having trouble pulling his team together in time."

"You're kidding."

"Sorry boss. You'd better talk to him."

Phil pressed a button on his mobile and passed the phone to Jones, who paused on the top step of the entrance atrium and waited for the call to connect.

Giles answered immediately.

"Phil?" he asked, his words nearly drowned out by the sound of sirens.

"No Giles, it's me, David. What's happening?"

"We had a bit of a delay, but we're on our way now. Be at the museum in thirty minutes or so."

"Cutting it a bit fine, Giles. What happened?"

"Takes them time to draw equipment and weapons. The armourer won't release ammunition in advance of a shout. No matter the situation, we can't bypass the regulations. There's another problem though."

"Which is?"

"I only have three men available. We don't have the full deployment to cover the agreed plans."

Hell, what next?

"Right, okay, we'll work out something on site. The museum is around the corner from us so we'll be there before you. Silent approach, okay? Don't want to wake the neighbourhood or tip off Parrish."

"Okay, David. See you in a few."

Jones ended the call and marched towards the entrance doors. Ryan stubbed out his cigarette in the full-to-overflowing smoker's bin and passed Jones a stab vest, which had been draped over the entrance railings.

Phil and Ryan followed Jones into a foyer crowded with uniformed officers. Sergeant Vic Doland faced twelve uniformed constables who stood in a rank at ease, awaiting their pre-match instructions.

Jones gave them all an encouraging smile, pushed his head through the opening in the stab vest, and yanked on the Velcro straps. The baseball cap with the white POLICE lettering that regulations insisted all plain-clothed officers wear during an armed operation could wait—he hated hats.

"Phil, where's Alex?" he asked quietly.

"Drawing her weapon," Phil whispered. "I thought it wise in case Inspector Danforth was delayed. Inspector Wilkie signed the authorisation chit for the firearm."

"Excellent. Did you call Superintendent Peyton, or the DCC?"

"No, boss. Didn't you?" Phil asked, eyes wide and innocent.

"Couldn't get through," Jones fibbed. "I'll ask the duty sergeant to keep trying his landline as soon as I have a moment."

Alex and Inspector Wilkie pushed through the doors leading from the basement. Constable Adeoye followed close behind. His comforting presence lifted Jones' spirit. Adeoye was a man he could trust.

Wilkie called his officers to attention.

Jones addressed them all, keeping his voice controlled but firm. "There's no time for a full briefing, so listen carefully. The ARU is on its way to the museum, but we'll reach the scene first. We have a watching brief until they arrive. Inspector Wilkie and Sergeant Doland will give you your orders when on site. Keep your heads down. No heroics. I don't want any of you hurt. Do I make myself clear?"

Some of the constables shuffled. Others shared nervous glances. Vic Doland gave them the evil stare, and they snapped back to attention.

Jones continued. "Okay, we had plans in place for this operation, but things have moved beyond that. You should all know the area around the Stafford Museum well enough, and if you aren't familiar with your own beat, Sergeant Doland will want to know why." The remark raised smirks from the more experienced officers, but the younger ones remained white faced and immobile.

While Jones spoke, two Ford Transit personnel carriers rigged for riot control with bull bars and retractable windscreen grilles, and an unmarked Range Rover, pulled up outside.

"Okay," Jones said, "let's move. Constable Adeoye, you're with us."

Adeoye's eyes widened for a moment before he said, "Yes, sir."

———

THE RANGE ROVER WITH JONES, Phil, Wash, Alex, and a silent Constable Adeoye arrived at the south end of Walton Street, Perry Bar. Inspector Wilkie's contingent had used a circuitous route and took up hidden positions in a side road half a mile away on the north and west ends. All had an excellent view of the Stafford Museum's impressive frontage.

The quiet road of grand residential and even grander business buildings in the Georgian style, basked in the bright orange glow of well-maintained streetlights. Parked cars lined both sides of the wide thoroughfare. Gaps between the vehicles allowed access to driveways and alleys that led to the rear of the larger buildings, one of which belonged to the Stafford Museum. The streetlights were great for observation, but not so good for a covert approach. Sunrise wouldn't arrive for another forty-five minutes. With luck, everything would be over well before daylight.

"Looks quiet," Phil said, from his position in the driving seat.

"Should do at this hour," Jones answered.

"No sign of the ARU yet," said Ryan, squeezed between Alex and Constable Adeoye. "What are we going to do, boss?"

"Wait right here until they arrive," Jones answered. "Parrish isn't averse to using firearms and I'm not risking anyone's lives to save a few trinkets." He stopped himself from mentioning the missing Angela Glennie, and turned towards the back. "Constable Adeoye, how are you doing?"

"Fine, sir."

"Relax, son. You're not on parade now." The man's mountainous shoulders remained stiff and he stared straight ahead. "And, as a temporary member of the SCU, I can't keep calling you 'Constable Adeoye'. What's your given name?"

"Benjamin sir, but people call me Ben."

"As in, Big Ben, right?" Wash asked.

"Yes, sure is."

"I'd never have guessed," said Phil, adding a slight grin.

"Did you need me for anything in particular, sir?" Adeoye asked, allowing his wide shoulders to relax by a full millimetre.

"Nothing in particular, Ben," Jones answered, and faced forwards to concentrate on the view through the windscreen. "I like the way you handled yourself during the Richardson arrest and thought you might like a front seat for the main event."

"Thank you, sir."

Phil twisted through one-eighty degrees, grunting at the tight squeeze between his belly and the steering wheel. "Nothing to do with the fact that Parrish never does a job without that monster, Hutch, at his side, eh boss?"

"Nothing whatsoever," Jones said, keeping a straight face.

Ryan's hook-nosed grin oozed wickedness.

"Here you go, Ben. Take a butcher's at this ugly mother. Huge, eh?" he said, and angled his tablet for Adeoye to see what Jones assumed was a photo of Parrish's chief minder. "Still happy the boss ordered you to volunteer?"

Ben took the tablet and studied the screen. A light shone in his dark brown eyes. "Delighted, Wash." He handed back the device and sucked his teeth. "My baby sister could take him before breakfast."

"Really?"

"Yeah. Look at his left eye. All that scar tissue. The man's big, but he's slow. Else he wouldn't keep getting hit."

Ryan cackled, punched Ben's arm gently, and mimed having broken his knuckles on the constable's massive biceps.

Alex rolled her eyes at her fellow DC's antics. "I would like to meet your sister, Benjamin."

"I bet you would," Ryan said, winking.

"Ben," Jones interrupted, "there is something you and Alex can do, assuming you fancy stretching your legs?"

"Name it, sir."

"Good man." Jones turned to face the back once more, leaving Phil to keep watch on the front. "Ryan, can you bring up the aerial photos of the museum and its grounds on that thing?"

Ryan tapped the screen and passed the device to Jones, who studied the photo for a moment.

"See that?" He dabbed a finger onto the panel. The picture disappeared and morphed into a screensaver of Ryan's version of a topless model—a Ferrari cabriolet of some sort.

"Oh for pity's sake, Ryan," Jones said. "Get the picture back."

The young DC sighed and moved his fingers over the screen. "I have shown you this before, boss. Look, here you go."

Jones refused to take the tablet back, but allowed his finger to hover over the area on the photo he wanted to target.

"See that long rectangle in the garden two buildings along from the museum? It's a row of lockup garages. Inspector Danforth was going to position one of his snipers up there. If you go the long way around, down this side street, you should be able to gain access though the builder's yard, there. See it?"

Alex and Ben nodded. Ryan frowned, probably upset at having to defer to the newest and temporary member of the team. Jones didn't bother to explain that Alex had the firearm for protection, and Ben had recent military fieldcraft training, and could help her scale obstacles, the wall between the merchant's yard and the garages, for instance. He doubted that Ryan had the strength to lift the powerfully built Alex, but Ben Adeoye certainly did.

"You'll have a great view of the museum's back garden and car parking area from there, but for God's sake keep your heads down. Alex?"

"Yes, boss?"

"Are you ready for this?"

She met Jones' gaze full square. "Of course. Did you think I wouldn't be prepared?"

"Excellent. I want a running commentary of any activity. Take a comms unit, but test it first."

Alex pressed the send button on her police radio handset twice, which their earpieces picked up as static double-clicks.

"Perfect. Phil?"

"Yes, boss?"

"You're the nearest in size to Ben, mind switching jackets? I can't send him out there in a police uniform. Too obvious a target."

"If you pay for any damage, like if it falls apart, or gets drilled full of bullet holes," Phil said and stepped out of the car. He shrugged off his new jacket, handed it over, and grimaced at the way the seams stretched when Ben pulled it on.

"Off you go, and take care," Jones said, and watched them disappear down a side street.

"Bloody hell," said Phil, when they were out of earshot. "He's a powerful beggar. I'd love to see him and Hutch go a couple of rounds, Marquis of Queensbury style."

Jones shook his head. "Wouldn't happen. Ben's a former Two-Para. They don't play by anybody's rules but their own."

"Neither does Hutch, judging by the file the NCA has on him."

"Ben Adeoye has army training. My money's on the Para every time, but if it comes to a fight, it'll mean we've messed up some-where. Ryan, you okay?"

"Yes, boss. Didn't realise Big Ben was ex-military. He'll look after our Alex."

"And she him," Phil muttered. "What's taking the ARU? Should be here by now."

The clock on the dashboard showed 04:28.

"Easy, Philip. We've only been here a few minutes. They'll be along soon."

"Look up," said Ryan, pointing at the view through the windscreen.

Car headlights illuminated the houses on the west side of Walton Street. They originated from a side road north of the museum, close to where Inspector Wilkie's team were parked in the van. The car's tyres squealed as it made the fast left-hand turn.

"That's not the ARU," said Phil.

"No way," Wash confirmed. "That beauty's a Jaguar XF, and someone's added an after-market exhaust system. Sounds horrible, and that was a terrible bit of oversteer and slide on that corner. They should've beefed up the suspension, too. Definitely isn't ARU."

The Jaguar headed towards them before braking hard. Its nose dipped and the lights bobbed as the car made a fast right-hander and disappeared into the Stafford Museum's side alley.

Damn it, where are you, Giles?

"I'm betting that was Parrish and the rest of the JT1 Crew. Phil, call Inspector Wilkie. Tell him to roll out the stingers and block his end of the street. He also needs to stop any civilian traffic." He reached for the radio mic. "Alex, are you there. Over."

"*Alex here, boss. Over.*" She sounded breathless.

"Company's arrived. How far are you from the garages, over?"

"*One hundred metres,*" she answered, "*but we've found a better place. Much closer. Over.*"

"How close? Over." Fear tingled at Jones' scalp.

"*Don't worry, boss. We are behind an outbuilding, a shed. Ben's keeping guard. We can see the entire rear courtyard and parking bays. Did you see the Jaguar arrive? Over.*"

"Yes. What's happening? Over."

"*Three men are getting out. Parrish, Hutch, and another man almost as large as Hutch. Parrish carries a weapon. I can't make the identification, an Uzi perhaps. They're wearing black military uniforms, similar to the ARU, and are carrying* ryggsäckar, *... rucksacks. They look heavy. Over.*"

"Might be the explosives," Phil said to Jones, who nodded.

"Alex, what are they up to now? Over."

"*Parrish is leading them to the rear entrance of the museum. Hutch is carrying a one-metre long metal bar with a flat blade on one end. Over.*"

"Anybody know what that is?" Phil asked. "The bar, I mean."

Before Jones could answer, Ryan piped up with, "Sounds like a fire-fighter's Halligan bar to me. Used to gain access to locked houses. Won't be any use on the museum doors, though. They look like wood, but are made of steel reinforced with full-length through-bolts and retained by sockets bedded into concrete. I'd love to watch them try. It's why Parrish needed Freeman to open them from inside. Wonder what's happened to our friendly jewel thief."

"*Boss,*" Alex called. "*Parrish opened the museum doors! He turned the handle and it opened. They are now inside and the door closed behind them. What should we do? Over.*"

"Looks like Freeman's done the business," Phil said, sharing a look with Ryan that showed a grudging respect for the locksmith. "I wonder how he's doing with the vault and the Monarch."

"If he fails, we'll likely hear a naff-off big explosion any minute now," Wash said, adding, "and the alarms are going to give the neighbours an early wakeup call."

Jones checked the time. 04:37.

"Alex, stay where you are until the ARU arrives. What's happening with the Jaguar? Over."

"*It has turned to face the exit. The engine's still running. Over.*"

Chapter Forty-Eight

SATURDAY 9TH JULY – *Pre-dawn*
Perry Bar, Birmingham

JONES PAUSED FOR A MOMENT. Control was spiralling down the plughole, and with control gone, the chances of ending the operation without bloodshed were disappearing too.

A devastating thought hit him hard.

The moment Parrish had the Rajmahl Collection and the *Sultana's Face* in his greedy mitts, he'd probably have no further need for a cracksmith. Freeman would die, and that meant certain death for Angela Glennie. Although Jones had never met the woman, he felt for her plight. Nobody deserved that fate and, despite himself, he'd grown to respect the likeable Freeman.

Hell.

Jones threw open his door.

"Boss," Phil said, "what we doing?"

"You're getting out while I roll the car down the hill and block that alleyway." Nobody moved. "Out, now. Move!"

He pushed Phil into action.

Phil and Ryan piled out of the Range Rover as Jones ran around the front and jumped into the driver's seat. He released the hand-brake and the Range Rover rolled down the slight hill under its own weight. The heavy wheel forced him to fire up the engine to activate power steering, but he kept the car in neutral and the revs on low idle.

Wash and Phil followed at walking and then jogging pace as the car's momentum increased its speed from four, to eight, and then to ten miles-per-hour. Jones noted, with relief, that his men used the Range Rover as a shield between themselves and the museum. In the driver's seat, Jones was the most exposed, which was fair enough —sort of.

At eleven miles-per-hour, the Rover's speed levelled out. Phil started dropping behind, but Wash kept pace, barely blowing.

With one hundred metres to his target, headlights brightened his rear-view mirror. Jones twitched the steering wheel to the right to block the approaching vehicle's passage. "Wash," he called through the open window. "Flag down that driver. We can't let him through."

By the time Jones' words were out, the approaching vehicle slowed, its headlights flashed twice, and it pulled to a stop on the brow of the hill.

The radio burst into activity and Giles Danforth's deep and plummy voice filled the cabin. *"DCI Jones, is that you in the Range Rover?"*

Jones didn't have time to pick up the press-to-talk microphone. "Sorry, Giles," he muttered, "be right with you."

Giles continued. *"David, what do you think you're … ah I see."*

Jones aimed the Range Rover at the space between the parked cars recently used by the speeding Jaguar, and bumped it against the far kerb, making it come to rest diagonally across the gap. The side road descended, curved to the right, and the corner of the museum hid Parrish's Jag from view.

Jones rolled out of the car, keeping his head below the roofline in case Parrish's driver decided to check his escape route and pop the Jag's nose out from around the corner. He didn't fancy being on the receiving end of the driver taking a pot shot at the idiot blocking his only escape route. Keeping low, he returned to Phil and Wash, who had stopped half way down the hill. Phil blew hard and rested his hands on his knees.

Giles and his men arrived at a fast jog.

———

"NICE MOTOR," Giles offered, his eyes glued to his field glasses and pointing them at the Jaguar. "Looks like Parrish might be a patriot. Believes in using British motors for his getaway cars. Probably wouldn't be seen dead in a Beemer."

Jones didn't have the heart to remind Giles that an Indian conglomerate currently owned Jaguar Cars.

In the fifteen minutes since the ARU's arrival, Jones had ceded operational control to Giles, but, as a matter of courtesy, the Inspector made sure to run every decision past Jones first. He did insist that Jones wear his baseball cap, much to Jones' annoyance.

"Safety first, David," had been the ARU man's response to Jones' half-hearted dissent.

Giles had sent one of his men to the garages where Alex and Adeoye should have been, a second to stand guard at the Range Rover barrier, and the third to cover the museum's front entrance. He and Jones had replaced Alex and Ben at what they dubbed the Forward Observation Post. Jones positioned his team in reserve with the second ARU officer.

From the FOP, Jones could easily make out both the rear of the museum and the side road with his diagonally parked Range Rover.

He leaned against a wooden garden shed and peeked around the edge while Giles took a one-kneed stance below him and stared through the field glasses. He gave a running commentary to his team members and for Jones' benefit.

"Can't see the driver for the tinted windows, but the engine's still running," Giles reported.

Dressed in a matt black quasi-military uniform—munitions belt, body armour, boots and visored helmet—Giles lowered the binoculars. "I don't like this working on the fly," he said, keeping his voice low. They both knew how far sound travelled at night. "Any idea why Parrish moved up the timetable?"

Jones shook his head and fiddled with the cap's peak. He couldn't make the damned thing sit comfortably.

"According to Freeman, he's done this before. Likes to keep his men on their toes. Good security measure too. On the plus side, he's a cautious sod and wouldn't go ahead with the job if he thought we were onto him."

"Agreed. He's been planning this heist for the best part of two years," Giles said. "The way I read his NCA psych profile, there's no way he'd abort unless he definitely knew Freeman had spoken to us. And in that event …."

Jones finished the sentence for Giles. "In that event, Freeman would be dead and in no position to warn me about the change in schedule. On top of that, Angela Glennie would be in the same condition."

"What about Superintendent Knightly and that rather fetching Inspector?" Giles grinned without turning his head.

"I tried calling the Superintendent on the way here," said Jones, "but couldn't get through."

Giles nodded. "He's incommunicado. Apparently, the NCA has more than one case on at a time." As Giles smiled, his teeth flashed in the light from the streetlamps. "I did manage to speak to the Super's assistant. They can't get here until mid-morning, but still have teams keeping tabs on Parrish's houses in case he gives us the slip here or they spot Angela Glennie. Christ, what that poor lass must be going through."

'Poor lass' is right, but don't go there, Jones.

Jones checked his watch yet again.

"They've been inside for half-an-hour. How long would it take them to set the explosives on the Monarch if Freeman can't open it?"

"No idea. Depends on what they're using and whether they know what they're doing." Giles raised the binoculars again. "It could take a while. They don't want to damage the merchandise.

On the other hand, your mate, Sean Freeman, might have cracked the safe already. In which case they could be out as soon as they load those rucksacks Alex told you about."

"Let's get one thing straight," Jones said, and stabbed the air between them with his index finger. "Sean Freeman's no mate of mine. I have some sympathy for his situation, but I'm still bagging him the moment we've taken Parrish."

"Easy, David. I'm kidding." The teeth flashed again. "You're wound up a little tight, mate. Things are going to be fine."

"Of course I'm wound up. There's a young woman out there somewhere scared half to death. Assuming she's not …."

Stop it!

"So, what's the plan?" Jones asked.

"Wait them out. Can't go charging in. Parrish and his men are armed and I don't want this to degenerate into a siege. We have half a dozen potential hostages inside the museum as well as Freeman."

"Damn it. I hate waiting around feeling this helpless."

"Me too."

Chapter Forty-Nine

SATURDAY 9TH JULY – *Dawn*
Perry Bar, Birmingham

DAWN CRACKED THE EASTERN HORIZON, bringing with it a light dew. The longer nothing happened, the more slowly the minutes ticked past. At one stage, Jones was so certain his Seiko had stopped, he asked Giles to confirm the time. Parrish and his men had been inside the museum over an hour.

Since then, nothing had happened—no lights, no sirens, no loud bangs.

Nothing.

At any moment, Jones expected to hear the muffled crump of an explosion and a barrage of alarms to indicate the destruction of the Monarch and the taking of its precious load. But the longer the delay, the more convinced he became that something had gone horribly wrong with Parrish's plan.

Giles kept in touch with his men and his base through the personal comms units complete with throat mike. He gave them a running commentary. Jones did the same for his team, but used the handheld radio unit. For added security, the ARU used a closed comms system with a separate waveband. Jones was unable to hear any of their comms traffic, but could follow Giles' part of it.

The damp seeped into his bones. Jones clamped his teeth together to stop them chattering.

Giles nudged him. "David. Something's happening."

"What?" Jones sidestepped to the edge of the shed and craned his neck to view the Jaguar.

"Driver's getting out. Must be wondering why it's taking so long."

"Don't blame him."

Jones used his personal Carl Zeiss 10x binoculars. Enough light bathed the scene for the glasses to work reasonably well. The driver —slim, in his mid-thirties with a mane of black hair and a shaggy beard—stood in the 'V' formed by the Jag's open door and its body-work. He checked his wristwatch, spoke into a mobile phone, checked his watch again, and then stared up at the brightening sky.

Here was a man with a decision to make. Should he stay or go? If he scarpered, he risked the terrible wrath of his psychotic boss. If he stayed he flirted with arrest. Tough choice.

Giles chortled.

"Poor bugger's crapping himself. Ah look, he's trying the phone again. I bet he's calling Parrish, but that won't work. The museum's electronics block radio transmissions. Landlines only in there."

"Right," said Jones, smiling. "Let's see what 'Lewis Hamilton' does next. This is better than the cinema."

The driver ducked back into the car and slammed the door. The Jag's engine roared, rear wheels spun and the car jumped forward. Jones reached for his radio to warn Phil and the team at the Range Rover, but the Jag screeched to a halt before it reached the corner, and then reversed back to the launch spot.

"Changed his mind," Giles muttered, and described the action to his men. "More scared of upsetting Parrish than spending a decade in a cell."

Lewis Hamilton jumped out of the Jag and sprinted to the Museum's rear doors. He placed his ear against a door panel and held it there for a few seconds before stepping away. The man scratched at the top of his head and turned to give the Jag a look of pure longing, but the fear of Parrish must have taken over again. The driver stepped forward and grabbed the twin handles to the doors.

He screamed.

Spasms seized his body. His back arched. He jerked again, released his grip on the handle, and slumped to the ground in a twitching, shuddering heap.

"What the hell?" Giles said, and turned puzzled eyes on Jones. "Did you see that?"

"I'm not blind, Giles."

"I mean, did *I* just see that?"

Jones nodded. "Either Lewis Hamilton had a heart attack, or those handles are electrified. Think it's time for us to do a little police work, don't you?"

Giles called his men forward, but kept his weapon trained on the front doors. Jones phoned for an ambulance. Lewis Hamilton, who lay in a flailing, gasping, shuddering pile, might have hurt himself in the fall. Poor lad.

Phil and the others edged around the Range Rover and started following the ARU man down the side road, but a signal from Jones stopped them before they turned the corner at the bottom of the hill. It was clear from their bemused expressions and the way they shook their heads and shrugged, that they had as much clue as Jones did.

At any moment, the rear museum doors could fly open to spew out Parrish and the others. The JT1 Crew had entered the museum armed for battle and might be prepared to fight their way out.

Using military hand signals that Jones remembered from his truncated army career, Giles orchestrated his team's approach. He moved in from the front, keeping in a half crouch and making use of the available cover—a large metal dumpster and the low wall. The officer from the Range Rover, who carried his assault rifle left-handed, kept his back to the museum wall to minimise his profile. The sniper from the garage climbed down from the roof and mirrored "Lefty's" actions, and the three ARU men moved in a trident claw formation, matching each other for pace.

Giles took up a one-kneed stance behind the Jag. He trained his weapon on the double doors and gave a series of rapid instructions. Lefty dropped to his knee and raised his weapon. "Sniper" rushed forward at a low crouch, rolled Lewis Hamilton onto his front, and dragged him facedown by his collar, out of the line of fire.

Once safely out of sight of the museum's doors, Sniper frisked Lewis for weapons before securing his hands behind his back with a thick cable tie. He didn't waste time handling his package with care and finished by binding another cable tie around the driver's ankles. The whole process took less than a minute and impressed the heck out of Jones. For his part, Lewis didn't seem to mind the rough handling.

From his position behind the shed, Jones could see everything, but hear nothing of importance. The wind rustled the grass at his feet, the ambient traffic noise increased, but his eyes were riveted to the scene playing before him, which was a movie with the sound turned down. He raised the comms unit to his mouth and spoke quietly. "Phil, can you hear me? Over."

"*Loud and clear, boss. Over.*" Phil's voice was hushed and breathless.

"Can you see what's going on? Over."

"*Not everything. The museum doors are recessed, but I can see the driver and the ARU man on the other side. What do you want us to do? Over.*"

"Send Ryan and Alex around to the front of the building to support the third ARU officer. Inspector Danforth and his men are about to affect an entry. I don't want Parrish and the others slipping out the front. You and Ben stay where you are for the moment. Over."

"*Right you are, boss. Over.*"

"Jones, out."

He lowered the radio and waited for the tricky part.

Jones hated being a spectator at his own operation. The pressure built as he stood and stared, wishing he could take part, but relieved not to have a weapon in his hands again. His rifle-toting army days had ended more than thirty years earlier and he didn't fancy a reprise.

Giles, still part hidden behind the Jag, gave his man the thumbs-up. Lefty ran, bent low, to the rear doors. Down on one knee again, he swung the rifle around his back, the webbing strap holding it firm, and took an object the size and shape of a mobile phone from a pouch on his utility belt. He touched the end of the device to the door handle, raised his arm, and stuck out his thumb. Jones took the signal to mean the handle was safe, no longer holding a charge.

Lefty jerked, opened his hand in a "stop, wait" gesture, and pressed his ear against the door. His body locked in concentration, and then his lips moved.

"Repeat that, over." Giles said, loud enough for Jones to hear from some fifty metres away. "You have to be kidding," he added.

Giles' loud-voiced break in radio protocol shocked Jones, who was now desperate to know what Lefty had heard behind the doors. He stepped out from behind the shed as Giles stood, still aiming his rifle at the doors, but pointed well away from Lefty.

"Now!" Giles shouted.

Lefty reached up, turned the handle, and pushed.

The Stafford Museum exploded into light and sound.

Chapter Fifty

SATURDAY 9TH JULY – *Dawn*
Perry Bar, Birmingham

THE STAFFORD MUSEUM'S floodlights flashed on, and the wailing cacophony of the sirens forced Jones to cover his ears. Every window in the rear of the building blazed with a brilliant white glow.

Three figures stumbled through the open door, Parrish, Hutch, and a third man, who, from the NCA's photo file and Freeman's verbal description, proved to be Adamovic. They raised arms to shield their eyes against the floodlights' glare, heads turning left and right, blinded.

"Armed police, armed police," shouted Giles, roaring above the bedlam. "Lower your weapons to the ground and come out with your hands up. Do it now."

Adamovic lowered his sawn-off shotgun, dropped to the ground, and lay prone with his arms out from his sides, hands open and the left side of his face pressed into the gravel. He performed the action so well, it was almost as though he'd done it a few times before.

Parrish, red-faced and wild-eyed, covered his ears with his hands and screamed obscenities at anyone and no one. Jones heard the word "Freeman" a number of times, interspersed with a few colourful expletives.

Jones concentrated on Hutch, the dutiful minder and Parrish's lifelong protector. What would the thug do?

Hutch ducked, screamed, "Fucking Freeman!" and punched his fists into Parrish's back. The diminutive gang boss screamed and fell sprawling to the ground, and the man-mountain took off at high speed.

"Stop!" Giles yelled and took aim.

Lefty, still kneeling, took the full force of Hutch on the hoof, and hit the museum brickwork with a sickening, bone-jarring crunch.

"Stop or I'll shoot!" Giles called.

Jones knew Giles wouldn't—couldn't—fire into the back of an unarmed man, especially a fleeing man who presented no immediate danger. Jones started to run, although he knew it was futile. Hutch would be long gone by the time Jones reached the car park.

"Ryan," Jones yelled into his radio, "Hutch is headed your way. Look out!"

Hutch, a flurry of driving arms and pumping legs, turned the corner, and ran straight into Ben Adeoye's swinging right forearm.

The "clothesline" arm connecting with the monster's Adam's apple took Hutch off his feet. He hit the tarmac and stayed there.

Jones could swear he felt the ground shake from some thirty metres away.

By the time Jones reached the corner, he'd slowed to a nonchalant stroll. Ryan and Ben had rolled Hutch onto his front—it took them both to move him—and cuffed his hands behind his back. Jones was surprised the manacles stretched large enough to accommodate the fallen man's tree trunk thick wrists. He was equally astonished to find that Hutch's head hadn't left his shoulders with the force of Ben's well-timed blow. They heaved Hutch to his feet and supported the dazed lump all the way back to his partners-in-failure.

Wrapped up neat and tidy, the JT1 Crew made a sorry sight as they sat cross-legged and shackled in the middle of the near-empty car park. The dishevelled driver had recovered enough to sit up, but he still looked dazed.

Parrish rocked forward and back, mumbling. Jones feared for his psychological stability. He wrote a mental note to have a psych evaluation performed ahead of the first formal interview. He also considered putting in a request for the West Midlands Police to recruit a full time psychologist after all the nut jobs they'd dealt with over the past few weeks. Kelvin Richardson, Alby Pope, poor Reg Prendergast, and now Digby Parrish, had all exhibited signs of psychological incapacity that week. Was it something in the Birmingham water?

The museum's sirens cut off and left Jones' ears ringing. The spotlights stayed on, but were less blinding since the arrival of a full and bright dawn.

Before long, a bulbous man sporting a drooping grey walrus moustache and wearing the dark blue uniform of a museum security guard—complete with a splodge of "scrambled egg" on the band of his peaked cap—arrived. He appeared around the same corner that Ryan and Ben had recently turned. Two other men in similar livery tried to follow, but Walrus shooed them back. He stopped at the kerb, jutted out his head, frowned, and smoothed out his moustache before heading straight towards Jones with all the fluid grace of a man treading water while wearing concrete wellie boots.

Upon reaching Jones, Walrus stopped, pushed the cap to the back of his head, and stood arms akimbo, feet wide apart. The question on his lips remained unasked as he took in the scene in slack-jawed surprise.

Jones held up his hand, index finger extended, and spoke into his radio. "Inspector Wilkie, are you receiving me? Over."

"*Yes, sir. Over,*" Wilkie responded.

"Did you follow any of that comms traffic? Over."

"*Just about, sir. Over.*"

"You can call up the cattle wagon now. We have four prisoners desperate to see the inside of a holding cell. Over."

"*Only four, sir? Any sign of Sean Freeman? Over.*"

"None so far. Keep your eyes open in case he strolls out the front entrance as though he owned the place. Doubt that'll happen, though. I have a sneaking suspicion our Mr Freeman was never in the museum. At least not tonight. Jones out."

Walrus, who had begun to turn purple, found his voice. "Are you in charge here, officer?" he demanded.

Jones struggled to keep a straight face, but held up his warrant card.

"DCI Jones, West Midlands Police Service. And you are?"

"Chief Security Officer Beatty. What the bloody hell's happening here, Jones?" The man's jowls shook. "I mean, this is private property. You can't go chasing your joy riders down here."

"Are you serious, sir?" Jones asked. "You see those men?" He waved a hand at Parrish and his crew. "They've been inside your high security building since half-past-four. You didn't know?"

Beatty's rotund and mobile face rolled through the gamut of emotions from frowning confusion, to narrow-eyed, screw-lipped disbelief. "Don't be ridiculous, man. No one's been inside the museum but me and my men since the day shift went home at eight o'clock yesterday evening."

Jones sighed and told the story with exaggerated patience. He finished by asking whether Beatty or his men ever performed any security sweeps.

"Of course we do, man. Every half hour, on each floor."

"Including the car park and rear reception area?"

"Well …" Beatty blanched. Clearly a colourful chap. "No. There's nothing of value in that area, and CCTV surveillance covers the rear annex. I have people watching the video monitors twenty-four-seven. The screens have been clear all evening."

A closed loop video stream.

The answers to Jones' internal questions started to flow.

"Do you mind if I go inside the rear foyer and have a quick look?"

Beatty's eyes narrowed.

"Let me see that ID again first."

The words "horse" and "stable door" sprang into Jones' mind, but he showed the card again. Beatty, with some reluctance, allowed Jones into the dark recesses of his realm.

Once through the doors Jones had stared at for the previous hour, more answers arrived. Apart from the doors through which Jones and Beatty had just walked, the windowless "Goods Receiving Bay" had only one other means of exit—a pair of doors directly opposite the rear entrance. Jones smiled as the story began to unfold in his mind.

A reception counter with a floor-to-ceiling grill and a stout metal gate intersected the room two thirds of the way back. The brick walls, painted grey, lent all the welcoming ambience of a prison visiting room. With both sets of double doors locked, the atrium-cum-goods receiving area had become a mantrap.

This particular mantrap looked as though a tornado had touched down hard—and stayed around to party with a dozen of its closest mates. Papers, telephones, and other electronic equipment lay scattered around the room in various states of destruction. Parrish and his men had ransacked the two desks behind the counter. What had they been looking for, a key to give them access into the building, or one to set them free?

Jones turned to Beatty. "You didn't notice any of this occurring on your CCTV monitors, I suppose?"

Beatty shook his head and leaned heavily against the rear wall.

"I think you'd better call someone in to overhaul your security system, sir."

"We had the whole place rewired last year."

Jones sighed. "In that case, I think we'll need to have a word with the contractors at some stage."

Assuming they're still in business.

A discarded rucksack and scorched area around the locks on the internal doors aroused Jones' interest. After a brief inspection, he called Giles for a second opinion.

The big man arrived quickly, studied the residue for a moment, and leaned close to sniff the putty. "Stuff around the handle looks and smells like C5. I'd bet they tried to blow their way into the access corridor. Wonder why the detonators didn't work?"

"I have a pretty good idea," Jones answered.

"You reckon your mate, Freeman, spiked them?" Giles asked, smiling. "The handles on the rear doors too?"

"The thought had crossed my mind. Did you notice the extra thick wiring loom feeding the electronic lock?"

Giles studied the area Jones indicated. "Ah, I see. Judging from the way the Jag driver folded up, that handle would have belted out the same charge as a stun gun." Giles pursed his lips. "Fifty thousand volts would have passed through his body. No wonder he still looks a little distracted. Plays havoc with the crown jewels, or so I'm led to believe."

"Well not to worry," Jones said. "If Lewis is married he won't be entitled to any conjugal visits where he's going."

"When did he have time to set this up?" Giles asked. "Freeman I mean."

"Don't you see, Giles?"

"No. Care to enlighten me?"

"I bet you my next month's paycheque Sean Freeman was one of the team who installed this system."

"You mean…?"

Jones nodded and spoke through gritted teeth. "Sean Freeman's been planning this operation almost as long as Parrish has. The sod's been playing us. Playing me!"

"But why?" Giles asked, opening his hands in a shrug. "Nothing's been taken."

Jones dragged a hand though his hair. "That's where you're wrong, Giles. Parrish is sitting on the ground out there. *He's* been taken."

"That's what this is about? An underworld vendetta?"

"Who knows?" Jones answered, frowning and shaking his head.

"And the woman, Angela Glennie?"

Jones rubbed a hand through his hair. Fatigue started weighing heavily, dragging him down. "I have absolutely no idea."

"Okay, David," Giles said, pointing to the door. "You'd better take Mr Beatty out of here and evacuate the building. My men and I will secure the C5 until your friend Captain Williams arrives with his bomb crew. Even though the stuff's relatively harmless without working detonators, I can't leave it lying around unattended for anyone to trip over." He raised his hand as Jones opened his mouth to speak. "No, don't say it. I'll take plenty of photos for evidence and make sure my men don't mess up your crime scene."

Jones nodded. "I know you will. I was going to say be careful, but I know you'll do that too. In the meantime, I'll have Mr Beatty evacuate the building. It'll give the man something important to do and keep him out from under our feet."

Chapter Fifty-One

SATURDAY 9TH JULY – *Early morning*
Perry Bar, Birmingham

THE SUN SHOWED its welcome face above the Perry Bar rooftops, adding warmth as well as light to Jones' mood. Over the previous half hour, the traffic on the nearby M6 had built from a sporadic rumble to a continuous grumbling roar—Birmingham's equivalent to heavy surf on a pebble beach.

While Giles reported the outcome of the operation to his superiors after handing control of the scene back to Jones, his men maintained a guard over the explosives.

Jones' team, including Ben Adeoye, stood in a close huddle, reviewing the morning's events. Jones kept himself slightly apart and studied Parrish who had calmed a little—at least he no longer drooled.

Ryan pointed at the still groggy driver. "Looks as though Freeman set the phasers to stun, boss?"

"Hmm?" Jones asked, although not really listening. He was

concentrating on the procession of four prisoners as the uniformed officers led them towards a waiting van.

"What was that, Ryan?" he added.

"Star Trek reference, boss. You won't have heard of it."

"Don't be ridiculous, son. I named my first ever goldfish Tiberius."

Ryan frowned and pulled in his pointed chin. "Why?"

"Call yourself a Star Trek buff? Tiberius was the captain of the Enterprise."

"Nah boss, you're wrong. That was Jean-Luc Picard."

"Go search Mr Google, youngster."

"Kidding, boss," Ryan scoffed, and the others cheered. "James Tiberius Kirk, I know."

"You are a funny man, DC Washington. Perhaps you chose the wrong career. You should be playing the Edinburgh Comedy Fringe."

Ryan lost the grin until Jones said, straight-faced, "I can take a joke, laddie. Can't you?"

The audience fell about and Ryan relaxed. Even Alex, normally above testosterone-fuelled banter, added her low chuckle to the mix. Ben Adeoye clapped Ryan on the back, an action that nearly knocked the poor lad off his feet, but he recovered enough to point at Hutch who twisted sideways to squeeze through the rear doors of the police wagon.

"Steady Ben," Ryan said, "or I'll set Hutch on you."

Hutch struggled against the two officers holding him. "Lucky punch, you fucking black bastard!" He tried to shout, but his voice came out strained after his throat's enforced meeting with Ben's forearm. "I'm going to tear you apart."

Ben faced the prisoner and crossed his arms. "Next time sir, I'll give you a formal introduction. Then we can have a proper dance."

A red-faced Hutch roared and threw his shoulder against the metal cage into which his guards had packed him. The van rocked on its heavy-duty suspension, but the cage door held.

Giles, having completed his call, approached Jones.

"The bomb squad won't be long. I'll go keep my men company.

You'll have my report on your desk by close of play today, sir." He leaned closer and lowered his voice. "And don't forget, Beth and I'll expect you next Saturday."

Jones nodded. "Right you are, Giles. Looking forward to it. Good job here, by the way. Nicely done. I'll pop over to your office later in the day and thank your men personally."

"Thanks, David, but it's not necessary. This is what we do, and we love it."

"How's your man, the left-hander? Took a fair old blow when he hit the wall."

"Ah, he's fine. Well protected in all this gear. More embarrassed than anything else. Wanted to take the big guy down by himself. He's going to suffer some hazing for a while, but everything's cool."

After Giles left, Phil issued instructions for Alex and Ryan to start interviewing the museum security guards. Police work had to continue.

Jones summoned Ben Adeoye, who jogged across and snapped to attention.

"Stand easy, Ben. Just wanted to say you did a fine job this morning."

The temporary member of the SCU grinned. "Thank you, Chief Inspector. Haven't had so much fun since Afghanistan."

"How's your forearm? You gave Hutch a fair old clout."

"Barely felt the blow land, sir. Never hurts when you get the timing right."

"I'll take your word for it. Anyway, we're going to be here for a while, but you're due off shift at eight so it's probably best for you to return to your mates. But I won't forget your support come appraisal time."

"Thank you, sir."

He gave Jones a smart salute and turned away to seek the rest of his team and receive his orders from Inspector Wilkie.

Phil appeared at Jones' side. "Charlie's going to be pissed he missed the action, boss."

"If I know Charlie Pelham, he'll have found enough action in Edinburgh last night. Just a sec, Phil," he said, and marched across the car park to speak with Parrish, the last in line for a place in the cage. He pulled the man to one aside.

"Where's Angela Glennie?"

Parrish blinked and tried to focus on Jones' face. "Who?"

"The Scottish woman you abducted last Tuesday evening? Sean Freeman's girlfriend."

"What the fuck you talking about?" Parrish lunged at Jones, but the restraints hampered his movements. Jones sidestepped, but left his leg in place. Parrish tripped and fell hard against the side of the van.

"Fucking Freeman! It's all down to Freeman. He's fucking dead meat!" Parrish screamed and kicked out at Jones. "Dead, you hear me!"

Two uniformed constables jumped forward and pinned Parrish to the van by his arms. Once they'd adjusted their holds, they forced the raving gangster into the cage next to his big henchman.

All the while, Parrish kept screaming, "I'm going to fucking kill him. Hunt him down and tear out his heart. Fucking bastard's dead meat."

"You'll have to find him first," Jones mumbled. "As will I."

Chapter Fifty-Two

SATURDAY 9TH JULY – *Sean Freeman*
London, England

BANG ON TIME, Angela pulled her little Fiat Panda to a stop at a junction three streets north of Parrish's mansion. Freeman opened the tailgate, threw in his backpack, much lighter without the blunderbuss or the carbon fibre rods, and jumped into the passenger seat.

"I love a girl who keeps her appointments," he said, beaming.

"Hi babe, what are you doing here?"

"Popped in at a mate's place to pick up something for our trip."

"Didn't he mind you calling so early?"

"Nah, DB Parrish is an old friend of the family," he said, leaned over, and kissed her cheek. "Now, off we go. Heathrow's that-a-way."

He directed her south and couldn't resist using a route that would take them past the house he'd just robbed.

Angela's hair fell forward in a wavy dark veil. She brushed it back from her face and flipped it over her shoulder. Freeman caught

361

the fresh fragrance of her shampoo—so much better than floor polish and cigar smoke.

"In the meantime," he said, "I've a call to make. Can I borrow your mobile? Mine doesn't work anymore. Electromagnetic pulses play havoc with electronics."

"There you go again, babe. Speaking in riddles. Phone's in my handbag. Help yourself."

Freeman checked his watch, which still ticked with clockwork precision, immune to little but a broken mainspring.

Angela stopped the Fiat at a red light. Two police cars screamed through the junction, blue lights flashing, two-tone sirens wailing. The cars passed them heading in the opposite direction. Freeman watched them through the Fiat's wing mirror as they pulled up outside Parrish's mansion. The dishy blonde, Inspector Eldritch, jumped out of the lead car's passenger side, two men followed her from the other car. They trooped up the steps and she started hammering on the front doors.

The traffic lights turned green. Angela pulled away and Freeman punched the buttons on her mobile.

Chapter Fifty-Three

Perry Bar, Birmingham

JONES AND PHIL sat in the front of the Range Rover. Phil had parked it on Walton Street to take in the great view of the museum's impressive frontage, together with a large portion of Birmingham's City Centre, which shone bright in the clean morning air.

"What the bloody hell happened in there, boss?" Phil asked. "I mean, where's Sean Freeman?"

Jones started to tell Phil what he learned in the loading bay and what he'd surmised when the mobile vibrated in his pocket. He withdrew it and hit the connect key.

"Jones here."

"Hello, Mr Jones. How are you diddling this fine Saturday morning?"

"Freeman! Where the hell are you?"

Phil's head snapped around. He whispered, "Put it on speaker," and Jones obliged.

"Sorry to have messed you about, Mr Jones. How did it go at the museum?"

"As if you didn't know," Jones said, allowing a cynical note to seep into his voice. "We have Parrish and his men safe and sound."

"Cool," Freeman said. "Did big Hutch give you any trouble?"

"Not much."

"Do you know how he earned his nickname?"

"No idea." Jones squeezed the mobile so hard that the case creaked in protest. "At first, I thought his surname might be Hutchinson, but it's Greg Wolverton."

"He keeps rabbits as pets."

"Come again?"

"Dear old Hutch breeds rabbits. Who'd have thought, eh?"

Jones' patience snapped.

"Damn it, Freeman. Answer my question. Where are you?"

"Can't tell you that, I'm afraid, Mr Jones. I'm a wanted man, remember?"

A woman in the background spoke, but Jones couldn't make out the words clearly. Phil reached across and pressed the "mute" button. "He's in a car, boss, and there's a woman with him."

"I know that, Philip. I'm not deaf."

"Want me to call the Comms Centre and try to trace the call?"

Jones nodded.

"Mr Jones, are you still there?"

Jones released the mute.

"Yes, I'm listening."

"Don't bother trying to trace this call. I'm on the move and you won't find me unless I want to be found."

"So why d'you phone? I thought we had an arrangement?"

"Yes … about that," Freeman said. "I'm really sorry, but you'll understand why I did what I did in a minute."

The man sounded genuinely embarrassed, but he'd fooled Jones once already.

"I'm all ears, Freeman. Surprise me."

"Didn't find the present I left down the back of the settee in your front room yet, then?"

Jones closed his eyes and pictured the scene with the three of them in his lounge, Freeman, Phil, and Jones.

"Not planted another bomb have you?"

Freeman laughed.

"Oh dear, you crack me up. As if I'd do that to you, Mr Jones. Once was enough. No. Down the left-hand side of the couch you'll find a memory stick."

"Go on!" Jones demanded.

"On the stick," Freeman continued, "you'll find everything you need to put Digby Parrish away for a very long time."

Phil stopped tapping into his tablet long enough to shake his head in disbelief.

"We already have him for attempted armed robbery and your confession for all the other robberies … ah, I see."

"Yes, quite. Without my taking the stand, I doubt a judge will allow my taped confession into evidence. That's why I thought you might need a little something extra. Call it my parting gift."

"Goody. I love presents. What exactly is on the memory stick?"

"More than enough to keep you and the Crown Prosecution Service interested for the whole court case. Taped conversations with jewellery fences and drugs dealers. A video clip of him and Hutch killing a man called Ivan Pelski."

"What's that?" Jones asked.

Phil's eyes turned into slits.

"They killed Ivan Pelski. It was horrible, Mr Jones. I didn't see the footage until after the event so I couldn't do anything to stop it. I tapped into Parrish's home security system a month after I joined *Parrish Enterprises*. Wanted to go to the police with the tape and bugger the consequences, but couldn't trust anyone in the force. I hadn't met you yet."

"Why'd Parrish kill Pelski?"

"No idea. Caught him with his hand in the cookie jar, I guess. I don't know where they buried him either, but I'm sure Inspector Eldritch will find something of value in Parrish's safe."

"What was that about Inspector Eldritch?" Jones asked.

"I've just seen her entering Parrish's Golders Green mansion after receiving an anonymous tip about an ongoing burglary from a helpful citizen. She's going to find an open safe. Inside the safe will be a huge cache of stolen jewels and a few other interesting bits and pieces, including a paper trail going back fifteen years. You might not have guessed, but Parrish is a fastidious record keeper." Again, Freeman laughed. "I love it when a plan comes together."

"Might I ask a question?"

"You just did, Mr Jones."

"Very funny, you should get together with one of my officers. You and he would have the audience rolling in the aisles," Jones said, making his voice as dry as desert sand. "Mind telling me how you broke into Parrish's inner sanctum? From what I read in the NCA files, the Parrish house boasts more security and electronic surveillance than the Stafford Museum."

"Piece of cake. I used my blunderbuss, an EMP discharger. Knocked out every piece of electronic equipment in the house. Probably messed up the neighbourhood's alarm clocks and satellite recorders too. Pity 'bout that, but needs must, as they say."

"EMP?" Jones said. "An electromagnetic pulse? Hang on a minute. Top-of-the-range security systems have countermeasures for EMPs. Why didn't Parrish install them?"

"Very good, Mr Jones. You clearly understand this stuff. As you may know, legitimate firms use offsite redundancy. The minute there's an interruption to the signal between the sites, the system sends an automated alarm to the nearest police station."

"Okay, I get it. The last thing Parrish wanted was police officers traipsing through his home, right?"

"Exactly. The arrogant bugger was so cocksure … pardon my language … that no one would dare turn him over, his gaff turned out to be the easiest break-in I ever tackled."

"So that's it? You're going to disappear off into the sunset with the takings from a couple of dozen jewel robberies?"

"Absolutely not, Mr Jones. The very idea. In fact, I left every 'bonus' Parrish paid me in the safe. It's all accounted for in his records. I did, however, keep the salary from the legit end of things though. I don't want anything from that bastard I didn't earn honestly."

"So, you're leaving the country with next to nothing?"

"Well, I didn't exactly say that now, did I?" Again he laughed. "I've taken a total of two million, three hundred thousand pounds worth of bearer bonds from Parrish's safe, which is the value of the insurance policy due my father after we lost our business. It should be enough to keep Angela and me going while we settle into our new lives."

"Angela Glennie," Jones said. "Is she with you now?"

"Yes, Mr Jones … Darling, mind saying hello to my friend, Detective Chief Inspector Jones?"

"Who?" a woman asked.

Jones and Phil exchanged glances. Phil broke out one of his cock-eyed smiles. Jones ground his teeth.

"Please, babe," Freeman said. "DCI Jones needs to know you're safe. Say hello."

"Um, hello," a woman said—a woman with a strong Scottish accent.

"Ms Glennie?"

"Aye."

"Would you mind telling me where you've been for the past few days?"

"I've been staying in Sean's London flat. Why?"

"You were never kidnapped?"

"What? Kidnapped? No, of course not. What's all this about? Sean, is this man a real police officer?"

"Of course I am," said Jones, almost shouting in frustration. "Who did you think Freeman's been talking to for the past few minutes?"

"You're not a screenwriter discussing a movie plot?"

Angela Glennie sounded lost and genuinely confused, although, as an actress, Jones couldn't be sure she wasn't playing him as deftly as Freeman had done back in his cottage. Reluctantly, he let the thought go.

"Sean?" Angela said. "What the heck's g'n on here, babe?"

"I'll tell you later, love. Concentrate on your driving. You just ran a red light." A car horn blared through the phone's speaker and died away. "We could do without being rammed or being stopped by the boys in blue," Freeman added through another laugh.

"Sorry, babe."

"To answer what might be your next question, Mr Jones," Freeman continued, "I'm afraid the telephone conversation between Parrish and the so-called kidnapper was faked. I spliced into the NCA's phone tap and layered in the recording."

"And no doubt it was you who tipped off the NCA about Parrish being the leader of the JT1 mob last month?"

"Yep. I've been planning to get back at him ever since he stitched up my father back in the late nineties and cost us our shop."

Phil's frown matched the way Jones felt.

"What exactly happened to your father?" Jones asked.

"A few years ago, Parrish needed a good locksmith and tried to get Dad to join his team. When Dad refused, Parrish put him in hospital and forced him out of business, out of spite. We lost everything. I was in school at the time, couldn't do a thing to help. But I'm not a kid anymore. At least Dad's okay now."

The new threads of information began to weave in Jones' head. He could see the whole of Freeman's plan meshing together and forming a complete blanket. "You used the present when referring to your father. He's still alive?"

"Oh yes, Mr Jones. He recovered from Hutch's beating well enough, although he lost his spleen and a kidney and still has to take antibiotics to ward off infection. I set him up in a new shop last year. New Zealand, or was it Australia? Or it could have been in Manchester. Oh dear, my memory's terrible these days." Again, a laugh followed the latest revelation.

When he'd calmed down, Jones asked, "Who was John Freeman, the coma patient?"

"Ah yes, poor John." Freeman's tone turned sombre. "An unfortunate man I found during my online searches. He suffered what the doctors call a 'major cerebrovascular incident', that's a stroke to you and me. Didn't have any living family or medical insurance and ended up in St Margaret's. Worse than death, if you ask me. Nobody should live like that."

"Bloody hell," Phil cut in. "You used a coma patient as part of a scheme to get back at Parrish? That's a bit callous isn't it?"

"Hello. Is that you, Mr Cryer?"

"It is."

"How you doing?"

"Answer the question," Phil insisted.

"Well, yes, and I felt guilty about it to begin with, Mr Cryer, but I did take good care of John Freeman. Spent time with him. I like to think he appreciated the companionship. And don't forget, for the last eighteen months he had the best possible care, courtesy of Digby Parrish. No, I think John Freeman would have thanked me, if he were able to speak. At least I hope so."

Phil frowned and mouthed something unrepeatable through clenched teeth.

"What's up, Phil?" Jones whispered.

"Yes, Mr Cryer," Freeman added. "Do you have another question for me?"

"I investigated your records and your family background, starting with John Freeman. It was all there. National insurance number, tax codes filed until the stroke stopped him working. I checked your parents, aunts, uncles, siblings. Everything was in order, right down to yours and their school reports and exam results."

"How far back did you go?" Freeman asked.

Jones could almost see a smile on the young man's face, and his anger bubbled up again. Freeman had played him and deserved the credit of a job well done, but it wasn't easy to swallow.

"I went back as far as John Freeman's parents," Phil answered avoiding Jones' eyes. "Your alleged grandparents."

"And there you have it, Mr Cryer. You didn't go far enough. My … colleague created a legend going back to the Second World War and my so-called great-grandparents. The research took years, and then we had to pepper the information onto the net. A labour of love, you might say. A labour of hate would be more accurate, but we did have to create the best possible cover to fool Parrish."

"This is all very elaborate," Jones said. "Was it worth all that time, just to break a toad like Digby Parrish?"

Freeman didn't answer for a moment. Jones took the opportunity to monitor the crime scene.

Ben Adeoye stood in the centre of a small group. His arm shot out as he re-enacted his part in the Hutch takedown. The sun warmed the Range Rover's cabin enough to make Jones shrug out of his jacket.

"Freeman," he said. "Are you still there?"

"Yes, Mr Jones, I'm still here. Actually, I was wondered how best to answer your question." Freeman paused again before adding, "In short, it was worth every second. After the beating my dad took, he was a broken man. Nobody attacks my family and gets away with it … and there is another thing."

"Which is?" Jones asked.

"Tommy and Gordy MacAndrews."

"The shotgun-toting goons from the second Edinburgh job?"

"Yes. I don't think they'll ever surface."

"You think they're dead?"

"Yeah. Hutch went missing for a day shortly after the Throck-morton raid. I reckon Parrish sent him to Scotland on a clean-up operation. There may be a record of it in Parrish's files. I didn't have time to read them all this morning. I'm sorry for the MacAndrews boys. They were stupid, but didn't deserve to die. I tried to warn them off but they wouldn't listen. I couldn't let things continue. Parrish had to be stopped. You do understand, don't you, Mr Jones?"

"Yes, Sean. I think I do."

"Hey, you called me, Sean!"

"A onetime only deal, son. Don't let our paths cross again."

"I won't. By the way, Inspector Eldritch is a bit tasty, Mr Jones. Ever thought of asking her out?"

Jones groaned. "Oh hell, you too? What is it with people trying to set me up on dates?

Jones pointed a finger at Phil, daring him to comment.

"You're a good man, Mr Jones. You deserve a good woman at your side. I have Angela, why shouldn't you have someone, too?"

Jones couldn't think of a way to respond without resorting to a torrent of expletives, and that, he would never do.

"By the way, what's my surname again, Mr Jones?" Freeman asked, still chuckling.

"Freeman," Jones answered, understanding the point.

"That's right David, but it's not my name, it's my status. Freeman. Cheers, Mr Jones. Have a good life."

The line went dead.

"The cheeky little sod," Jones said, but smiled as he spoke.

"Don't quote me on this boss, but I'm happy the bugger's getting away."

Jones wrinkled his nose. "That's no way for a future DI to talk, Philip. Don't ever let me hear you say anything like that again, understand?"

"Yes, boss. Certainly, boss. Anything you say, boss." Phil waved a lazy salute. "So, you're just going to let him toddle off, free as a bird?"

"Do you have any idea where he is?"

"Yep." Phil raised his tablet. "We kept him talking long enough for comms to a trace the call. He must have forgotten he was using Angela Glennie's mobile and she's on a contract."

"Really," Jones said. "Now that is interesting. Where is the young scumbag?"

"Comms can't pinpoint the exact location, but they have come up with a one-mile radius."

"Which is?"

"London, south of the river, and you know what that means."

Jones nodded. "He's headed for Heathrow or Gatwick, or Dover. He's leaving the country."

"That's what I thought," Phil said, and dropped the tablet into his lap. "Want me to call Superintendent Knightly, or send out an All Ports Warning?"

Jones rubbed his chin and stared through the windscreen again.

Ben Adeoye had finished his reconstruction to what looked like hearty praise from his mates. Vic Doland issued instructions from the museum entrance and the group dispersed, presumably to head back to the station for an end of shift debriefing and to complete their logbooks.

"Boss?"

"Hmm?"

"Superintendent Knightly, the All Ports Warning?"

"Oh yes, right. I'll call him from the office. I left my mobile there and can't remember his number. I only hope they'll be in time to catch the young scamp."

Phil stared at the mobile in Jones' hand. "So, you're letting him go?"

"Now would I do such a thing?" Jones said, shaking his head and frowning. "Besides, I can't see Freeman making it that easy for us. We don't even know his real name, or what he looks like now. Back to the station please. We have a shed load of interviews ahead of us. So much paperwork, so little time."

Phil fired up the motor, but his mobile beeped out an old-style SOS ring tone before he could pull away. "Oh God, that's Manda. She never calls me at work."

Jones' heart flipped.

"What's wrong?"

Uncharacteristically, Phil fumbled with the phone and dropped it into his footwell. He struggled to retrieve it and had to open the driver's door to make room. With the mobile grasped in a trembling hand, he read the text. "Oh Christ, she's gone into labour." He turned terrified eyes on Jones. "It's a month early!"

"Swap seats, I'm driving!" Jones dived out of the car and ran around the front. "Where is she?"

Phil climbed out of the car and stood by the open driver's door, white-faced and shaking. He shook his head and frowned. "I ... Oh, she's on her way to St Elizabeth's."

"Get in, man. Passenger seat."

Phil hesitated and Jones pushed him into action, dived into the driver's seat, and had the wheels spinning the instant Phil slammed his door closed. "Seatbelt, Philip."

Jones snapped on the blues and two-tones, and floored the throttle. He'd received a similar call back in 1975, and prayed to all he knew that the outcome would be different this time around.

Epilogue

MANDA CRYER HELD up the little white bundle to show him a red thing, dark-haired and wrinkled. With eyes closed and tiny hands resting against its cheek, the little lad didn't look too impressive.

"Isn't he beautiful, David?"

Jones nodded, unable to speak for the lump of rock crammed into his throat. Most parents considered their children the most wonderful things on the planet. He certainly had with his own darling boy, Paul, who'd lived a whole lifetime in thirteen minutes.

Oh, God.

He stared at the eight-year-old Jamie Cryer, curled up asleep on the visitor's chair. According to her baby pictures, Jamie had been as wrinkled and prune-like as this new-born when she first arrived in the world, so there was still hope for the poor lad.

Manda, flushed but beaming, had recovered well from the eight-hour labour, every second of which, Jones had spent pacing the corridor outside the delivery suite, guarding Jamie while, presum-

374

ably, Phil held Manda's hand. To hell with interviewing Parrish and the rest of the JT1 Crew. They could wait. The case against them couldn't have been much stronger.

At least Manda looked in better condition than did her red-faced, glassy-eyed husband.

"Go on, Phil," she said, "ask him."

Jones cocked an eyebrow and smiled at the brand new father.

"Well, Philip? You're not going to ask me to baby-sit Jamie again. Not after the last time. My building site home's no place for a kiddie. And I'm too old to cope with all her energy."

Liar, liar, pants on ....

"No boss," Phil answered. "It's not that."

Jones tried to hide his disappointment.

"What is it then, my tongue-tied second-in command?"

"We'd like to call him David in your honour. Would you mind?"

"What? I ... I don't know what to say other than ... yes, I bloody well would mind."

"Boss?"

"David," Manda said, hurt clouding her eyes. "Why not?"

Because it's not the name I was born with.

Unable to explain the real reason, Jones latched on to the first excuse he could find. "Why saddle the poor lad with such a dull name? Mind if I make an alternative suggestion?"

Phil and Manda exchanged glances. Manda said, "Okay. What did you have in mind?"

"How about Paul?"

Manda looked first at Phil and then at the baby. "Why Paul?"

"I've always liked the name. It means 'small', and this little fellow's no giant."

She smiled and kissed her son's forehead. "What do you think, Phil?"

The baby yawned and Phil grinned.

"Look at that. He doesn't seem to mind, and neither do I. Paul it is. Thanks, David."

"No, Phil, Manda, thank you for the huge honour. He's a lucky boy to have such wonderful parents. May ... er, I hold him?"

Without hesitation, Manda offered up the tiny bundle and for the briefest of moments, Jones returned to a London hospital in 1975. He blinked hard, kissed the baby's forehead, and handed him back, but not before vowing to protect Paul Cryer with his life. Something he hadn't been able to do for his own darling son.

The End

Next in the DCI Jones series

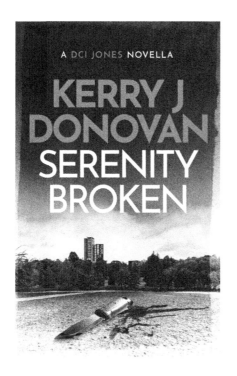

fusebooks.com/serenitybroken

The DCI Jones series

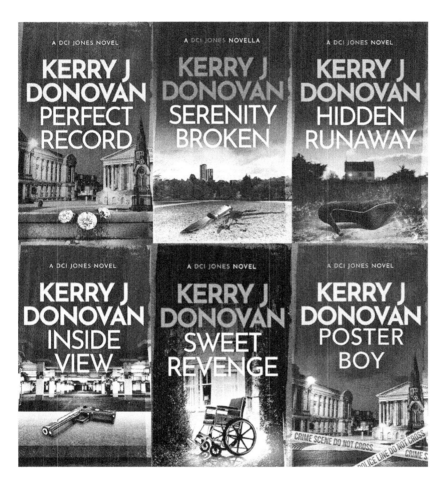

fusebooks.com/dcijones

PLEASE LEAVE A REVIEW

If you enjoyed Perfect Record, it would mean a lot to Kerry if you were able to leave a review. Reviews are an important way for books to find new readers. Thank you.

fusebooks.com/perfectrecord

ABOUT KERRY J DONOVAN

#1 International Best-seller with *Ryan Kaine: On the Run*, Kerry was born in Dublin. He currently lives in a cottage in the heart of rural Brittany. He has three children and four grandchildren, all of whom live in England. As an absentee granddad, Kerry is hugely thankful for the advent of video calling.

Kerry earned a first class honours degree in Human Biology, and has a PhD in Sport and Exercise Sciences. A former scientific advisor to The Office of the Deputy Prime Minister, he helped UK emergency first-responders prepare for chemical attacks in the wake of 9/11. He is also a former furniture designer/maker.

kerryjdonovan.com

Printed in Great Britain
by Amazon

25012840R00223